Best Wishes
to
Wes & Ruth Robinson,
Aloysius P. Sharon,
Alan Stang

The Name of the King

THE NAME OF THE KING

Aloysius P. Sharon

The Hunt for the Last, Worst Nazi War Criminal

Patton House
Los Angeles, California

Patton House
P.O. Box 261642
Encino, CA 91426
(818) 996-2585

First Edition

The Name of the King is a work of fiction. All characters and events described or depicted herein are fictitious creations of the author, except for historical events and personages, living or dead. Any resemblance to other, actual incidents or individuals is not intended and coincidental.

International Standard Book Number: 0-9670606-0-5
Library of Congress Catalog Card Number: 99-70122

Table of Contents

One: Confession 1
Two: Confrontation 6
Three: Exorcism 11
Four: Conjugal Heaven 20
Five: Conjugal Hell 25
Six: Brief Encounter 32
Seven: Bad Blood 38
Eight: Masquerade 47
Nine: The Deal 57
Ten: Swindle 63
Eleven: Polyakov's Arm 72
Twelve: Lords of Creation 81
Thirteen: *Der Führer* 90
Fourteen: The Arabs 94
Fifteen: Bank Heist 98
Sixteen: Samba Lesson 106
Seventeen: Return of the Native 112
Eighteen: Flim Flam 121
Nineteen: Nymphomaniac 129
Twenty: Romance 136
Twenty One: Casing the Jernt 145
Twenty Two: Prodigal Son 153
Twenty Three: Messiah 157

Twenty Four: Conversion 163
Twenty Five: The Raid 167
Twenty Six: Dreams of Glory 173
Twenty Seven: Under Cover 181
Twenty Eight: Sisterhood 188
Twenty Nine: Tax Man 196
Thirty: Unmasked 204
Thirty One: The Beast 211
Thirty Two: Baptism 220
Thirty Three: Fool's Gold 226
Thirty Four: Identity Crisis 239
Thirty Five: Breathing Together 251
Thirty Six: Lifeguard 258
Thirty Seven: Reunion 267
Thirty Eight: Vengeance 274
Thirty Nine: Collapse 288
Forty: Victory 295
About the Author: 303

Chapter One
Confession

It was on Easter Sunday--no doubt a coincidence--that Abe Goldstein finally admitted he was Jesus Christ. He didn't want to be Jesus Christ, God knows--he was Jewish--and in fact he had denied that he was Jesus Christ for months. Had someone told him just last Christmas, in 1977, that he--Abe Goldstein--was Jesus Christ, he would have been properly scandalized, and would have assumed that whoever had said it was demented.

Yet, against his will, he had admitted it, if only to himself, because the dream had been too real, more than a dream, more than a nightmare. It had been more real than his waking life. Abe had been seated on a throne, in a cloud of flying angels. One of his feet had rested on the earth. People in lines as long as eternity waited before him to be judged. Moses and Elijah had stood beside him and had deferred to him. Who else could he be? And weren't dreams as real as daylight in The Bible?

Then, starting in Easter Week, there was the voice, a majestic voice, full of humor, compassion and authority, reverberating through his mind, not just when he was trying to sleep beside Shirley in his modest home in the Bronx, but during the day, when he was at work, driving a garbage truck through the streets of New York. That's the way it was for Abe.

He wondered what it meant, and while he wondered the voice became a hammer, beating his head upon an anvil, goading him, forcing him to yield. He could not hear what his fellow workers said; Moe Stern, his dear friend, among them. His boss, McGillicuddy, spoke and gave orders, and Abe smiled and nodded, especially obsequious, pretending to hear, pretending to obey as always, when in fact he had not heard a thing and could only pray he was doing what McGillicuddy wanted. God forbid it wasn't. What would he tell Francis X. McGillicuddy then? *Sorry, boss, but I heard this voice; it says I'm Jesus Christ.* McGillicuddy was more Catholic than the Pope. Abe could already see him walking away, shaking his head and muttering about the Jews. McGillicuddy was already angry with him, because he had let Abe use the new computer in his office, and Abe had let it eat his files. Abe drove his truck in fear that he would have an accident. The doomsday voice even drowned out the traffic, not an easy thing to do in New York. If only Abe could get some sleep, sleep without dreams, without the voice.

Why me, God? Abe asked. *God, why me*? He didn't believe in Jesus Christ. Didn't the rabbis say he was just another false messiah? Bible times had been full of them. In fact, so were modern times. If God insisted Abe be someone else, why couldn't he be Moses or Elijah? *Why not Abraham, God?* Besides, if Jesus were really everything the gentiles said he was, shouldn't God pick a nuclear physicist, a general, a great surgeon or a movie star?

At last, on Easter morning, when Shirley and the kids were still asleep, Abe had stood in a corner of his small living room behind the plastic plant and admitted, I AM. Why he had said exactly that, he didn't know. Those were the only words he spoke to the voice booming through his mind, and instantly, to his intense relief, it stopped, as if finally appeased. The voice had smiled. *Thank you, Abe. You catch on fast. Take the day off.*

Abe had waited, flinching, then had staggered and sat down. He had never realized what a joy silence was. It was like a palpable thing, like a woman's hand--not Shirley's--caressing him.

Thank you, God, he said. *Oh, God, thank you. I'll be anyone you like.*

Good idea, Abe. I'm glad you thought of it.

But shouldn't you pick somebody more important, God? I'm short, I'm overweight, I'm going bald, I'm missing some teeth and I drive a garbage truck. Shouldn't you at least pick somebody taller? I can't even lead my wife.

A universal problem, said the voice. *It's supposed to be that way since Eden. Since you people like your wives' advice so much, I want you to enjoy a lot of it.*

But, God . . . .

You're also argumentative. All of you are, even the best. Did you know that?

No, God.

Moses couldn't speak, said the voice. *Jonah couldn't pay attention, Simon Bar-jona couldn't keep the faith and Thomas couldn't believe. You Jews have made a mess of free will.*

I'm sorry, God.

Jesus was a carpenter and now you drive a garbage truck. Understand? Before time was, you are. You alone give everlasting life.

Whatever you say, God, said Abe. Now that he was able to think again, he remembered that nobody knew he was Jesus Christ. The voice seemed satisfied that Abe alone knew it, so there was no need to tell anyone else. Why worry? He would tell himself he was anyone the voice wanted him to be, the Archbishop of

Canterbury included. Abe was pleased with himself, smiled and said nothing to God. He wasn't usually so cunning.

But it wasn't that simple. When is it? Abe's new identity--which he had acknowledged in his living room--was like a seed taking root. After a week of silent bliss and long nights of sleep, his mood changed. *Why* had God made him Jesus Christ? Was Abe's recognition of the fact all there was to it? Would a man as important as God go to all this trouble for nothing? The questions became as menacing as the endless voice had been painful. Didn't it make sense to believe that God had made him Jesus Christ for a purpose, and that the purpose had not yet been revealed? Abe had lived 32 years without knowing who he was or would become. The revelation had scared him out of more than three years' growth. Could the Lord be planning to scare him again? Was Abe's unwilling admission of his new identity just a chapter in this bizarre story?

God, please, no more, said Abe. *Just being Jesus Christ is enough.* But there was no answer. For the first time in all the years they had known him, McGillicuddy and his fellow workers noticed a dramatic change in Abe. He had always been so sunny, so carefree. Many people had envied his disposition and called him "Mr. Sunshine." Now he was morose. He had been gregarious, quick with a joke. Now he didn't talk. His colleagues whispered and wondered whether they should ask him what was wrong. They didn't know he was cringing, waiting to be squashed.

God, please, do it now, he pleaded. *Get it over with.*

But there was no answer, and Abe's torment increased. Doom was approaching. That was obvious. It was already almost tangible, and there was no place to hide. Where can you hide from God? The fear and silence were now as painful as the voice. God had made him Jesus Christ, because the Lord had a robust sense of humor, and this was just another of his jokes, like man himself. Now, the Lord would let him squirm. It was the story of his life.

Slowly Abe realized that, despite the danger, he had to tell someone else his troubles. Another mind would have a different perspective and probably would see things Abe had missed. Maybe such a person--the right person--could intercede on his behalf, even exorcise his new identity. Who was both safe enough and smart enough to tell? Abe considered and rejected several prospects. Shirley of course was out of the question. The only subjects she could discuss were Mah-jongg and Miami, and not very well. Suppose he went to St. Simon Stock, pretended to be Catholic and confessed. The priest wouldn't see him, wouldn't know who he was, but would tell him vigorously he wasn't Jesus Christ. Abe would tell God it wasn't his fault; that the argument was now between God and the Roman Catholic Church. Since God is Jewish, he wouldn't be angry with Abe for getting the church into trouble. It was tempting. Abe had never known he was so clever. But the thought of doing it inspired him with fear. Suppose the priest realized he was a ringer while he was still trapped in the confessional.

The Name of the King
4

Suppose the Catholics wouldn't let him go, forced him to convert. They would make him say the rosary. Sooner or later, Shirley would catch him, and his life, now a living hell, would become an inferno.

Abe thought a few days before he realized Moe Stern was the man. Of course! So often, solutions were right under one's nose, if one only cared to look. Sure, Moe was another garbage truck driver, but he was smart. He was an educated man, a high school graduate. Moe religiously (no pun intended) read every issue of *Reader's Digest*. Once, at a fund-raiser, he had shaken hands with the borough president of the Bronx. He was even an international traveler. A couple of years before, just for the adventure, he had taken the bus to Montreal. Finally, he was accessible. And, he was a Jew.

"Moe, I need some advice."

Moe was flattered. Who doesn't like to give advice? The trouble was that people rarely asked for it, and took umbrage when it was volunteered. Moe wanted to advise someone important and draw a big check, like the Washington advisers he religiously read about in *Reader's Digest.*

"Sure, guy. What's up?"

They were sitting in an all-night diner. They had just come off their shift. They were alone. Abe was as nervous as a hooker at communion. He had confidence in Moe, yes. But, so far, the horrible secret lived only in Abe's mind. Now, he was going to tell it to someone else, and the act of doing so--to exorcise it--would paradoxically give it substance. Thank God he had taken time to figure out a plan.

"Moe, I'm Jesus Christ."

Abe put his head in his hands and squeezed in frustration, as if trying to crack a walnut. That hadn't been what he had meant to say, at all. He had decided to set the stage by discussing the "nightmare" in detail, the terror, the lack of sleep, his fight with God. His new identity would be the most humiliating confession he had ever made, in an otherwise uneventful life, but Moe would realize he was a victim, not a perpetrator. They were both Jews. It would be easy to sell the theory that he was being victimized by the gentiles. Both of them had been raised with such stories. Wasn't the Hitler Holocaust an egregious example, even now in 1978? However, Abe had kicked his own plan into the garbage. Why?

Moe Stern put down his cup. "You're Jesus Christ."

"That's right."

"You're not Abe Goldstein?"

"I am Abe Goldstein, Moe. I was. I'm also Jesus Christ. I just found out."

"How did you find out?"

"From God."

"God told you you're Jesus Christ?"

"Correct."

Confession
5

Moe considered. Advising Abe Goldstein would be a pallid substitute for advising President Carter, which was Moe's secret dream. On the other hand, it would keep him in practice, just in case the President called. Indeed, suppose--just suppose--Abe turned out to be right. Weren't the Christians always talking about the so-called Second Coming? If they were right, somebody had to be Jesus Christ. Why not Abe? Advising President Carter would probably pay a lot better, but it would be a pallid substitute for advising God, who, thank God, was Jewish.

"If George Burns can be God, you can be Jesus Christ," Moe decided. "He's just as good as you are--just as Jewish. Abe, the only difference between you and George Burns is that he has more *chutzpah*, more sex appeal, more hair and more money."

"Moe, I'm serious. There are lots of people I could have told. I picked you because I need help. You're the only one who knows."

"Hey, guy, I'm sorry. I stand corrected. So, what do I call you now? Abe, Jesus or just plain God?"

"Moe, you still don't get it. I don't want to be Jesus Christ."

Moe again put down his cup. "If you don't want to be Jesus Christ, how come that's who you are?"

Abe told him the whole story: the dream, or, rather, the "nightmare," the voice, the conversations, all the things he had planned to tell first to prepare Moe for the shock.

Moe smiled. "Good news! If this were the year 30, and we were sitting in an all-night diner in Jerusalem eating pickled herring, and you thought you were Jesus Christ, I'm guessing you'd have real *tsouris*. You'd probably be stoned. Today? No problem. You can be anyone you like. People don't believe any more."

"At least I won't be stoned."

"No, you're going to be crucified."

"Moe!"

"Just a little joke. Take it easy, guy. Look, Abe, you said the voice now leaves you alone. Why not just ignore it. Let it fade away. Pretend you're Abe Goldstein. No one will suspect you were ever Jesus Christ. You don't look anything like him, anyway."

"I know, but that's not good enough, Moe. This thing's hanging over me. I can't sleep. I have to get rid of it."

"Okay. Don't panic. Let's be logical. I have an idea. Go to your rabbi. Fighting Jesus Christ is his business. Take it to him."

"I don't have a rabbi, Moe. I don't go to temple."

"You call yourself a Jew, but you don't go to temple?"

"I don't call myself anything but Jesus Christ, Moe."

"All right, I'll take you to mine. But, I warn you, Abe. He's tough."

Chapter Two
Confrontation

Abe and Moe sat with Rabbi Stanley B. Garlick in his office. The rabbi had served this Brooklyn congregation for many years and was a man of vast learning and experience. He was suspicious, but Moe had been a member many of those years, and was a small, but steady, contributor, always eager to buy expensive seats for the High Holy Days. Now, the rabbi looked at him and his companion so long and so intently, that they became uncomfortable, which was the general idea.

"How may I serve you, Moe?" he said at last.

"Rabbi, this is my friend, Abe Goldstein. He has a serious problem."

"I'm sure he does. Where do you go to *schule*, Mr. Goldstein?"

"I don't go to *schule*, rabbi."

"You don't go to *schule*? Not anywhere?"

"No."

"Moe, you're right. He has a problem. In light of this incriminating admission, Mr. Abe Goldstein, may I ask you why--if we're not good enough for you; if *no one* is good enough for you--are you here?"

The rabbi was used to dealing with wise guys. They came into his office all the time, all of them Jews, proud as perdition of their unbelief. Here in New York--in fact everywhere in the country--Christians treated him with respect, even deference, because the Jews were "the people of The Book." He had heard there were some *momsers* who said the Holocaust was a fraud, but he had never met them. It was probably just a rumor. His most dangerous adversaries were Jews. It was an epidemic, but where did it come from? The rabbi knew that behind it was something sinister, something he couldn't see, part of the age-old conspiracy to destroy the Jews. In fact weren't the Jews themselves committing suicide with Christian girls? Christian girls were the greatest threat to Judaism since the Inquisition and Hitler. The rabbi routinely warned *bar mitzvah* boys about them. Not enough Jewish parents understood that the Christians sent their daughters to deceive their sons into marriage, because everyone knew Jewish boys were the best providers, the best husbands and fathers, and, let's face it, the best lovers, and would treat their daughters like Jewish American Princesses.

Over the years, he had learned how to protect himself. For instance, when someone he didn't know came into his office and sat down, the rabbi kept him waiting until he became uncomfortable. Then the rabbi overpowered him. He was doing that now--trying to do it--but Moe and this Abe Goldstein, who didn't go to *schule*, were such *schlemazels*, they didn't know they were being overpowered.

"He's here *because* he doesn't go to *schule*," said Moe.

The rabbi brightened. "He's ready to join?"

"He's Jesus Christ."

Moe almost kicked himself. He had planned to back into the subject slowly, with circumspection. Instead, he was following in Abe's elephantine footsteps. What on earth had made him say that?

Like a man who has suddenly discovered he is sitting in the first car of a roller coaster nearing apogee, the rabbi grabbed the arms of his chair in a death grip. His mood had been bad when the conversation started. He had just returned from a fruitless trip to a distant public hospital, where he had been told that the lady he was there to see, Mrs. Joyce Harris, had without warning checked out and left. Yet, she had still been in the throes of recovery from a shattered hip. According to the administrator, she had left with relatives. But she had no relatives. That was why Garlick had gone to see her. She hadn't even called to tell him. Was it the rabbi's imagination, or had several of his older people recently disappeared like Mrs. Harris? Now, his mood turned from somber to black, but he prayed that *Addonai* would give him self-control.

"Since when are you a wise guy, Moe?"

"Rabbi, I'm not a wise guy. That's who this is."

"Moe, did I ever tell you why I became a rabbi?"

"No."

"I'm going to. I became a rabbi because of my grandfather. My grandfather was a dentist who had been a barber and there was a ritual to my visits. They always started in the office in the dental chair at the far end of his apartment, which seemed to me as a child almost as long as forever. My grandfather put a bowl on my head, gave me a haircut and then fixed my teeth.

"Then we would trek halfway down the apartment to the living room, where he gave me moral instruction supported by liberal references to *torah*. Finally, we adjourned to the kitchen, where my grandmother stood among the steaming pots at the stove, and I ate under her direction, while my grandfather smiled and nodded with immense dignity. He was a full-service grandfather, all right."

He paused, enjoying the fond recollection. Abe's head sank low, concealing his tears. The rabbi's story was so happy and therefore so sad, so alien to anything Abe had ever known, evoking a family hunger that could not be satisfied.

"What a happy story," said Moe, who, like the rabbi, had been born in America and therefore couldn't understand.

Too absorbed to notice Abe's emotion, Garlick continued, "My grandfather told me that, if I became a rabbi, people would shout my name with deference when I walked down the street. They would invite me in to eat. When I appeared on stage, he said, they would applaud. When I appeared in temple, they would shut up.

"So, I gave up my boyhood dream of hunting secret Nazis, and became a rabbi. And, sure enough, everything is happening as my grandfather said. When I walk down the street, people call out my name. They're honored. After they hide the pork chops and bacon, they invite me in to dine. When I walk on stage, they applaud. In *schule*, they shut up. I don't know how my grandfather could have been so perspicacious."

"Your grandfather could prognosticate," said Moe, thanking God for *Reader's Digest*, where "prognosticate" had followed "perspicacious" in a recent test of word power.

"But, as perspicacious as he was, there was one thing he didn't tell me. Do you know what that thing was, Moe?"

"No, rabbi, but I want to know. Don't you, Abe?"

"No."

"He didn't tell me that 30 years later, a *nudnik* named Abe Goldstein--who is not even a member--a man who obviously has a *goyische kopf*, would walk in here smirking and say he's Jesus Christ."

Abe's face fell to his chest. "I came here for help, rabbi," he whispered.

"He didn't tell me that a Judas named Moe Stern would bring him to my office."

"Rabbi, I'm confused," said Moe. "Is that a compliment or not?"

"Not," said Abe.

"Quick question, rabbi," said Moe. "If he was as bad as I think you think he was, what did he do?"

"Do you have a grandfather?" the rabbi asked, ignoring him.

"I did," said Abe. "Two."

"Were they Jewish?"

Abe bristled, something he rarely did. "Rabbi, nobody in my family has not been Jewish."

"You're looking at a full-blooded prince of the Hebrew nation," said Moe.

The rabbi relented, enough to say, "Tell me about yourself."

Abe was encouraged. Maybe the rabbi would help, after all. "I was born in Europe, in what they called a `Displaced Persons' camp. I drive a garbage truck with Moe. I live in the Bronx with my wife, Shirley, who is Jewish and belongs to Hadassah. Our children go to *cheder*."

"And your parents?"

"I never knew my father. I still don't know his name. I never knew my grandfathers. Only my mother escaped."

It was an unspoken rebuke, of course. While young Stanley B. Garlick had been safe in New York, pursued by competing Christian girls sent by their parents--who knew he would be the best provider, the best husband and father, and, let's face it, the best lover--Abe's mother had endured the Holocaust, a credential that could even survive a son who was Jesus Christ. Rabbi Garlick had found the key.

"Does your mother--your mother who endured the Holocaust because she is Jewish--know you are Jesus Christ?"

"No."

"Why don't you tell her?"

"Because I'm telling you."

"Why would an Abe Goldstein want to be Jesus Christ, anyway? Can't you be one of our people? Why not Moses or Elijah? Why not Abraham, for whom you are named? They're not good enough for you?"

"I don't want to be Jesus Christ, rabbi. That's the problem."

"So, who told you that's who you are?"

"God."

"God told you you're Jesus Christ?"

"Yes."

"How? Did he call you collect?"

"He spoke."

"Do you believe in Jesus Christ?"

"No."

The rabbi smiled. He was surprised. He had been building with relish toward a rousing brawl. He was a "reform" rabbi, who affected urbanity and compromise, but inside the reform rabbi was an orthodox version struggling to get out. Abe's submissive manner meant there would be no rousing brawl today.

However, Abe's answer contained the seeds of its own destruction. Yes, he said he didn't believe in Jesus Christ. Fine! But would God make him someone he didn't believe in? Would God make him someone *God* didn't believe in? The rabbi had been a rabbi for many years, and knew how God works. God did not inspire unbelief. Abe's denial of Jesus Christ didn't mean much. Hadn't Moses demeaned his own forensic prowess until reminded of Who had made his tongue? Moses had even dared argue with God, yet God had made him prophet. Jonah had run, but God had had him swallowed by a whale. Could Abe believe, despite his denial, even without knowing it, even without wanting to believe?

The Name of the King
10

"Then, what's the problem?" the rabbi asked. "You can't be someone you don't believe in. That's logic."

"*Why* don't we believe in him, rabbi?"

"Why? Because we're Jews, of course. Why else?"

"Wasn't Jesus king of the Jews?"

"Gentile propaganda! I suppose God told you that, too."

"Yes."

"King of the Jews," said Moe. "I didn't know that."

"What are you, some kind of theologian?" said the rabbi. "Where did you find him, Moe?"

"You shouldn't have seen that movie," Moe whispered.

"Tell me about the miracles," said Abe.

Taken by surprise, Rabbi Stanley B. Garlick momentarily lost control. His gorge rose, to wherever rising gorges go. "What kind of Jew are you?" he thundered. "I won't permit you to play your *goyische* games here."

What goyische games? Why was the rabbi so angry at him? Abe didn't know. All he was doing was asking questions based on what God had said. "Remember, rabbi, nobody in my family has ever not been Jewish."

"Yes, and nobody doesn't like Sara Lee. So what?"

"Moe said you could help me. I guess he was wrong."

"You're headed for big trouble, Abe Goldstein, or whoever you think you are. If you really were Jesus Christ, you'd know a lot more than you do."

Chapter Three
Exorcism

Abe sat in a psychiatrist's office. Moe had suggested it, feeling uncomfortable after the fiasco with the rabbi, and insurance had paid for it, so it was free. Moe had convinced Abe that people who see psychiatrists aren't necessarily crazy. Abe had made the appointment to humor him.

"Tell me about your father," said psychiatrist George Bogart.

"You mean my father on earth, or my Father in heaven?"

The psychiatrist smiled. "Let's start with your father on earth."

"I can't."

"It's a secret?"

"No. I just don't know anything."

"Let's start with something easy. How tall is he?"

"I don't know. I've never seen him."

"You've never seen your father?"

"No."

"Have you ever seen a picture of your father, Mr. Goldstein?"

"No."

"Were you raised in an orphanage? Are you adopted?"

"No. I was raised by my mom."

"Have you ever asked her about your father?"

"Sure. But she isn't talking."

Bogart nodded. He understood. Mr. Goldstein's parents weren't married. Of course his mother wasn't talking! He had been raised without a father and had adopted God. His decision to become Jesus made the connection sturdier and gave him the power he lacked. The problem was totally pedestrian, after all.

"Tell me about your mother, Mr. Goldstein."

"Sure. What do you want to know?"

"How well do you get along?"

"We get along fine, if we stay a few feet apart."

The Name of the King
12

"I think I don't understand."

"My mother has never hugged me; won't even squeeze my arm."

"That's a very common problem. People who can't reach out and touch someone."

"I'm the only one she can't touch. Of course, she has no friends."

"Not once in your whole life?"

"Not that I remember. The best she can do is hold me at arm's length and pat my back."

"Have you ever asked her why?"

"Sure. She isn't talking."

"How old are you, Mr. Goldstein?"

"I'm 32."

Hmm! Maybe Bogart had been wrong about him. Abe had opened an especially enticing vein. How thick were his good humor and tranquility? Did they conceal a psychiatric gold mine? Like every psychiatrist, Bogart was constantly searching for the classic case that would put him next to Freud. Could this be it?

"Mr. Goldstein, would you be willing to take some tests?"

"Sure, but I never was any good at them."

A few weeks passed. Abe sat in the psychiatrist's office again. Bogart was puzzled. Far from being a classic case, Mr. Goldstein had "passed" all the tests, from the Rorschach to the Minnesota Multiphasic and Stanford-Binet, and so on, with supernormal marks. The psychiatrist had expected otherwise. Having dared to hope that he was handling movie material--maybe another "Three Faces of Eve"--Bogart was understandably ambivalent about the results, but the fact that his own Oedipus Complex had been successfully resolved, with the aid of psychoanalysis, forestalled the danger that the disappointment would regress him to latent infantility, or worse.

Indeed, the strangest thing about Mr. Goldstein was that he seemed considerably more "normal" than everybody else. He thought he was Jesus Christ. Well, so what! Among Bogart`s other patients right now, were a couple of Napoleons--Napoleon was a traditional favorite--a George Washington, an Albert Einstein who could not explain why he knew no mathematics beyond long division, and even two Abraham Lincolns. There was even a Mary, Queen of Scots, who spoke English with a Slavic accent. *Explain that to me*, Bogart thought.

One of his patients was a "Harry Houdini," who revealed that he hadn't died when everyone thought he had. He had merely disappeared, and his disappearance was his greatest trick, which included the fact that he didn't look anything like Houdini. He was presently preparing his return to the stage. During every session, he pleaded with Bogart to allow him to prove that he could escape any restraint.

Exorcism
13

Because of their delusions, these people could not function "normally"; the Napoleons had a dangerous propensity for war, and the Washington kept turning up at the White House demanding that President Carter be removed. Unlike them, Mr. Goldstein could function, no doubt because he "didn't want" to be Jesus. It was an interesting gambit, obviously designed to conceal aberration, but quite transparent, the classic symptom of paranoid schizophrenia; against his will, "alien forces had taken control" of Mr. Goldstein's head. Indeed, wasn't his provocative "normalcy" symptomatic of itself? No one was normal. The fact that he was "normal" proved something was wrong. How "normal" could a man be, if he has to think about garbage all day?

But, if he could function, if he could work--which he obviously could--why not let him alone? Why lock him up and drive him crazy? Now, Bogart looked across his desk at Abe. Abe looked at him steadily, without challenge, smiling slightly, with a warmth that made the young doctor uncomfortable. It told him that, paradoxically, Mr. Goldstein's delusion was deepening.

"Mr. Goldstein, I have news that may disappoint you," said Bogart.

"There's no cure?"

"We can't find anything wrong with you."

Abe thought this over for a long time. "In other words, doctor, I am Jesus Christ? God is right?"

How easy it would be to go astray in this profession, Bogart thought. So many of his patients were genuinely brilliant. It was imperative to remember that their brilliance was often a function of their delusions. "Great wits are sure to madness near allied."

"Let me skillfully evade that question, Mr. Goldstein. Remember all those tests you took?"

"The ink blots that looked like ink blots?"

The ink blots were a mildly embarrassing blot on Bogart's psychiatric escutcheon. Despite his best efforts, Abe had been unable to see anything more in them than ink.

"Among others. What I mean when I say we can't find anything wrong with you, is that the tests show you to be a tad more normal than I am."

"Does that mean you're crazy, doctor?"

"Most psychiatrists are crazy. That's why they entered the profession."

"Because, if you are, I can recommend a good psychiatrist."

"You are most kind, Mr. Goldstein, but I don't trust them. I use a chiropractor."

"I was hoping you could tell me I'm not Jesus Christ."

"I know you were, Mr. Goldstein. You said that. But we don't do it that way. If I just tell you you're not Jesus Christ, would you believe me?"

"No, you're right. It wouldn't be enough. I've told myself many times I'm not Jesus Christ, but because of the dream and the voice I don't believe me. I was just hoping that, since you're a doctor, a psychiatrist . . . ."

"The way we do it, Mr. Goldstein, is to help you realize that you're not who you think you are."

Abe brightened. "Then there's hope?"

"I would be less than ethical, Mr. Goldstein, if I failed to tell you that my record with Jesus Christs is something that sorely needs prayer. Jesus Christs are stiff-necked, like their fellow Jews of old. I have a much better record with Napoleons."

"Doc, I need help. I can't stand this much more."

Was there anything Bogart could do for Abe Goldstein? To give him the help he said he wanted, could mean taking him from his family. It would mean the usual drugs. It might mean incapacitation, with no sure hope of recovery. Some patients emerged from drug therapy worse than before. Of course, that was something the profession didn't like to discuss. Do no harm, said the physician's oath. Let well enough alone. There was so much the profession didn't want to discuss. It was changing. Bogart was losing faith, constantly arguing with his colleagues. The present campaign for "death with dignity" was disturbing. Why? Wasn't death with dignity humane, even a Hippocratic goal? Bogart didn't know why he was troubled. Certainly the bizarre disappearance of Mrs. Harris was a factor. Bogart had been unable to find anything out. The relative who came to get her had mentioned a vacation in Europe. Dr. Bogart needed one himself.

Abe had told him about the film festival where he had seen the revival. What was it called? "King of Kings?" Bogart hadn't seen it, and didn't plan to. He was an atheist, and such subjects bored him. Maybe Mr. Goldstein's delusion was nothing more than a delayed reaction to the film.

"We need to see how this thing develops," said Bogart. "Go home, but keep in touch. If it gets worse, we'll do what we must." The doctor liked Abe. Too bad! Bogart was afraid he would see Abe again.

So, now, Abe sat again in the all-night diner with Moe Stern, and was back where he'd started. Abe wasn't sure how he felt. He knew he was supposed to be depressed, but he wasn't. In fact, he felt a new exhilaration.

"I have an idea," said Moe.

"You had an idea, Moe. You had two ideas."

"So I made a mistake. Who do you think I am? Jesus Christ?"

"I'm sorry."

"So listen. What do you know about Jesus Christ?"

"Nothing, except what I saw in that movie. That's how I know this is all a mistake."

"Abe, I read the New Testament."

Exorcism
15

"You read the New Testament?" Abe felt a combination of curiosity and fear. Jews did not read the so-called "New Testament." First of all, there was no such thing. As always, Abe was impressed by Moe's daring.

"I did it for you, Abe."

"How did you get a copy?"

"From one of those street preachers in Bryant Park, next to the library. I wore dark glasses and one of my son's magic-store beards. He passed it to me from inside his coat. There's no way anyone can trace it to me. You know what the rabbi would say if he knew?"

"He'd be mad?"

"Mad! Abe, have you ever grabbed a bone from a pit bull? Have you ever told Hulk Hogan he was queer?"

"No, but I did tell Shirley she couldn't have that Persian lamb coat."

"That's right. I forgot. Abe, you may be Jesus Christ, but you have *chutzpah*."

"Moe, I'm not Jesus Christ."

"That's right. I forgot."

"Moe," Abe whispered. "What did it say?"

"What did what say, Abe?"

"The New Testament, Moe. Remember? The one you got in Bryant Park. Moe, what's happening to you?"

"Did you know that Jesus Christ was a rabbi?"

"Jesus was a rabbi?"

"Did you know he was king of the Jews?"

"Moe, that's what the movie said. I asked you about it, and you said the movie was *goyische* junk. If you knew that, why did you let me say those things to the rabbi?"

"Abe, do you want to hear what the book says, or not?"

"I want to hear what it says, but I don't."

"The book says he was one of us, Abe. The Jews told the king to kill him."

"The Jews told the king to kill a Jew?"

"Sure. We're a stiff-necked people. If no one's killing us, we'll do it ourselves."

"Why?"

"Abe, the solution is standing right under our nose. Remember the miracles?"

"Yes, Moe, I remember the miracles. I remember that when I mentioned the miracles, the rabbi kicked us out of his office. Do you remember that, Moe?"

"People came to Jesus with leprosy, with bleeding, with blindness, even death, and he cured them. Lazarus had been dead so long, he stank like a Chicago election, but Jesus raised him from the grave. The book says that was one of the proofs he was Messiah. That was why his fellow Jews hated him so much. Abe, don't you see what we have to do?"

"I have to be killed?"

"No, Abe. You don't have to be killed. You have to try to perform a miracle, really try. You really have to embarrass yourself. Understand?"

"No."

"When you fail, we'll have proof that you aren't really Jesus Christ. You'll show it to God. He'll admit He made a mistake."

"How could God make a mistake?"

"Abe, do you want to be Jesus Christ, or don't you? Isn't George Burns God as much as you're Jesus Christ? Didn't George Burns admit he made the avocado pit too big? Isn't George Jewish?"

"Where would we find leprosy in this country these days?" Abe asked.

"We don't need leprosy," said Moe. "There's plenty of cancer and syphilis."

"God, thank you, thank you, for cancer and syphilis. Who am I to look such gifts in the mouth?"

"Let's go to Bellevue. It's close."

"Moe, did you happen to know that syphilis is contagious? Did you happen to know that your skin falls off? And you don't have to be a funny boy to get it. I heard that on the radio."

It was a good point. Abe wasn't usually so clever. Moe was not a funny boy, and he definitely didn't want his skin to fall off. "So, Mr. Know-It-All, what do you suggest?"

"Let's go to a cemetery. The people are dead. They can't hurt us anymore. I promise I'll make myself look like an idiot. I read about one in New Jersey, near Morristown."

Moe didn't want his skin to fall off, but he also didn't want to go to a cemetery. In his mind's eye, he saw Abe reciting incantations over a grave. Nearby, mourners and gravediggers attached to other graves watched. Moe heard singing, but the voices were dead. Wings flapped--Moe was sure he felt them on his face--and his hair stood erect. Besides, suppose, just suppose, God hadn't made a mistake. The chances of that were good. What other mistake had He made besides the avocado? What if Abe really were Jesus Christ! No, Moe definitely didn't want to conduct the exorcism in a cemetery.

"New Jersey!" he exclaimed. "Abe, use your head. How would we get there? We don't have a car. We'd have to take the subway, the bus and the tube, then another bus. It would take four hours, if we ever got there at all. They'd find our bodies in Paramus. Is that where you want to die, Abe? In Paramus?"

"There's a cemetery right near my house."

"Abe, Abe, that cemetery belongs to the church. Who do you think is buried there? Jews? Do you want to resurrect a gentile? God might just do it in spite. And it's probably illegal."

Exorcism
17

"We can do it at night."

The hair Moe had left now stood at full attention. There was a limit to friendship, and they had now arrived. As sure as God had made little, green avocados, with oversized pits, Moe Stern would not appear in a Christian cemetery--or even one run by the chief rabbi of Jerusalem--at night, even if God personally told him that in return his four daughters would marry Donald Trump. It was unlike Abe to suggest anything so bizarre. Abe seemed to be laughing at him gently, which was also unlike him.

"Why don't we fly to the sun?" said Moe. "We'll do that at night, too. We'll have nothing to fear."

By now, the night was giving way to day. People on their way to work were filling up the streets. Moe and Abe waited until they arrived, and then took a bus down Second Avenue to Bellevue, where the two evangelists announced their presence to the powers-that-be. Moe wisely didn't tell them that Abe was Jesus Christ. Shortly, they found themselves sitting by a bed.

"They didn't even ask for i.d.," Moe whispered.

"They believed what you said."

"What did I say?"

"You said we were medical missionaries."

"I know."

The man in the bed was comatose, and appeared to have been horribly mutilated, either by disease or by accident.

"Moe, shouldn't you have asked what this man has?"

"The worse the better, whatever it is," Moe said. "All right, lay on your hands."

"Meaning what?"

"Let's see." Moe referred to an impressive volume. "He's sick all over. Hold his head."

"Moe, I don't want to hold his head. He's loaded with disease. I could catch pus."

"Abe, there has to be physical contact. It says so right here. If you're worried about disease, you shouldn't be a garbageman."

"You hold his head, Moe. This is your idea."

"Abe, Abe, I'm not Jesus Christ, remember? You are. What would it prove if I hold his head? Now, do you want to be freed from this curse, or don't you?"

"Sure, Moe, sure. I'm sorry. I'm still not used to being Jesus Christ."

Abe tentatively took the man's head in his hands. As he had feared, it was repulsive, spongy, like old cottage cheese. There was a smell, the cloying, ancient smell of putrefying flesh. Abe knew it would cling to him forever. His fingers touched something wet. It ran over them and he recoiled. He was able to maintain the necessary contact only with great difficulty.

The Name of the King
18

Moe retreated to the door to avoid contamination. "Are you laying on your hands, Abe?"

"Yeah. Both hands are laid on. Hurry, Moe. What do I do now?"

"Tell him he's cured."

"That's all?" Abe could not believe it. As we have seen, Abe was not a diligent templegoer, but he certainly knew that Judaism is full of colorful ritual. Moe was the maven on Christianity, sure, but surely there was more to it than that.

"That's it," said Moe. "Tell him to get up and walk."

It was dark and quiet in the corner behind the screen. No one else was near. Abe's mouth began to form the words, but he still didn't know what he was supposed to say. Abe thanked the one and only God that the victim was in a coma, too far gone to testify against them.

At that moment, the victim opened his eyes. They were colorless and watery. Like every other aperture in his diseased carcass, they leaked. "Who are you?" he whispered.

"That's Jesus Christ," said Moe, instantly surprised he had said it.

"Moe!" Abe shouted as loudly as a whisper allows. What was happening to Moe? It wasn't like him to blurt such nonsense.

The victim closed his eyes. The tension noticeably left his body. A smile seeped across his face.

"You came," he whispered.

"Do it, Abe. Do it now."

"What do I say, Moe?"

"I don't know, Abe. You're Jesus Christ."

Abe pressed the paper-thin flesh at the temples. The sooner he said something, Moe would let him turn the fetorous victim loose, and the growing risk of infection would cease.

"By the power vested in me as Jesus Christ, rabbi and king of the Jews, and under authority of the laws of the City and State of New York and of the United States government, with God as my witness, I hereby, herewith and et cetera pronounce you cured of everything, from asthma to yaws, including whatever it is you have now, free of charge."

There was a stillness in the corner, heavy and portentous. Something was about to happen. Abe cringed and closed his eyes. Moe's opened wide, his pupils like frisbees floating on milk. A minute passed. Two. Five. Ten. Half an hour had passed when Moe rose.

"Abe, we did it," he exulted. "You're free." Moe didn't say so--he didn't need to--but Abe was free because of his advice.

Abe had to admit it looked good. The victim was back in a coma. He still had no color. He hadn't gotten up and walked. If there was any change at all, he seemed even more moribund. Abe's failure was a complete success. *Thank you,*

Exorcism
19

God, thank you, thank you! Now they had the proof that the voice had been a fantasy, more than vivid, yes, but nothing more. The dream had been a nightmare. As Moe had said, Abe was free. He wasn't Jesus Christ.

Why then was he suffering anticlimax worse than severe postpartum depression? Why was he sad? Shouldn't he be dancing like King David? He felt empty, as if he'd lost his purpose. Yes, he didn't want to be Jesus Christ--he was immensely relieved to hear Moe testify that he wasn't Jesus Christ--but it would have been a blessing to cure this poor man of his problem, whatever it was. What a pity they couldn't have it both ways. It seemed to Abe that he was profiting from the victim's misfortune.

Like conspirators up to no good, they skulked from the hospital, parted and finally went home. Where else would Abe go?

Chapter Four
Conjugal Heaven

Shirley was at it again. "*I* had to marry a garbageman. Was I crazy, Abe? Tell me. I want to know."

"Please, Shirl. Let me sleep."

"All right. I'll let you sleep. I know perfectly well that you work at night so you won't have to talk."

"Shirl, that's crazy. You know `perfectly well' I work at night because that's where McGillicuddy puts me."

"So I *am* crazy. Thank you. That's what I thought." Shirley's bovine eyes shone with triumph. "But it just so happens I read *Cosmo*. Did you know they know all about you, Abe? You're not fooling anyone."

Why did she do it? It had nothing to do with menstruation. Once a month wouldn't be so bad, but she did it all the time. Was it part of being a frustrated Jewish American Princess?

"Please, Shirl. Let me sleep."

"You should have stopped me, Abe. If you'd ever had any feeling for me, you would have. The fact that you didn't, proves you don't. If you loved me as much as you said you did, how could you suggest marriage? Why didn't you tell me you had this fetish for garbage? Whoever heard of a Jewish garbageman, anyway? A Jew is supposed to be a dentist, a lawyer, an accountant. A Jew is supposed to make money.

"You should have left and joined the Foreign Legion. That's what it's for. There's plenty of garbage in the Sahara. I could have married Sid Bloberg. You know what he is today, Abe? I met his wife the other day, coming out of K-Mart, with her nose as high as the rear end of a horse. She hates me, of course. She knows I could have married Sid.

"Do you know what he is? Are you going to answer me, Abe, or not? Because if you're not, I honestly don't see any reason why I should waste valuable energy trying to save our marriage by communicating, like *Cosmopolitan* says. I asked you whether you know what Sid Bloberg is."

Conjugal Heaven
21

Abe wanted to save the marriage for three reasons: first, he couldn't afford another wife; second, he was Jewish; third, he was just as crazy as she was. "Okay, Shirl. I'll communicate. Yes, I know what Sid Bloberg is. He's a royal *schmuck*. End of communication."

"He's a tax collector for I.R.S., is what he is, Mr. Know-It-All. He's somebody. He doesn't come home smelling of garbage."

"He stinks anyway, Shirl. He's a spy."

"So what! He's an important government official."

"You should have married Hitler. He was an important government official too."

"I warn you, Abe. I won't sit still and be insulted. Where were you, anyway? Do you know what time it is? Just look at the clock."

"I was at Bellevue Hospital, Shirl."

"That's where you belong. I hope you had your head examined. *Why* were you at Bellevue Hospital? May I ask? I'm only your wife, Abe. That's all."

Well, why *had* he been at Bellevue Hospital? To exorcise Jesus Christ by failing to perform a miracle? He was tempted to tell her that, to drive her even crazier than she was. "If you really want to know, Shirl, I went to visit a sick friend."

"Why don't you apply at I.R.S.? Of course, they wouldn't give you a job like Sid's. He's smart. He's a computer *mayven.* He practically invented them. You can't even type. You know where Sid once took me, Abe? To the Catskills. We spent the whole day. We actually ate at Grossinger's. Where do *you* take me, Abe? Can you tell me in God's name why we had to see that movie? Was that any place for a Jew to be? You *are* a Jew, aren't you, Abe?"

"The movie said Jesus was king of the Jews, Shirl."

"Sure it said that, Abe. Don't you know why? Do you have any brains at all? It said that to con dumb *Yids* like you. Don't you know who makes those movies, Abe? Gentiles! That's why Hollywood lies."

"Shirl, Shirl, is Metro-Goldwyn-Mayer a gentile? Is he? Is George Burns a gentile? Is Sydney Pollock a gentile? Sydney Pollock, Shirl."

"I happen to know that Robert Redford is."

"Sure he is, Shirl. He's a token *goy*."

She continued, perorated, even fulminated and embellished, but, after a while, Abe could no longer hear the words. Thank God, that always happened. It was a safety valve. The voice itself, without the meaning, was bad enough, like a continuous car crash. Her large, covetous eyes trembled. Her small head bobbed in imbecilic menace on her long neck. Abe told himself to pretend he was in a World War II foxhole and hunker down, but he couldn't. He had a death wish.

"Then why do the Christians attack Hollywood, Shirl? Why do they hate Hollywood so much? Tell me that, Madam Expert."

Shirley opened her mouth, then closed it. She had no answer, but Abe knew his triumph would not be worth the pain. Her face turned red. Pressure was building in her, as in a boiler, and her face was the gauge. The only thing he didn't know was when she would explode. "Oh, woe is me," she said. "Woe is me." She swayed as she lamented--she always did that--and Abe fell asleep at last to the lullaby of her keening.

The next afternoon, Moe called. His voice was solemn, masking shock. "Turn on channel two," he whispered.

A face Abe barely recognized was there, a lively face, full of color. "They can say what they like," said the face. "I know who cured me. I was cured by Jesus Christ."

The camera cut to a commentator who was trying to suppress a smile. "He answered your prayers?"

"Man, He was *here*! He spoke to me, said I was cured. He held my head in His hands. The doc tried hard, I know, but until Jesus came, it amounted to nothin'. And if even one thing I've said ain't true, my name ain't Honky Ryan."

The camera cut to the commentator again. Now, he was chuckling. "Welcome back, Horatius Ryan."

The camera cut again to a doctor in a white coat and stethoscope, who spoke in the crisp, pseudo-British style of a New Delhi Indian educated at Cambridge. "If Mr. Ryan chooses to believe he was cured by Jesus Christ, I'm certainly not going to argue with him. In this democracy of ours, we should encourage every line of thought, and Christianity is no exception. What we need to know however is whether the new Polyakov compound we tested on him--with his permission, of course--had anything to do with it."

"Doctor, the compound you tested comes from Polyakov Pharmaceuticals?"

"Correct. In West Germany."

"Shouldn't its immense reputation make the compound the most likely reason for the cure?"

"One would like to think so, but, you see, we only had time to use it once. Not enough."

"Whoever or whatever saved Horatius Ryan--thank you. Ken Walker, eyewitness news. Good afternoon."

Abe turned off the television. The drapes were closed and he sat in the dark. Thank God Shirley hadn't seen it. But, how did he know that? How could he be sure she hadn't seen it, just because she wasn't home? In fact, suppose McGillicuddy had seen it. Suppose he used it as an excuse to fire Abe. The only thing Abe knew how to do was drive a garbage truck. Who else would hire him?

Fear was in the room. It sat in the corner, behind the large, plastic plant, watching him, smiling, waiting to tear out his intestines. Suppose the same report was on the evening news and one of his nemeses did see it? Abe brightened. So what! The report hadn't mentioned him. Why on earth would anyone think Abe was involved? If anyone asked him about it, he'd play dumb. If anyone tried to connect him, he'd deny it.

It was the medicine, he thought. The new medicine from Polyakov, in Munich. It had to be. Abe thought it several times, trying to convince himself, failing to squelch the oozing panic in his stomach.

Moe called again. "How were we to know about the medicine?"

"It *was* the medicine, Moe. It *had* to be the medicine."

"Sure, *you* know that, Abe. *I* know it. But we don't *know*."

"Moe, you picked a gentile. Why?"

"Abe, use your head. Would Jesus save a Jew? Besides, I had to tell them we were missionaries. Remember? Have you ever heard of a Jewish missionary?"

"And if the rabbi finds out?"

"Have you ever grabbed a bone from a pit bull? Have you ever told Hulk Hogan he was queer?"

"Moe, he'll talk. He's talking now."

"What do you suggest we do, Abe? Kill him?"

"We'll pay him off."

"With what? Free garbage?"

"Couldn't we just take him prisoner?"

"Abe, we need another test."

"What good would that do, Moe? We'd never know for sure. There would always be a doctor who'd take credit for his `cure.' When the real Jesus Christ was laying on his hands, things like leprosy were hopeless. The doctors didn't try."

"You're right. We need a really hopeless case. Abe, I've got it. Let's go down to the school for the blind."

The next morning, they sat opposite a black man named Bill Chase, who had been blind since birth. There was no chance Bill would ever see. His problem was beyond the reach of medical science and he was taking no treatment.

"Do you believe you could ever see?" asked Abe.

Bill Chase smiled. "Only Jesus Christ Himself could give me sight."

They did not comment. Why confuse or offend him? They were sitting in a garden on school grounds. The city's noise seemed far away. Water ran at their feet in a tiny brook. Abe bent, extracted some mud and kneaded it, preparing a poultice.

"What are you doing, Abe?" Moe asked.

"I don't know. Strange. I don't know what I'm doing, but I do it."

The Name of the King
24

Abe put the mud on Chase's eyes. It stuck there. Water cascaded down his face. "It feels like mud."

"That's what it is, Bill. Sit here for a while. The only one who could give you sight will do so. Wash off the mud in the brook, and you will see. Tell no one we were here. Let the people think it happened by itself."

Bill Chase laughed. Abe had made the most ridiculous statement Bill had ever heard. The doctors had never told him exactly why he couldn't see, but he knew it was impossible, after years of ineffective treatment. The administrators had asked him to meet these men, to talk about the school. The office had said they were grant-makers from a wealthy foundation, who, if properly impressed, might send some money. The office had not said they would put mud on his face and tell him his sight would be restored.

So, he laughed, and, as he did so, the two would-not-be faith-healers melted into the trees and disappeared. Abe was so happy, he even rode the subway with pleasure, too preoccupied with happiness to guess which of his fellow passengers were muggers. It was over at last. Moe had been right. Abe felt guilt because they had taken advantage of Bill as they had the man at Bellevue, but, because they had, Abe could now return to normal life, such as it was.

"Let's go to my place and celebrate," he said. "This is a great day." He was so happy, he even forgot about Shirley.

Chapter Five
Conjugal Hell

They found the place full of police. Shirley had called them to report a burglar, and they had him cornered on the couch. The "burglar" was Honky Ryan, still cured.

"I'm not a burglar," he was still insisting, when Abe and Moe arrived.

"Of course you're not a burglar, lad," said Sergeant Bobby Combs. "We were just wondering what you were looking for on the Goldstein back porch. I know the Fordham Road bus doesn't stop here. Maybe you were transferring to the Westchester El."

Combs couldn't wait to hear Ryan's explanation. Burglars caught in *flagrante delicto* said the craziest things. Recently, a woman had found a burglar (or worse) in her closet, and had shot him when he knocked her down on the bed. The burglar later told Combs that he had been waiting for a cab, had begun to suspect the closet was not a hack stand, had become disoriented and claustrophobic because of a chronic health condition, and had no idea why the woman had shot him when he tripped leaving the closet and accidentally knocked her down. The burglar's attorney had recently filed suit against the lady's insurance company on a contingency basis, and of course she would do time on the gun charge, to emphasize the folly of taking the law into one's own hands.

"I told you, Sarge," said Honky Ryan. "I'm looking for Abe Goldstein."

"*Why* are you looking for Abe Goldstein?"

"Did you happen to know he's Jesus Christ?"

Combs gave Honky Ryan a droll smile. At last he understood. It was a simple nut case, not his line at all. He would call the hospital people and be done with it. What a pity Honky was a fellow Irishman. He was embarrassing his noble race in front of these Jews. Everybody knew that Jesus Christ was Roman Catholic.

The Name of the King
26

Shirley Goldstein sat on the love seat. Her mouth hung open. The bottom of her jaw almost touched her knees. Her eyes bulged. What was left of her mind was leaking from her ears. She was speechless, not an easy condition to arrange.

"Let's get to the bottom of this, Honky," said Combs. "This looks like himself now. Let's ask him who he thinks he is."

"Sure."

"Who are you, sir?"

"I'm Abe Goldstein. That's my wife, Shirl."

"Can you prove it, Abe?"

"Sure. Here's my chauffeur's license. I drive a garbage truck for the Department of Sanitation."

"Would you happen to know my cousin McGillicuddy?"

"He's my boss."

"Are you now, or have you ever been, Jesus Christ?"

"No."

Honky Ryan exploded. "He's lying."

"Jesus Christ lying?" said Combs.

"Sergeant, we're Jews," said Moe. "Why would we pretend to be Jesus Christ?"

"A good point," said Combs. "Everybody knows Jesus Christ is Roman Catholic."

"There must be a law against such accusations," said Moe. "It's McCarthyism."

"Are you calling Jesus Christ a Communist?" said Combs, who had been trained at the academy not to lose his temper. "Because, if you are, this billy club says you won't get away with it."

"What's McCarthyism?" asked Abe.

"Abe, what have you done now?" Shirley whispered, starting to recover.

"You still don't get it, do you?" said Ryan. "Look at me, man. Didn't you see me on television yesterday?"

"I've seen you somewhere," said Bobby Combs. "Was it in the Post Office?"

"Look, he cured me. I was almost dead--incurable, in Bellevue Hospital--and he cured me."

"How?"

"He just touched my head and said I was cured."

"But, man, that's no proof he's Jesus Christ."

"A voice said he was."

"Sure it did. You were delirious. I've heard voices myself."

"So have I," said Abe.

Conjugal Hell
27

"Remember the California preacher who healed the sick on TV?" Combs asked. "He said he heard a voice, and he did. It was his wife, on a microphone stuck in his ear."

Shirley moaned. Life as she knew it was coming to an end. Hadn't Abe told her he'd visited a "sick friend" at Bellevue? Obviously this confession was proof of his guilt--but what was he guilty of? He certainly wasn't Jesus Christ.

The door opened. A black man came in, looking around the room, searching, an activity compounded by his electric-black eyes. They were like revolving neon quoits, like twin volcanoes preparing to erupt. The others stared at them, mesmerized, sure they would do so.

"I'm looking for Abe Goldstein," he said.

"Sure you are," said Combs. "Everybody's looking for Abe Goldstein. Abe Goldstein is a very popular man."

"And who might you be?"

"When I got here I thought I was a New York policeman, but now I'm not sure."

"So that's what you look like." Electric-Eyes visually feasted on Combs.

"He's Abe Goldstein," said Moe, pointing.

"Moe!" said Abe.

"Abe Goldstein!" said Electric-Eyes. The searchlight eyes caressed Abe's face. Abe sensed approaching doom.

"No!" said Abe. "I'm not Abe Goldstein. I've never been Abe Goldstein. I don't even know who Abe Goldstein is."

"You're not Abe Goldstein?" said Shirley. "But when we were married you said you were. Who are you, Abe?"

"He's Jesus Christ," said Moe.

"Moe!" said Abe.

"I think the lady has a good question," said Combs. "If you're not Jesus Christ, and if you're not Abe Goldstein, who are you?"

"I don't remember."

Electric-Eyes pointed at Abe. "He's lying. I recognize his voice."

"Lying again, Abe?" said Combs. "Doesn't that prove you're not Jesus Christ?"

"Who are you?" Moe demanded of Electric-Eyes.

"A good question," said Combs. "I was afraid to ask.

"Don't you recognize me, Moe? You were there."

"Would somebody tell me why we're supposed to recognize everybody who walks in that door?" asked Combs.

"Maybe it's because I've changed," said Electric-Eyes. "But I recognize you. You and your friend gave me sight. I can see. I can see." Electric-Eyes frolicked around the room among them. "You're a New York policeman." He pointed. "You're Horatius Ryan. He healed you, too. I saw it on the radio. Lady,

I'm sorry, I don't have any idea who you are, but I'll believe anything you say. I'm Bill Chase--I see the flowers--and you, you're Abe Goldstein, and you might as well be Jesus Christ."

"Abe, what have you done?" whispered Shirley. She called him Abe from habit. She had to call him something. She moaned. Her family had always berated her for marrying Abe. What would they say when they found out she didn't know who he was?

Abe appealed to Electric-Eyes and Honky. "Please, please. Don't tell anybody else."

It was a long time before they all agreed to leave the house. Even so, when Abe looked furtively through the Venetian blinds a couple of times, he saw Ryan and Chase skulking through the trees. There was no danger that Shirley would call the police again. She sat on the sofa in a trance. Her mouth still hung open. She would catch many flies before dawn.

He took the night off. While dressing early the next morning, he heard sounds outside. Bill and Honky were still there, pointing at the house. Ingrates! Had they stayed all night? A couple of television cameras stood on the lawn. Someone knocked on the door. "Mr. Goldstein?" said an authoritative voice. "Charles Wasserman. *New York Herald.*" The voice softened. "*Landsmann*?"

Abe ran to the television, turned it on and saw--his face. Where had they gotten that picture? He looked like the guilty man in a police lineup. He turned it off before he could hear what was being said and began running aimlessly around the room. The telephone rang.

"Hello?"

"Mr. Goldstein?" It was a voice of immense, but honeyed, power. Was it God, now talking on the phone? Why did God now talk with an Italian accent?

"Yes."

"Vincent Blandino, Superior Pictures, in Hollywood. We must buy your utterly inspiring story. Who is your agent?"

Abe hung up, ran to a window and peered through the blinds. The back yard was clear. He climbed the fence into the next yard, kept ahead of the dog, cut through the alley and ran.

At work, the dispatcher said McGillicuddy wanted to see him. That large dignitary sat behind his desk, smiling broadly. Abe could almost see canary feathers on his lips. McGillicuddy handed him a paper.

"What's this?" Abe asked.

"Suspension," McGillicuddy chortled.

"Suspension! For what?" How could a man who just last year had won the Metropolitan Sanitation Association's Garbageman of the Year award--for the second time--be suspended? Suspension meant that he no longer would feel the power of the truck through his hands. The breeze would no longer caress his departing hair.

Conjugal Hell
29

"Psychiatric evaluation. You're to report there right away. Here's the address. Don't tell them I sent you." McGillicuddy folded his arms, his satisfaction as large as he was. Abe had no right to be Garbageman of the Year.

"There's nothing wrong with me, Mac. You know that."

"I'll tell you what I know, Abe. I know I have a responsibility to the people of the City of New York. You know how much one of our trucks weighs, Abe? You know what could happen if one of them got loose? Every one of our drivers is personally certified by me, Frank McGillicuddy, and I won't risk my reputation on a driver who has delusions. It's all in the regulations, Abe, if you'd care to have a look." McGillicuddy extended a large, dog-eared volume.

What could Abe say? Hadn't he himself worried about an accident when the voice was reverberating through his mind? Thank God that didn't happen any more.

"You mean, I'm fired?"

"You're suspended. If I had the power to fire you, I would, but you're entitled to a hearing. The shrink will decide what happens to you next."

"Why do you hate me so much, Mac?"

"I don't hate you, Abe. It says here in the regs. that I can't hate you, so I don't. It says I should love you, so I do. I don't want it said of Frank McGillicuddy that he made Jesus Christ drive a garbage truck."

The next thing Abe knew, he was walking aimlessly down the sidewalk, hands in his pockets, hunched over, hat brim low. He didn't want anyone to see him. He was a total failure. He had ruined his life. He wasn't even good enough to drive a garbage truck. No one would hire him now. Shirley was right. She had been right all along. Abe descended into the subway and rode home. It was late in the day. The sun was setting. The thermometer was falling. It would be a nippy night, even this late in the spring. He shivered.

Now he was crossing the grass to the front door. All he had to do was get inside. He would lock the door and hide, never come out. What was the point in seeing the psychiatrist? He had seen a psychiatrist. He already knew he was a failure. He didn't need another psychiatrist to tell him that's what he was.

Abe's key wouldn't work the lock. That had never happened. What was wrong? He jiggled it, pushed and pulled without success. He knocked.

"Shirl?" he said.

"Go away, Abe." Her voice was so close that he started. She was sitting on the floor, inside, against the door.

"Open up, Shirl."

"You don't live here any more, Abe. You left a long time ago. Remember?"

"Shirl, what are you talking about? I went to work. I've been gone a few hours. Are you crazy?"

"No, Abe, I'm not crazy. You are. But I'll tell you what I'm talking about. I'm talking about the fact that I never dreamed a human being could be humiliated as much as you've humiliated me. I'm talking about the fact that what you're doing now is *even worse* than handling garbage. You're a crook, Abe, a faker, a swindler."

As she listened to herself say what she had been thinking so long, she realized how bad her suffering actually was, and the sound of her voice enraged her.

"You call yourself a Jew?" she screamed. "You're no Jew. If you really were a Jew, at least you'd be Meyer Lansky."

"Why am I not a Jew, Shirl?"

"You know why. Pretending to be Jesus Christ."

"Shirl, I'm not pretending to be Jesus Christ. I was appointed."

"See? Listen to yourself."

"What do you want me to do, Shirl?"

"I want you to leave, Abe, or whoever you are."

"Are you talking divorce, Shirl?"

"Yes, I'm talking divorce, you bastard."

"And you call that Jewish?"

"Don't you dare lecture me about what's Jewish, you no-good, rotten skunk."

"What about the kids, Shirl?"

"We'll move. We'll change our name. They're still young. Maybe they'll recover."

"Don't they need a father, Shirl?"

"Yes, you bastard, you no-good, *goyische,* rotten skunk, they do need a father. What are you?"

"Could I at least have my clothes, Shirl?"

"Sure. I burned them. The ashes are in the can at the curb. Help yourself."

What could he say? Hadn't he just been telling himself she was right? Sure she had kicked him out. What else should a total failure expect?

He slunk away from the door, crossed the grass and reached the sidewalk. Sure enough, the ashes that had once been his clothing were in the can. He looked both ways. He had never reached the sidewalk without knowing where to go, but now, even this early in his banishment, he didn't. How could a man who had no home, no job, no family, no friends, no clothes and no destination, know which way to go? *Why me, God*? he asked, as he had so many times.

He was an inoffensive, undemanding man. He had the usual, human weaknesses--envy, venality, carnality--nothing more, certainly not pride. Once in a while--not often--he saw another woman who caused a weakness in his knees, but he had never done anything about it. He had never deliberately hurt anyone. *God, what did I do?*

Are you about ready to stop fooling around?

Conjugal Hell
31

God, what do you mean? Abe felt terror that mounted to panic. He got behind a hedge and fell to his knees. *God, how am I fooling around? Please, stop me.*

No problem, Abe. I have all day.

Abe took the first subway train that came along, rode a while, got off and walked. He had no idea where he was or was going. What difference did it make? He reached Central Park and walked along Central Park West. The rich, the powerful, the influential, the witty and beautiful, walked there, too, and paid him just enough attention to wish that he were gone. Bums in various stages of dissolution were there, bums like Abe, who belonged on Columbus Avenue.

He got tired, lay down on a bench and fell asleep. When he awoke, it was the dawn of a glorious day. It was warm. Birds were singing in the trees. Bees were sipping nectar; the very air was perfume--and his shoes were gone.

Chapter Six
Brief Encounter

"Did you get the money, professor?"

In anyone else, *Herr Doktor* Professor Heinz Vörst would have seen impertinence. One did not ask such questions of the director of the Department of Heredity at the Kaiser Wilhelm Institute, especially if one were merely 18 and smiled provocatively; but Horst Krüger was *Herr Doktor's* best student. Vörst often told him his troubles. Despite the age difference, they were so *simpático.*

"Yes, young friend. I got it. The Institute will not collapse. Our historic work continues, despite the disgrace."

"Disgrace, professor? You? I don't understand."

"In America, I am called `the world's most renowned eugenic psychiatrist.' In New York, I was lavishly praised by the Selkirk Foundation. The so-called 'birth control' people are printing our work. The Schoonhoven Foundation's generosity has saved us. But here? In our own country? In the year 1930, so-called modern times? We are ignored. We are tolerated. We are made the butt of stupid night club jokes. Only in America could I find enough support."

"If only we could be like the Americans. Why can't we?"

The professor removed his *pince nez* with thumb and forefinger. It was an exquisite gesture he had learned in France, and Krüger had gotten used to it. By now, he knew, it would introduce a profound statement. Sure enough, the professor shrugged and sighed with deprecation. He was impressed. Young Horst was showing the promise he expected.

"A logical question. An important question." The professor smiled. "The answer is that we can't be like the Americans because we are ruled by frightened, little men."

"But if euthanasia is so humane . . . ."

Vörst pointed with his *pince-nez*. "Precisely. It *is* humane. It is the best way to solve the problem of lives not worth living. That is why they do not want it. They want other countries to surpass us. They want our country on its knees, humiliated, bankrupt, broken by the cost. And they want to use this problem for the purpose."

It would have been difficult for an eighteen-year-old skeptic to withstand this. Vörst had been saying it for years, softly, slyly, as subtle as the Chinese water torture, just a drop at a time. But Horst Krüger was not a skeptic. He believed. His entire being cried out for vengeance.

"The bastards. They are traitors."

"Yes. They are traitors."

"Who are these people, *Herr* Dr. Professor?"

"Don't you know, my young friend?" A piece of chalk was in his hand. He turned to the blackboard and drew a shape, deliberately making it screech until the sound echoed painfully in the otherwise empty lecture hall like the hellish chanting of long dead teutonic souls. When he had finished, Krüger saw an obscenely large, six-pointed star.

Herr Dr. Vörst looked at him like a conspirator. They shared a smile and breathed as one. Vörst was pleased. He had chosen well. They were so *simpático*. Perhaps at some point Vörst would tell him the true purpose of his work, now known only to himself and Adolf Hitler. The Führer had suggested he develop someone like Krüger--someone with the loyalty of a virus and the pedigree of Thor--just in case. "Suppose you die," the Führer had whispered.

"You will make a fine physician," said Vörst.

The thrill of being treated as an equal, as a colleague, by a man who had been in jail with Hitler, was intoxicating, and had the effect of making Krüger act older than his years.

"Have you thought of emigration?" Krüger asked.

"To America?"

"Yes. They treated you so well."

"The thought is tempting, I must confess. America is our sister. Did you know that because of emigration the Americans once considered adopting German as their native language? England has been her traditional enemy from the start, and still would be had not Churchill arranged the Lusitania fraud. No doubt that is why America has done such fine work. While we struggle and sink under the intolerable weight of useless eaters, the Americans have refined sterilization to an art. You must read Madison Grant's *Passing of the Great Race* and Lothrop Stoddard's *Revolt Against Civilization: The Menace of the Under Man*. Here. Take them. But our rightful place is here. If we abandon the Fatherland, our name would be a curse. There is much to do."

There *was* much to do, and Krüger did it, but for some years, even after he won his medical degree, he suffered. Were he less true to his principles, there would have been no problem. His father, a Lutheran pastor, had considerable influence, along with a modest "fortune" his industrialist grandfather had brought home from South Africa, which the pastor was dissipating among the "deserving needy." However, Krüger wasn't one of them. His father disapproved of young Horst's patriotic activities, to such an extent that he refused to finance them, which caused an inevitable rupture.

His hands trembled early in 1933, when he read as follows in the *Munchener Medizinische Wochenschrift*: "Six thousand physicians are looking for work and bread in Berlin . . . ." While almost 60% of the doctors in that city were Jews--something the Americans wouldn't tolerate--his taxable income fell to 9,470 RM in 1934.

It was not until the Nuremberg laws of September, 1935, that Krüger's fortunes began to turn around. Jewish doctors, now stripped of citizenship, were fired. Aryan doctors replaced them. Vörst, now the chief architect of Hitler's "racial hygiene" legislation, and completely vindicated, found his prize pupil an important post in the Party's new Office of Racial Policy, where Krüger supervised the production of dossiers on every inhabitant of metropolitan Munich. Now that "sexual traffic" was illegal, it was imperative to know who had Jewish blood and how much.

The work was a joy. The money was good. The boss was a young physician, Dr. Walter Gross, an aggressive speaker appointed in May, 1934, by Rudolf Hess himself, despite which his appearance was classically Semitic. Meeting him in the street, one would have instinctively called him a Jew.

Krüger could not relax in his presence. The effort of concealing his suspicion was intense. He consulted the latest Aryan scientific findings in phrenology, ear lobes, even gait. Most of them proved Dr. Gross was a fraud. Yet, recruiting the services of his own department, Krüger was able to trace Gross's lineage back to Wotan. Something was wrong. How could genealogy contradict science? The effort made Krüger one of the nation's foremost experts in both.

It was 1937. Krüger sponsored a contest in cooperation with the National Socialist Teachers' Association and the Propaganda Ministry, to inspire high school teachers to investigate the racial roots of local families. It brought him praise from Walter Gross. Vörst too was pleased. Other important people began to recognize his name. The *Arzteblatt für Berlin* told of a teacher in the contest who had found a Jew among the distant ancestors of a certain family, which didn't know he had been baptized in 1817. Another article discussed Krüger's campaign for "death with dignity," and quoted him at length: "There is no point of view, not legal, social, moral nor religious, which can justify the failure to legalize euthanasia for people who desperately desire death with dignity. I consider such legalization a simple duty of compassion. To deny the incurable patient the peaceful death he much desires is no longer compassion but the opposite."

Krüger put the paper down and left the office with satisfaction. It was a glorious day, brisk, windy, a Teutonic day. He was strolling through the

Pinakothek, surely one of the world's best museums, losing himself in the exhibits, wandering through the halls.

A girl deflected his attention, a tall girl, young, with a notebook, no doubt a student at the University of Munich. She was slender, everything about her was slender, from her long legs to her aristocratic face. She was fair, almost pale, blue-eyed, blonde, blonde enough to make Himmler gasp, and Krüger did so. He watched her through a window. She was outside, hair blowing in the wind, lips parted, teeth white. She looked like a woman on a Nazi recruiting poster, the most sublime Aryan specimen he had ever seen.

Mesmerized, he nevertheless tore himself away and ran for the exit. When he finally got to the place she had stood, she was gone. He scoured the neighborhood. He went to the university with growing desperation. Without a name, the registrar could do nothing. At last, beaten, utterly desolate, he gave up, mourning the love he had lost, but never had. Trying to forget, he immersed himself even more deeply in his work.

A couple of months later, he was standing on a platform, waiting for a train. After a brief illness, his father had died. Krüger was returning to Gunzburg, something of a conquering hero, to comfort his mother and take control of the estate.

About a coach length away, someone in a big hat was noisily rummaging in a handbag. Mildly interested, Krüger saw long legs beneath a fashionable frock. She finished, took her hat off and shook out her hair, cascading like an alpine stream from a mysterious, pristine source.

It was *she*. Her hair was still in motion, sublimely feminine and free. The air was on fire. He couldn't breathe. His mouth went dry, his body eaten up by fever. He was weak and put a hand out, looking for support.

She saw him, actually ensnared him in her glance. Surprise was on her face, surprise slowly combining with delight. She smiled. He saw teeth, or, rather, pearls on a string. She was actually coming toward him. Krüger knew that he would die.

"Oh," she said, arriving, flustered. "Sorry. You look like someone else."

"Would that I were he."

A scent enveloped Krüger. She was even more beautiful beside him. He was almost too taken aback to salute and "heil" Hitler.

"Let's pretend you are."

"All right. Let's pretend."

"No. Even better, let's pretend I came to meet you. That way you can be yourself."

"Splendid. Whom did you think I was?"

"An acquaintance I haven't seen for some time. No one important." She was lying, of course. Her face told him that. Why must women always lie? Why was she so nervous? Was the man she had been there to meet now waiting on the platform?

"A handsome acquaintance?"

"Handsome. Yes." She laughed.

The train had come. Still talking, they boarded and, quite naturally, sat down side by side, where the conversation ceased.

"Have you spent much time in Gunzburg?" he asked, trying to revive it.

"I've never been there. Is that where you're going?"

"Yes. My father died. I must see my mother and settle the estate."

"I'm sorry. No wonder you are sad."

"Am I sad? I didn't know that."

"You look almost forlorn."

"No. I am almost ecstatic."

"But, . . . your father."

"My father was a factotum of the Christian slave religion and an apologist for the Jews."

He was testing her, of course. The rebirth of the Reich paradoxically meant there were so many people one couldn't trust. To his delight, she took his arm. "How sad."

"Tell me about yourself," he said.

"No. I'd rather hear about you."

"Very well." He handed her his card. What man, however benighted, swinish, contemptible or thick, invited to discuss himself by the most beautiful, exciting woman he has ever met, would decline? "As you see," he tapped the card, "I am Horst Krüger, a physician, in the service of the Führer at the Office of Racial Policy." Krüger launched into a rendition of his "research" and racial theories; his adoration of the Führer; his ambitions; his reflections on National Socialist Woman; none of which would edify or even entertain.

"I have a passion for opera," he told her. "Do you?"

"Yes."

"Who is your favorite composer?"

"Wagner, of course."

"Of course! You look like a valkyrie. Why?"

"Silly. Because that's what I am."

Krüger was as close to heaven as one can be on this earth without leaving. Another increment, however small, and he would be gone. In his mind's eye, he saw her on his arm, wearing pearls, dressed in black, bowing as he presented her to the Führer.

"I also love poetry. I used to love Heine. '*Ich weiss nicht was soll es bedeuten, das ich so traurig bin.*' Lovely. Of course, that was before I knew he was a Jew."

"Thank God we found out."

Brief Encounter
37

"Do you know why I'm telling you all this?" he asked.

"You're a man, so you like to talk about yourself."

"Not only that. I'm telling you all this because I have decided to marry you."

She jumped up, like a doe surprised by a hunter as she bent to drink from a lake. "We're here. I must go."

Sure enough, they were stopping at Dachau. Such a lovely town. The ride had been so short. Krüger had been so entranced by the sound of his voice and profundities; he hadn't noticed. He grabbed her wrist.

"No. You can't. I've proposed. You are mine."

"Next time."

"When? Where?"

"Next week. Same train."

Next week, same train. He settled back against the cushions, lulled by the magic of her voice, ecstatic because he had won an assignation, longing for the moment when he would use her to launch a line of Siegfrieds. The train began to move. Suddenly, his eyes opened. He jumped up and looked anxiously out the window. He still didn't know who she was, or where to find her. He didn't even know her name. What had she done to him? He was usually so punctilious about details. He searched the receding platform. She was gone. Dachau, too, disappeared in the trees. Was she merely a phantasm, a sorceress? He groaned. There was no way he could wait a week.

Chapter Seven
Bad Blood

"Unfortunately, there appears to be an irregularity, *Herr Doktor.*"

"Irregularity? Preposterous! What on earth are you talking about, Bruckner?"

Gerhard Bruckner had made a minor, political career by being nice. Ideology interested him as little as a kick in the pants. In the United States, he would have been a justice of the peace, or a member of the Cedar Rapids City Council. All of which did no good in these times, when everything was ideological, and nice equaled stupid.

Krüger wore the characteristic, mocking smile. Bruckner had always disliked him. He had a mean streak as wide as a couple of *autobahns*. As a child, he had been fond of practical jokes, thinking himself immune from criticism as the offspring of the pastor, and had once done something very mean to Bruckner's daughter in church, snipping off a pigtail as it hung over a pew. She had come home, heartsick, the offended item in her hands. Krüger's father had whipped him to the point of blood and breathlessness. It had done no good.

"It is so good to have you back, *Herr Doktor*. If only the circumstances were happier."

"The circumstances will be perfectly adequate, Bruckner, when you settle the estate."

"The papers will be on your desk in Munich in the morning, *Herr Doktor*."

"Why can't I take them along?"

"Because I don't have them now," Bruckner lied. He didn't want to be there when Krüger saw the documents, which lay in a manila folder within easy reach in a desk drawer.

Krüger was furious. "I shall wait no longer," he said at the door. Irregularity, indeed!

But, when he looked at the papers a few days later, his outrage fled, replaced by horror. Like all of us, Krüger had suffered embarrassment, even humiliation, in his time. For instance, his father had insisted on making a Jew their family doctor. Krüger had never seen the man without a cigar. Always as a child, during consultations, Krüger had watched his cigar ash grow, waggling provocatively while he palpated, prodded and advised. Krüger had wondered whether it would fall into his playground wounds before the doctor could leave it in the tray. It never had, but the recollection made Krüger shudder, especially today. Only a Jew would think of smoking during a medical consultation. Indeed, the discomfort of being touched, even handled, by a Jew was still oppressive. The doctor had dared display his World War I Iron Cross in a prominent place in his waiting room. Inexcusable impudence! Worse, Krüger had made the mistake of asking him for a hospital appointment. The Jew had given it instead to his daughter's Jew fiancé. The humiliation of being snubbed by a Jew had been intense.

Yet, in his entire life, he could not recall a greater horror than what now mocked him on the page. Using Krüger's own genealogical techniques, in which he took such pride, Bruckner had discovered that, in 1771, one of Krüger's ancestors had been Jewish, and hadn't even bothered to convert.

Of course, Bruckner had been astounded, in view of *Herr Doktor's* present reputation. He didn't care if Krüger were descended from a Ubangi, or even a baboon (which he probably was); Bruckner had conducted the investigation in routine deference to the National Socialist rhetoric he ridiculed in private. The problem was that, once he had the findings, he hadn't known what to do. He was an innocent bystander around whom some idiot had built a pen of wild dogs. Whatever he did could be wrong and could be fatal. Someone would be angry with an anger that could not be overcome with *schnapps*.

He preferred to let the matter lie, perhaps destroy the documents, not even mention it to Krüger, who had grown into something dangerous. Bruckner had called Munich to verify that. But the people above Krüger had more power and were even more dangerous, and Bruckner was supposed to give the documents to them. Suppose they found out. Wouldn't his malfeasance utterly destroy the Nazi "loyalty" he had so assiduously faked? Bruckner had heard there was a "concentration camp" near Munich in a town called Dachau--he had passed through it many times, but had never gotten off the train--to which people who committed crimes like the destruction of documents were sent. He shuddered. Indeed, were the truth later to come out, wouldn't Krüger be furious because Bruckner hadn't warned him?

Bruckner had decided to be a "good Nazi," and tell the truth. Hadn't Krüger's father always taught that truth was the best policy? Probably nothing would come of it. How important was an ancestor in 1771 anyway, for God's sake? The only reason it wasn't a joke was that the National Socialist idiots were in power. If the young doctor took issue, "good Nazi" Bruckner would spout some Nazi nonsense.

The Name of the King
40

Then Bruckner had his brainstorm. He would both report the documents and conceal them. Wasn't Krüger a big cheese in the Office of Racial Policy? Bruckner would turn the documents over to him, and he could do as he liked. Wasn't the Office of Racial Policy in charge of such matters? Who could complain? In fact, Krüger would probably be grateful.

What Bruckner didn't understand were the racial requirements for high Nazi office. He didn't fully appreciate the distinction between the "small" and "large" certificates of ancestry. If Krüger's ambition could have been satisfied with routine government employment under the Civil Service Law of 1933, the small *Abstammungsnachweis* would have more than sufficed. All it required was that not more than one of an individual's four grandparents be a full Jew. Needless to say, National Socialist membership required a higher standard even of wives, promulgated by the very Office of Racial Policy where Krüger worked, certifying no Jewish blood whatsoever since January 1, 1800. So far so good. The requirement that proved to be Bruckner's undoing was the fact that the Führer corps of the SS required documented purity back to 1750, which Krüger's 1771 Jewish ancestor could not be blamed for, not having known that in 1933, goaded beyond endurance in the aftermath of the Treaty of Versailles, Germany would go collectively insane.

Krüger stared mindlessly at the proof of the intruder. Even his name was there: Polyakov. Krüger couldn't say it. What had he looked like? The typical short, bloated, hook-nosed Semite? What criminal things had he done? Krüger shuddered. His first reaction was disbelief. Surely there was something wrong with the documents. But there wasn't. By now, wasn't he an expert who lectured the professors? He had looked at such documents a thousand times. He had learned to smell a forgery as far as he could smell a Jew.

Krüger looked at the documents and saw his life go up in smoke. Could he reach the upper echelons of the Party with them hanging from his neck? Impossible! He would lose everything he'd worked for. He would be stripped of rank and utterly cast out. Krüger studied his hands with loathing, as if he were the victim of some fulsome disease. The horrid question asked itself, would not be denied. Was he a Jew? Krüger literally groaned. Surely his experience and training had overcome the disgusting infusion of Jewish blood. No! Such a justification paid deference to environment, rather than heredity, a Communist idea. Krüger groaned with redoubled *angst*, compounded by the fact that the campaign for death with dignity had lately been drawing flak, launched no doubt by hidden Jews. By now, the campaign was so well identified as his, he could not let it fail, especially since Vörst had privately explained its crucial importance to the plan.

That night he addressed the annual banquet of a society of influential engineers, all of whom were big contributors to the Party. "The question of whether we should spend all of this money on ballast type persons of no value was not important in previous years because the state had sufficient money. Now, conditions are different, and we really have to deal with this question."

So perfect was his discipline, no one knew he was in funk, and he suffered through the week. Almost too late, he remembered. The girl! The valkyrie soulmate he had chosen. It was almost time to meet her at the station. In fear and frenzy, he rushed there, arriving just in time. The train was stopping at the platform, making smoke. People talked, waiting to board. Conductors looked at their watches. Soon, she would come.

But she didn't. Krüger made a circuit of the platform without success, finally boarding the already moving train. He walked through all the cars. There was no sign of her. The ride to Dachau was interminable. Thanks to his duties, he knew the town well. He got off there, went into shops and asked about her. No one knew a thing. Maybe she was ill. Maybe she had missed the train. That was what he told himself.

That week, he got nothing done. He tried, but could not focus. Thank God he had picked such a competent staff. He spent the entire week just waiting for the day. When it came, he went to the station quite early and waited. She did not come. Again he rode the train to Dachau, walked through the cars and got off. Again he asked people about her. He didn't know what else to do.

The next week, he did it again. Returning to Munich, he went to the university, wandering the halls, seeking a clue, convinced she was a student there. He wound up at his desk, late in the evening, after everyone had gone, haggard, numb, trying to decipher what had happened. She knew he wanted her. He had even proposed. She had experienced his personal attraction and been enveloped in his charm. He had given her his card, so she knew of his importance. Yet, she had refused to appear or even call, which was unthinkable.

At last he got around to Bruckner. Only one explanation for the impossible snub occurred to Krüger. Bruckner, in Gunzburg, knew the girl from Dachau. She had told him of their meeting, of Krüger's proposal, of this chance to serve the cause. And Bruckner had told her of the Jew in Krüger's blood, which inevitably had caused her to recoil. Wasn't she the ultimate *Aryan* maiden? Wasn't it her sublime purity that had stunned Krüger into such disorientation that he had neglected even to ask her name? Of course she had fled and probably torn up his card. What else would an *Aryan* maiden do? Krüger's Jewish ancestor faded into history. Blood was less important than the triumph of the will. He had to find her.

Krüger called Bruckner in Gunzburg. "To whom else have you given this information?"

"No one, *Herr Doktor*. Is there someone else you would like me to inform?" Bruckner's voice was jovial, humorous, intimate and insinuating. He was lying, of course. He had told the girl. Krüger's psychiatric training made that clear. Krüger had to do something about him. All he needed was a plan.

The Name of the King
42

* * *

For a long time, he had resisted, in the firm belief that the children were alarmists. After all, German was the language of Goethe, of Schubert, of Heine and Beethoven; Germany was the most humane civilization on this benighted earth. Yes, there were aberrations, bad ones; in time, they would be corrected. Germany's good sense would prevail. The rumors of "concentration camps" were too grotesque to believe. Years ago, in 1927, he thought, he had spent some time in Dachau. Such a pleasant town!

Besides, whatever was happening wouldn't touch him personally. Joshua Erhard was a country doctor, far removed from the centers of influence. He was a Jew, yes, but he had always enjoyed a good relationship with the gentiles of Gunzburg. Wasn't he the family doctor for the local Lutheran pastor? Hadn't he saved the pastor's son after the horse had kicked him in the head? How on earth that *nudnik* had become a doctor was a mystery. His father, the pastor, had asked Erhard to refuse him the hospital appointment he had sought, and Erhard had warily acceded, giving it instead to Frieda's fiancé.

Erhard picked up the Iron Cross he displayed proudly in his waiting room and looked at it fondly, recalling his service in the war. *Hauptmann* Joshua Erhard! *Jawohl*! Its weight was reassuring, proof that the present unpleasantness would pass. He was a loyal German and his country had been deceived by the punitive Treaty of Versailles. No wonder there were problems. Hadn't he predicted them when the infamous treaty saw the light?

He had yielded only when the practice of medicine by Jews, at least in the countryside, had become almost impossible, despite his appeals to Gerhard Bruckner. What could he do? Flee to Berlin, like many other Jewish doctors, hoping that the cosmopolitan capital would be more hospitable? He hated Berlin. He was a country doctor, but the country no longer wanted him.

At last, he had agreed to leave. Frieda and his son-in-law David Polyakov had made the arrangements. David, too, had been reluctant, sharing his father-in-law's beliefs. It had taken so long. Without the money from David's family, it would have been impossible. They had boarded at Rotterdam. The celebration when they sailed had been exceeded only by the euphoria when they arrived in New York Harbor, in the protection of the Statue of Liberty. Frieda knew so much about it. Erhard was surprised. While they waited for processing at immigration, she had regaled them with the Statue's history, her meaning and construction. "The torch has been closed since 1916 because of crowds. It accommodates only eight or ten people." She even knew the entire Emma Lazarus poem by heart, not just the famous, few lines carved in Miss Liberty's pedestal. Erhard's sense of oppression cautiously receded. They even had joked about what they would do first in the promised land, the three of them contending to make the most outrageous proposal.

"And you David?" asked Erhard. "What will you do?"

"I want to stand at the torch, which has been closed since 1916, and read Torah."

"Hurrah!" said Frieda, clapping hands.

Perhaps because the promise was so bright, the betrayal was so devastating; the betrayal made the poetry a lie. Under the eyes of Miss Liberty, they were declared "undesirables." In 1934, influential foundations had proposed stronger immigration restrictions against Jews fleeing Nazi Germany. By the time Erhard, his daughter and son-in-law arrived, the quota of 24,430 a year had been filled. They were sent back. The trip had accomplished nothing.

Now, Erhard stood in his own house, in his own country, no longer a citizen, and without a place or profession. He had made some whispered calls; with apologies had been furtively denied. Even in the modest time they had been gone, it seemed, the profession had changed. Rumor said that doctors were doing strange things. Could he do them? The Hippocratic Oath wasn't binding any more. The sanctity of life that was his *raison d'être* as a doctor and a Jew lay in the trash, replaced by "useless eaters" no good to themselves or society, incurable idiots and the hopelessly insane, "who are mentally dead and therefore not truly human, who don't even know they are loved," yet drain the nation of scarce resources, "especially in these years of worldwide depression," but who have no rights to lose because they have none. An article in a popular magazine devoted to German sport and health condemned Christianity for the "present perversion of German thought." A doctor named Vörst, a eugenicist at the Kaiser Wilhelm Institute called upon the nation's psychiatrists to provide a humane and patriotic solution: "There is a higher morality, a state morality. We have neglected to see that the state is an organism, like the human organism and has corresponding laws. As doctors, we know that, in the interest of the whole human organism, less valuable members must be pushed out."

"Papa? Papa?"

Frieda had been talking to him. She was pulling his sleeve. "Yes, *liebchen.* What did you say?"

"We must try again."

"Have you forgotten, *liebchen*? *Fräulein* Liberty doesn't want us. No one wants us. We are undesirables."

"What should we do, then, Papa?"

"I don't know. Stay here."

"What would we do here, Papa? On September 30th, your medical license will be revoked under the new law. You and David will no longer be doctors, but attendants."

Erhard snorted bitterly. "After 31 years of practice. An attendant! *Heil* Hitler!"

"You will only be allowed to treat Jews, with permission."

"Is it true?" he asked David.

"Yes." Frieda gave thanks that the forthcoming cancellation of his license had persuaded him at last.

"How can David make a living?" she asked

Erhard nodded. "You are right, *liebchen.* Thank you for opening my eyes. I'm not only ignorant, I'm stupid. I have practiced so long. Another few years do not matter. You are young. You are not yet so stupid. Perhaps there is a remote corner of the world not yet purified that would tolerate a Jewish doctor. Where would you go?"

"Switzerland. Not far," said David.

"A humane people, like the Germans and Americans. Could you get in?"

"My family has money in Zurich. We would only need to get there."

"It is good to have money in Zurich. Yes, perhaps it could be done. Neither of you looks Jewish. Such a stupid thing to say--today almost everything is stupid--but it is true. Things that are totally idiotic, totally meaningless in normal times, now are important. Yes, try it."

"You must come with us, Papa."

"No. I look Jewish. I must stay away from you."

"Papa, because I don't look Jewish, there is great danger here. Something happened before we left."

She handed him a card. "Horst Krüger," he read. "*Arzt.* Office of Racial Policy. Yes. That's no surprise. The *nudnik* would work there."

"You know him, Papa?"

"Don't you remember, *liebchen*? He is the pastor's son."

"No. We'd never met--until he gave me his card." Frieda told her father what had happened. "I had to lie to get away. He said he was coming here to settle an estate. I got off just in time in Dachau. He frightened me, Papa. His eyes. His manner. So domineering. So acquisitive. Like a wolf. Someone who'll do anything to get what he wants. Believe me, Papa, it isn't easy looking like Sieglinde. What's wrong with him?"

"He's a Nazi. He was a Nazi as a child. Before Hitler."

* * *

As soon as he heard of the new program conceived at the Brandenburg psychiatric hospital near Berlin, Krüger volunteered. It was humane. Viktor Brack kept emphasizing that. That was why Jewish children were excluded. Jews did not deserve the "merciful act."

Bad Blood
45

Krüger couldn't understand the need for subterfuge. Wasn't the program saving German money? Wasn't it doing valuable research? Children with physical or mental problems were sorted for "selection." Those selected for extermination were marked with a plus. Humane death was administered slowly, so it could be disguised as pneumonia or bronchitis. Hermann Pfannmuller, at Eglfing-Haar, preferred starvation, and death of "natural causes," which was least likely to provoke the foreign press or "the gentlemen in Switzerland" (the Red Cross). To hell with them! Who cared what they thought!

All the institutions then sent a letter, telling parents their children had died suddenly of brain edema, appendicitis, etc., and that to prevent epidemic the body had been cremated. Some parents made trouble asking how their children could have died of appendicitis when the appendix had already been removed. Krüger shook his head. Were he running the program, such defective paperwork would not be tolerated. Besides, why not tell the parents what good work the government was doing? Wouldn't they be grateful?

When the program was expanded to include adult mental patients, the weak and inferior, Krüger saw his chance. He called Bruckner.

"As an influential, local official, you need to see what we are doing for the Reich, Herr Bruckner."

"Yes, I want to see what you are doing."

"You will visit Brandenburg as my guest. *Heil* Hitler."

From the beginning, Bruckner had lived in terror. The documents had brought no repercussions, but, recently, he had found his mistake. Should he tell Krüger? Yes, the idiot would be happy to hear the news, but wouldn't he also be angry because Bruckner had caused him such "suffering?" Wouldn't the fact that the documents had fooled him yield embarrassment Bruckner would cause? Hadn't Bruckner used Krüger's methods? Bruckner hadn't known what to do. He had no one to confide in. Frieda was the only person he had told. Krüger's call brought immense relief. Bruckner decided to say nothing. There would be no repercussions if he didn't resurrect the "scandal" again. Didn't *Herr* Doktor's most cordial invitation prove that? Bruckner was flattered. The people with the power considered him important. It was good to have influential friends.

Indeed, when he developed the sudden headache and horrific breathing problem at lunch in the doctor's office, Krüger had been most solicitous. "Has this ever happened before?" he asked, starting to write in a file. "Any family history?"

"Never. Please do something. Stop the pain!"

The pain was intolerable. The injection relieved it. Bruckner felt gratitude as intense as the pain. There was another injection, producing a pleasant lassitude. The room receded. His dear friend Krüger was still writing in the file. Bruckner tried to thank him, but could not shape the sounds, managing at best to produce a meaningless noise, which seemed far away.

The Name of the King
46

Now, he and Krüger were walking down the hall. He couldn't properly control his limbs. Krüger had to help. He was in another room and someone else was helping him undress. He was sitting on a bench, looking at a tile floor. Others sat around him. They were naked. Why? In fact, why were they behaving so obtusely? Didn't they even have the sense to be embarrassed? One was even drooling. Were they crazy? What was this place? What had happened to his dear friend Krüger? Bruckner shivered, feeling cold without his clothes.

Krüger watched with the other doctors through the square peep hole. After a few minutes, they cleared the room of gas. Special SS men loaded the corpses on stretchers and delivered them to the crematoria. Brack was radiant. The experiment was an unqualified success. "You have seen the future. With this simple, procedure, we have solved the Fatherland's economic and population problems. The growing danger of being overrun by genetically diseased defectives has been squelched. Permit me to remind you, distinguished colleagues, that the operation should be conducted only by physicians. The needle belongs only in the doctor's hand."

Krüger nodded. Brack was right.

Chapter Eight
Masquerade

e don't know where he is. We don't know what he is--today. But, we know he's out there--somewhere. We know he's alive. Simon's investigators have reliable witnesses. He has been seen."

At the mention of the hallowed name, the audience stirred. There were several, notable exhalations. The famous, flaming scar, that began under the speaker's thick, brown hair at the temple, and flowed down his pink cheek to the jawbone like a river of fire, was throbbing red.

". . . And so I pledge you half my fortune--certified if you will by financial statement--to the man who brings Horst Krüger to justice. I do this not just for the obvious reason that I am a graduate of Auschwitz and one of his victims. I do it for the others who could not be with us tonight--but who are surely here in spirit. I do it because I promised *Addonai* I would do it--and I shall do it, or my name isn't David Polyakov." His voice had risen to a trumpet crescendo, but now he chuckled and it fell. "And my name *is* David Polyakov."

There was silence as the double twist took effect. Then, one by one and table by table, the banqueters rose, nodding, smiling and applauding. Polyakov's self-deprecation, combined with an impish self-promotion, was so characteristic, and was an important element of his notable success. But he had earned the right to self-promotion. He deserved to be promoted. Had there ever been such a philanthropist? Yes, there were many who mentioned the need to catch Nazi war criminals; some even helped. But who as of this year of 5738 (1978 to Christian readers) had appeared before this august Jewish organization, meeting today in Garmisch-Partenkirchen--before an audience that just happened to include the French Ambassador to Israel--and pledged half a fortune that was worth two or three, to apprehend a man Simon Wiesenthal had hunted for years, a man who had rivaled Dr. Josef Mengele for cruelty. Polyakov had been honored by the

Israeli government for his efforts, and was the most famous former inmate of Auschwitz.

He left the dais and moved through the clapping hands, squeezing selected shoulders and kissing certain cheeks, working the crowd like a candidate for office. Although he had built a relatively small stake into a fortune of more than $2 billion, he was as modest as he was brilliant and never forgot his roots. Cynics said in wonder that he was too good to be true. He warmly greeted the French ambassador, who was purring.

"Thank you, David. Thank you. Thank you," said the ambassador, who was Jewish himself and against all reason had lived with guilt since he had seen the *gestapo* haul away his parents.

"You are too kind, Excellency," said Polyakov. "I am just a poor, but lucky Jew, giving thanks as he can."

Who would think of challenging a point in Polyakov's biography, in view of his stunning largesse. Not for him were the silly embellishments that found their way into the résumés of so many public men. He had mastered Hebrew as an adult. He was an authority on the Talmud. He even spoke Yiddish, and was originally from Poland. Wasn't he one of the top, lay Jewish scholars in Germany?

"An observation comes to mind," said the ambassador, who was a man of some perception, "but I'm afraid to make it."

"You? Afraid?" smiled Polyakov. "After what you have been through? Nonsense." Polyakov put a protective arm around the ambassador's shoulders. "Tell me what it is."

Polyakov put his ear near the ambassador's mouth, alert to the unlikely event that the coming comment might require damage control. His excellency was impressed. Polyakov obviously knew what he'd been through, and was responding with the warmth that was so characteristic of the man.

"Despite our long association, I have never heard you make a speech before tonight. As I heard you dominate the crowd, as I saw you remake them into one being with one mind by feeding the hunger we all share--as I saw strong men cry--I realized with ironic wonder that you enjoy the same forensic genius and force of will as Adolf Hitler--with the sublime difference that he used those things for total evil, while you use them for good."

Emotion rarely got the best of the man called David Polyakov, but it did so now. He shook the ambassador's hand warmly, and felt the same combination of loathing, self-contempt and exultation he had felt for 33 years, from the beginning: loathing because of where he was, self-contempt for what he was doing, and exultation because he had been able to pull it off. He knew he shouldn't feel the self-contempt, but he did. He was a man of war, a man of single combat, on whom guile and politics had been forced.

Masquerade
49

* * *

It was early in November, 1944, and Horst Krüger sat in his office in Auschwitz, where he had volunteered for service. He was sad. The war was coming to an end. The Soviets were approaching. Now came the shocking news that the camp was to be closed. Why couldn't the others see what was happening? He sympathized with the propaganda coming from Berlin--wanted to believe it--but knew it wasn't true. It was the product of inertia; the original, motive force was gone. The Führer was surrounded by traitors and incompetents.

Worse, the war was going to end with the glorious objective unachieved. Just the other evening, Vörst had called him to say the research was going well, but "we need more subjects. We need more time." Vörst expected Krüger to deliver. How?

No one suspected the Final Solution's secret purpose. No one knew the Jews were just the means to an end. Certainly there was no lack of Jews; there were whole towns of them untouched. There were millions in New York, the biggest Jewish city in the world, breeding like a fungus, fouling everything they touched, pretending to be what they were not. They had utterly destroyed America, from which Krüger had expected so much. As late as 1936, Harry Laughlin had come to Heidelberg for an honorary doctorate; had gone home with the film "Erbkrank" ("The Genetically Diseased"), and shown it to the staff of his foundation. Laughlin had intended to make a similar film for the Americans, but, of course, the Jews had put a stop to that. The Americans were thoroughly corrupt. The Jews had even infiltrated the American officer corps. Now, the war would end. Without the camps they would grow back like a cancer. Without the camps, the research would have to stop. Precious time would be lost. If the Führer were to die . . . .

Everything depended on Krüger. Were he to falter, civilization would collapse. What should he do? What would the Führer do? Yes, like the others Krüger could fight on to the end, hopelessly, in a quixotic rear-guard action, as part of some silly drivel about "honor." That would amount, in effect, to collaborating in one's own murder or humiliating imprisonment by Jews. It would be tantamount to suicide, making a fanatic's joke of his ideals. It was crucial in this turbulence to keep his gaze fixed on the goal--and the goal was to resurrect the Party. The goal was to immortalize the Führer. The mongrelizers were unimportant. They would breed themselves into imbecility, which the Americans had already done. In time to come, when the world emerged from the nightmare of mongrelization and saw the wisdom of Nazi population policy, the Führer would be there to save it.

All Krüger had to do was ensure that the program survived; the goal remained the same, but the means had to change. He poured a glass of schnapps and looked at his hand as he brought it to his lips. The Führer had shaken it, had squeezed his arm in thanks. Krüger now deservedly regarded it as a sacred part of his anatomy. Later, he had seen the Führer drink a toad's blood, in celebration of his leadership in the super-secret Ultima Thule. The Führer had invited Krüger to participate, an indescribable honor by which means their two souls had become one, an indissoluble teutonic union so alien to Christianity, the weakling Jew religion of his childhood.

Could Krüger just disappear? Yes, he could do that. The documents necessary to prepare a new identity would be no problem. He could just walk away. Rumor had it that some were already doing so. But he had no money. How would he live?

He looked at his watch. It was time to see Frieda. Krüger had arranged for her assignment to "Canada," the absurdly named section of Auschwitz-Birkenau where inmates, mostly women, collected and stored the valuables the Nazis had persuaded the deportees to bring. "It is not against the rules to take personal effects," they had announced. So much more effective than suggesting that the victims bring their jewelry. Many had brought as much as they could carry, hoping thereby to curry favor. Krüger chuckled. Subterfuge had its uses.

She was working at her place when he arrived, so absorbed she didn't notice him, unstitching linings, looking for the loot, trying to forget where she was, hating what she was doing, somewhat bedraggled, still a valkyrie. As always, he marveled. Walter Gross had troubled him, but the fact that Frieda was a Jewess, still shook Krüger's Nazi faith. Her face defied all Nazi science.

But her behavior confirmed it. She had tricked him, played him for a fool. Like all Jews, she was a chiseler. She had led him on, and he had proposed. Then she had jilted him and disappeared. He shuddered. He knew what she was, but still felt a powerful attraction. Why? Because of what Bruckner had discovered? No! It could not be! Krüger still didn't know for sure whether Bruckner had told her before he was dispatched. There was no way to ask.

At last she saw him watching her and blushed, perfectly aware that he was keeping her alive, that, but for him, she would long since have joined the others in the chimneys. In fact, "Canada" was a paradise compared to "normal life" in Birkenau. What did he want? All he ever did was stare. He was furious because she had misled him on the train. Well, what did he expect! He was a Nazi. Wasn't she a Jew? Was it her fault that her husband looked like him? Was it her fault that she looked like a valkyrie? Why didn't he kill her and be done with it? Frieda felt the shame Krüger wanted her to feel. He understood the "Jewish mind."

Today was different. He spoke to her. "Good news, *liebchen.* Your father is arriving. He was posing as a German, even daring to treat *Aryans*. He even had the papers. Just think. He was so happy when we told him you were here."

A welter of emotions besieged her. Her father called her "*liebchen.*" The same word on Krüger's lips was an assault. When had she last seen her father? Wasn't it the day he had forced her and David to leave? Her father couldn't join them; his sister was too weak. They had tried to get to Switzerland, had arrived at Lake Constance, where they were caught on the train and kicked into the snow. Was David still alive, here somewhere in the camp? Krüger knew, but of course she couldn't ask him.

She longed to see her father, longed to hug his neck and smell his tobacco and cologne. She was a little girl, who needed help. But her father would be powerless here. Krüger would use him as a weapon to subdue her. She trembled. Krüger was chortling. Had he noticed? She desperately wanted to see her father, but not here.

Krüger left. Frieda found herself on the lawn with the other girls. Such an exquisite lawn, so thick, almost lush. The camp administration took pains to keep it fertilized and mowed. Lolling on it dressed in the finery they had appropriated from the confiscated luggage, the reasonably nourished girls completed a reassuring vista. Despite the horrors of the train trip--on which so many died--and the obviously bad manners of the Nazis, what could be so wrong here in the camp, if pretty girls in gay frocks were lounging on a lawn that wore a manicure probably better than the Führer's?

The band was playing. Composed of virtuosos from all Europe playing for their lives, it inspired the Birkenau slaves with rousing marches when they trudged back and forth to work, performing with a fervor that Sousa would have feared. Now, they were welcoming a new shipment with Strauss. Krüger loved Strauss. His waltzes were so gay. Besides, wasn't he Austrian, like the Führer?

The new arrivals were passing by, women, children and old men too weak to work, "useless eaters" bound for Crematorium II without "selection." A little girl pushed a toy pram that no doubt contained a doll. Her mother carried an infant whose bonnet she adjusted for the sun. Someone else's little boy demanded that his mother watch him somersault. Everyone was placid. The adults felt relief. Thank God the horrid trip was over.

"Do you girls work in those factories?" someone called, pointing at the chimneys.

"What do they make there?" yelled someone else.

The girls on the lawn waved in response. What else should they have done? Scream across the electrified fence that these new arrivals, so happy to be off the train, were strolling toward extermination? The girls would either join them or be shot. The victims would suffer even more. Their ignorance intact, they would endure only a few minutes' pain. Inside "Local B," the "Bath Director" would give them towels and soap, there would be signs in every European language under the clothes hangers warning them to remember the numbers of their hangers, "if you want your things when you leave," and, herding into the "bath," they would see the *potemkin* shower heads. The pretense was worth it; a riot would have been unpleasant.

The Name of the King
52

Unlike the others, Frieda did not wave, weaving her own pretense that she was thereby not at fault, perfectly aware that her presence in the tableau made her an accessory; indeed, even the gown she wore was stolen goods. Frieda watched stonily while her fellows hummed along with Strauss, her tingling skin aflame with guilt. Why did she live, while others died?

She was perfectly aware that Krüger knew what she was feeling, wanted her to feel it--indeed, was keeping her in "Canada" to feel it--but her knowledge did no good. She was alive and was guilty.

The women and children were fairly well-fed. They had obviously come from home. Behind them were some men who seemed elderly. It was often hard to guess someone's age there; people looked much older than they were. These men obviously had come from some other camp. They were gaunt, shambling, like the one opposite her now, eyes blank, face dead, obviously a "Muselmann," a zombie, so different because of deprivation from what he probably had been, despite which his appearance was familiar.

Frieda tried to scream. The Muselmann was her father. She opened her mouth and threw her head back, but the sound would not come out. It choked her. She coughed. She could not stop. Krüger appeared and took her father from the line, pulling him with two fingers by the sleeve like a child.

"Papa!"

The other girls stopped humming Strauss. The new arrivals looked to see who was shouting. A soldier fearing trouble forced them to continue. A female SS officer--a lesbian like her beautiful boss, who was the commandant of all the women--reached eagerly for her pistol; Krüger patted her, persuaded her to calm. Frieda couldn't see that he was smiling. He didn't need to look at her to know she had been touched. He had ostentatiously saved her father from the "showers," and would expect something in return. Alone, she was invulnerable, but now she was not alone.

Her voice, so alive, so vibrant in contrast to the horror, revived her father. Dimly, he recalled the loving sound. His head came up. His eyes connected, flooding with intelligence. No longer a Muselmann, he searched for her. So much the better, thought Krüger, roughly pulling him away. He had a plan.

The sky darkened. Smoke was coming from the chimneys. The smell, always pervasive, became intolerable. They gagged. Frieda held her breath, which did no good.

A couple of nights later, Ruda started having pains. They all had managed to conceal her pregnancy, but now her time had come, and news of the birth would condemn her and the infant. Only if it were stillborn would Ruda be spared. The others laid her down on a blanket in one of the bottom *koias* of the barrack. The infirmary was out of the question. Even were it possible, antisepsis there was utterly lacking, and the risk of infection was great.

Masquerade
53

Someone produced a flat piece of wood she had found at the garbage dump, and put it in Ruda's mouth. "You cannot scream, Ruda. Bite on this."

A couple of the older women had some experience as midwives. For hours, they worked on Ruda, who growled like a dog and broke some teeth biting on the wood, and long after midnight the child, a boy, arrived. The women passed him around with furtive exclamations. That a baby could be born here was certainly a miracle, but soon their situation overwhelmed it. A pregnancy could be concealed by clever women; a baby could not, however stupid the men. When the child was discovered, he and Ruda, and maybe all the others, would be killed. The women, even Ruda, looked at each other, shuddering with guilt.

"What can we do?" asked Jacqueline.

No one spoke. "You know what we must do," said Frieda at last. "Do you understand? Well, do you?" The others nodded. Jacqueline began to cry. "Do you agree, Ruda?" Frieda asked her.

"Yes." But Ruda could not look at her.

"Who will do it?" Frieda asked. "Jacqueline?"

Jacqueline shook her head. All the others turned away, despite the growing danger. Not knowing where he was, the infant bawled lustily, dissipating Ruda's heroic efforts to keep him still.

Frieda covered his mouth with a palm and squeezed his nose. He struggled so that she had to press hard. Like his mother and the other women, he was fighting to survive, too ignorant to understand that was impossible. At last he was quiet and Frieda removed her hand.

"Your baby was stillborn," she said. "I'm sorry."

"Now we, too, are murderers," said Jacqueline.

A couple of days later, Krüger had her brought to his office. Her father was there, still basking in the memory of her voice, no longer a Muselmann. Yet, in the presence of their captor, despite themselves, they were quite reserved. Krüger polluted even their reunion.

"I understand there was some trouble Monday night," he said.

So he knew. He always knew. As always, he was playing Nazi games. "None I know about," she said.

"She handled it," Krüger told Erhard. "Your daughter is so competent. Yet, she won't cooperate. I have done so much for her. As you see, she's well fed. But she won't let me help her. She's a foolish child. I thought perhaps that you, her father, could help her see reason."

Erhard had forgotten Frieda's encounter with Krüger on the train. Who besides a specialist in criminal psychiatry could know it was important? Of course, he was totally unaware of the bizarre relationship between them. Yet, he had a father's intuition. Wasn't Krüger the same *nudnik* he had known at home?

"Perhaps," said Erhard. "If we could be alone."

"A good idea, doctor," said Krüger. "Let us try it."

The Name of the King
54

He rose and left the room. Erhard and Frieda embraced, inhaling each other, whispering, knowing that, in a moment, Krüger would return. Indeed, the door was ajar. Was he listening?

"Papa, where have you come from?"

"Dachau. Such a pleasant town. I spent some time there in 1927. I stayed at the . . . ."

"When did they . . . ?

"Soon after you left. *Liebchen,* are you . . . ?"

"Yes, I'm dead. We Jews were wrong, Papa. There *is* a hell."

"And David?"

"I don't know. Krüger does, but of course he's not talking."

"*Liebchen,* you must live."

Frieda smiled. Her father had such quaint ideas. He was a man of the past, of another world. These days, no one lived.

"Really, Papa? Why?"

"You must live to tell the world what happened."

"The world would not believe me, Papa. It doesn't now. Remember? David wanted to read Torah from the Statue of Liberty."

Her father bowed his head. "Yes."

"This is the only world we have. Only here in hell can we defeat the Beast."

Erhard nodded. How wise she had become, like Queen Esther. The last time he had seen her, she had still been a little girl. She still was. They stopped whispering and held each other close. Erhard had expected they would have so much to say--especially here where the banal struggle for the requirements of daily life became supreme--but everything worth saying had been said. He hugged her with the pitiful remainder of his strength, caressed her cheek and golden hair. Frieda had showed him what he had to do.

Krüger returned, beaming. "Well, doctor, have you and Frieda talked?"

Erhard nodded. "It is all arranged."

"Splendid! You'll work in the infirmary. Perhaps you could help in our pioneer experiments on twins. I'll see about your rations. Go now. The corporal will escort you."

Erhard squeezed her hand and left. She blanched. What was arranged? He hadn't understood. He hadn't understood anything, which was so unlike him. Krüger didn't understand either. Indeed, he put his hand on hers.

"I've waited so long, *liebchen,*" he said. "It's your fault. You've been so mean. We must act quickly. We've lost so much time."

Desperate for time and the need to keep him at bay, she blurted, "Suppose it isn't as good as you think."

Instantly, she realized she had made a mistake, but she could not call the comment back. What a stupid thing to say! The bizarre reunion had shaken her. What would her father do? It was dangerous to be with loved ones in hell.

Masquerade
55

"Impossible!" said Krüger. He was pouring some *schnapps*. "Fate made you mine."

Her father had done this. She was angry with him, which frightened her. Her intolerable situation was becoming impossible. She was frantic. What could she do?

"No! I am David's."

"David is dead."

It was the first word she had heard of her husband since the arrest. She ignored it. If she ignored it, David would be alive.

"Do you want me so much because you are a Jew?"

The bottle in Krüger's hand stopped in mid-flight. Frieda's desperation had found a weakness. "So Bruckner had time to talk."

"I asked him what he knew."

"You see? You wanted to know about me. All the more reason I must have you. But I am not a Jew. I am as responsible for someone a couple of centuries ago, as I am for Cain. No, *liebchen*, I want you because of the day on the train from Munich when we were betrothed. Remember? I want you because you don't want me."

"If you are not responsible for your ancestors, why am I responsible for mine?"

Krüger had not known she was so subtle. The discovery added to her charm. Outside, there was a shout. Frieda heard her name and followed Krüger through the door. Erhard was running, with a vigor that belied his decrepit condition. What was he thinking of? When she understood, she shouted, too.

"Papa, no!"

"I'm leaving now, darling. My time is passed. Win!"

An officer drew his pistol and fired. Erhard fell. Soldiers were running. But the wound was superficial, in the leg, not good enough. Krüger would patch him up and return him to hell. Was this the best they could do? He was up, running again, bandy-legged now, rolling down into the moat that surrounded every *lager*. It had rained for a couple of days, the water was high and he dog-paddled across it. A machine gun was firing. Erhard heard splashes.

Why didn't they just let him do what he obviously was doing? Why the panic? Wouldn't he be just as dead? Yes, but the decision would be his. It would mean that they had lost control. For the same reason, Krüger wanted Frieda.

At last a bullet found him. He coughed, spewing blood, thrashing. The moat turned red, the water foaming. He gained the far bank and, with a final effort, reached. His hand closed around the wire in triumph. He was free.

Justly famous German efficiency took over. The massive current in the electrified fence savaged Erhard's body like a doll. The *lager* was quiet again. The newcomers stared in speechless horror. Krüger and the others were dismayed, despite themselves. As Erhard had expected, they had lost. Frieda's head fell. What a stupid child she was. It was she who hadn't understood. Her father had understood everything.

Chapter Nine
The Deal

In deference to her "victory," Krüger did not come for several days. At least, she was able to steal from the new arrivals in peace. She was a thief, she was a murderess, and now she had driven her father to suicide, all courtesy of Krüger. What more could she do? The only thing left to think about was David. Had her tormentor told the truth?

In his office, Krüger wound his American Victrola and put a record on the turntable. His love of music had followed him even here. Soon, "*Wie schön ist das Leben*" filled the room. How pleasant. He looked out the window. It was getting dark, but he could still see the men he had assigned to clean the latrines. Each latrine was a paved ditch about a yard deep, over which were mounted a couple of cement chests about 30 inches high, each chest offering two holes. There were hundreds of them, but not enough to satisfy the demand. For some inmates who were forced to rely on holes in the ground, the paved ditches were the ultimate in plumbing.

There was no paper and chronic enteritis was endemic. The water supply was polluted. Swarms of insects carried disease; epidemics of dysentery and typhoid spared no one.

All this needed to be cleaned every day, "in the interest of public health," which was Krüger's province, and he invariably chose Jewish intellectuals--doctors, lawyers, professors and businessmen--for the purpose. They hated having dirty hands. The Jewish antipathy to manual labor was notorious, a symptom of their spurious "superiority."

Well, by the *Führer*, Horst Krüger was one pure-bred *Aryan* who wasn't going to let them get away with it! How interesting it was to watch, standing far enough away so that his tall boots remained unblemished. In their eyes he saw a doglike appeal. Most of them trembled with self-revulsion, knowing that if they were the men they had pretended to be they would rebel. Some had become Muselmanns, gone insane, eyes blank, mouths spewing drool.

The Name of the King
58

Krüger left his office and strolled past the latrines. Acknowledging his presence, the Jews worked faster and harder. Except for Polyakov. Always it was necessary to add those three words, "Except for Polyakov." It was unbearable.

"*Guten abend, Herr Scheissminister,*" Krüger said.

Polyakov stopped work, smiled and looked at Krüger without flinching. "*Ja, ich bin der Scheissminister*. Did you want something, Horst?" Not, "Did you want something, *Hauptsturmfuhrer*?" or even "*Herr* Krüger." He was utterly without fear, which Krüger could not understand, and, because he could not understand it, he himself felt afraid.

Krüger knew with total certainty that, were he to make the mistake of telling Polyakov he was going to be killed, the Jew would reply calmly, "Kill me, then, Horst." Krüger had schemed himself into a corner. Because of the intolerable conditions he had imposed, the Jew, like Erhard, would consider death a happy escape, a victory.

Krüger shook with fury. He dissembled, and smiled. "Only to watch you work."

"Watch, then."

But Polyakov did not resume the work that Krüger had said he was there to watch. He was baiting Krüger, taunting him, daring him to act, despite the fact that Krüger had already made sure Polyakov could never satisfy a woman. Vörst had taken care of it a testicle at a time as part of the "research." That was why Krüger wanted Frieda and Polyakov to live; why he had waited at the arrival ramp to assign them to labor, not extermination; why he discreetly made sure their diets were sufficient. He wanted them both to survive the camp. He wanted to be at their reunion, when Polyakov had to tell her the truth. How high in the air would she hold her nose then? How much would she suffer when she learned she would spawn no more Jews?

Yet, Polyakov smiled, and his smile was an insult. With difficulty, Krüger suppressed the desire to smash it from his face. To do so would have been an admission of defeat. Despite his total power over Polyakov, despite everything he had done, Krüger wondered against his will whether Polyakov had won the struggle between them. The suspicion corroded him, but there was nothing he could do, and the word from the fronts only added to the pressure. Yes, Polyakov would be released, but, when he was released, he would have power, despite the surgery. The Jews in the latrine, and their front men, the Americans, would win.

Krüger stayed as long as necessary, pretending to be calm, then returned to his office and ordered Polyakov's file. Perhaps it would explain the mystery of the man.

The file contained more information about Polyakov than he probably knew himself. Krüger stared at his measurements, medical history and fingerprints. He was the surviving son of an immensely wealthy Jewish family with considerable property in Germany--since confiscated--and millions in Switzerland. A handwritten entry showed how much they had, but not where in Switzerland it was. The bastard! Their money no doubt came from gouging honest German businessmen. Weren't the Jews notorious for keeping their fingers on the scales? No wonder they had millions in Switzerland. Did the fact that Polyakov shared the same family name--and the same Jew dog religion--with Krüger's incriminating ancestor mean they were related? Was that why they looked so much alike? Krüger shuddered.

Millions in Switzerland. Millions Polyakov and Frieda would enjoy. A supremely daring idea erupted in Krüger's mind. Could it work? After all, according to the documents, which didn't lie, Krüger's ancestor had been a Polyakov. Didn't that mean Krüger was entitled to those millions? A few minutes later, Polyakov stood before his desk. As always, his mere presence was offensive. He was emaciated. There was an ugly rash on his neck. He stank. His stench was so breathtaking that it even overcame the pungent odor of burning flesh. Far worse than all of this was the fact that he still was undefeated.

"Sit down," said Krüger.

To be here at all, was utterly incredible. There were chairs, rugs, pictures on the walls, accoutrements of civilization among which Krüger was the only false note. "*Wie schön ist das Leben*" wafted from the Victrola. To be invited to sit, so routine in the real world, was unthinkable here in hell. Polyakov did as directed and waited.

"You look ill," said Krüger with satisfaction. "You're scrawny. Any complaints about the food?"

"No. The food is quite adequate."

Krüger's question had been a mistake. *Of course* Polyakov would not complain. Always, everywhere, Polyakov was scheming. Having answered Krüger's question, he waited again.

"Do you want to live, Polyakov?"

"What do you want?"

Typically, Polyakov had cut through all the sauerkraut to the bone. His audacity was intolerable. Krüger had brought him to his office and invited him to sit. Was he so insane that he didn't remember where he was and with whom? More than ever, Krüger wanted to twist Polyakov's red, ropy, skinny neck like a chicken's, and watch his shrieking corpse run around the room while he died.

"You have money in Switzerland," Krüger said, waving a hand before Polyakov could respond. "Don't bother repeating that you'll never tell where it is. I know that our people couldn't force you to talk. It's all here." Polyakov saw his file on Krüger's desk. It was open, and the document on top was his marriage certificate. "The present phase of the war will soon end," Krüger said. "It is time to make other arrangements. I propose a trade. An exchange."

Polyakov smiled. "You have nothing I want."

The Name of the King
60

"Your life?"

"My life is over. I'm dead. So are you. You killed us both. We're in hell. As I said, you have nothing I want."

"Do you want your wife?"

Polyakov blanched. At last! Krüger exulted. He had found the key. There always was one, if a man had enough patience. Krüger did have something Polyakov wanted.

"I haven't heard of her for years," whispered Polyakov. He was revealing himself for the first time, but he had no choice. Even Nazis sometimes told the truth, if only by accident.

"She is alive and she is here," said Krüger.

"Where?"

"In Canada.'"

"I don't believe you," Polyakov said.

"You don't have to believe me. I'll let you meet."

"All right, if she's alive, I'll buy her."

"Perhaps. If you persuade me. How much is she worth?"

"You're the extortionist. Tell me what you want."

"Maybe you'd rather not buy her, after all, Polyakov. Maybe you prefer your money, a failing of your race. No problem. Go back to work. I'll sell her somewhere else."

"Why would I buy my wife in here?"

"Because she would be delivered out there." Krüger pointed out the window and laughed. "Although I can't imagine what you would do with her."

Polyakov flushed painfully with shame and guilt. He was dead. Krüger had killed him with emasculation, in the name of Himmler's crazy schemes. With Frieda dead, there was nothing to live for, and no loss. Frieda alive would restore him to life, but their reunion would be a disaster. He would be killed again. This time, Frieda's love for him would do it.

A searing question came to mind, a question he could not ask. Had Krüger done the same thing to her? Another inmate had told him of rows of women strapped to operating tables for hours, awaiting "*Herr* Professor." Had Frieda been one of them?

If she was, it was Polyakov's fault, as much as her father's. For years, Frieda had implored him to leave Germany. For years--even after the *Anschluss*, even after *Kristallnacht*--he had refused, like her father. He had told her there was nothing to fear; that she was imagining things; that no one could be as evil as she said Hitler was; that he had brought stability to business and restored value to the mark--that, after all, the Allies *had* mistreated Germany in the Treaty of Versailles. Hadn't her father been an officer in the Imperial German Army in World War I? Didn't he proudly display his Iron Cross in the sitting room?

The Deal
61

At last, in 1941, they had fled, hoping to find a way across Lake Constance to Switzerland. They had been caught. Polyakov had been taken to Berlin and eventually to Auschwitz. Frieda vaguely remembered a castle, an underground corridor, a ramp and then a truck. There were so many others in the truck. She was naked--they were all naked--and she couldn't breathe. Then there was daylight again. She was falling, and the others were falling on top of her. The foulest thing she had ever smelled assailed her: the stench of putrefying corpses covered with their wastes, combined with chlorine. She had lain there through the night, unable to move, but when morning came, galvanized by her discovery that she lay face to face with a corpse, she had dug herself out. When found, she had been wandering naked through the woods near Chelmno.

In Auschwitz, a modicum of sanity returned, but she never could remember what had happened. Frieda hadn't seen her husband since they had been caught. Was he dead?

Polyakov now knew she had been right about the Nazis, but his knowledge was too late, useless. His pallid face flushed with guilt. Was she alive? If so, she would know that he had killed her. She was a Jewish woman, and would die without children. Worse, she would die without children even if they were released and reunited. Polyakov had killed her by refusing to listen to her warnings. His name would die out, along with the rest of his family. The joy of his discovery that Frieda was alive curdled.

Krüger waited, savoring the moment. "When you were caught, you were headed to Switzerland," he said at last, pointing at the file. "To visit your money, no doubt. This time, you will arrive, because I shall accompany you. You will arrange the withdrawal of ten million Swiss francs in cash. As you see, I know exactly what you have."

"And my wife?"

"She will be released--if you think she is worth ten million francs. If you don't, someone else will."

"What assurance would I have that you would do as you say?"

Krüger smiled. "The best assurance possible--the word of an officer of the Third Reich."

"The word of an officer of the Third Reich?" David Polyakov began to laugh--the thought was so absurd, he could not squelch it--softly at first; then with gusto. He hadn't enjoyed such a belly laugh in years, not since long before the misfortune of meeting Krüger. Now, Polyakov laughed in his face.

The Nazi's certified *Aryan* blood boiled again. He had to suppress it. The war had left him unable to conduct a normal conversation with a Jew, but this was business.

"You misunderstand," said Krüger. "You and I shall go to Switzerland, where you will make the arrangements, to be consummated only by the appearance of your wife, who will wait for us on the German side of the border.

We shall then return for her, and the three of us will go back to Switzerland. Your wife will accompany me to the bank to complete the transfer of funds, and you will be free on neutral ground. So, you see, Polyakov, it is I who must trust you."

Chapter Ten
Swindle

"This is a rather large transfer," said Pierre Gely, senior vice president of the Zurich Bank Corporation.

He was suspicious. Something was wrong, and he even had an idea what it was, but he couldn't prove it, and the two men who sat in his office wouldn't help him. They were a strange combination of resemblance and incongruity. They looked a lot alike in the face. They were of the same build and height. They would even have been of the same weight, if their diets for years had not been so obviously different. One of them was pink, exuded authority and had Nazi written all over him. The other was diffident, dead-white and emaciated. Gely could not imagine that they had anything in common.

Yet, the man who resembled a corpse was the one who had the money in the bank. His handwriting and his knowledge of the code words proved it. There had been no activity in his account since the beginning of the war--some years now--so long that Gely and Polyakov had never met. Gely had only recently been named senior vice president of the bank.

Polyakov was a Jew, of course. What else could he be? Had he been an inmate of one of the camps? The European newspapers, even some of the foreign Jewish organizations, still pretended they didn't exist, but Pierre Gely knew damn well they did. One of the dividends of conducting people's secret affairs was that one learned so much else that was meant to be secret.

Was this very large withdrawal the work of extortion? It would just about deplete the account. Did the Nazi have something to do with the camps? He wasn't talking and neither was Polyakov. There was nothing Gely could put a finger on but intuition, which he didn't trust, and he couldn't very well accuse the Nazi if Polyakov wouldn't help.

Krüger smiled a response to Gely's comment. "Is anything wrong, *monsieur*?"

The Name of the King
64

"Not at all, *mein Herr*. Just passing time." They were speaking French. Gely's use of German to address Krüger was as far as he dared go. It was far enough; Krüger caught it, and he dilated with happiness because Gely knew what was happening and could do nothing about it.

"You must see many unusual things here these days, because of the war," said Polyakov, trying to reassure Gely.

"I do."

It was just what Gely had been thinking. So many furtive people had lately sat in his office and lied. He knew they were lying, and they knew he knew, but he faithfully played out his part in the charade. Now that the war was clearly coming to an end, there were more such people, each with his own story Gely lusted to know. This strange couple was just the latest.

"I'll need some time to arrange this much cash," said Gely, blandly trying to punish the Nazi. "Will that make a problem, *Herr* Maginot?"

As sure as he knew anything, Gely knew that the Nazi's name wasn't Maginot, and that he had adopted it not only to pretend he was French, but because it was the name of the infamous French defense line the Germans had overrun--but that was the name the Nazi had given. The banker couldn't accuse him of anything on the basis of a feeling. This was a bank, where 2+2=4, not the office of Dr. Sigmund Freud.

"Not at all," said Krüger. "Take a whole day. Remember the arrangement."

"Of course. The arrangement. Let me consult my notes. The funds are to be transferred only in the presence of Mrs. Polyakov, who will sign the requisite forms. Here in the record is a sample of her signature. I assume Mrs. Polyakov will be able to identify herself."

"Yes," said Polyakov.

Frustration was devouring the banker. Wasn't it obvious what this farce was? But what could he do about it without the victim's cooperation? And Polyakov was not going to gamble with his wife. Gely looked at "Maginot," who smiled, not a real smile, but a badly drawn caricature pasted on his face, meant to convey its falsity.

"Maginot" said, "If you require any more identification, *Monsieur* Gely, you will find these numbers tattooed on her arm. She is being released from prison in Germany." He handed Gely a paper.

I'll bet, thought Gely. And who is releasing her? What numbers are tattooed on *your* arm? Did "Maginot" wear the infamous SS tattoo? Gely had to remind himself that such things were none of his business. He was a banker--a neutral banker--not a British intelligence officer or a priest.

"May I have your card?" said the Nazi. "You are handling this delicate matter so well. I believe we have not seen the last of each other."

Swindle
65

* * *

All the way back to Germany, Polyakov had expected a double-cross. What else could he expect from a Nazi? Since when would a Nazi--an Auschwitz Nazi--keep his word to a Jew, a Jew whose job was cleaning latrines? Polyakov knew there would be a double-cross--he just didn't know when--but he had agreed to Krüger's proposition for Frieda. If there was any chance to save her, he had to take it.

To his surprise, Krüger had done as he promised. Frieda was alive, as he had said. Like Polyakov, she had been separated from the other inmates for many weeks. Long before the Soviets arrived, Krüger took Frieda from the camp. His uniform and the papers he had prepared did their job. There had been fresh clothing and travel documents at the inn in Katowice. Then, he had flown with her to Berlin, and driven her to Sachsenhausen, near Oranienburg, 25 miles northwest of the capital, where he installed her in Barracks 19 as a factotum in the final phase of Operation Bernhard, while he arranged their departure.

Historians and monetary experts will recall Bernhard as one of the most secret Nazi operations of the war. In August, 1942, Barracks 19 was suddenly cleared. Inmates awaiting extermination were sent elsewhere for the purpose. Others built a barbed wire wall ten feet high around the compound, which even regular camp guards were forbidden to enter. Instead, a squad of *Totenkopf* "Death's Head" SS killers was installed to provide security.

They never failed, no doubt because of their justly famous devotion to duty, further purified by the warning that any of them who revealed what was happening inside would be sent immediately to do battle at Stalingrad or some other choice post. Inside the compound, 30 Jews salvaged from death camps throughout Europe were assembled, their mission to counterfeit millions in British and then American currency. "Money bombs" were to be dropped into those economies, to destroy them with inflation.

The *Totenkopf* guards were surprised to learn that these 30 Jews were no longer *untermenschen* and all the other things the Nazis called them. Now, they were valued collaborators. Their diet would be excellent. They would be allowed cigarettes. When Hitler imposed his National Socialist world government, these Jews would live in special areas and continue working for it.

Unlike the others, all carefully hand-picked, Frieda had no special talent for it, but Bernhard offered plausibility to Krüger's wish to improve her diet and restore her health. Since she was the only woman involved in the last days of the operation, the barracks of course had to be remodeled for the purpose. The fact that SS Major Bernhard Krüger, in whose honor Bernhard was named, was Horst's cousin, did no harm, and explains why Frieda's name never appeared in official records.

Needless to say, Krüger did not give Polyakov, her husband, the same treatment. All Krüger had promised to do was keep him alive, which he did.

The Name of the King
66

Krüger had him flown to Munich and installed at Dachau, some thirty miles away, telling anyone who asked that he was part of a racial experiment mandated by Himmler. Who had time to check while the Third Reich collapsed? Besides, Himmler was always implementing crazy ideas. Recently, he had sent an explorer to Tibet, to discover a rumored pure Germanic race.

Von Runstedt had failed at Bastogne. The fronts were collapsing. Berlin was dying, blocks of historic buildings reduced by Allied air raids to smoking piles of bricks. The trip to the station took a couple of hours. On the way, they clearly heard the cries of the trapped and dying in the cellars. It was early morning, but the smoke was so thick, they couldn't see. The air was full of bits of paper, and other charred detritus. Familiar streets, devastated by bomb craters and severed water mains, were impassable. Rivets exploded like machine gun fire. Rescue teams sickened by the stench poked at corpses soldered to the pavements by the heat. Frieda looked at Krüger. He was smiling, so happy to be right. The world was ending, giving place to the new. Krüger knew that Vörst would do his part.

At the station, they had to wait another hour. Then, she was sitting opposite Krüger aboard the train, the train that would take them south to Munich and her husband. All the way down south, he tried to engage her in conversation, while she feasted on the signs and tried to remember her geography. She had lived in the other world so long, everything seemed bizarre.

At last they were in Munich. They left the train. There was the breathtaking moment when she sat in a large touring car with David. He had not seen his wife for more than four years, since the day they had been caught. He was amazed to see how well she looked. Krüger's change in diet, including vitamin supplements, was producing good effects. Polyakov had expected a scarecrow like himself, but Frieda was filling out, even recovering her beauty, full of promise but for her eyes, where Polyakov saw death.

All the way down south, they simply stared at each other, each feasting on the proof that the other was alive, waiting to speak until they were alone. Anything they said in Krüger's presence would be contaminated. He sat next to her, very near, and she was sure he stank of pork.

Krüger's medical bag was on the seat. Polyakov looked at it with a combination of nostalgia and loathing, nostalgia for his stillborn private practice, loathing for what medicine in Krüger's hands had become. Krüger opened it, withdrew a couple of syringes and prepared them. "Your arm," he said.

A protest flew to Polyakov's lips. He suppressed it. What good could it do? "The one with the numbers?" he asked.

"Always a wisecrack, eh, Polyakov?"

"Is it poison?" David asked.

Krüger did not respond. He finished with Polyakov in silence and Frieda held out her arm.

Swindle
67

The car stopped and Polyakov awoke. Frieda was stretching. She had been asleep too. Krüger opened the door. "We're here."

"Where?" said Polyakov.

He looked out the window and saw trees. Far away, he saw snow and mountains. There was nothing else, no hint of a structure. They certainly were not in Zurich. Polyakov realized that he didn't even know which country they were in. The last city he remembered of any size was Munich. Had they passed through customs when he was asleep? It was dawn. How long had they been sedated?

"Wait for me," said Krüger. "Everything is arranged." He hustled Polyakov out of the car.

"Where?" asked Polyakov, confused.

Krüger pointed. "There. Under that tree."

Frieda protested and tried to get out. He restrained her, and put the car in gear. In a moment, it was gone and the silence closed in. Polyakov went to the tree, as Krüger had directed. It was cold, especially for a man whose resistance was gone and who was not properly dressed. The wind rose, which increased the discomfort. Perhaps, if he could walk, it would be better. But, he could not walk. He had to be standing at the tree when Frieda returned. Stamping his feet was an *ersatz* substitute for walking, but after a while they lost sensation. He heard them crunching in the snow, but felt nothing. Was it doing any good?

Obviously, Krüger wasn't going far. Otherwise, he wouldn't have left David there; which meant that he had to be very near civilization. Why didn't anyone else pass on the road? The silence was becoming oppressive.

Hours passed, maybe minutes. David felt his spirit rise, tugging at his would-be corpse, already close to free from his corruption. He thought he heard Frieda's voice, but still had sense enough to know he was hallucinating. Now he understood. Krüger wasn't coming back. Polyakov, the Jew, was being victimized again. Good! He still hadn't told Frieda. He didn't know how. How could he tell her Krüger had made him a eunuch? How could he tell her she would never have a child? Maybe it would be best to die here. She would never know. Death by freezing was said to be painless. *Was anything said about it in medical school? I can't recall.* At the camp, Krüger had conducted freezing experiments; had told David and some others to carry the corpses of a couple of Soviet officers he had left outside naked in tubs of ice water overnight. Polyakov had heard their cries. Why had they complained? They should have thanked Krüger for a humane departure. Would they rather have been gassed? People are never satisfied. Polyakov already could feel nothing.

He stopped stamping and swatting himself and fell to his knees. He tried to bury himself in snow; but, the snow was sticky and would not yield, and he lacked the strength to work it. He closed his eyes and prayed for *Addonai* to take him.

The Name of the King
68

He was still rocking back and forth when Krüger found him. Krüger stood him up. "You didn't have to pray. Let's go."

Head lolling, limbs flaccid, he somehow made it to the car. The movement and the painful warmth revived him.

"Where is Frieda?"

"At the inn. She is waiting for you. Come."

They drove almost three hours. The road narrowed. They were high up in the mountains. Krüger drummed on the steering wheel with delight, loving the way the car held the road. It was a German touring car, the kind the Führer loved. What a pity he would have to leave it. He stopped and got out.

"This is the place, Polyakov."

Krüger struck off across the snow, loving the lash of cold on his face, not even bothering to look back at Polyakov. What else could Polyakov do but follow? He tried, but Auschwitz took its toll. He could not keep up. There was no path. The snow was deep and claimed his feet. They were high up and the air was thin. Krüger whistled while he trekked, but Polyakov floundered, struggled for breath and fell behind.

"Hurry!" Krüger shouted over his shoulder. "Frieda is waiting. We don't have much time."

"I can't," gasped Polyakov. "I must rest." He fell in the snow.

"I cannot wait. Let it not be said that I failed to keep my bargain."

"Wait!" croaked Polyakov. "I'm coming." He staggered to his feet and tottered on.

Krüger could not recall exactly when or where he had gotten the idea. Maybe it was something the banker in Zurich had said. Maybe it was just the fact that, as Polyakov slowly recovered from his long residence in hell, he and Krüger again looked more and more alike. As always, Krüger tried to dismiss the resemblance and failed. How could a Jew--a Polish Jew, no less--look so much like an *Aryan* leader, if they were not related?

Along with the eerie resemblance, a question arose. What would Krüger do after he received the 10,000,000 francs? He had lacked the time to think that far. Yes, he would have 10,000,000 francs, but he would be a so-called "war criminal." What would all his money be worth? The Allies would hunt him for the rest of his life. He knew their plans. Their pronouncements were turning ominous. The policy of "unconditional surrender" proved that Eisenhower was probably a secret Jew. If they caught Krüger, they would take his money. Polyakov would get it back. Yes, that was the decisive fact. Polyakov would get it back! The Jew would win.

Krüger needed a cover, somewhere to hide. Better yet, he needed to hide in the open. What would his money be worth, if he couldn't enjoy it, if he had to live on the run? Well, how does one hide in the open? Didn't the great revolutionaries say that the best place to hide was under the enemy's guns, so close that one couldn't be hit? Didn't Mao Tse-tung, whose Long March, and whose version of Socialism, National Socialist Krüger grudgingly admired, teach that the best place to hide was among the enemy, "like a fish in the sea?" Krüger saw that the shocking resemblance to Polyakov was a blessing. Wasn't it obvious what he had to do? Let the others flee to impotence in the jungles of Brazil. To a man of refinement, a man of teutonic culture--the only kind--what Krüger had to do would be distasteful, yes, but it would beat the Jews at their own game.

They had walked for hours. It was early afternoon, but it seemed dark. The sky was the color of blackboard slate. It was cold, cold that made a mockery of Polyakov's worn clothing. They passed a stone arch and crossed a broad, treeless field. Despite the danger of avalanche, Krüger broke into song, song that made a mockery of music. Behind him, Polyakov fell in the snow, wheezing with the unaccustomed effort. Krüger saw, smiled, but did not stop. Polyakov pulled himself erect and followed, staggering, arms dangling uselessly, mouth hanging slack. They entered a wood--leafless birch standing erect--and Polyakov fell again. He could not go on.

After a while, Krüger came back. With the toe of his boot, he prodded Polyakov, tentatively, as if he were an animal hit by a car, lying abandoned on the shoulder of a road.

"Come along, now," said Krüger, almost gently. "It isn't far. Frieda is waiting."

But Polyakov couldn't rise, couldn't even answer. Krüger got him to his feet and carried him, skinny arms and legs dangling like overcooked spaghetti. "Let it never be said that Horst Krüger failed in his duty," Krüger said.

He strode on smartly, barely paying deference to his load. He was remarkably strong. He knew he could march through the snow carrying Polyakov forever. Vörst's experiments were already bearing fruit.

Bouncing on his shoulder like a bizarre collection of rags, Polyakov grudgingly began to think well of him. Wasn't Krüger doing everything he'd promised--even more? He hadn't promised to carry Polyakov, but he was carrying him. Polyakov chided himself both for his mistrust, and for his bizarre, new feelings. Yes, Krüger was doing as he'd said, but wasn't he robbing Polyakov?

At last, there was a small lodge, completely hidden by some firs. They went in. Krüger dumped Polyakov and blew on his hands. It was almost as cold in here as it was outside, but Polyakov, gasping on the floor, revived.

"Where are we?" asked Polyakov. "What is this place?"

"This is where you start your new life."

"Where is my wife?"

"It's cold," said Krüger. "Build a fire."

There was kindling already in the fireplace and with fumbling fingers Polyakov did so. Krüger sat for a few minutes, toasting his hands, dreaming dreams of total conquest, while the effort of carrying Polyakov wore off. To facilitate the process, he took a glass of *schnapps*.

"You're getting fat, Polyakov," he said. "You're heavier than I thought. I've been feeding you too much."

Polyakov did not answer. Krüger clapped his knees and rose.

"It's time." He took a brand-new shovel from a corner and went outside. Polyakov followed.

"Where is my wife?" said Polyakov again. "Let's go into Zurich and finish our business."

"We shall finish our business, Polyakov, but not in Zurich. Here. Now." Krüger smiled. How dumb could this Jew be?

It started to snow, the flakes large and sticky. A breeze, brisk and icy, whistled dirges through the trees. Far away, an animal howled. At last, Polyakov understood, and he was immensely bitter because he had been so stupid.

"You're going to kill me, aren't you?"

"Yes."

"You've planned to kill me all along."

"Yes."

Krüger had always looked with contempt at face-saving euphemisms. "Final Solution," indeed. Himmler had been a weakling. His squeamishness had trivialized the Führer. He should have said proudly that he was ridding the world of Yiddish scum. His schoolteacher concern for the welfare of animals had always made Krüger sick.

"Yes, I'm going to kill you. You should thank me for letting you live this long. You won't, of course. How could a Jew understand gratitude?"

Polyakov smiled. "So much for the word of an officer of the Third Reich."

"This is exactly what I promised. This is what you said you want. But of course a Jew is never satisfied."

"I want freedom."

"That's what you'll get, Polyakov. Freedom from the war. Freedom from Germany. Freedom from National Socialism. Freedom from me. Isn't all that what you want?"

"And my wife?"

"Be reasonable, Polyakov. What can you do for her? You're not a man. You never were. I just made it official. You can't give her children. You can't even give her a good time. With you, she would have to take lovers, or be condemned to a life of frustration. But I can do much. I have ten million francs and I'm the real David Polyakov. I'm going to be a much better David Polyakov than you were. I'm going to preserve your family name. If you had any decency, you'd stop bitching, and thank me for giving your kids such pure *Aryan* blood."

Krüger pushed him off the porch and walked a few yards, testing. "This is the place." He handed Polyakov the shovel. "Dig. I'll watch from inside. It's cold." Krüger turned to go inside.

The wind rose, as if in comment. Polyakov was sure he heard whispering in it. "You dig," he said.

"What did you say?"

"I said, `You dig.'" Polyakov handed him the shovel, and so nonplused was Krüger that he took it.

"Why, you skinny, impertinent, Yiddish bastard. I'll . . . ."

Polyakov laughed, as he had in Krüger's office. "You'll what?"

The two men looked at each other, and Krüger saw that Polyakov was acting dishonorably, as always. There had never been a Jew with honor.

"I'll watch from inside. It's cold," said Polyakov. "Better still, kill me first. Then you dig."

He was about to die, but he was making jokes. He looked at Krüger boldly. The insult in his glance was overwhelming. Digging while Polyakov watched would be intolerable, of course, but killing him first would not be much better. Polyakov would die with the sweet knowledge that Krüger would have to dig later, alone in the cold, listening to the voices calling in the trees, mocking him, telling him to make the grave deep enough to keep Polyakov warm.

The dirty, little Yid typically was trying to deny Krüger victory. He was beyond suffering, beyond fear, which meant that killing him would not be victory, but defeat. However, Auschwitz and the Allies were behind them. They could not go back. Polyakov's death would at least put a stop to his insufferable, Yiddish jokes, and remove his ghastly face from Krüger's eyes.

"Where am I?" asked Polyakov. "Germany? I hope so. You've already ruined it. There would be no harm done. Tell me. I always like to know where I am when I die."

Chapter Eleven
Polyakov's Arm

Krüger roared, ran at Polyakov, raised the shovel and swung. Polyakov gasped softly, clutched his throat, staggered and fell. Blood pumped out around his head on the snow, like a halo in a late medieval painting. Krüger hit him again, again and again. There was a popping sound. A haze of blood and brain stood in the air. Krüger kept hitting him until the man who had been Polyakov no longer had a face.

Then Krüger turned his attention to Polyakov's arm, the one with the tattoo. The ink was of course indelible, installed with a metal-tipped stylus. He had to expunge the concentration camp numbers. If Polyakov's body--what remained of it--ever were found, there could be no numbers that would lead to a name. There was room in this world for only one David Polyakov, and that was Krüger.

Krüger hacked at Polyakov's elbow with the shovel. He would cut the arm off, carry it away and throw it to some dogs. No incriminating trace of it would be found. The destruction of the number would resurrect David Polyakov.

For Krüger, this was something new. He wasn't squeamish like Himmler--far from it--but someone else had always done his killing. It wasn't nearly as messy and unpleasant as he had thought, something like pulling wings off a chicken. But this wing refused to come. However hard he tried, he couldn't separate the tendons. Was the cold the reason or was the arm's willfulness part of the mystery of Polyakov that he had never understood?

There was a handaxe inside the lodge at the fireplace. With mounting exasperation, he got it and went to work again, but, although the tool thwacked loudly and made considerable gore, he could not liberate the incriminating arm. It was inexplicable.

Fire! Of course! He would burn it off, and, by doing so, make a sacrifice to the *Führer*. Krüger carried the bloody corpse inside the lodge, threw it on the rug, and thrust the arm into the fire. He took the *schnapps* from the cupboard, sat down and enjoyed another drink. The reassuring smell of burning, human flesh filled the room, a smell that for Krüger was pregnant with nostalgia. It had permeated the environs of Auschwitz as far as Katowice. He had last smelled it in Berlin, which somewhat tainted the nostalgia. Krüger went outside and continued to enjoy his drink on the porch, wishing only for some comrades to join him in savoring the moment.

But time was passing. He had to get along to Zurich with Frieda for their appointment at the bank. He went inside, threw his glass into the fireplace in celebration, paid silent obeisance to the *Führer*, and bent to look at Polyakov's arm.

Krüger gasped and recoiled in horror. It was not easy to make Krüger do this, but he did it. Polyakov's arm had been burned, all right, horribly--it was charred--but the telltale number, and a circular patch of skin framing it, was intact. In fact, because of the contrast, the number was even easier to see than before. Polyakov was dead, but the mystery remained. It was as if some unknown force had countermanded the *Aryan* sacrifice Krüger had meant the incineration to be. He swore. The bastards who did the tattoos had done too good a job.

No matter. Krüger picked up Polyakov again, carried him back outside, and again threw the body on the ground. He picked up the shovel. He would bury Polyakov himself. No one would ever find him in this God-forsaken place. Nothing and no one ever came here but worms.

But the ground predictably was frozen. It was immensely hard to dig. Krüger threw down the shovel in disgust. Such work was not meant for a German officer--a physician and intellectual, the flower of German culture--whose arm the *Führer* personally had clasped, but for Jews, for gypsies, for retardates and Slavs. Obviously, God, who is an *Aryan* and perfectly aware of this, had intervened. Krüger would bring someone later to do the job.

He looked at his watch. He had to change and get to Zurich. His preparations had even included practice runs. To be in good time, he would have to leave now. This was one appointment he couldn't miss.

He walked back to the car, again enjoying the brisk air. What a delight it was to be alive and without troubles on such a glorious day. He drove to the little inn, made himself presentable and picked up Frieda.

"I won't go anywhere without David," she said. "Where is he?"

"Did you know that you are still in Germany? I don't need your acquiescence. I could take you by force."

"Then do it--by force."

Krüger smiled. "Happily, there's no need, *Frau* Polyakov. Your husband is free. I have kept my word. He's waiting for you nearby."

It was easy to say this. Wasn't it the truth? Krüger was not a psychopath who lied just for fun. He always told the truth when he didn't have to lie. Polyakov was free and he was waiting nearby. "To be reunited, you need only keep our appointment at the bank. Afterward, I shall call my colleagues, who will send him along. I've arranged a room for you in Zurich. He will join you there."

"All right. Let's go." She could not look at him. She talked to the wall, telling herself that the horror would soon end.

"Why are you so distant, Frieda? I don't understand. Haven't I done everything I promised? Didn't I treat you well? Was it my fault I fell in love with you?"

No, of course it wasn't. It was hers. His desire for her was as strong as it had ever been. It hung in the air like something she could touch. He looked at her now and trembled with desire. She was filling out so well. Her hair was coming in again, fine and blonde, like the sun. So many Jews had frizzy hair like the Zulus--to whom Himmler's investigators had learned the Jews were related--and the predatory nose that had launched more than a thousand Nazi cartoonists. Frieda, on the contrary, was perfect. Her dainty nose pointed up, not down. Her legs were long, her features elegant. She was a classic *Aryan*, except that she was a Jew, which, to Krüger, made her exotic. Maybe that was the quality that had kept her appeal intact, even after so many years at the camp, especially now that she was returning to normal. What had seduced him from the beginning was the perverse, powerful lure of the forbidden; that, and all those lovely millions of francs in the bank. Certainly he could have taken her by force, but he didn't want to do that. He wanted her to receive him voluntarily, yet she had tried to humiliate him from the start, even daring him to kill her at the camp. Why? Why would she scorn a chance to marry a true *Aryan*?

She shuddered. He was standing at the door across the spacious room, yet, because they were alone, he seemed quite close. It was perfectly quiet, but she would have known he was there, even with her eyes closed. Because the horror was now ending, bitter things she wanted to say came to mind, about how he had destroyed their lives, when all they had wanted was to be left alone. She wanted to tell him how foul a pig he was.

She restrained herself, afraid that if she said something she would go too far. Without Krüger, she could not see David, and she wanted to see David more than anything on earth.

"Why would a Nazi fall in love with me?" She spoke the key words acidly. Her hands flew to her throat. She had not meant to say anything, and had not known she would, but her bitterness had escaped like bile under pressure from a valve.

Krüger smiled. "Yes, I'm a Nazi. I'll always be a Nazi thanks to you. You gave the ultimate meaning to my devotion to the Party. Because of you I realized the genius of the Führer. Frieda, darling, I give you humble thanks."

"No!" Frieda's face fell into her hands. He was telling her that what had happened to them was her own fault, that she had created this monster that stank of the crypt. No! His remark was utterly without logic, characteristically self-serving and insane. But, despite all reason, she felt guilt. Could there be some truth to what he said? Had she helped make him the monster he was? She shuddered again, too consumed to say more.

"Shall we go, *liebchen*?" said Krüger. "David is waiting."

At the bank, Krüger put the suitcases beside the desk. "I assume everything is in order, Monsieur Gely?"

Gely held in one hand something that hung on a chain around his neck. He let it go to open the file on his desk, and Krüger saw that it was the star of David. Gely was a Jew! Krüger retched invisibly. They were everywhere! People who looked perfectly normal could turn out to be Jews. Hadn't Frieda taught him that? He had fallen in love with her without knowing she was a Jew. When he found out, it was too late. No one could be trusted. Nowhere was it safe.

Yet, there had been something suspicious about this man from the start. Was it an odor? Here in Zurich, just a few miles from hallowed German ground, he had been beyond Krüger's reach. Krüger didn't know that Gely had borrowed the star of David from a Jewish colleague for the occasion.

"*Certainement*, Herr `Maginot,'" said Gely. "This is the Zurich Bank Corporation, for good reason the largest in Switzerland. Things are *always* in order here." Was Gely emphasizing the name "Maginot" to prove he knew it was a fraud? His impotence in the obvious charade was lacerating his Gallic heart, in which long slumbering memories of teutonic invasions had awakened. "Maginot" opened the suitcase on the desk, and Gely saw the gaping jaws of Nazi Germany, preparing to swallow even more.

"I am most impressed with your efficiency, Monsieur Gely," said Krüger. "It is almost German. You are a credit to your race."

Gely bristled. "To which race do you refer?"

"You are a Jew, aren't you?"

"Yes," Gely lied. "I am today." Concealed under his shirt, he wore a wooden cross on a chain around his neck.

Gely's remark was lost on Krüger. "In my country, too, you Jews wear yellow stars."

"Which country is that?" asked Gely, amused, glad now that he had worn the gold star.

"France."

"France," mused Gely, feigning surprise. "Despite your name, I had thought it was Germany. You never said. In France, we Jews no longer wear yellow stars--unless we choose to. As you see, I choose to."

"Yes. I see. And I remember."

"In any event, let us thank the Jewish God we are not in your country." By now, Gely was enjoying himself too much to notice Krüger's threat.

There was an awkward silence. "As you see, *Herr* 'Maginot,' I have implemented *Monsieur* Polyakov's instructions exactly. The record is to contain none of the details of the transfer. It will show only a withdrawal of ten million Swiss francs, and a balance of 12,416."

"Excellent," said Krüger. "*très bien*, I believe."

"There is just one more thing," said Gely. "Frankly, it's embarrassing, *Madame* Polyakov. I don't know how to ask. May I say that your husband suggested I do so."

"The numbers."

"Yes. Thank you for not making me explain."

"Your discomfort proves you are a civilized man, *Monsieur* Gely, for which I in turn thank you. Please be at ease. We are two civilized people forced into an uncivilized situation not of our making. You have no cause to apologize. Thank you for being a Jew today."

Frieda undid her long sleeve and showed him her forearm. Gely blushed as much as he would have had she removed her brassiere, mumbled something she couldn't hear, and compared the numbers on her arm to the numbers Polyakov had written on the notepaper. They matched, as he had known they would. He had no doubt at all that the woman with the numbers on her arm was Mrs. Polyakov, but he wanted to know and to remember as much as he could.

"My instructions say I am to give you this, *Herr* 'Maginot.'" Gely handed Krüger the notepaper, and pushed a button on his desk. Two men came in with the cash, while the Nazi burned the paper in an ash tray. Gely pushed another paper across the desk. "If you will just sign this receipt, *Herr* 'Maginot,' the transfer will be complete. I believe the denominations are as you requested."

Gely did not add that he had recorded the serial numbers of the bills, in case anyone discreetly wanted to know.

"*Naturellement*," chortled Krüger, loading packages of fresh currency into the suitcases. As he did so, his hubris grew. He was a man of total will and power, a consummate Nazi. Wasn't he outwitting one of the largest banks in Europe? Gely the Jew knew what Krüger was doing, but, so perfect was the plan, that Gely couldn't stop him. Gely childishly thought he would irritate Krüger by hinting that he knew. He didn't understand that Krüger *wanted* him to know.

"Don't you want to count it, *Herr* 'Maginot?'" asked Gely.

"Not at all, *mon cher Monsieur* Gely. This is the Zurich Bank Corporation, where things are always in order. In any event, we shall soon meet again. I have no doubt of it."

Gely sneered. He had no intention of ever seeing this unsavory Nazi again. He rose in frustration as the last of the bills disappeared inside the suitcases, and Krüger maneuvered Frieda to the door. Gely saw with exasperation that "Maginot" wasn't going to leave her alone.

"My respects to your husband," Gely called as they left.

They were back in the car. "Now that you have robbed us, take me to my husband," she whispered.

Krüger chortled, a protective arm around the suitcases. "All right." He drove with one hand, fast and very well, talking, talking, impressed with himself. Frieda covertly marveled with distaste at how much this Nazi and her husband looked alike. Before he died, Bruckner told her he had made a mistake. The Jew circa 1771 had been someone else's ancestor. Krüger was as pure an *Aryan* as Thor, but Bruckner's documents had fooled him. Now, Frieda wouldn't tell him, because the mistake caused him pain. So, there was no way to explain the resemblance. They were even the same age, within a month.

He stopped at the hotel. "Let's go to your room," he said. "There is something I must show you." He got the key and they went up.

"Take me to my husband," she said doggedly. "We have done everything you said." What could he show her that she might want to see? Who cared?

"Of course you have, *liebchen*. All in good time. First, look at this. The sections I've underlined. It's always better to be prepared." Krüger put a file in her lap, opened it and tapped a page. She didn't want to look, but it was there. It would have been recognized as a government file in any country on earth, thick, official, festooned with stamps and seals. There were many numbered photographs of her husband.

She read a few minutes. Her hands shook. Her mouth trembled. Krüger saw tears falling on the paper. She could read no more, but she could not look up. If she looked up, she would see the beast. What did he really look like? Certainly not like David. His real face was no doubt a gargoyle's that would give pause to Quasimodo. Through some satanic power of hypnosis he had made himself appealing. It was inexcusable to show him weakness, but there was nothing she could do.

Krüger said kindly, "I was sure you would want to know it, dear Frieda. Was I right?"

She kept looking at the papers, even turning pages, but it was obvious that her tears made them impossible to see. "You sadistic, inhuman bastard," she whispered.

"At this point, dear, dear Frieda, there is no use discussing the reasons for it. We both know. Recriminations would just make bad feeling and damage our relationship. It was necessary."

"What relationship, you sauerkraut bastard?" She was out of control now, shaking. She could not stop.

"Frieda! Please! You'll hurt yourself."

"*Mein Gott*! Why? Because I wouldn't go to bed with you? Because I wouldn't be an hour's playmate? Why didn't you just kill him? Why didn't you just kill us both?"

"You are talking about science, Frieda, state policy, too boring to discuss here. Whatever the reason, he is no longer a man, as you see. Because he loves you, he asked me to take care of you, to take his identity, to become David

Polyakov. In return for that identity, I would carry on his name, a matter of importance to you Jews. He asks you to understand that he can do nothing for you. He is no longer a man and no longer has money. He can't bear to see you again. There are winners and losers, dear Frieda, and blood makes me a winner."

She still couldn't look up. She whispered, "My husband, David Polyakov, asked you to marry me?"

"Yes. He spoke of the remarkable resemblance we enjoy. I was skeptical, at first, but his regard for you persuaded me. If you convince me, too, perhaps we could make it work."

Frieda held her head, groaning. The pain was too intense. This was worse than anything she had ever experienced at Auschwitz. "Please, God, take me," she whispered.

"There is also the fact that Polyakov isn't even a German. What is he? May I see the file? Ah, yes, Poland. Of course. Ghetto refuse! You are a German, as am I. Your father was a German doctor. How on earth could a German woman become involved with a 'Polak'? Was there any good reason besides the money?"

"Jews in Poland are not 'Polaks.'"

"Yet, Jews in Germany wanted to be Germans. Why?"

"You revoked my citizenship. Remember?"

"Clearly because they recognize *Aryan* superiority. They may be *untermenschen*, but they're smart." Krüger chuckled. He had a gift for repartee.

Frieda shuddered. "Herr Krüger, I don't pretend to know what you want, but I do know that my husband--however mutilated--wouldn't give me to another man. I do know he wouldn't give me to a concentration camp sadist."

"Why do you hate me so much, Frieda? I don't understand."

Frieda shook with waves of terror. The fact that Krüger didn't understand why she hated him so much, was proof that he was utterly insane. She didn't know what to say, and couldn't speak anyway. Could the Nazi see her shake? If so, he might suspect what she was thinking, which could be dangerous. Frieda had read that calling attention to someone's insanity often led to violence.

"Did you know, my dear *Frau* Polyakov, that your friends the British invented the so-called 'concentration camp?' They did, and used it to good effect in the Boer War. Until they 'concentrated' the Boer women and children--many of whom were Germans, by the way--they kept losing. All we Germans have done is perfect the technique--as honest men we give the British the credit--but, because of our obvious superiority, envious men like your husband, blame us. The Allies are perfectly aware of our humane program of purification. They've said nothing, and their silence is approval. They know their friends the British invented it.

"Did you know that your President Roosevelt has said nothing and has refused to admit Jews? He has made so-called 'anti-semitic' remarks to ingratiate himself with the Arabs--yet the Allies do not disclaim him. He's a 'goy,' but American Jews believe he is their savior. Your 'birth control' people and their eugenics advocate selective breeding to improve the race, and abortion for the unfit. So do we. Their organization--what is it called?--has printed several essays by our leading racial scientists. Yet, American propagandists call them heroines, while envious, little men like your husband condemn us. As in all things, the German position--the position of the Third Reich--is devoid of such hypocrisy. The *Aryan* calls a Jew a Jew."

Frieda paid no attention to his driveling, but was glad for it. She pretended to be listening. She had to stall. The Nazi was lying about her husband. She had to see him.

"Where is my husband? If what you say is true, he must tell me so himself."

"I told you, Frieda. Polyakov told me he couldn't bear the pain. He asked me to do it. I agreed, for old times' sake."

"Why didn't he say a word about it on the train?"

"I don't know."

"You're lying," she exploded. "You've been lying from the start. You never intended to keep your word. You couldn't. You're a Nazi bastard. A Nazi bastard can't tell the truth."

"I'm sorry you feel that way, Frieda. You have been horribly misled. David will be displeased."

Frieda screamed again that Krüger was a Nazi bastard and was lying. She knew she was doing the worst possible thing, but she had lost control. "I wouldn't believe it if my husband told me so himself. I'd rather die than have you touch me. You're the real *untermensch.*"

"Frieda, I appeal to you. As you know, I have a Jewish ancestor myself."

"You don't. Bruckner made a mistake. He told me so."

"Did he! I'm so happy. Thank you, dear Frieda, for the news. I never lost faith my blood was pure. Despite the lack of kinship, I have now become a Jew."

Enraged that she had made him happy, Frieda screamed every foul name she had ever heard and ransacked her memory for more. Still, it was not enough. "Take me to my husband, you bastard!"

Kruger was disappointed. What a pity! She would have fit so well into his plans, but she was a Jewess and was stupid. "As you wish," he said. "Your husband is waiting. Come. Let us join him. You will see too late that I speak the truth."

He clapped his knees, rose and opened the door. Frieda sprang up. *Thank God*! At last she would see David.

A few weeks later, the *Volksrecht* reported the disappearance of Pierre Gely, senior vice president of the Zurich Bank Corporation. The *Thurgauer Zeitung* and the *Neue Zurcher Zeitung* picked the story up, but it had to compete with the electrifying announcement of the German surrender. On an inside page, a few lines characterized the disappearance as "strange"--what disappearance isn't?--and described M. Gely as an immensely popular banker, "a pillar of his church and community affairs," with no known enemies. Whether or not the disappearance had anything to do with the welcome news about the war wasn't known. A week later, a motorist found Gely's body, across the border in Germany on the shoulder of a road, which only compounded the mystery. It was never solved.

Chapter Twelve
Lords of Creation

"Your story is utterly *fantastique*," marveled the French Ambassador to Israel.

"That doesn't mean it isn't true," joked "Polyakov."

The French Ambassador laughed. "Polyakov" was so *charmant*, almost French! "Would that it were not," said the Ambassador. "I don't believe I've ever heard a story so horrifying, and at the same time so inspirational. I wonder why no one has ever thought of telling it on film."

"Vincent Blandino, at Superior Pictures in Hollywood, has approached me. I may agree, if I can get the right leading man."

"Whom do you want, dear *Monsieur* Polyakov?"

"Robert Redford. I'm told we used to look very much alike."

"You still do, especially the profile, except that *Monsieur* Redford lamentably now looks older than you. Frankly, my dear *Monsieur* Polyakov, I am at a loss to understand how a man who has survived so much, who has suffered as much as you have . . . ."

". . . and who has been around as long as I have . . . ."

". . . can look as young and as good as you look."

Of course, Robert Redford didn't have that long scar on his face. It was obviously part of the suffering the Ambassador had mentioned. No one ever asked about it--the risk of offending "Polyakov" was too great--and neither did the French Ambassador.

"I'd be happy to tell you my age, Your Excellency, since you ask. I'm 66."

"Sixty six! *Fantastique*! You don't look a day over 40, if that."

"Clean living, Excellency. Clean women. But, most important, clean thoughts."

"Did you ever regain your memory, *Monsieur* Polyakov?"

"Some of it. After treatment. There are blank spots to this day. The Americans found me and told me who I was, who I am." He pointed to his forearm. "Thank God they were able to trace me through the numbers."

"Numbers do not lie."

"Correct, Excellency. Unfortunately, liars have been known to number."

The French Ambassador to Israel chortled. Polyakov was so witty, so quick. He showed no symptoms at all of the ponderous, teutonic sense of humor.

He had thought of everything, including the surgeon who had made the few necessary changes on his face: lengthening the nose and slightly thickening the lips. Krüger had told him to leave the facial scar alone. It was a badge of sorts, a blazing memento of "Nazi brutality." More than anything else people saw, it proved who he was; what he was.

Needless to say, the surgeon had also tattooed Polyakov's concentration camp number on Krüger's arm, and removed his SS tattoo. Krüger convinced him to cover both his upper arms with scars, to obliterate the mark the SS tattoo had made. Two scarred arms would inhibit any suspicion that the incriminating number had been removed from either one. The swelling and inflammation the Jews had whined about at Auschwitz, Krüger welcomed. Yet, he had shuddered when the surgeon worked on the arm the Führer had clasped.

Since Krüger did not intend to remain celibate, and since there was always the risk of a chance medical exam, he had even had himself circumcised, and the pain had been intense. No wonder the Jews were so stiff-necked. They hated the Nazis for humiliating them, but loved to humiliate themselves.

What a pity that such a talented and loyal, *Aryan* surgeon had to die, but dead doctors don't talk. Under Jewish torture he would have remembered these bizarre procedures--perhaps even remembered the numbers--had not Krüger wisely taken the precaution of terminating him "with extreme prejudice," in the language of C.I.A. To his credit, the doctor had welcomed his own death, secure in the knowledge that he was dying for the Reich.

For the same reason, but with considerably more pleasure, "Polyakov" had killed the banker, Pierre Gely. Gely also would have remembered too much. He had put his nose where it didn't belong--had impersonated a Jew--and suffered the consequences. Gely had been so righteous and proud of his joke. In his last moments, he had realized that the joke was on him. Most of the world's troubles were caused by people who couldn't mind their own business.

Because of his "amnesia," "Polyakov" "couldn't remember" why he had scars on his face and upper arms. The scars were there when American forces found him wandering in France. Clever American doctors had included the disfigurements in his file, marking them down to Nazi torture at Auschwitz, or an unknown "accident." A distinguished American psychiatrist wrote therein that the horror of what “Polyakov” had seen and survived, had "overloaded his psychological circuits" and explained his "amnesia."

The transformation was complete. Krüger had disappeared. "Polyakov" remained. As the French Ambassador had said, his survival was a "miracle," his story a fountainhead of inspiration. From time to time over the years, journalists wondered in features and television "specials," what had happened to Krüger. Without a corpse with the SS tattoo on its arm--without the number--the people chasing Krüger could not assume he was dead. Wiesenthal and the Israelis looked for Bormann, then Eichmann, Mengele and Vörst. "Polyakov" directed and liberally financed the search for Krüger, which had given him no small reputation as a "Nazi-hunter." On several occasions in several places over the years, Krüger had "left only minutes" before "Polyakov" arrived. Was it his fault that Krüger was too clever to be caught?

The only thing he feared was that the one person who could expose him might appear. For many years, he had sought that person, seeking to complete the executions of Polyakov, the surgeon and Gely. He could never find her. Yet, with the growing list of his achievements--his Jewish philanthropies; his success in business; his official citations from the Israeli government; in short, the remarkable story the reader has enjoyed in a couple of biographies and a television special--that person suddenly emerging from the obscurity of thirty three years with such a ridiculous accusation, would look more and more like a crank.

The Jews he necessarily spent so much time with, did not dream how much he loathed them. They were every bit as corrupt as the *Führer* had said they were, constantly grubbing for money. There could never be any place for them in National Socialism. From time to time, the old, excruciating question arose: Had he taken the coward's way out? Was everything he told himself a sham? He was a warrior. Shouldn't he have died in battle, like so many of his colleagues?

Their deaths were noble, yes, but they were gone. They could not rebuild the Reich, like Krüger. It was easy to die, a trifle. It was hard to live, especially as he did. As always, the imagined tramp of marching feet swept away his doubts. The Führer would salute him. He had fooled his enemies, pretended he was one of them--had spat in their faces--for more than thirty years. When he finally told them the truth, they would be mortified unto death. "Polyakov" already could taste his triumph.

Yet, although he looked no more than 40, if that--thanks to Heinz--as the ambassador had said, he was 66. Once in a while, even now, in 1978, he read stories about Japanese officers, still loyal to the Emperor, who had waited for victory all these years in some forgotten jungle, not knowing the war was over; not knowing that Japan had won with the computer chip what it had lost on the battlefield. When found, they went home and were welcomed as heroes. Krüger, too, had been hiding all these years in a jungle, but, if found, he would not be welcomed home. He would be disgraced, jailed, tried and probably executed. Regret was creeping in. He knew it was dangerous to permit that, but it was. He needed a sign, a sign from the sleeping heroes of the *Vaterland*, something to prove, if only to himself, that his patience would not be in vain.

The Name of the King
84

Krüger left the reception, called for his car--a Mercedes-Benz limousine, of course--told his chauffeur to get on the *autobahn* and drove up to Munich. What a lovely city, scene of one of the *Führer's* greatest triumphs, where he had shown the world that the British are cowards. That was why Krüger had chosen it for his headquarters. Now, he rode up fifty flights to his office, looked through some memos and made some calls. The light on the massive doomsday phone started flashing. He lifted the receiver, listened to the recorded message and frowned. In a moment, he bounded up another flight to the pad on the roof, and choppered to the castle, one of the most enchanting spots on the Rhine, especially now, in the early evening.

Everything seemed normal. As usual, Vörst was waiting for him in the study, and handed him a glass. "To Adolf Hitler," said Vörst.

"To the *Führer* and the Fourth Reich."

A large portrait of Hitler standing triumphally in a touring car hung on the wall over the mantle. They raised their glasses and drank to him.

"How is he?" Krüger asked gently.

Vörst's eyes misted. "No change."

"How long must we wait, Heinz? How long?"

"I don't know."

They drank again. "Delightful," said Krüger. "What is it?"

"A trifle, really. Nothing serious. A Moselle."

"Immensely pleasing."

"Of course. You come from München?"

"Yes. I was in Garmisch today. I pledged half my fortune to the Jew who brings me to justice."

"Your reputation for generosity is deserved."

"Like so many young people today, I am trying to find myself." Both men laughed.

"When were you last in Berlin?" asked Vörst.

Berlin had been Krüger's favorite German city. Then, it had been the center of imperial Nazi might. Now, it was an occupied, divided city, a reminder of Germany's defeat, however temporary. Now, Krüger didn't like to go there. He remembered the sickening day he had left Berlin with Frieda.

"Last week. It was unavoidable."

"Last week! Horst, what was it like?"

The question proved that Vörst was melancholy, too, and cut Krüger's heart like a scalpel. Yes, he felt a growing *angst*, his spirit drooped, but at least he could travel--as chairman of the Company, he had been everywhere--and he could socialize. He had never married--a wife would know too much--but he had women, elegant, fastidious women, both Jew and gentile, of different ages and conjugal conditions, but all of considerable wealth, who considered a love affair with a man so remarkable a coup.

Lords of Creation
85

On the contrary, Heinz Vörst, a scientific genius, former director of the Department of Heredity at the Kaiser Wilhelm Institute, Krüger's teacher, one of the top architects of the Führer's racial program, a father of the *Einsatzgruppen*, had spent much of his life in prison. Caught after the Munich *putsch* in the 'Twenties, he had been locked up with Hitler. Caught again after the war crimes trials, he had been imprisoned with Hess. He was the only man outside a few top Allied and German commanders, who knew the truth about Hess's mysterious jump into England; who knew the secret Hess would be locked up for life to prevent him from revealing. Awaiting death by hanging, Vörst had escaped. Needless to say, Jewish organizations were furious. They would have been even more furious had they known that he had escaped with Krüger's help.

For twenty seven years, Vörst had lived in the castle. Krüger had bought it for the purpose. Neither the gawking foreigners who toured it at "Polyakov's" invitation--a brilliant cover--nor even the guides who conducted them, had any inkling that they were not seeing it all; that in a wing of the castle they didn't even know was off-limits, Heinz Vörst was continuing his "research."

It was Vörst who had developed the compound that was keeping Krüger so young. Indeed, Vörst himself, now 85, looked like a man in his early fifties. He had not left his wing of the castle since Krüger had brought him there in 1951. He couldn't, precisely because he looked only a little older than he had looked as the physician in charge of "racial research" at Auschwitz--only a little different--and he was still a fugitive. An appearance in public would be an invitation to arrest. So, Heinz Vörst was still in prison, if prison is a place one cannot leave.

Three or four men--devoted Nazis--maintained the property, but even they had never been told that Vörst lived in the castle. The only man allowed to see Heinz Vörst all these years--the only man who knew he was alive--had been Krüger himself. There was a housekeeper, but she had no family, no friends and no reason to leave--so she didn't know that she, too, was a prisoner. She had been selected for her bad eyes, her stupidity and her loyalty to Hitler.

Yes, Vörst was a bookish man. He spent hours--sometimes days--alone in his lab, investigating things that man should not know, but he was also a social man, gregarious, who looked not at all like the utterly insane scientist is popularly supposed to look. He was a large man with a beer belly, the florid complexion and veiny nose of a serious tippler, who could easily have found work even now as a bouncer in a cheap whore house. In his youth, still svelte, he had spent many weekends climbing in *lederhosen* and leather shorts, and rolling village maidens in the hay.

For more than thirty years, he had been denied most of this, denied recognition, denied travel, denied association with every Nazi but Krüger. What was Krüger's suffering next to his? Heinz had sacrificed everything to the Cause. What right had Krüger to complain?

The Name of the King
86

Of course, Heinz did have women. He had made plain to Krüger that he could not continue without them. His conversations with Horst had a bouquet like fine knackwurst, it was true, but they were too infrequent--because of Company demands on his comrade-in-arms in Munich--and, even at their best, could not have prevented the progression of his insanity. Only women could do that, and they were crucial to the plan.

Krüger found them in the red-light districts of cities like Hamburg, Dusseldorf, Amsterdam, even Paris--which gave him a chance to practice his French--hookers nobody but their *maquereaux* would miss. He had never been noticed. If he had been, well, who would deny a bit of relaxation to such a benefactor of humanity? Almost without exception, the women were riddled with Sexually Transmitted Diseases, of course. Vörst cured them, treated them to every luxury for months--sublime food, a royal wardrobe and quarters, celestial entertainment featuring Vörst playing German *lieder* on a celesta--and, when he needed their vital organs, or when they finally became boring, as all women did, whichever came first, to humane execution. Over the years, 58 such women had died in his arms, worshipping him as they did so. They could not know when recruited that, having seen the face of Satan, they could not leave hell alive. They could not know that Vörst needed their organs for the Plan. The Plan had already claimed millions. What was another hooker?

"There are rumors that Brezhnev will permit the destruction of the Wall," Krüger said.

"Brezhnev," said Vörst. "Slavic garbage."

"Yes."

"Why would he do that?" asked Vörst.

"To neutralize N.A.T.O. and lull the West. To pave the way for a new Bolshevik offensive."

"Outrageous! Surely the West won't fall for it."

"They will, my dear Heinz. They will fall for it, because they are as stupid as they are decadent and corrupt."

Vörst filled their glasses and they toasted Hitler again. "Ach! Berlin!" Vörst mused. "The holy city. Irrefutable proof of the superiority of German civilization. So many memories. By any chance, Horst, did you visit the bunker?"

"It no longer exists." Krüger knew that reminiscing was inordinately dangerous. It led to melancholy. Yet, like a drunk who knows that drink is killing him, but drinks, he couldn't stop reminiscing any more than could Vörst.

"The *Führer's* bunker no longer exists? Since when?"

"I don't remember."

"All this time, you haven't told me."

"I wanted to shield you, Heinz. It's too painful to recall."

"Surely, Horst, there is a marker, a sign, perhaps a plaque."

Lords of Creation
87

"No. Nothing. They have obliterated any trace."

"They are still afraid of him," Vörst exulted. "With good reason, as they shall see."

"They have constructed new housing on the site," Krüger said stonily. He knew he had said too much; had made another mistake--but Vörst was the only human being he could discuss such things with, and Krüger could not leave them unmentioned.

"New housing? On the site of the bunker? Horst, my dear friend, I don't know how to ask this. Is it just possible . . . is it possible . . . that . . . ?"

"That Jews live there? On the site of the bunker? It is not only possible, Heinz, it is probable."

Vörst's hands went to his face. His shoulders heaved. He began to cry. "Is there no outrage the barbarians will not commit?"

"Apparently not."

"The romance is gone," he bawled. "They trash everything noble, cheapen every sentiment, reduce everything to commerce."

Krüger squeezed his shoulder. "We must be strong."

"*Ja.*"

"Why did you bring me here, Heinz? The code you used is extremely urgent."

"With good reason. We must have more organ material."

"Still more material? Why so much?"

Vörst went to the phonograph and pushed a button. The stately, but electrifying, cadences of the *Horst Wessel* filled the room, complete with a robust, *Aryan* choir. Krüger could almost hear marching boots; could almost see endless, irresistible waves of the *Wehrmacht* occupying *lebensraum.* Vörst took a position beneath the portrait of Hitler.

"As you know, my dear Horst, the active ingredient in the compound derives from the proper combination and administration of certain human organ extract. Despite the treason of Jewish front men like Rommel, despite the mock investigations and lying historians, despite the preposterous war crimes trials, our enemies have never discovered the true purpose of our experiments at Auschwitz. You will remember that both Himmler and Goering took the cyanide capsules we all carried, rather than reveal it. Hess, God bless him, has never talked, despite systematic Jewish brainwashing with drugs.

"All these years, I have been refining the process. You see the remarkable results whenever you look into a mirror or make love. Now, my friend, now, we stand at the door of no doubt the most staggering discovery in the history of medicine: eternal life, life without end, everlasting, for us, the master race, the true and only chosen people. Think of it, Horst. You, I, and the few others we initiate, will literally live forever. We shall vindicate the *Führer*, once and for all. We shall destroy the Allies and the mongrelizers simply by outlasting them.

The Name of the King
88

"What is the continuing allure of the Jews and their slave religion? What is the secret to the blasphemous success of their contemptible, Christian lickspittles? Why is Jesus, the Jewish charlatan, so universally revered? Isn't it because of his pathetic promise of everlasting life? So desperate, so consuming and universal, is this lust for eternal life, that the whining weakling is still respected although he couldn't even save himself.

"But, now, Horst, you and I will give eternal life in fact; not the contemptible, Christian fraud, the imitation--not "pie in the sky, by and by"--but life here on earth where it was meant to be lived, life that is wholesome, robust, and, above all, *Aryan.* We have conquered nature, Horst. We have dethroned their spineless god. Who alone can give eternal life? Isn't it God Himself? And won't the eternal life we offer come as a gift from the *Führer* Himself? Won't the world see at last who the true God really is?

"For years, I couldn't solve the final problem. The perfected compound successfully retards aging, yes. In two or three mortal years, we have been aging only one--but we still age. All we had done was slow the process down. In a century, Horst, with the compound as it is, you might look 70. In a few hundred years, you could look really old. Ha, ha! A good joke, *nein*? I was not able to stop aging completely." Vörst smiled archly. "Until now."

Krüger came out of his chair. "You have finally succeeded, *mein freund*, as we knew you would, after all these years?"

"On paper. Everything checks and rechecks. But, I must make more tests. I need more organ material, much more. It is time again for *blitzkrieg, Komandant.* Ah, for the dear, old days of Auschwitz, when we could work in peace, when the do-gooders knew better than to open their yaps, when we had all the human matter we needed, when the Jews served a useful purpose. For them, such basic, human rights as privacy don't exist."

"Your playmates, Heinz . . . ."

"So charming. I tell them all they keep me young. And they do. More than they know. Mine is a consuming passion. But a couple every year or so, while sufficient for my pleasure, is no longer adequate for our noble purpose. I need groups of at least a dozen."

"A dozen would be difficult, Heinz. Is there no other way?"

"I should tell you this, Horst. My *in vivo* calculations show that, if we do not advance, we shall retreat. The effect we have achieved is impressive, yes, but it is temporary; if we do not advance to immortality, we shall age again--even faster than before."

"No stalemate. Total war."

"Correct. Total war. The thing we were born for. The thing we love more than anything on earth, except the *Führer.*"

Krüger blanched. "What would defeat do to him?" he whispered.

Vörst shook his head. "Utter corruption. Total dissolution."

"Would extract of these organs, perhaps pulverized, work?"

"*Nein*. We knew that already back in Auschwitz. The tissue must be taken from living donors. I leave the problem in your immensely capable hands."

"I'll take action at once, Herr *Doktor*."

But it wasn't going to be as easy as he had led Vörst to believe. The women Krüger had brought him for years, either hog-tied and drugged or utterly deceived, were women no one else wanted--hookers and worse--but even such welcome disappearances required investigation and preparation. Sometimes the police asked questions. If Krüger were to truck out a dozen such women, there could be an uproar that would beggar Jack the Ripper.

What was needed was another public relations coup like the one they had launched in the beginning, in which they had convinced the gullible world that their hatred of Jews was the only reason for the camps. The world did not know why they hated Jews so much; did not know that the Jews and their Christian lickspittles were a threat to the "new" Nazi religion.

Indeed, the Nazi "apostles" had succeeded in concealing not just the true reason, but even the subterfuge, to such an extent, that many Jews had reported voluntarily, with their suitcases, enraptured by stories of "resettlement" to a "new life." Most of them hadn't caught on even when told to disrobe for "delousing." Some had even waited submissively all night, afraid of losing their places in line, nothing like today's Israelis. The Führer had achieved perhaps the greatest disinformation coup since the Bible's excoriation of Pharaoh.

"You know what I need," said Vörst.

Krüger smiled. "Have I ever failed you, Heinz? In more than forty years since Kaiser Wilhelm?"

"Never! Good! That's done. I'll dismiss it from mind. Will you dine with me this evening, Horst? We are having one of your forbidden favorites, a delectable pork roast."

"Unfortunately, I must return to *München*. There is trouble in New York."

"What sort of trouble?"

"I don't know yet. That's why I must go back."

"I shall think of you, *mein freund*, as I savor each delightful *Aryan* morsel. Before you leave, shall we pay our respects?"

Krüger straightened and checked the knot in his tie. He was nervous, and it was not easy to make him nervous. "*Jawohl*!"

Chapter Thirteen
Der Fuhrer

There was a stuffed eagle on a table and Vörst pushed one of its eyes. He always enjoyed doing that so much, because it was a bald eagle, an American symbol, and Vörst easily imagined that it caused the eagle pain. The fireplace swung into the wall. There was a tiny room, then a passage. They walked inside and down some stairs. The fireplace swung shut. There was a door, steel and very heavy. Vörst produced a key. There was a corridor sloping downward, there were suspicious dogs--German Shepherds, of course--and another, equally impregnable door. Again Vörst produced a key. Both men took an extra breath.

Inside, it was cold, about the temperature of a meat locker, so cold that they donned fur parkas at the door for the purpose. It was a room meant for ceremony, designed for intimidation. The ceiling was high; it disappeared in the dark. For all anyone could tell, it reached to the sky. There were a couple of Tiffany lamps in the corners, giving little light. There was an I.V. rig against the wall. There was heavy, uncomfortable furniture. There was an altar. Across it lay a reasonable facsimile of the Spear of Destiny, the occult symbol of teutonic rule. Behind it, on the wall, was a grinning portrait of the Goat of Mendes. There was a flame on the floor at the crux of a swastika, apparently serviced by a gas jet.

And, on an elaborate throne beside the altar, under a brocaded valance, dressed in the exquisitely tailored uniform and full regalia of a field marshal of the *Wehrmacht*, sat Adolf Hitler, despite the official findings of the *Amtsgericht* of Berchtesgaden in 1954.

It is distasteful, but, unfortunately, it is necessary, to dwell on these details, because of the egregious misinformation on the subject extruded by writers with otherwise acceptable reputations, writers we have no wish to embarrass and shall not name, who have told everyone foolish enough to listen that Hitler "committed suicide" in his bunker in Berlin. They are victims--albeit willing victims--of Nazi propaganda, and should develop the integrity to examine their own motives. Some authors will say anything to sell a book.

On the contrary, the authenticated truth of what you now read here, is known to the few men who run the renamed K.G.B. in Moscow, MI-6 in London, C.I.A. in Washington, and, of course, to German intelligence and Mossad. Yet, since this is the first public revelation of the facts--based upon personal interviews with the unimpeachable sources cited above--along with the corroborative certified documents from their archives--it is important to state that we are not talking euphemistically about a Mme. Tussaud wax figure. We are not talking about a National Socialist version of the plastic *potemkin* fake the Soviets displayed for decades in the utterly mislabeled architectural hoax they called “Lenin’s Tomb.” We are not talking about a sculpture. We are talking about Adolf Hitler himself--in physical person--the man who enslaved Europe and fought the world for years, who shocked its conscience and killed millions in concentration camps--but who did no such thing as "commit suicide in the command bunker underneath Berlin." It had not been easy to fool writers as truly clever as the ones we have mentioned, but the reader will note, if they did not, that no authenticated Hitler corpse was ever found at the site of the alleged suicide.

Yes, the Communists have their “Lenin's Tomb,” but Hitler was alive--dormant, hibernating, in suspension if you will, but certainly alive--needing only the mystic spark of Odin to reascend to full awareness. Krüger had brought him to the castle in 1949. Because of our contractual commitment to C.I.A. and other agencies--default in which could subject us to federal prosecution--we are not yet authorized to reveal where he was kept in the four years between the end of the war and his arrival at the castle. Likewise, we are still allowed to tell you nothing about the ludicrous contretemps that reduced him to somnolence. Hitler was nowhere near the bunker when the end came--when the end came because of "treason by Jewish front men like Rommel." He was on his way to the secret headquarters prepared for the next phase of the war, expertly disguised as a pimp, in the protective company of a troupe of garish, young women trained to dissemble, when Vörst, likewise disguised, staunch in the belief that everyone on earth, except the *Führer*, was his personal property, attempted to inspect the no doubt fascinating mammaries of an immensely dignified *hausfrau* whose husband unfortunately happened to be present. In the ensuing turmoil, the *Führer*, for once perfectly blameless, sustained a mystifying blow to the head. Had other writers and their ilk taken the trouble to reveal this, inevitable recrimination in the ranks could well have stultified the worldwide Nazi resurgence that threatens us today.

For 27 dogged, faithful years, Vörst had administered the compound daily, with the incredible result that Hitler looked only slightly older than he had when Spike Jones and his City Slickers were traveling to the bank with bags of money singing, "Right in *Der Führer's* Face." His legs were crossed. A long, lovingly polished boot hung to the floor. Vörst cut his hair and trimmed the famous mustache himself, with the result that he was impeccably groomed. An elbow rested on the arm of his throne, a hand on his chin, in the style of Rodin's "Thinker."

And his eyes--the eyes that had transfixed the largest crowds in Europe--were open.

The *Führer* stared at them, and stared, his gaze a burning poker in their hearts. He saw into their very souls, saw things even they didn't know were there. At any moment, he would erupt in judgment as of old; the scream that had brought strong men to hearing impairment and reduced them to shaking ruins like survivors of a rock concert, would flood this secret temple with sonic boom. The two disciples fervently willed it to happen. They knew it wouldn't, but were intimidated anyway. Hitler leaned forward, listening, waiting, waiting for the summons.

"I must have more material," whispered Vörst. "He will awaken."

"Yes." Krüger trembled. No one else on earth could make him do so. When the *Führer* awakened, Krüger could shed his putrid identity as Polyakov and be himself.

The eternal flame at the crux of the swastika flickered and Vörst gasped. The inexplicable spasm passed; the flame again stood tall and still, like the Spear of Destiny itself. "The fact that this flame has burned without interruption for more than twenty five years is a triumph in itself," Vörst whispered. "It is a symbol of our continuity and purity, of our right to rule. Were it ever to go out, we would be dead."

Something spiritual was in the room, Krüger was sure. The teutonic gods in Valhalla were beckoning. What was it Bormann had said? "If we are destined, like the old Nibelungs, to perish in King Attila's hall . . . ." Good, old Bormann! Where was he now?

Later that evening, after Krüger had gone, Vörst watched a movie with his latest, little friend. She pointed at the television screen. "Gor' blimey, 'ho are those funny, little men with the eyes?"

How refreshing she was. In all his long life, Vörst had never sampled an English tart. She was an utter barbarian. Krüger had found her by accident in Piccadilly Circus. What of it? The war with England was long over. Didn't Krüger still exercise his curious passion for Jewesses? Yet the war against the Jews was still vibrantly alive. Needless to say, the English lady's mammaries were stupendous.

"Those are Japanese, my child."

"Japanese, you say. Gor' blimey, what are the little buggers doing?"

"They are fighting the Americans."

Der Fuhrer
93

It was a war movie--Vörst loved war movies--and Vörst was rooting, naturally, for the Japanese. They were inferior to the *Aryans*, of course, but they did believe in racial purity, they had fought the Americans, and Vörst hated the Americans. All the years he had been locked up with Hess, they had pretended not to know that his name should be pronounced something like the English word "First," pronouncing it instead like "Vurst," as in knockwurst, or like "Worst." They were mongrel peasants of the lowest sort, totally impervious to culture.

"Did they ever fight the Yanks for real?"

"Oh, yes."

"When?"

"In World War II."

"Never 'eard of it. 'ho won?"

She had been trained to live only for the day. Her memory began anew every morning, a "tabula rasa" that would have enraptured John Locke. Nothing had happened before last night. If he let her return to London, she would be able to tell nothing about her spree, except that it was "bloody swell." She had seen the portrait of Hitler in the study, and had asked Vörst who it was. For the first time in many years, Vörst began to think he was in love.

Chapter Fourteen
The Arabs

"What sort of trouble?" Krüger asked.

Schwartz leaned eagerly across Krüger's desk. He was tall, blond, pink, athletic, immensely competent and loyal to the Company, even fanatic, superficially a perfect Aryan, but he was a Jew. Schwartz was one of Polyakov Pharmaceutical's senior vice presidents, but he had no idea who Krüger really was.

"We don't know for sure, *Herr* Polyakov. It's the strangest thing I've ever heard."

"Stop philosophizing, man. Give me some facts. Who is the man? What is he? What has he actually done?"

"He's a 'faith healer,' I think they call it."

"Christian nonsense!" Krüger said with special gusto. He rarely got the chance to say something he really believed, so now he allowed himself to call it nonsense because "Polyakov" was a Jew, and so was Schwartz. "What would a faith healer have to do with us?"

"He has achieved some so-called 'cures.' He has emptied a couple of convalescent homes. In one case, the police, expecting a disturbance, found the residents dancing on the lawn. It doesn't amount to much--as yet--but they were chronic patients. Our U.S. sales manager says they were substantial--and profitable--users of our products. Rejuvenall, for instance."

"Rejuvenall?"

"Cleared last year by F.D.A. Our new, anti-aging product. The detail men say it's very popular. With regular use, proper diet and sufficient exercise, a man of 60 could look 55."

"Ah, yes. Rejuvenall. Our age retardant. Another pearl before swine." Krüger chuckled. Jewish chemists at his Munich plant had developed it, and he had let them have their fun. It was harmless, little more than a placebo, but, because of its name, developed by the pompous, Jewish geniuses at his Madison Avenue advertising agency, the idiot public had decided it was worth the price.

If they knew what Vörst had produced, they would go berserk. Needless to say, Krüger didn't tell Schwartz, whose degree was in statistics, that Rejuvenall was nothing but a name. It amounted to no more than a blip in the Company's profit picture.

"They were substantial users, *Herr* Polyakov. Not any more. Not since they took the so-called cure. As I say, it doesn't amount to much overall, but sales are not maturing as projected in that restricted area. Foresight tells me we need to act, in case the problem wants to get out of hand."

"Wise. Very wise. I approve." Schwartz was very clever, for a Jew.

"Thank you, *Herr* Polyakov. I am so grateful for your comment. As you know, *Herr* Polyakov, I live for the Company. I am proud to have devoted my life to our ethical pharmaceuticals. They are a cause one can believe in. In all humility, I must say . . . ."

"Exactly what does this 'faith healer' do?"

"He appears without warning and tells the sick they are cured--and they believe him. They get dressed and go home."

"Outrageous! Has anyone thought of examining them? Does anyone have any brains in New York?"

"Some of them have been discreetly examined by a distinguished, interdisciplinary panel at Sloan-Kettering. Without exception, they are free of disease. There is no trace of Alzheimer's. They even go back to work and get married. Needless to say, *Herr* Polyakov, these findings have not been published, although *Lancet* knows about them. They are locked in the safe at the Institute."

"Incredible. They probably were never sick in the first place, but the doctors said they were. That's why there is so much less sickness when the doctors go on strike. Most people don't know that the purpose of modern medicine is not to cure, but to treat. Doctors are among the biggest frauds on earth. Without us, they would still be wearing bones in their noses and bleeding with leeches."

"Those very words have been running through my mind, *Herr* Polyakov. Still, this thing could hurt us."

"Well, why do I have to do something about it? Aren't there police in New York?"

"They are having trouble, *Herr* Polyakov. Something the Americans call 'civil rights.'"

"I've never heard of them. What on earth are 'civil rights?'"

Schwartz was a product of post-war anti-Nazi Germany and had tried for years to understand "David Polyakov," but he had failed. "Polyakov" was a Jew, but he thought like something else. "Civil rights are powers the government cannot take away," said Schwartz. "Powers given by God."

"A bizarre concept. Quite un-German. In this case, who is the charlatan responsible?"

"His name is . . . . Let me see; yes, his name is Abe Goldstein. Abraham, to be exact. At the moment, that is all we know."

Abraham Goldstein. Of course. A Jew! Whatever anyone did, however noble, didn't a Jew always stick his large, snotty beak into it and defile it? Wasn't that the story of Krüger's life? Wasn't it the story of civilization? The problem in New York was obviously another extrusion of the hopelessly corrupt Yiddish-Christian sub-culture that had subverted the United States.

Krüger smiled. His voice fell. "You mean, a *landsmann*, a fellow Jew, is doing this to us?"

Schwartz nodded. His head fell. "Yes."

"Cheer up! He may be only posing as a Jew. We must know everything about him. Call the Arabs."

A month or so later, Yusuf and Ahmed sat before him. Those were the only names they used, and Krüger knew perfectly well they were phony. So what! His own name was phony. Krüger remembered a time after the war, when half the population of Europe was using assumed names, because the other half was hunting them. Who his investigators were for sure, he didn't know, but they were Arabs, they probably were concealing the fact that they hated Jews, because they thought Krüger was one--and they had already conducted a couple of delicate intelligence missions for him with amazing competence.

Krüger told Schwartz, who was hiding his chagrin, that, as a "committed Zionist," he dealt with them, "reluctantly," because they were so valuable. If only they didn't have such prominent, Semitic beaks. What strange tricks Odin plays. He relied on them because they were intensely loyal to him for the strongest reason: money--which he paid them liberally. He had never asked, and didn't want to know, how they accomplished what they did. Now, he was eager to hear what they had discovered. New York sales of Rejuvenall had fallen even more since Schwartz had first identified the problem. Krüger had given him no hint of the true reasons he was concerned. With characteristic genius, he had solved the problem Vörst had summoned him to the castle to discuss, and with the same solution was advancing the strategy agreed on with their colleagues in New York. Rejuvenall was helpful in covering their tracks.

"What have you learned, gentlemen?" Krüger asked. "What do we know about this charlatan?"

"There is nothing to know, *Herr* Polyakov," said Ahmed. "His name really is Abraham Goldstein."

"Imagine someone using his real name," said Yusuf.

"Preposterous!" joked Krüger.

"Nothing is known about his father," said Ahmed. "He apparently died when Abraham was very young. The widow, Abraham's mother, still lives in the

Bronx. Abraham Goldstein drives a garbage truck in New York. At least, he did before embarking on his new career. Until now, he has never done anything of note. His wife is Shirley, and they have two children, but because of his delusion she kicked him out."

"A man so unspeakably degenerate, so weak, so hopelessly depraved, that his wife can kick him out, can nevertheless make so much trouble for the Company? How?"

"Abraham is the father of Islam," said Yusuf. "But Abraham Goldstein is not a Muslim. No one whose wife kicks him out could be a Muslim."

"You spoke of a delusion."

"I did. Abraham Goldstein, a Jew like yourself, believes he is Jesus Christ, another Jew. Psychiatrists in the United States say such delusions are quite common. We don't understand, *Herr* Polyakov. Islam has no such problem. No one believes he is Mohammed. Could you explain? You are a Jew."

Krüger smiled. "This is good news, gentlemen. He is a lunatic. Nothing more. We have no problem," he said to Schwartz. "He must be caught and hospitalized, given proper medication. The Company will gladly pay his bills."

"It isn't that easy," Ahmed said. "He has allies. The New York police have failed."

"Amateurs," said Krüger. "Savages. How did they win the war?"

"Which war?" said Ahmed.

"We think you should go to New York," Yusuf said. "Perhaps your presence would inspire the Americans."

"Impossible!" snorted Krüger. New York was the symbol of everything he hated, the "mystery Babylon" of his satanic belief, the largest Jewish city on earth. He felt unclean whenever he was there. The fact that it existed was an insult. But, if his mission were important enough, why couldn't he go? Certainly he could not tell the Arabs.

Schwartz's intuition saved him. "Apparently you do not know this, gentlemen, but *Herr* Polyakov has more to do as Chairman of the largest ethical pharmaceutical house on earth, whose U.S. subsidiary alone is one of the most formidable listings on the New York Stock Exchange, a Company whose formulations have saved millions of people from unhappy lives and untimely deaths . . . ."

"Yes, yes, Mr. Schwartz," said Krüger, immensely pleased. "Gentlemen," he told them all, "I expect you to do what is necessary to bring Mr. Goldstein's career to a close."

The light on the doomsday phone started flashing. It was Vörst again.

Chapter Fifteen
Bank Heist

"Spats" Davis walked into the bank and smiled. It was dangerous for him to be there, dangerous and redundant--as always, he had planned the job down to the most picayune detail--but the danger was an aphrodisiac he could not resist, and the mystery of banking was even more intense. Maybe this time the solution to the mystery would emerge. "Spats" knew he was looking at it but couldn't see it.

It was a branch office, deep in the heart of Flatbush. Spats had never worked anywhere near there and would not be expected. The haul would be small, but he didn't need the money. The point of the job was simply to keep the boys in practice, besides which Spats was one of the lucky few who love their work. It was ten a.m. on a Monday morning. Only a couple of other customers were there. The usual, armed guard was lounging in a corner. Except for him, all the workers Spats saw were women. That was another thing he loved about banks. They were full of women. Spats loved women; there was less chance a woman would try to be a hero, although you never knew these days. It was quiet, like the temple that it was.

Spats looked lovingly, but covertly, at the vault. The product of a revolution in the science of security, it stood, not in the sub-basement behind many steel doors, but a few feet away in the bank lobby, facing the impressive plate glass windows, squat, sleek, distended with cash. Who would dare rob a safe in plain sight?

Spats went to a desk, pretended to complete a form and approached a teller, a stunning red head with considerable hair. According to her name plate, she was Elizabeth Ann McGillicuddy.

"Good morning, Miss McGillicuddy," he said cheerily. The appellation "Ms." was then coming into vogue, assuring an even playing field for the battle of the genders, but Spats, old-fashioned to a fault, eschewed even playing fields on principle, so much so that even a lukewarm feminist would have called him offensively porcine.

Elizabeth Ann, who was both quite nubile and socially unreconstructed, sensed this was a man who stubbornly stuck to the old ways, and quivered. His accent came from somewhere in Europe, but where?

"Good morning to you. Please let me help you." She was quite taken with him. She had never seen a man so handsome, even on cable or the silver screen. He reminded her of an actor who had played a German officer in a World War Two movie she had seen the other night--was it Robert Redford?--except that this man's hair was black.

"I'm wondering whether my money is safe in your bank," said Spats.

Elizabeth Ann drew herself up. "Sir, your money is as safe here as it would be in the hands of Congress itself. As you see," she pointed to a couple of signs, "we are members of both the F.D.I.C. and the National Reserve System. And if all that fails, there is always Mr. Wolf." She pointed to the guard.

"Ah, yes, Mr. Wolf. A true killing machine. Nevertheless, I believe I'd like to make a withdrawal."

"Certainly, sir. Have you made out the slip?" The slip would tell her his name. Later, she would look in the records and learn everything about him she could.

Spats smiled and pushed the paper across the counter. It was completely filled out, and when she saw the number he had written there, she gasped.

"It's a lot of money."

"Isn't it. Why fool around."

"I've never handled a transaction this big. I don't know whether we have the cash."

"Trust me, Elizabeth Ann. You do."

He put a hand over hers. Her balance departed. Thank God she was sitting down. Would she faint? He was sublimely confident, utterly in charge, his cologne a caress. Elizabeth Ann was mortified to feel herself blush, starting deep in the roots of her voluminous hair. The fact that he was so handsome, so powerful and had so much money in the bank caused her flat stomach to churn and increased her embarrassment. Could he read her stomach and the roots of her hair? Despite her youth, Elizabeth Ann had already survived several would-be suitors, whose suits had failed to conceal ulterior designs on her flesh. She was searching for a man who was remarkably handsome, sublimely confident, utterly in charge and immensely wealthy, a man who longed to father many robust sons--policemen and politicians--within the bonds of holy matrimony; a man whose cologne was a caress, and who suffered from a loneliness that could be dissipated only by Elizabeth Ann McGillicuddy. The man she was searching for would listen, listen, listen to her, and, when she reluctantly drew breath, would show her his soul. Such a man had never walked in to Elizabeth Ann's remote branch bank here in darkest Flatbush. Now one had. What could she do to keep him there?

The Name of the King
100

Elizabeth Ann consulted her monitor and frowned. "I think there's some mistake, Mr. . . . Mr. . . . ." She looked at the slip, afraid to say the name, afraid that if she said it, she would laugh.

"Percy Hornswoggle. Ridiculous, isn't it? My real name's John Smith. I changed it because I couldn't get a hotel room."

"I can't find any record of your account, Mr. Hornswoggle."

"That's because I don't have one, Elizabeth Ann. I don't trust your bank's policy on Third World loans. Did you know that Veribanc puts you in the yellow zone? I'm surprised at you. What's a nice girl like you doing in a jernt like this? But, as long as we're both here, why don't you give it to me, anyway." Spats put his sample case on the counter. "Just put the lovely, little packages in here."

"But, Mr. Hornswoggle, I can't give you money if you don't have an account. Don't you know that?"

As she said this, the other members of the gang filtered in, perfectly on time, all carrying twelve-gauge shotguns--probably in violation of several New York City ordinances--and wearing Jimmy Carter rubber masks. Spats deplored violence as much as Field Marshal Rommel, despite which a show of force was necessary to convince his customers he meant it. Mr. Wolf, the killing machine, was sitting on the floor. At last, Elizabeth Ann, despite her consummate, crushing naiveté, understood.

"Oh, dear," she said.

"You'll be happy to know that all of them are Democrats," said Spats, nodding at his men. "I was offered some Gerald Ford faces at a major discount, but chose these in deference to the President. Go ahead and push your security button, Elizabeth Ann."

She did so, unobtrusively, while she filled the case, not knowing that the alarm had been disarmed. She stacked the currency neatly in the case, blushing while Spats nodded with delight. She was mortified beyond redemption. Many other girls would not have been, but Elizabeth Ann was a girl who always did what she was told, courtesy of her father, Francis X. McGillicuddy, and, only a few seconds ago, she had been fantasizing recklessly about marriage to this man, despite the obvious difference in their ages. He appeared to be of middle age, in his forties. Didn't this prove she was utterly licentious and lost?

"Did you push your security button, Elizabeth Ann?"

"No."

"Did you put that nasty, orange dye in the case?"

"No."

These were lies, of course. Of course she had pushed the security button. Of course she had put the nasty, orange dye in the case. Hadn't she been trained by the Treasury Department to do just that and deny everything?

"Elizabeth Ann, I shall write to your employer, recommending your enthusiasm and competence. You are a credit to your job classification." Spats closed and locked the case. "You have been a true delight to work with. The Democratic Party thanks you." He bowed and kissed her hand, his lips caressing the third finger at the junction of the hand, where he encountered a most enchanting scent. Then he strolled toward the doors, waved at the security cameras and was gone. The men with the Jimmy Carter faces backed out. Everything was normal again. The entire operation, starting from the time she knew what was happening--the only sensible way to figure it--had taken no more than a couple of minutes. Mr. Wolf, the killing machine, minus his .357, got to his feet unhurt, smiling. Sitting on the floor and doing nothing had been just as easy as the man who had called him during one of Eloise's screaming fits had promised it would be. Spats believed in total information, like the fact that Wolf was in the hole because his wife had committed to cosmetic hip surgery for cellulite, a procedure which the bank's employee major medical plan does not cover. Only yesterday, Wolf's bookmaker, a large man of disgusting habits, whose kid brother presently was a member of Spats's entourage, had given him a three-day ultimatum. What was an honest working man making little more than minimum wage to do? The man who had called had not explained that the feds would easily trace the defective alarm to Mr. Wolf, but he would have plenty of time to figure it out in stir. The gratitude he now felt for the man who had bribed him would change, but the feds never found the short, fat man Wolf eagerly described, praying for a plea bargain.

Elizabeth Ann gave the police--including Sergeant Bobby Combs, her cousin--a good description to put beside what they saw on the security cameras. That was one of the things the Treasury Department had taught her to do. He was tall, at least 6'3". He had black hair, slightly graying at the temples, which probably meant he was in his middle forties. His eyes were dark brown. He was husky and weighed about 210. He looked like an actor she had recently seen in a movie, and had a German accent. The F.B.I. would guess it was a fraud--but they wouldn't know. It was not an easy accent to duplicate. Sadly, he would be stained with the indelible, orange dye that would also ruin the money. He had been so charming, so gallant. No one had kissed her hand since she was a child. He would be caught, of course, and thrown into jail where he belonged. She would visit him there, and give him a Bible, which would cause him to repent. The others had worn Jimmy Carter masks and were Democrats.

The police found a witness outside, who said he had seen the gang--five or six in number--pile into a tan, four-door, late model car, but by that time they wore no masks and carried no shotguns, so the witness didn't know they were a gang and paid them no mind. The trouble was that, by the time the "Finest" could get it on the radio, the car had been driven into an alley, up a ramp into a moving van, which left the neighborhood sedately as the squad cars arrived.

Inside the van, Spats and his colleagues listened to the police on the radio. As always, the cops were confused. He would wait until later to remove his disguise, starting with the black wig, continuing with the body padding and the contact lenses that had made his eyes brown, and finishing with the "elevator" shoes that had made him taller than he was. When he finished, he would still be tall--but only an even six feet--about 190, blond, blue-eyed and slender, and would be thirty three years old. That was one of the reasons Spats was so successful. No one knew who he was, or what he really looked like.

Amateurs believed successful disguise meant making some dramatic change. They didn't understand that a disguise shouldn't look like one. It was impossible to convince them that too much was no good. They didn't realize a new identity lay in the little things, like a slight change in hairdo or height, even a change in context or emphasis. They thought a successful disguise meant a clown face by Barnum & Bailey. They didn't understand that the main element in a successful disguise is the certainty that it works. Spats had brought the art of disguise to new heights. Even the men in his gang didn't know what he looked like or who he was, didn't have his phone number and couldn't call. Once, after such a job, a new man, a wise guy, had reached for his wig and tried to learn his identity. The police had found his corpse in a garbage can in Canarsie, and no one had raised the question again.

So, nobody squealed, because nobody knew anything and nobody wanted to. Spats's entourage knew at least that what they saw was a disguise, simply because the boss always looked different on a job. The feds didn't even know that. The only reason they knew that the same gang was doing all the heists was the "m.o.," the *modus operandi*, the consummate attention to detail. Spats Davis's fingerprints were all over each job, except that there were no fingerprints.

Elizabeth Ann remained in his mind. She had deceived him. She had looked him in the face and lied, and smiled when she did it, in the face of what she had no doubt learned in church. She had denied pushing the button and putting the dye in his case. Of course, unknown to the government, Spats had developed a technique to remove the cash without activating the dye, despite which he was aghast at her behavior, an emotion no doubt magnified by the memory of her scent. He rarely if ever had to face such treachery. She was just doing what she had been trained to do, of course, but the fact that a girl with such a face, with such a figure, with such hair--a girl whose scent had been like a caress--could betray every civilized agreement with a smile, probably also including the Geneva Convention, meant that the world was coming to a bad end. It was enough to destroy one's faith in humanity and fair play. Spats deflated as low as he ever got, and stayed that way, utterly disillusioned, for at least a minute. Then, his false emotion was gone. But she remained.

Even his name was an invention. By now, no one remembered that his real name was Charles, and that for years he had been nicknamed "Chuck." It had been impossible to make a name for himself in crime with such absurd, back-to-back monikers. Many people thought "Chuck" Wilson was an accountant, or, at best, a Post Office clerk. There had been three Charles Wilsons of note: a couple of Congressmen and a Secretary of Defense who had said that what was good for General Motors was good for the country. No wonder the Mafia had turned Chuck Wilson down, even though he did a respectable impression of Marlon Brando. Not being Italian was bad enough. The godfathers, the *consiglioris*, the *capos di tutti*, even the lowly street soldiers and headbusters, refused to fellowship, even to break bread, with a man who had such a bizarre handle. It would have been bad luck.

To build a successful criminal career, one needed a proper nickname. Among the celebrities in his gang were Louie the Enemy, who had never had a friend and spoke through permanently clenched teeth, Jim Stink, who had never bathed voluntarily, Guzik the Goniff, a compulsive thief, and Tartoo the Hip Jew, whose perfect attendance and largesse at synagogue were the pride of Rabbi Stanley B. Garlick, who had no idea what Tartoo did for a living. Needless to say, there were a Moose and a Hawk. No gang worthy of the name would be without one.

Not until he had started calling himself "Spats Davis," had Chuck Wilson inspired confidence. Of course, he had never worn the ridiculous contraptions called spats, but they evoked the era of the Twenties, which was exotic. There was always the chance that, if provoked, a man named "Spats" would ream a grapefruit on your nose.

For several years, the gang had been conducting major robberies, and the cops were going crazy. Payrolls were a favorite. It was Spats who had whacked Lufthansa for $5,000,000 plus at J.F.K. on December 11, 1978. It was Spats who, just eight days later, hit Wells Fargo for $3,000,000 on Staten Island. Yet, nothing was as alluring as a bank--because of the mystery.

The cash he withdrew from time to time--like the transaction he had just concluded with Elizabeth Ann--was only part of banking's appeal. The bank, a private corporation, could create credit, as good as cash, at will. In the beginning, it had done so with the ink well, later with the typewriter. Now, the bank created credit with the computer. Why was it illegal for Spats to do the same thing? Why couldn't he form a corporation for the purpose? That was the mystery, and his curiosity would not let him rest.

The next few weeks had been carefully planned. His tickets to Rio and hotel reservations arrived. The suckers who were going to "buy" the ranch he didn't own in the *Mato Grosso* were already there and waiting to give him their money--in dollars, need we add. The longer they waited, the greater the chance they would discover that the "lawyers" they had hired to investigate the deal, were not lawyers, and were not even Brazilians, but were in fact Portuguese bunco artists Spats had met on the docks in New York. Now the Portuguese were demanding a huge piece of the sting. They were crooks. This was not an easy way to make a living.

Yet, it had been so easy to get started. As a child, he had stolen from his mother, so cleverly that she had never found anything missing. She was just too stupid to know what she had. Later, he boosted from department stores and sold what he stole. As a teenager, he had stolen his grandmother's house. She had had bad eyes by then and was a little addled anyway, and had believed him when he told her she was signing a contract to buy magazines, which would help him win a free trip to the nation's Capitol to visit the Washington Monument. He knew his grandmother had a weakness for obelisks. By the time her lawyers and the district attorney found out what had happened, the house had been sold. Yet his grandmother never spoke to him again. Good riddance! So many people didn't have a sense of humor, like the people who had bought it. What did they expect for such a price? Title insurance? What was his grandmother complaining about, anyway? She had her house back, didn't she? Was it his fault that she couldn't take a joke?

Spats had never known his father. His mother had, and she wasn't talking. In fact, she went out of her way to encourage a mystery. She wouldn't say who he was, or what he was, or how long she had known him, or even whether he was still alive. Had they been married, or was Spats a self-made bastard? During the war, she had driven a Red Cross ambulance in Europe, but she never talked about it. Since then, all she ever did was go to her job and go home. He didn't even know what she did, and she wanted no part of him. Was that the reason Spats became what he was? Otherwise, he had had a pleasant childhood. In this Age of Psychoanalysis, no one was sufficiently unsophisticated to realize that he had become a career criminal just because he loved crime.

Still in his teens, he stole Social Security checks from mail boxes. All you had to do was follow the mailman on the swift completion of his appointed rounds, except that you couldn't do the same mailboxes twice. It was easy work, but he had quit after hitting a Social Security "beneficiary" in the head when she caught him in the act and objected. Even that early, young Chuck already knew that the government would replace the check, so it wasn't worth going to the hospital for. People did such stupid things.

Chuck had nothing against violence. It was he who had dropped the cat from the roof of the apartment house in front of a schoolmate and her friends. All nine lives ran out. He had never heard such wonderful screaming, but he preferred to eschew violence himself. You used violence when you couldn't outsmart somebody; it meant weakness. There were some anxious days after he hit the old lady in the head, and he followed her progress in the press. To get even, she might die, and give birth to a charge of Murder One. She recovered, however, too confused to describe her assailant, which was important, because, in those days, the future Spats still looked like himself.

Bank Heist
105

Things had always broken like that for Chuck, become Spats. He was tall, naturally blond, athletic, consummately handsome, like a Viking, and as intelligent as he was striking. He read a lot. Anyone listening to him would have been amazed to learn that he had left school abruptly in the eighth grade, when someone turned up pregnant. It wasn't his fault she was the teacher. A guy wasn't safe anywhere nowadays. He had grown into a man who looked like a leader, a man people asked for advice and gave trust, a man they willingly gave their money. There were only two kinds of people: Chuck and everyone else. In this Age of Institutionalization, he was a true individualist.

After the misunderstanding at the mailbox, Chuck had returned to real estate as it related to insurance. The country was suffering from one of the periodic recessions that necessarily afflict Free Enterprise. Businessmen were hurting. For a substantial fee, Chuck and his gang burned their establishments down, so expertly that, while the Fire Department investigators knew what had happened, they couldn't prove it. Chuck had read a best-seller which maintained that an investor should magnify his success by making the same money work in many ways. So, he established a company called Manhattan Restorations, which restored insured businesses that had mysteriously suffered fires, and provided him a respectable facade, no pun intended. To establish credibility with insurance companies and attract capital from banks, he formed another company called Manhattan Fiscal and Physical Management, whose only real purpose was to promote Manhattan Restorations. The fact that Louie the Enemy, using the absurd pseudonym "Louis Benson," was president of the captive company, was one of those strange quirks fiscal and physical life in New York is heir to.

Yet, his thoughts always returned to the banks, probably because he just didn't understand. If someone deposited $100, and the reserve requirement was 10%, the system eventually could lend $1,000. Where did the other $900 come from? Weren't the banks themselves kiting checks? Spats suspected the existence of an immensely lucrative racket he should be part of, but he couldn't figure out what it was.

So, Spats had to content himself with robbing the robbers and buying property abroad, still far from the pinnacle of his profession. No one was making a movie or writing a book about him. He had not even been called as a witness in a congressional investigation. He had not been exposed by “Sixty Minutes,” and he was annoyed. He was caught in a contradiction, a victim of his own artistry. He wanted to remain anonymous, so he could blend into a crowd, and, at the same time, longed for the recognition his artistry deserved.

Chapter Sixteen
Samba Lesson

Spats raised his glass and sipped the wine. It was a *Liebfraumilch*, very pleasing. He wasn't sure why, but he almost always chose German vintages. They were robust. Like all the other men at the large, round banquet tables, he wore a tuxedo. He was just as much at home at a "penguin party," as he was at the docks. The women wore the latest creations from Scaasi and Givenchy, vivaciously pretending not to compete with each other. Soon, their gowns would turn up on the plain pipe-racks of resale shops on upper Madison Avenue, at INCREDIBLE SAVINGS--if you act now!--because it would be more humiliating than rape and clitoral circumcision to be seen in the same ensemble twice.

He was very happy. The Rio deal was humming like an africanized bee. Despite the risk, he had made the investors wait--to increase their longing--and they had waited. They really wanted that ranch in the *Mato Grosso*. Just this morning, Jim Stink, deloused and fumigated, had boarded a plane at Kennedy. All he had to do was pick up the cash.

The waiters cleared the dishes and the program began. The occasion was a fiscal seminar sponsored by a prestigious New World Order “think tank,” on the eve of Senate consideration of the new treaty with Japan. Spats made a point of attending such affairs with such people. It was important for a con man to stay *au courant*. By now, his face was familiar. Besides, wasn't each of them just as much a crook as he was? The only difference was that Spats was honest about it. The others had the inherited connections to make their crimes look like philanthropy.

The main speaker, for instance, Albert Holley, president of the New York National Reserve Bank. He had to be a crook. How else could he have made so much money in government service? How did a crook become president of the New York Reserve?

"People often ask me about the rumor that our currency will be redesigned," said Holley. "Ladies and gentlemen, it's no rumor. Our currency must be redesigned for three reasons. First, to make it compatible with the other, major, convertible world currencies. Second, to inhibit counterfeiting. And, third, to force the underground economy--which, as I'm sure you know, means the drug racket--into the open."

There was polite applause, which Spats joined. He suspected that the issue of currency compatibility was road apples, but he could only guess what was behind it. Like everything connected to banking, it was a mystery, but he knew it wasn't the magic of compound interest.

"Currency compatibility is a necessary step on the road toward an international currency and the humane civilization all of us seek. The next generation of photocopiers will make it possible to counterfeit United States currency with astounding authenticity. And I'm sure I don't have to elucidate on the drug racket. Friends, it's quite simple. You are either for the drug racket, or you're against it. If you're against it, you'll support whatever is necessary to fight it. Our children deserve no less."

Needless to say, such a denouement deserved a standing ovation, which it got. Anyone who didn't participate deserved whatever suspicion he provoked. Prominent among Holley's activities was his leadership of an organization that applied considerable, public pressure on behalf of the government's unconditional war on drugs.

Later, when the women had withdrawn, Spats offered Holley his card. "Charles Wilson," he said. "Manhattan Restorations."

"Interesting. What do you restore?"

"Whatever needs it and can pay."

"Can you do anything about this horrifying dewlap?" Holley pulled at the sagging skin beneath his chin.

"Not much, I'm afraid. Our license covers only architecture, and we try to stay within the law."

"My wife says I'm an old ruin. Will that help?"

"I was taken by your remarks about the new copiers," said Spats. "Are they really as fearsome as you say?"

"Even more so. We experimented ourselves and were horrified. Even an expert would have trouble weeding out their notes."

"Are you talking about brand-name copiers it's legal to buy?"

"Perfectly legal. Of course, there's a catch."

"Isn't there always."

"You have to have the right paper."

"Where do you get that?"

"You don't. The Crane Company sells only to the government."

"But, if there's as much counterfeiting as you say . . . ."

"Between you and me, there isn't. There's less of it than ever."

"I guess I just don't understand."

"The people who work off the books are what we want. They're creating chaos. If we let the people just do what they want, pretty soon they'll get the idea they run things. Our good friends at I.R.S. are wanting to bury the Underground Economy. The change will no doubt inspire them to dance on its grave."

"Thank God I pay my taxes on time."

"I'm going to pass your card along to my wife, Mr. Wilson. She's a president herself, of a group that renovates historic buildings. I wish I could recall the name."

A factotum appeared with a message for Holley on a tray. He excused himself, which was just as well; it was time for Spats to go home and call Louie. Tomorrow, he would order a new copier.

"Dey got Jim," Louie said.

"Who got Jim? What are you talking about, Lou?"

"At de airport in Miami."

"Did they get the cash?"

"Yeh. Dat's why dey did it. Said it was phony."

"Counterfeit?"

"Right. Dey said it was made on a copy machine. Crazy, ain't it?"

"So, where is Jim?"

"In da federal slam in Miami. You want I should call our liar in West Palm?"

Spats was tempted to cast Jim adrift, but, facing many years in the slam, where he would be forced to bathe, he would talk. Spats of course would be immune, but the gang could be hurt.

"Call him."

"Boss? Wouldn't it be easier ta make da stuff on a copier dan whackin' da banks?"

No wonder the "investors" had waited so long. They had been waiting to unload a suitcase of hot cash. Of course, Spats hadn't owned the property he had "sold," which meant that the deal had been crooked both ways, but the fact that they had snookered him stood by itself. They didn't know he didn't own the ranch; didn't know he was swindling them. For all they knew, they had buncoed an honest businessman. Who and what were they?

A couple of weeks later, Spats sat in a chopper opposite the "investors." It was a "Jolly Green Giant," the kind they had used in Vietnam. Needless to say, Spats had not served in the war. There was no money in it, and a man could get hurt. Below, there was nothing, nothing but trees, not a road or a water tower, no dominion, no pollution. They were flying over the Brazilian jungle, already far from civilization, where the Brazilians themselves were considered foreign invaders.

The "investors" were thoroughly tied to their seats. They belonged to a New York "family," of course. Didn't they always. The Portuguese had had no way of knowing that. Spats had been contemptuous of Italians since his bid for membership in the Mafia had been rejected. Now, he would send them a message.

"I tol' ya, Spats, it wasn't our idea," shouted one. The chug-chug of the chopper made it difficult to hear. "It's what dey tol' us."

"Shaddup, Eddie," said the other.

"I know that, boys," said Spats. "You had nothing to do with it. You were waiting for the bus."

"Whadda we have ta do?" Eddie shouted.

"Shaddup."

"Sure," said Spats "I know. *Omerta*. The code of silence. I'm impressed."

"No, Spats. I mean it. Don' listen to him. He's crazy."

"Hey, Eddie," the other shouted. "*Scifozo*! Are you lookin' for trouble?"

"Joe, are you crazy? Whadda ya tink we're in now?"

"He has a point," said Spats. "What do you think you're in now, Joe?"

"Answer him, Joe," Eddie screamed. "Don't make him mad."

"Good thinking, Eddie, but too late. I'm mad now. Because of you, one of my men is in the slam in Miami, and I don't have cash I've already spent. You guys are crooks. You should be ashamed."

Joe laughed. "Do unto udders before dey do unto you."

Spats laughed too. "I admire you, Joe. You're a real soldier."

The chopper door was open and Spats looked out. "Boring, isn't it," he mused, lounging on the bench. "They say it goes on for thousands of miles, and you come out in Peru. Even the Brazilians don't know what's down there." Spats chuckled. "But I do. Little fish with big teeth that eat your meat to the bone, even your pecker. Snakes that squeeze you to death. Natives with bones in their ears. Just like Disneyland. Should I go on?"

"I'm convinced," said Eddie.

"Don' say a woid," said Joe.

"This is as good a place as any," said Spats. The Moose and the Hawk were standing up, farther back in the chopper, holding on like straphangers in the New York subway. Spats gestured and they brought Joe to the door.

"I was glad to meet you, Joe," said Spats. "Any last words?"

Joe was a soldier, and a soldier doesn't talk. If there was one thing he had learned in the Family, that was it. If you talked, your tongue was torn out with the pliers, and fed to the dogs. Joe had actually seen that happen. Besides, Spats wasn't really a man of the rackets. Didn't the Godfather poisonally toin him down? Joe had expected Spats to be as pretty as a hooker, and dressed like a pimp. Instead, he was a bald man about 55, with a salt-and-pepper beard and a limp. He was just a glorified bunco man, as the Godfather had said. He was yellow, and, at the last minute, he would fold. All Joe had to do until then was bluff. Joe had been told for years that he was indestructible, and he believed it.

But, now, as Joe stood at the chopper door, Spats's bozos holding his arms, his feet a couple of inches from everlasting perdition, he realized that he had made a mistake. Spats *wasn't* bluffing. He was going to do exactly as he said, and down below were those fish, the snakes and the natives--if Joe lived to face them. Sure, Joe was supposed to keep his mouth shut--but not now. *Omerta* had its limits.

"Now, just a damn minute," he said.

It was too late. Spats was a sixth-dan black belt; as Joe spoke, Spats slammed the edge of a foot into the small of his back and pushed. Joe spread-eagled out the door. He was still talking, with even more animation, despite which the rest of what he said is lost to history and cannot be recorded here. The others watched him fall, until he disappeared in the jungle below.

Spats turned to Eddie. "I guess that leaves you."

"Yeh, Spats. Anyting. Just ask."

"I was wondering, Eddie. Who's your boss?"

Eddie named the family he worked for, the boss who had given him the orders, and considerable inside information about who was doing what to whom, in which Spats was totally uninterested. Eddie glowed with relief. The fact that he was now telling Spats what he wanted to know--and that Crazy Joe was no longer there to interrupt--was proof of a reprieve.

"Why, Eddie? Is there no honor among thieves?"

"Spats, I'm afraid to say."

"Don't be afraid, Eddie. You're doing fine."

"He said dey want to take you down, 'cause you're gettin' too big. You're a pain in da behind. Dat's what he said."

"How did they do it, Eddie?"

"Do what, Spats?"

"Make those hundreds."

"Wid a copier."

"A photocopier?"

"Da one dat takes da pictures, yeah. Dat's what dey said."

"What kind of copier was it?"

"Spats, I dunno. I swear to God. I wasn't dere. Joe knew, but he jus' stepped out."

"Where did they get the paper, Eddie?"

"I dunno. I'm just an errand boy. I dunno where dey got da paper."

"Since when do the scum bags you work for print paper?"

"Dey don't, Spats. Dey do drugs. Da government declared war on us. Dis was a job dey put out on contract."

"You've done well, Eddie. As well as you could."

Eddie smiled. "It's okay, den, Spats?"

"Sure, it's okay. Boys!"

Samba Lesson
111

The Moose and the Hawk untied Eddie from the bench, and began to put a parachute on his back.

Eddie was alarmed. "Spats, whadda dey doin'?"

"Between me and Joe there was something personal," said Spats. "Eddie, I just want you to know that between me and you there isn't. I like you."

"Get your damn paws off me!"

"It's business, Eddie. Haven't you been to the movies?"

"Are we doin' dis right, Boss?" asked the Moose.

"I don't have any idea," said Spats. "Just do your best, and we'll pray that it opens."

"Spats, you said it was okay," Eddie screamed.

"It is, Eddie. That's why I'm giving you the 'chute. You'll be alive when you hit the ground--if you know how to hit. And you do know how, because you're a hit man, Eddie. Just hook up there and jump. Of course, maybe you won't want to be alive. I don't know how friendly the natives are. It's up to you."

Eddie already stood in the door. He was crying. "Spats. Spats. Please. I got a wife and kids."

"Eddie, look, be reasonable. You know you can't just walk away. It would be bad for you. It would be bad for morale. Buck up. All you have to do is walk out. It's only a couple or three hundred miles--maybe more--and you'll be a better man for it. Come and see me in New York, and tell me all about it."

Spats nodded and the Hawk pushed Eddie out. He fell clear and the 'chute opened. "Thank God," Spats whispered.

The three men watched while the chopper circled, until the 'chute flattened out on the trees. Spats could almost see Eddie hanging from the treetops, yelling for someone to get him down. Soon, no doubt, someone would.

"Let's get back to town, boys," said Spats. "While you're here, you'll probably want to learn the samba."

Chapter Seventeen
Return of the Native

It had not been easy to walk out of the *Mato Grosso.* Yes, Eddie was a jungle creature, and the jungle he prowled was more dangerous, but the East River did not contain fish that could eat everything but one's bones in less time than it took to cook a flapjack, chirping while they did so. There were Manhattan snakes, but they walked on two legs, weren't 25 feet long, and didn't squeeze you to death. Canarsie housed no tribes that had never seen a white man.

Thank God the natives who had found him still in the parachute, hanging from a tree, shouting, had realized he was a god. For unnumbered centuries, their wise men had promised he would come, from heaven through the trees, and now here was proof. Who else could have such bizarre skin and talk such strange jabber? Who else but a god could suspend himself from a tree, by means of a contraption no living man had seen? Indeed, hadn't one of the natives seen him jump from a large bird, from an altitude no living man could attain? Besides, it was well known that the tribe consisted of the only human beings on earth, so Eddie could not be a man.

Many people had tried to kill Eddie lately. In New York, the *capo di tutti* himself had demeaned his ancestry and manhood, promising despite his pleas to whack him with extreme prejudice if Eddie failed again. The boss had been impressed when Eddie pointed out that "Just One More Chance" was playing softly on the stereo. Thank God the boss was superstitious. He had crossed himself.

But Eddie *had* failed again. Despite his pleas, Spats had thrown him from the chopper. If he ever got back to New York, what would he tell the boss? That the paper wasn't good enough to fool Miami customs? That Spats had found out? Wouldn't the boss ask why Spats had iced Joe but left Eddie alive? Right then and there, hanging from the tree, Eddie promised God that, if he survived, he would religiously go to confession once a year during Christmas week. In fact, he raised God to twice a year, once during Easter, when he saw the natives, despite which he lost his potty training and resolve.

Afraid he would be angry, they gently brought him down. They were small people, and Eddie stood a head-and-a-half above them, which was helpful. Even the medicine person was impressed. Eddie's odor, so like his own, was music to his nose and most authentic.

Eddie caught on quickly. He may have lacked the killer instinct, but he wasn't stupid. According to venerated teachings transmitted through the generations without perversion--not easy without a written language--the god from the sky would impregnate a woman of the tribe, from which union would issue a king, who would lead them to heaven on earth. Despite the communication gap, as wide as the Amazon, one didn't have to be a professor of anthropology to know what it meant when they installed him on a throne and smilingly brought the nubile maidens to inspect.

He liked being a god. How long he would have stayed had not Original Sin intervened, is impossible to know. He missed so many things: pasta; pizza with anchovies; automobiles; television; cold beer; cold cash; cold air; cold conking; hot women named Angelina, who wore pantyhose, and, thanks to the miracle of depilation, had no curly hair on their legs. He disliked slimy things that squished underfoot and wound up on one's plate; insects that burrowed into his skin; sleeping in the open; humidity that left everything permanently wet. On the other hand, being a god was easy work, which required only that he sit and look regal when he wasn't pollinating, for which duty he cleverly chose the chief's daughter, the paucity of whose ensemble left little to imagine. The royal nuptials soon followed--including a ghastly beverage which did, however, have the kick of white lightning--and he went manfully to work.

In the short time he was there, he did learn something of the language, but, sadly, not enough. He didn't fully understand that the reason for his relationship with the princess was prophecy, not amusement, procreation, not recreation. He didn't understand that, because there could be only one king, he would be restricted to monogamy, a cultish practice he had heard of but never seen. More important, he didn't understand that, still according to prophecy, he would be returned to heaven by a grateful nation when the pregnancy became extant. The wise men didn't bother to explain it to him, assuming that, as a god, he knew it. Eddie was feeling quite proud of himself when the elders shouted hosannas while they debated the swelling royal tummy.

Pregnancy here was even more of a miracle than it is on Avenue A. The natives lacked even the elements of basic physiology, and were unaware of the connection between pregnancy and sex. As far as they knew, the miracle happened when a lucky couple ate sufficient grubs together in syncopation with the moon.

So, no one on earth was more surprised than Eddie, when his grateful hosts joyfully prepared to burn him at the stake. Within the smoke, he would reascend to heaven. His ashes would be scattered to the winds and return there by a different route. All of this was on the point of consummation, when some natives arrived with Joe's partly eaten corpse. Most of the legs and lower abdomen were gone, but more than enough remained to see that here was another god.

There was silence for a long time, followed by a frightful wail. The jabbering began. By now, Eddie knew enough to understand that the atmosphere was turning monotheistic with a vengeance. The prophecy did not include the arrival of two gods. Did the fact that this new god was not only dead but horribly defaced mean that the gods were not immortal? The tribesmen clamored around the medicine person, who conducted tests with some items, including a pickled eyeball, he took from a bag around his neck.

Ignored for the moment, reprieved from the stake, Eddie wriggled from his fiber bonds and plunged into the jungle, bound for anywhere, leaving home, hearth, erstwhile family, friends, tribe and fecund wife, all of whom soon were staggering drunk, the princess apparently unaware of Fetal Alcohol Syndrome. A facsimile of sanity returned the next day. They could have caught him, of course, but they were still fearful and confused. No one had seen him leave. They had no way of knowing he hadn't just disappeared through the tree tops the way he had come. He was not dead and mutilated, like the other god, but in full vigor.

A few months later, on schedule, the king arrived. He grew into a mighty man of valor, but failed to lead his people to the promised heaven on earth. They burned him to send a message of dissatisfaction to the gods. At last, reduced to about a dozen souls, the remnant was discovered by a couple of anthropologists from Yale, who introduced them to true civilization, which included some infectious diseases and a lawsuit about who would get the credit. The older people of the nation were placed in Brazilian institutions for study. The four young men wound up working in a *favela* in Sao Paulo. The ten year old, who, unknown but to God, was Eddie's grandson, showed remarkable aptitude, was brought to the United States, won a four year scholarship to Harvard, became a social activist and was elected to Congress, where he won the plaudits of his peers. Of course, all this happened many years later.

How Eddie got out will never be known. From time to time he remembered crashing through the jungle, strange sounds and smells, rain, suffocating heat and humidity, night noises, but they were disjointed, sensory impressions, things happening to someone else, which occurred in different order each time he recalled them, as in a kaleidoscope, and told no story. He remembered a birdlike screeching and water churning in a river, turning red, while a piglike animal bellowed and disappeared. He remembered a sudden, agonizing pain in his leg, rooting for grubs and killing thirst. But, except for the screaming, he remembered nothing after he awoke to find the snake wrapped around his arm. The only thing that kept him going was the memory of cold beer and linguini.

When sanity returned, he was in a bed, the air smelled antiseptic, and the loveliest woman he had ever seen was speaking to him softly in a language he recognized as Portuguese. All she and the other medical personnel in the hospital were able to tell him was that a Brazilian army vehicle had delivered him there. He was still in one piece, but the arm was permanently disfigured, and he suffered from an intestinal ailment the doctors could never identify.

Back in New York at last, Eddie fell on his knees, showed the *capo di tutti* his arm and pled for mercy. He looked so ghastly, Marcello let him live, rightly guessing that wasting a man so wounded would have disillusioned the boys. Also, Eddie was able to describe Spats, or so he thought. For the first time, thanks to Eddie, the boss knew what he looked like. He was a bald man about 55, with a salt-and-pepper beard and a limp. With the advantage of hindsight, the boss reflected that perhaps he should have welcomed Spats's bid for a home in the family. Now, it was too late. He would have to be whacked. Marcello couldn't understand why the boys couldn't find him, now that they knew what he looked like. The only man they had found who filled his description turned out to be the rabbi of a large synagogue in Queens.

Eddie visited his big sister, put his head on her kitchen table and cried while she stroked his hair and bit her lip. Under threat of non-stop badinage, sexual and other deprivation, Eddie's brother-in-law, a Family *capo*, talked Marcello into letting Eddie help launder money. The family had devised an elaborate scheme, quite by accident. The federal government was fighting the war against drugs. Among its weapons were property seizures and "money laundering" statutes. Honest citizens who themselves had successfully deceived I.R.S. on their returns wound up bidding for luxury mob automobiles at government auctions. The mob, which scrupulously paid its taxes in deference to Al Capone, assigned its lawyers and C.P.A.s to develop ways of transforming its substantial revenue, so it could be legitimately invested.

Oblivious of all this, Enzo Ghibellini, B.Ch.E., M.A., Ph.D., suffered in silence. He knew as much about *Cosa Nostra* as he did about the Calcutta sewing circle, but, because of the accident of his name, and the fact that he had been born and educated in Palermo and spoke Italian as well as Dante along with many other languages, he had for years endured stale Anglo-Saxon jokes and inane questions about his "connections" to the Mafia. Asking his tormentors how close they had been to Richard Nixon, had not cured the hollow feeling.

Much worse, although he was a professor of both chemical and electrical engineering, had a graduate degree in fine arts from the University of Bologna, where he had specialized in engraving, and held several patents for technology presently in use, he now faced dismissal from the prestigious University of

Manhattan, for "unethical conduct unbecoming a tenured professor," including "egregious sexual harassment."

Dr. Ghibellini knew all about sexual harassment. His former wife was a dancer he had met after only a week in this country. He had wandered into the club looking for dental floss, in the mistaken belief that the word "Topless" on the marquee referred to a chain of discount drug stores, and her demands had driven him to environmental angina and psychosomatic duodenal ulcer, which had taken all the expertise of psychiatrist George Bogart to cure. To her credit, Mrs. Ghibellini did her part in his recovery--as soon as she discovered he was broke--by cleaving to a promoter whose financial statement she had taken the precaution to request. At the moment, she was a waitress in a greasy spoon in Pleasanton, California, waiting for the promoter to finish a term for filing false financial statements with a bank, waiting to stick something sharp and metallic through his gizzard. Ghibellini no longer patronized exotic dancing, but, despite Bogart's cure, and no doubt in part because of his preoccupation with things scientific and artistic, he still didn't understand the ins and outs of a brassiere.

Now, he had discovered that the doctoral dissertation of his rival for the chairmanship of the department consisted in large part of wisdom she had liberally lifted from other authors without attribution. No wonder her writing was so good! Some of it was even his! Surely such plagiarism was "unethical conduct," etc. Ghibellini didn't understand that the clique behind her now controlled the administration. He didn't understand that her appointment was a rare opportunity to "strike a blow for women's rights." During centuries of oppression, females had been systematically denied technical education to keep them in subjection. Yes, she had perpetrated the plagiarism as alleged, but those centuries of oppression made *quid pro quo* irrelevant under the doctrine of gender reparations. University compliance officers, to whom every appointment was referred, certainly had no intention of eschewing this chance to make minority names for themselves, simply because some picayune, little foreigner, whose parents no doubt had been WithOutPaperS, stood in the way. You can't make an omelet without breaking eggs.

It must be admitted that Dr. Ghibellini was not blameless. Goaded to desperation by the forces of empowerment, he commented that his rival had lifted more than the stolen passages. He never did say she had "judiciously lifted her skirt," but that was what his enemies claimed he had said and they made it stick, despite the fact that Casanova himself would have embraced celibacy had she done any such thing. All of which proved that Enzo Ghibellini was a politically incorrect male chauvinist pig.

He faced ruin. What would he do if kicked out at the age of 61? Where would he go? Cured of women and married to his work, he didn't even have someone he could tell his problem, which wouldn't solve it, but would feel so good. Anyone on the faculty could be a spy for the clique. He couldn't tell a priest. What good would that do? The priest would probably say he was wrong; that he should do the Christian thing and make way for progress. The most important thing in his life right now was his nine year old nephew Alfredo, whose mother, Enzo's sister, and father, had been killed in an automobile accident in Rome. Enzo had adopted him and moved him to New York. The boy was doing well; had quickly learned English. For the first and only time in his life, Enzo reveled in the joys of parenthood. There would be a hearing soon. Were Enzo kicked out, he would lose his nephew's respect, which would be intolerable. He had never felt such rage and frustration, yet, such was his anxiety, he could not vent them.

For years, a distant relative had called him from time to time. Enzo didn't even know how they were related. Were they fourth cousins twice removed? What was his name? Marcello? Every time he called, he was immensely cordial, always asking Enzo warmly whether there was something he could do. How many people would be that friendly, especially here in New York? Marcello was certainly someone in whom he could confide. Enzo didn't even know what kind of work he did. He probably was a mailman or a truck driver. It didn't matter.

Enzo called the number he had left, and proposed they get together. Marcello welcomed the idea and suggested they meet in a restaurant. To Enzo's surprised delight, the restaurant was exquisite and Marcello seemed to have an entourage. After a superb dinner, he put a cigar in his mouth, and someone jumped forward to light it. Enzo deduced that he probably wasn't a mailman.

He was as cordial in person as he had been on the telephone. He listened, with sympathy, tenting his fingers while he weighed and considered. He asked questions. What was the woman's name? What was she? Where did she live?

He nodded. "You were right to come to me. We are cousins. Family."

"Thanks for listening. I had no one."

"Such corruption. What's happening to this country?" Marcello looked from one to the other of his smiling entourage, as if expecting an answer. "Eddie, you're a world traveler," he asked one. "What's happening?"

"I don't know," said Eddie.

"I'll tell you. It's the fault of the men. The women run things, because the men won't. Am I right, Eddie?"

"You're right." What else could Eddie say? Sure, the boss was talking about him, and what he said was true. There was no point risking death to deny it.

Enzo blushed and tried to become small. Marcello hadn't mentioned it, but he was talking about Enzo. Wasn't Enzo here because the women were running things? Hadn't Enzo let them do it?

"I'll ask around." said Marcello. "See what I can do."

Enzo was thrilled. He had not at all expected that Marcello could do something. All he had hoped to find was a willing ear. "I would be so grateful."

The relief was so intense that he forgot to ask himself what on earth his dear cousin could do.

Marcello put a hand over his. "Maybe one day *you* will listen to *me*."

"Of course! Please call on me!"

No one was more surprised than Enzo when the woman disappeared. There had been no trip planned, no convention to address as the new chairperson. There had been no confrontation. She hadn't stormed out and quit. Why should she? Hadn't she won? Hadn't Enzo been condemned at the hearing? She was there on Monday, giving orders as usual, reveling in her empowerment, and on Tuesday she was not. The dean of the college called the police, of course. They came, asked some ineffectual questions and accomplished nothing. What could they do? There was no blood, there were no prints, there were no signs of entry, no clues, nothing to prove a crime had been committed. For all anyone knew, she had taken a job as a circus geek, killing chickens with her teeth.

The coincidence strained credulity, and Ghibellini called Marcello as a courtesy to report it, barely suppressing his joy, still unaware that the offending feminist had been safely installed in an E.P.A.-approved landfill in Queens.

"Disappeared?" said Marcello. "You mean . . . gone?"

"Yes."

"Was it coincidence, dear cousin Enzo, or an answer to prayer?"

"I prayed, but I don't know."

"Let us hope that nothing nice has happened to her."

Marcello laughed. Enzo, realizing that it was all right to do so, gave vent to his triumph.

After a while, the administration at Manhattan began to realize that she wasn't coming back. The attitude toward Dr. Ghibellini changed. Before the disappearance, the clique had treated him with indifference or contempt. Now, when he arrived, the conversation dimmed. His enemies looked at him furtively, not with fear but with uncertainty. There was no reason to think he was involved in the disappearance, but he certainly was the beneficiary. There was a question they could not ask. It was enough.

A couple of months later, the findings of the hearing were reversed. It was a miracle! Thank God someone up there was persuaded to see reason. Enzo received another call from cousin Marcello. Would Enzo be able to give Marcello some help? Of course he would! They were family. There was nothing Enzo wouldn't do for Marcello.

Alan Greenspan had been chairman of the Council of Economic Advisers for Gerry Ford. Despite his Whip Inflation Now program, in which inflation would be whipped if enough Americans ate everything on their dinner plates, a builder had gone bankrupt on Long Island. Through a series of maneuvers that would be boring to explain, Marcello had inherited a subdivision, designed for the very wealthy but presently in a state of decay. Considerable money was at stake. The subdivision needed restoration, after which it would be sold. There would be substantial profit, but the operation would take time, which Marcello could not spare. Enzo was not only chairman of the Department of Engineering at the University, but an artist. Marcello understood that Enzo knew nothing about business, but he would have the benefit of Marcello's advice. Marcello would turn him over to Eddie, who would act as liaison. Enzo remembered Eddie. Would Enzo be willing to supervise and share in the profits?

Of course he would! It was legal, wasn't it? Enzo had never been as grateful to anyone in his life. His luck was too good to be true. No one understood how little a university professor was paid. Marcello had come to the right man. Nothing was more important than family.

A month passed. Dr. Enzo Ghibellini was in a fowl mood. No doubt that was why he ordered the goose shank. He had no way of knowing that before the meal ended his mood would turn foul. How could he? They were dining in one of the most pleasant spots on earth, Rienzi's, where the view of the city rivaled the four star food.

"Can you help me?" he asked.

"That depends on what you want restored," said Charles Montgomery Wilson, president of Manhattan Restorations, Inc. Chuck always brought his clients here, to underline the fact that he was not just a builder. He was a developer, an artist.

"Homes on Long Island. Not for everyone. Refuges for the discriminating few who still appreciate gracious country living. Accessible to the city, yet a world removed."

Chuck chuckled. "You sound like a brochure."

"Only a brochure could do justice to the truth."

"Show me the paperwork."

Ghibellini opened his attaché case and did so. Spats pored over plats, deeds, assignments, vendors' liens and photographs, and saw that what the professor wanted was not in his line. Manhattan Restorations was a cover, a specialty company, which did a house from time to time to prove he was "legit." This would be a project involving many homes. Only a real company could do it. Still, he was intrigued. The people who bought such homes were people Charles Montgomery Wilson should know.

"I should tell you, Dr. Ghibellini, I'm very expensive."

Ghibellini gestured at the documents. "I hope so. Someone who is cheap could not do the job."

"I'll need a financial statement and bank references. The usual due diligence."

"Of course. But unnecessary. We pay in cash. The whole thing, up front. You may put it in escrow with partial releases. Needless to say, we expect a substantial break on the price."

For a couple of weeks, Ghibellini had been training with Marcello's lawyer, but he still hadn't mastered the lingo. Had he said it right? He was a scientist, an engineer, a master engraver. What did he know about real estate? Thank God Marcello had told him not to worry. Enzo admitted he didn't understand the deal, but the fact that a lawyer was involved certainly proved it was legal.

Spats put his cup down. Cash! Cash meant freedom. This thing was getting more interesting. Was Ghibellini acting for himself, or did he have principals? Where would a professor get this kind of money? Was this a scam? There was no way now that Spats would turn the job down.

A waiter appeared at Ghibellini's elbow, and summoned him to the phone. "Uncle?" It was Fredo.

"How did you know I was here, Fredo?"

"They told me."

"Who told you?"

Enzo heard confusing noises. Fredo left the phone. Someone else was there. Enzo heard him breathing. A door closed. Had Fredo left the room? He and whoever was there breathed together.

"Enzo?" It was an unfamiliar voice.

"Yes."

"How's it going?"

"Fine."

"Good. Let us know if you need any help."

"Who are you?"

"We're at your place." The voice laughed. "Should I give you the number?"

Enzo shook as he hung up the phone. Fredo was in danger. The fact that the voice hadn't said so was even more frightening than a threat. He had to call the police! He reached again for the phone. But what would he tell the police? That a man had called from his home and offered his help? Maybe he should call Marcello. But suppose Marcello was behind it. Ghibellini realized there was no one he could tell. Still trembling, trying to master himself, he returned to his dinner conference with Spats, unaware that Marcello knew nothing whatever about the call.

Chapter Eighteen
Flim Flam

Eddie had the spirit of enterprise, but not the brains to go with it. As a god, he hadn't needed brains. In New York, as Marcello's soldier, he did. The problem was, he didn't have the brains to know he didn't have any. That was why he congratulated himself about the phone call. He hadn't actually threatened Ghibellini. All he had done was create an atmosphere. Hadn't he seen Marcello do it many times? The boss would be impressed.

It didn't occur to Eddie that an "atmosphere" wasn't needed, that Ghibellini was doing exactly what Marcello wanted without one. It didn't occur to Eddie that the phone call would tell even a man as naive as Ghibellini something wasn't kosher. Eddie had been a god in Brazil; he wanted to be a big man in New York.

For the same reason, the cash he gave Enzo was phony. He bought it from the same printer who had sold him the Rio paper. That had been Marcello's deal. This one was Eddie's. Enzo was a professor, too dumb to know the difference, the sap he gave it to wouldn't know either, and Eddie had bought it for 14% of the face--the market price--with the cash his brother-in-law had given him. Eddie was tired of being a flunky, tired of Marcello's remarks, tired of taking orders, tired of being treated like a go-fer. He had been a god, which changes a man and can even go to his head. A man with his spirit of enterprise is supposed to be the boss. Sure, the Rio caper had bombed. His mistake had been to give phony paper to Spats. This was different. Less than 24 hours after giving Ghibellini the doctored cash, Eddie was at J.F.K., ticket to Rio in hand, on his way to a *vita nova*, where there was no extradition.

Sad to relate, alert public servants at the airport confiscated Marcello's attaché full of cash, after Eddie neglected to complete Department of the Treasury Form 4790 (Report of International Transportation of Currency or Monetary Instruments), indicating that he was departing the country with more than $5,000. Who can keep track of so many regulations? At least the cash was genuine. Shorn of his stake, indignant with federal agents who refused to let him use it to make bail, terrified that Marcello would find him, afraid to use his one phone call even to call his big sister, Eddie nevertheless stood up manfully to interrogation in deference to *Omerta.*

Ever since the phone call, Ghibellini had been living in dread. Yes, Fredo had been safe when Enzo got home, had told his uncle how genial the visitor had been, and had suspected nothing. Fredo thought Eddie was Ghibellini's friend, but Enzo knew better. He knew a "fine, Italian hand" when he saw one. Didn't he have one himself? Wasn't he an honors graduate in engraving from the University of Bologna? But he didn't know what was wrong, which made his foreboding worse. Eddie hadn't said anything about his visit when he gave Enzo the cash, and Ghibellini had been afraid to ask. Now, Enzo was supposed to give the cash to Chuck Wilson. Obviously, the problem was related to the cash.

He called Marcello, who was already irritated when he picked up the phone. Eddie was supposed to call when he delivered the cash, but Eddie hadn't called. Eddie had disappeared. Eddie had already burned him once. Marcello had grudgingly given him the job only because Palumbo was grousing he would otherwise be denied sex. Why Palumbo didn't get rid of that broad, Marcello didn't know. How good a lay could she be? Had Eddie screwed up again?

The minute Enzo started talking, Marcello knew something was wrong. Enzo's voice was shaking. He was stuttering like a bootlegger at a Baptist convention.

"What happened?" asked Marcello.

"Nothing happened, Tony. What do you mean?"

"Where's Eddie?"

"Gone. Left for the airport."

"What airport?"

"He told the driver J.F.K."

"What driver?"

"The cab driver. In a cab you have a driver."

"He wasn't driving his own car?"

"Why would he drive his car, Tony? He went to the airport."

"He would drive his own car if he was coming back."

"He's not coming back?"

"Did he give you the cash?"

"Yes. I have it right here."

"All you have to do is deliver it."

"All right."

Marcello hung up. Why would Eddie go to the airport? Where was he going? It didn't matter. He had delivered the cash. Eddie finally had done something right, despite the fact that he remained a *scifozo*. Now, one of the visible extrusions of Marcello's family business, completely legit, like the fin of a shark, especially in its relations with I.R.S., would sell the refurbished subdivision for considerable profit, all sufficiently laundered for deposit in an institution protected by F.D.I.C., clean enough even for *Il Papa* to accept. He had even been able to pay less for cash. Marcello decided to do the same thing again. But why had cousin Enzo been stuttering like a teetotaler at a Mafia convention?

Enzo was still nervous when he gave Spats the cash. Marcello had told him not even to ask for a receipt, explaining that high class gents used the honor system, which Enzo found impressive. Of course, Spats checked a couple of bills at random under black light, technology he had ordered stolen from American Express for the purpose. Ever since Eddie had tried to flummox him in Rio, Spats had rivaled I.R.S. in his suspicion of cash. When both bills turned out to be phony, he checked some more, which left him incredulous. Ghibellini was a crook! Was it impossible to find an honest man these days? What was happening to the moral fiber of this country?

Despite the testimony of his own eyes, Spats couldn't believe it. Although his judgment of women had often proven defective, he remained confident that his judgment of men stood the test. Yet, Ghibellini had fooled him completely. Was he a consummate bunco artist? If so, why was he morose when he gave Spats the cash? Shouldn't he have smiled to preserve customer confidence? Shouldn't he have been as ecstatic as a woodpecker in a peg leg factory about the double lick he was hitting? He was going to make a profit on the subdivision that would beggar a robber baron, and he was going to do so with phony cash. Spats thought fondly of Eddie, who by now no doubt had long since been eaten by man or beast. Because of international paperwork, it would have been impossible to fly Ghibellini from New York to Rio, and then kick him out of a chopper into the Mato Grosso, but surely in deference to Eddie the least Spats could offer was a cement ash can, with proper interment on a scenic hill in the country that Enzo could haunt. Yet, there was a mystery here, which obviously would die with Ghibellini, and Spats loved a mystery. Mastering himself, he realized that the best thing to do was to wait, which his expertly managed cash flow, generously augmented by certain banking transactions, allowed him to do.

After a couple of days, Marcello cracked. No one had ever accused him of patience. He called Charles Montgomery Wilson, introducing himself as Bill Bender, Ghibellini's C.P.A.

"The doc wants to make sure you are happy. He sure is. He wants to use you again."

"Your call is very thoughtful, Mr. Bender. It tells me you are a man I want to do business with. You can make me happier. When do I get paid?"

"Hasn't he paid you yet?"

"No."

The Name of the King
124

Spats hadn't planned to say it. He had said it because of a sudden inspiration. Wasn't it the truth? He had not been paid. In return for all his hard work, Enzo had given him a load of counterfeit bills. These days, an honest workman had nowhere to turn. He had to rely on himself.

There was a long pause. Marcello heard chanting and the clanking of chains. He mumbled something unintelligible and hung up. Who was lying? Sure, Charles Montgomery Wilson belonged to all the fancy clubs in midtown, he knew all the people with clout, and had more credit than the bureau, but so what! Wasn't Enzo Chairman of the Department of Engineering at the University of Manhattan? In fact, wasn't Wilson an Anglo-Saxon, someone Marcello had never heard of until he found him in the phone book? Wasn't Enzo a fellow Italian, indeed, a Sicilian, who was a distant cousin? The answer was obvious.

A couple of days later, Enzo sat in his office with a woman he didn't know. She was taking some undergraduate courses at night and said she wanted curriculum advice. Hindsight would reveal it was a mistake to see her alone, but Enzo's systemic naiveté could not foresee what would happen. She had bad teeth accompanied by mausoleum breath magnified by bubble gum; a complexion that no doubt had launched a thousand quips; nails gnawed to the knuckle; fingers impregnated with nicotine to the wrist; and all the allure of a cholera victim in the final throes of dehydration, despite which she actually painted her nails purple while Enzo tried to talk, with the predictable effect that Enzo could not suppress his disgust. If only he had known she had been sent there to provoke him. Yes, his predecessor had disappeared, but the forces of liberated womanhood could not accept defeat.

"Whatsamatta, Doc," she asked, "you don' appreciate fine art?"

Yes, the city owned the university and the mayor had mandated "open enrollment," which meant that anyone could matriculate, but what was such a woman doing there? God almighty, there was a limit, even in New York! How dare she ask whether he appreciated fine art? Still under her influence, Enzo complained to the administration as soon as she left.

At home, a jar sat on the kitchen table. Inside, floating in some liquid, was a small, vaguely spherical, probably organic object, resembling nothing so much as a movie mutant in miniature from deep space. Who had put it there, and how had he done it? Enzo looked around and trembled, feeling like the typical victim of a burglary. But this was not a burglary. In a way, it was worse. Someone had left the jar to send Enzo a message, but what was the message?

Enzo was afraid to open the jar, could not even touch it, but he drove over to the medical school and did some research, not liking what he found. When he returned, the telephone was ringing. It was a hospital in White Plains.

"Good news, Dr. Ghibellini! The crisis is past, and was not as serious as we thought. It was a bizarre accident, but the boy shows every prospect of recovering completely. Thank God the passerby brought him here when he did.

There is every reason to believe he will live a normal life. It would be beneficial if you are here when he wakes up."

"What happened?" he whispered, knowing the answer, but not wanting to hear. It was too late. The doctor had already hung up. Enzo tried to do so, but was shaking too much to put the phone in the cradle. When he finally succeeded, it rang at once.

Palumbo was irritated when he called. Palumbo had persuaded Marcello to give Eddie the job despite the fiasco in Brazil, and now Eddie had not only screwed up; he had stolen from the family. On orders from Marcello, Palumbo had been to see Wilson, who confirmed what he had said on the phone. Were Eddie and Enzo in this together? Marcello had whacked many men for less, but Eddie was gone. Palumbo was here, available to Marcello's wrath. Palumbo's irritation combined with the fact that he was nowhere near as subtle as Eddie, to produce unpleasant results.

"Did ya get my message?"

"What have you done to Fredo?"

"A crazy accident. Thank God and St. Anthony of Padua I was dere to take him to da hospital. But it could be woise. He has anudder one. Dey said he'll recover and father a dozen *bambini*. Even his wife won't notice. Of cawse, if somethin' happens to da udder one, he'd be a soprano. Ya never know dese days. Do ya get my drift, Enzo, or do ya want me to stop beatin' around da begonias?"

"Why?" That was the only thing Ghibellini could squeeze out.

"By da way, Enzo, when are ya plannin' ta pay da man? Tomorrow won't be too late. Your friends are worried about ya."

What man? Pay what? Enzo didn't know what the voice was talking about. The only payoff he knew about was the one he had made.

"Please! What are you talking about?"

"Tomorrow." Palumbo hung up.

Enzo shook all the way to the hospital, and still was shaking when Fredo woke up screaming. "Tomorrow" came and went. Enzo never knew how he lived through it. He didn't know the name of the man who had called, didn't know his number, so couldn't call to tell him there had been some mistake. He was afraid to call Marcello. There was nothing he could do. Thank God at least that Enzo was Fredo's legal guardian, and that the university group insurance would take care of the horrendous medical bill. Enzo told the doctor to "spare no expense." The next afternoon, he went back to the medical school to research amputation, and concluded that at this late date an attempt to reattach the deleted article would be fruitless. Returning home, he buried the jar in the back yard. Fredo would never see it.

The first thing Spats did when he and Marcello hung up was to call Clayton, Willis and Jones, the "Big Eight" accounting firm that did his books, and ask whether there was a C.P.A. named Bill Bender. There wasn't, of course, so who had called? Obviously, someone on the inside who wanted information, someone who had been staggered to learn that Spats hadn't been paid. Was Ghibellini the victim of a double cross, or the perpetrator? Spats investigated and found that he was not only a professor of engineering, but a master engraver.

It was Friday evening, on the worst day of Enzo's life. He had gone to the university in the morning, found that his key would not admit him to his office, and called the dean, who explained that an "interdepartmental faculty committee" had decided to suspend him indefinitely, because there had been "too many complaints from women students about your blatant chauvinism," and "you have finally gone too far."

"What chauvinism? What complaints?"

"Professor Ghibellini, because of your legendary insensitivity, which I needn't remind you was the subject of the recent hearing, Ms. Alexandra Freitag is suing the university for sexual harassment. In consultation with university counsel, the committee concluded that your dubious expertise is not worth the risk."

"Who in God's name is Alexandra Freitag?"

"I should think you would remember. Ms. Freitag is the person you abused merely for doing her nails."

"Dean Chase, that woman belongs in an obedience class for pit bulls, not a university."

"'That woman' happens to hold an immensely responsible position in the federal government. Unfortunately, Dr. Ghibellini, your sexist remarks merely prove her point."

After lunch, which Ghibellini did not eat, he called the benefits administrator, who explained that his indefinite suspension had been made retroactive to the date of the suit, which meant that Fredo's bizarre "accident" wasn't covered after all. Certainly, Dr. Ghibellini had the right to "contest the determination." After "fact-finding," the university would convene a hearing, by which time he would be dead. As a precaution, he called the hospital and told the doctors to spare every unnecessary expense.

He now had no job, would owe a hospital bill big enough to build a new wing, and someone was threatening to complete the mutilation of Fredo--and perhaps even of Enzo himself--for reasons unknown.

By now, Enzo was afraid to answer the telephone. Ever since the jar, he had been afraid to enter his kitchen. Sure enough, when he came home, someone was sitting at the table drinking expresso he had made, someone who didn't look or sound anything like Chuck Wilson. As soon as he got rid of him, Enzo would pack his things and move.

"Make yourself at home, Enzo," said his latest visitor, cordially waving at a chair. Like Enzo, he had an Italian accent.

"I . . . I. . . I'm glad you're here," lied Enzo. "I didn't understand."

"Many people don't understand. Then it's too late."

"Who are you people?"

"Didn't you know? We're your friends."

"You're an enemy! You mutilated Fredo."

"We didn't mutilate Fredo. Somebody else did that."

"Why? What have I done?"

"I can get them off your back if you cooperate. Interested?"

"Yes! Yes! Tell me what to do."

Now for the test. Spats had been feeling his way in the conversation, saying little, learning much; he had devised the test after considerable thought. Spats took out a twenty dollar bill and put it down in front of Enzo.

"Is this for real?"

"You mean, is it counterfeit?"

"That's what I mean."

"How would I know that?"

"They tell me you're the greatest engraver in the world. Is it true?"

How could he deny it? "Of course it's true," he whispered.

"Could you make any more of these?"

Enzo had never told a living soul, but once, motivated simply by curiosity, he had tried his hand at a portion of Jackson's face on a twenty. Convinced he could outdo the Bureau of Engraving and Printing, he had destroyed the proof. Of course there had been nothing criminal in this. Every engraver, indeed, every printer, wonders about the same thing.

"With the proper equipment? Yes," Enzo chuckled. "Unfortunately, it's illegal."

Spats snorted. "What's illegal?"

"I don't follow."

"What does illegal mean?"

"Doesn't it mean against the law?"

"Illegal means someone else's bozos are in office. Legal means *your* bozos are in office."

Enzo shook his head. "I can't do it."

"Okay, Thanks for seeing me. The coffee was good. I'll let myself out. My best regards to Fredo." Spats rose.

"Wait a minute. Wait a minute. Give me time to think."

"Sure. Take the whole minute. I'm in no rush."

"Would there be any money in it?"

"Since you'd be printing $7,000,000, I'm guessing there would . Are you interested?"

"Seven million dollars!"

"More or less."

"And my nephew?"

"Home out of danger. Can you do it?"

"Yes, but . . . $7,000,000. I don't know."

"With your share you could pay a lot of bills."

"I don't know."

Had Dr. Ghibellini passed the test, or not? Had he printed the counterfeits he had brought to Spats? He was either the greatest dissembler since the serpent, or so dumb that he still didn't know the cash was bad. Could a man be that dumb? Spats decided to see just how far Enzo would take it.

Then Spats had the inspiration.

Chapter Nineteen
Nymphomaniac

A couple of months later, Elizabeth Ann McGillicuddy left the bank at five p.m. She always left the bank at five p.m. Elizabeth Ann was a creature of schedules and appointments. She loved routine. People who hated routine were "weird." She always was where she was supposed to be, never where she wasn't. She always did what she was supposed to do, the way she was supposed to do it. Elizabeth Ann was as uncomplicated as a woman can get, in other words about as simple as a heart bypass. For all these reasons, she had been less disturbed by the bank robbery than she had by the feelings it engendered. The revelation that she had feelings she hadn't known about and couldn't control was frightening.

She got on the bus and rode home to Bay Ridge. She browsed in a department store. She bought a belt. She said hello to someone she had gone to high school with. She remembered walking in a parking lot and a group of approaching men, all smiling at her. The last thing she remembered was a stinging in her hip. She gasped and put a hand to it. She couldn't walk, had to lean against a car. She was falling. Fortunately, the smiling men were there to catch her. When she awoke, she was in bed, but the bed was not her own. She had the grandmother of all headaches. And a man was sitting in the shadows, in an armchair in a corner. She could not see his face.

"Who are you?" she asked.

"You're supposed to ask *where* you are. Haven't you ever been to the movies?"

"Am I? Okay, where am I?"

"You're still a little groggy. Don't you know?"

"No. How could I?"

"That's right. How could you? You're not as groggy as I thought."

"So, where am I?"

"You're in my guest room."

"Why am I in your guest room?"

"We didn't know where else to put you. Don't you remember anything?"

"I remember walking. I remember some men. My leg hurt. That's all."

"Do you remember what you did?"

"What did I do?"

"Do you remember who I am?"

"No. Why am I here?"

"Can you tell me why you did it?"

Elizabeth Ann covered her face. "You're scaring me. You'd better stop."

"Do you have a headache?"

"Yes."

"I'm not surprised. The bank wants to avoid any scandal."

"What scandal?" Elizabeth Ann was terrified. Her father was not only a prominent Roman Catholic layman, but a supervisor for the Department of Sanitation. He did not believe in scandal.

The man in the corner got up, and came into the light. Elizabeth Ann saw that he was very handsome, tall, athletic, blond and blue-eyed, young, but mature. He sat on the bed. He smiled and she saw that he was infinitely sympathetic. His teeth were as white as a Ku Klux Klan bed sheet, straight from an ad for dental implants. In fact, he was the handsomest man she had ever seen, a man who made the bank robber look hopelessly gross, a man who would love nothing more than to bare his soul to the right woman, if she were not involved in scandal. She gasped. Again the suspicious feelings threatened to engulf her. He showed her a card, which she couldn't look at because of his cologne. Would he think he was too old for her?

"My i.d.," he said. "Always demand it. We can't be too careful." He showed her some pictures. "This is what we found. Whoever they are, they have the negatives."

The pictures were the most mortifying things she had ever seen. In full color, they showed a woman who wore only a garter belt, stockings and a large, satin bow in her hair, participating in horrifying sex acts, sex acts God had not intended, things she hadn't known were possible, things her mother had probably been too embarrassed to warn her about. For instance, the woman in the pictures was doing something unspeakably nasty with her mouth. They were pictures from Hell, taken by the Devil. Worse, although Elizabeth Ann couldn't see the man, she was the woman.

Elizabeth Ann had never been so embarrassed in her life. She couldn't remember doing any such things, but pictures don't lie, and the pictures showed her doing them. The fact that she couldn't remember doing them meant that she was out of control, utterly rotten with sin. Her face was on fire. Guilt burned like acid in her flat stomach. How could a person who had always obeyed her parents, who had always gone to church, who had never seen a movie more risqué than PG, who was twenty one--almost middle-aged--and still a virgin, be so horribly depraved? She knew that, despite all those precautions, the reason was the blasphemous urges she had felt when looking at certain men. Hadn't she felt that horrid urge even for the man who had robbed the bank? In fact, didn't she feel the same forbidden urge right now for the utterly gorgeous man who was sitting on the bed? What more proof did she need to know she was a nymphomaniac? Hadn't she looked the word up in the dictionary once, when her father was out of the house? Elizabeth Ann's father did not believe in sin and certainly not in sex, so Elizabeth Ann shut her eyes tightly and prayed that God would strike her down.

"How did this happen?" she asked.

"We don't know. That's what we need to find out."

She cried. "I've never done anything . . . . "

He nodded. "We know. They used drugs."

"Am I fired?" she whispered.

"No, but we want you to stay out of sight."

Staying out of sight was just what she wanted. She wanted to crawl into a hole, deep enough so that, when she died, no one could find her putrefying corpse. Her unexpected metamorphosis from someone who always did as expected, to someone who did unspeakable things she couldn't even remember, was a shock too gargantuan to handle. Her father, Frank, again came to mind, and she groaned. She could never see him again. At home, her mother's wedding dress, which fit her perfectly, was hanging in her closet. She could never wear it. She could never be married. Father Cecchetti would shoot her down on the steps of the church. She was already dead.

"I'll never be married in church," she said.

The man who was sitting on the bed took her hand. Elizabeth Ann discreetly tried to take it back. He knew what she had done, and had photographs to prove it. He was so handsome, so genteel. He would condemn her. He should condemn her. Instead, he smiled, patted her hand and nodded.

"Yes, you will."

Elizabeth Ann's stomach churned. She felt intense gratitude. Maybe she wasn't dead, after all. "Thank you," she whispered. "What's going to happen to me?"

"Great things, Elizabeth Ann." He put a couple of pills in her hand and gave her a glass of water. "Right now, you need to sleep."

"Yes. I need to sleep." It was so reassuring to do as he said. Sleep was oblivion. It would help her forget. She took the pills and washed them down.

But now it was night again, and she was awake. She was still in the room, still in the bed, it was dark, and she was doing unspeakable things again, the same things she had done in the pictures. The drugs were doing just as Dr. Ghibellini had promised they would. If she had been "normal," she would have been curious about the man who lay beside her. She didn't know and didn't care.

The unspeakable things she was doing did not perturb her in the least. She reveled in them. The qualms and contradictions of the morning had dissipated with the dew. Now, she was someone else and was at peace. She couldn't even remember what had bothered her that morning. She heard herself talking, but the voice that was usually so crisp and efficient made no sense at all.

A pleasant cologne hung in the air. It seemed familiar, but she had no way of knowing and didn't really care, which didn't bother her. The fact that she was a nymphomaniac no longer was a problem. The only thing she feared was that whoever was doing such marvelous things to her would stop. But, he didn't. Now, he began playing with her toes. The act was so intimate, and the sensation so excruciatingly delicious, that she screamed. She didn't know--and at the moment wouldn't have wanted to know--that she was part of a master plan.

Night after night, it was the same. She had no idea how much time had passed. She didn't know that, by now, she had almost completely dropped out of the news. She was just another unsolved disappearance, someone who would turn up on television from time to time. There were so many such people. Who could keep track of them, especially in New York?

* * *

Right at the start, there was a dispute, nothing insurmountable. Spats had bought the latest model of every major copier--the top of the line--explaining that Albert Holley himself had called them a threat. Dr. Ghibellini had listened patiently, politely, and then had dismissed them with contempt. Why would "Giuseppe" go to so much trouble to recruit him, if he didn't know that Enzo was an artist who could bring the Bureau of Engraving and Printing to its knees?

Spats explained that his interest in art was confined to the Tuesday evening lingerie show at a favorite roadhouse in Jersey, that time was of the essence, that what was contemplated made Dr. Ghibellini's no doubt sublime artistry redundant, and that if the copiers worked, they should go ahead and use them. Dr. Ghibellini contended that more precious time would be consumed in proving that the copiers didn't work, but agreed to a test, in which, sure enough, Fredo, now recovered, was questioned by officials at a branch of the Chase Manhattan Bank and released, minus the twenty he had been told to pass.

Spats couldn't understand how Holley could be so wrong. His crest fallen, he wondered how he was going to recoup his investment in the copiers, finally assigning Jim Stink to peddle them from a truck.

In the course of research, it was Enzo's turn to be chastened. Machines had been developed that could engrave as well as Dürer. The technology involved a selenium cell that contained a very photosensitive metalloid. Posing as a newspaper publisher, Spats bought Enzo one, and had it shipped from Europe. There was a Gestetner 212 offset lithograph machine, an eighteen-inch electric guillotine, a hand letterpress, numbering boxes and magnetic ink. Enzo told him what chemicals to buy. Spats installed him in a house in the Bronx, including a spacious basement workshop, and a backyard, where Fredo could play.

Enzo was happier than he had been since his arrival in the United States at the end of the war. Yes, he couldn't leave the premises for fear that one of Marcello's men would see him, but he didn't want to leave. He had all the money he needed for Fredo and himself, which wasn't much, and he was doing exactly what he wanted. How many people can say that much? When Giuseppe had coaxed him into it, that night in his apartment, Enzo had not realized how absorbing it would be. He could work in peace as long as he liked. Because the federal government had supported Freitag the demented feminoid rather than Enzo after all these years of loyal service, there was nothing wrong with what he was doing. In waking fantasy, he saw her tobacco-flecked lips; imagined he could whiff her dinosaur breath. He shuddered, giving thanks to St. Christopher he was safe.

The more he looked, the more he saw how ingeniously designed the dollar was. The filigree was remarkably elaborate, some letters white against a dark background, others the reverse. He looked at the seal under magnification, and was surprised to see that the points on a genuine bill were not sharp. There were ridges and hollows, which meant that the seal was done by letterpress, while most of the bill was engraved. Sometimes the seal wasn't even registered well. Was there a danger that his "Engravamatique" could make a bill that was too perfect?

Of course, the biggest problem was the paper, manufactured only by Crane, and sold only to the government. Spats tried to get some anonymously, but failed. Many people didn't know it contained tiny blue and red silk threads, added in fixed quantities. There was another problem. Most papers that otherwise could be suitable, fluoresce in black light. To proceed without solving the problem would have been utterly absurd.

Enzo went to see a woman he had met on the boat to America after the war. A German Jew, she had been part of the last phase of Operation Bernhard, at the Sachsenhausen concentration camp near Berlin, where the Nazis used Jews gleaned from death camps across Europe to counterfeit British and American currencies, in a scheme to destroy them by means of "money bombs." The Nazis could not know that, years after the war, the British and Americans would do to themselves precisely what Bernhard intended. In the beginning, Enzo and the woman had been together a short time as refugees. He was alone. She, too, was alone, but had a little son. Yet, although she was friendly enough, she did not respond. Something had happened to her too unspeakable to discuss, and perhaps the greater horror was that it still held her in thrall. Enzo hadn't seen her for years.

She knew nothing about the paper. She thought perhaps it was made by the Hahnemuehle plant of Schleicher & Schull, but wasn't sure. She did remember hearing that Nazi cryptographers had been stumped by the numerical and alphabetical sequences of American $20 bills, and that *Life* magazine had solved the problem for them in an article about the Bureau of Engraving, that included a chart of the system.

In London, he finally discovered Optimum 80. Lawyers used it for documents that were meant to last. Not only was it non-absorbent, it was made entirely of rags, rather than wood pulp, so that it was also non-fluorescent under ultra-violet light. To simulate the red and blue fibers, he first used nylon and wire. They failed. Then, he tried fibers from frayed lengths of household appliance cable, which worked.

Enzo added the letters from A to L, the numbers from 1 to 12, and the names of the banks. To make the bills silky, he not only dipped them in glycerine, but calendared them. Embossing was a problem. He solved it by cutting down a stock Stevenson and Blake border which he locked into a chase; then mounting the chase into a Chandler and Price platen press, and feeding the bills through. To be sure, he pressed them in a hand-press through thin cardboard against a brass plate he had engraved.

At last, he led Spats to a table, on which a couple of dozen twenties were displayed. "Study them," he said. "Take as long as you like." Enzo couldn't remember the last time he'd been so happy. He was Albrecht Dürer, showing a visiting nobleman through his studio.

Spats reached for one. "You may touch them," said Enzo, "but you can't pick them up."

Spats studied them with strong magnification, in a growing transport of delight. All of them looked perfect, the more so the closer he looked. His sensitive fingertips told him that the corners were perfectly embossed. He was suspicious.

"Professor, are you sure you're not playing games?"

"As the late, much imitated Benito Mussolini once said in another context, 'Trust me.'"

Spats took an hour and still couldn't tell the difference. Finally, at random, he picked one.

"No," said Enzo. "That one is genuine. Try again."

Spats picked another and another. He was wrong and wrong again. He was happy to be wrong, of course; in fact, all the bills were perfect, so he chose with growing awe. The possibility that there really was a phony among them, meant that Dr. Ghibellini was the greatest engraver since the invention of the art. Was that possible? He chose again.

Nymphomaniac
135

Now, half the bills were gone, but Spats still had not found the phony that Ghibellini said was there. "I can't take it any more," said Spats. "Which one is it?"

Enzo was smug, which he knew was bad taste, but he couldn't help it. "Now that you've picked half of them, the law of probability says you will find it soon. *Persevera et persevera.*"

"What?"

"Keep trying."

"No. Show me."

"You lack faith, my friend." Dr. Ghibellini picked one of the remaining notes and handed it to Spats.

"You're kidding," said Spats. He looked at it for a long time through the magnifying loupe and felt the corners. It was perfect. Spats didn't know what to think. Was he the victim of a scam, in which case he would whack this little "dago" himself, or should he rejoice? While he stared at the bill, Enzo turned it over in his hands.

The other side was blank.

Chapter Twenty
Romance

Spats had read that the experts called it a "syndrome," in which a hostage gradually adopts his captor's point of view. Whether or not this was a case of the syndrome, Spats didn't know, but Elizabeth Ann certainly had been doing just that, and she didn't even know she was a hostage. She no longer worried about her father. She no longer worried about getting married. She agreed with Spats in everything. She was such a clinging vine, he couldn't stand her. It was impossible to have a conversation with a woman who agreed with everything you said.

Now, for instance, she was waiting for him at the door of the vault, and she was smiling. She was gorgeous, utterly radiant, yes, and Spats felt the same involuntary heat of procreation he had felt when they first met, but she was going to launch another inane conversation, he was sure. She never stopped talking. She even talked in her sleep.

The guard who sat before the vault all night was there, large, sedate, thumbs in his belt. "Maximilian T. McGuiness, at your service," he whispered in Spats's ear. No one else was there to hear, but security had become a religion to McGuiness since he had embarked on this profession.

"He knows about the test and the need for confidentiality," said Elizabeth Ann. "I've explained everything."

Spats was pleasantly surprised. What she had said was exactly right. From the beginning, he had worried. Elizabeth Ann was the one essential element, but also the most dangerous. Now, he relaxed. She was behaving perfectly, even calling him by the name he had chosen for the job.

Spats said, "Ah, yes, McGuiness. I have read your file. You have an excellent record, and there is every reason to believe that your performance here tonight will add to it. There could be a promotion. Would you be interested?"

Maximilian T. McGuiness expanded like a float in a Thanksgiving Day parade. He had been raised in Uniontown, Pennsylvania to believe that loyal, efficient service would be rewarded, and here was proof, after just a week in the city and a few days on the job. "Use what you have," his dad had said at the bus stop, and young Maximilian had taken the paternal advice to heart. What he lacked in formal training, he more than made up for in size, a love of uniforms including belts he could stick his thumbs in, and an intelligence level low enough to protect him from insanity while he sat in a chair and looked through a plate glass window six nights a week, forbidden by explicit regulations even to read, which would have diverted his attention from the vault, but which, thank God, he didn't enjoy anyway. He certainly would not wind up like Wolf, the idiot he had replaced, who would do time for his participation in the recent robbery. No one at the bank was talking about it officially, of course, but McGuiness had put his ear to the wall and heard. How Wolf had been suckered into such insanity, Maximilian T. McGuiness could not imagine.

"If the truth be known, I would," he whispered, "and why shouldn't it? I have some ideas I'd like to discuss."

The man from the Federal Deposit Insurance Corporation inspired instant and perfect confidence. His hair was more salt than pepper, which proved his maturity, and there were deep lines in his face, which proved that he knew what he was talking about. He was compassionate. He had just proved that. Most overweight people were. Most important, although he was relatively short he exuded authority. Not only did he have seven kinds of i.d., he demanded that Maximilian inspect it. He was clearly as authentic as a Manchu Dynasty junk bond.

Spats looked at the vault the way Paolo looked at Francesca, the way Hillary looked at Mt. Everest, the way George S. Patton, Jr. looked at Karl Rudolf Gerd von Runstedt. It was sleek, pristine, elegant, as nubile as Elizabeth Ann had been until recently. It was open, yes, open. The reader will perhaps recall that industry publications at the time were talking about the "revolution in bank security." No longer was it necessary to ensconce the vault below ground behind yards of cement. There, tunneling, nocturnal robbers who had seen “Rififi,” could burrow at their leisure. The vault would be much safer in the lobby, facing the tall plate glass windows. Who would rob a vault in plain sight, where passersby could see? And, it was open, to express contempt for the idea. The massive door, a couple of feet thick, stood ajar, its exquisitely complicated electronic intestines on display behind a transparent shield. A sign explained them, mocking any tendency to covet. Only a tall steel gate covered the vault's lovely mouth. Who would rob a vault that was open? Yes, Miss McGillicuddy here had been robbed, but she was a teller. Indeed, who would be crazy enough to rob the bank again?

"Lets get to work," said Spats.

The boys filtered in, all cleaned up, all wearing the uniform of one of the biggest banks in the United States, grunting with the effort of carrying the heavy cases. Even Jim Stink, out on bail reduced to manageable dimensions by Spats's liar in West Palm, had bathed. Their armored car, authentic in every respect, stood at the curb.

"Oh, James, I'm so excited about this test," Elizabeth Ann effervesced. "You're right, it's necessary. Thank you so much for letting me participate. I know I'm going to justify your confidence."

Spats produced the key made by Dr. Ghibellini, for whom the problem had been child's play. "Allow me," said McGuiness. He took it with a flourish and slid it in the lock. It worked, of course. Only the new alarm system remained, based not just on ultrasonic sound detection, but on movement, via the so-called "Doppler effect." Emitting high-frequency waves inaudible to human ears, it would be triggered by the departure of a single twenty dollar bill, bringing the authentic bank officials and other busybodies to the scene. Needless to say, the portable electronic device designed by Dr. Ghibellini made it harmless. Everything was easy, if you knew what you were doing. When Marcello called again as expected, Spats had told him he had now been paid. Of course, Spats hadn't mentioned that to Enzo, who eagerly went into hiding, much happier than he had been as a professor, with the promise of more money than the entire engineering faculty had ever seen.

Spats signaled and the boys filed into the vault and went to work. Elizabeth Ann kept talking, of course, for which the drugs could not be blamed. The drugs released the Elizabeth Ann no one had known about, not even Elizabeth Ann herself, the real Elizabeth Ann worth suffering for. Without them, she would have been talking anyway. She would talk all night, if Spats let her do so. The bank officers would find her there, still talking, in the morning. At least she wasn't talking about God. She was an amazing combination of computerized efficiency and stunning naiveté.

But what could he do? God could not create a woman more suited to his purpose. When she had disappeared all those months ago, the bank of course had immediately checked her accounts. So soon after the robbery, the question logically arose of whether her disappearance was related. Needless to say, they were perfect to the penny, to the mill, except for Percy Hornswoggle's visit. When she reappeared, months later, Spats had told her to tell the truth: she had been kidnapped and unable to communicate. The kidnappers had wanted information about the bank. They had tortured her with drugs and unspeakable things, but she had refused to cooperate. In the end, they had let her go, disgusted. She believed, but couldn't prove, they were the same men who had robbed her. Her doctor wasn't sure she ever would recover.

The bank had lavishly welcomed her back as a heroine, to a branch in Manhattan, far from her home, with a substantial promotion and increase in pay. She had told her father the same thing, along with the fact that now it was time for her to live on her own. If she didn't have to face her father every day, and if she did everything Spats said, maybe she could live with the guilt of the other Elizabeth Ann. Spats had set her up in an apartment.

Frank McGillicuddy had bristled. He didn't know whether he was glad she had reappeared, or not. He was suspicious--he suspected everyone--but he knew only what she said, and it was too late to throw her out of the house. She was infernally circumspect, especially at the bank, but wasn't a bank officer supposed to be circumspect?

"Say nothing else," Spats had whispered, even though they were far from the bank, proving just how secret it was.

"Please, James. You frighten me. What's gone wrong?"

"Do you know who I am, Elizabeth Ann?" He had told her he was James K., for Kevin, Slagle. The boys had been primed to call him Jim in her presence.

"Certainly I know who you are, James. After my father, you're the finest man I've ever met. You're handsome to a fault, a great dancer, generous and genteel, and, most of all, forgiving. In fact, James, since you ask . . . ."

"Yes, yes, Elizabeth Ann, thank you." Did she always have to talk so much? Thank God the time had come to use her. "I mean, do you know what I do for a living?"

"You're with the bank."

"Not exactly. I'm senior vice president of the Federal Deposit Insurance Corporation."

Elizabeth Ann rolled her eyes. "James, Isn't F.D.I.C. bankrupt? I read that the chairman said it is."

"He's right, Elizabeth Ann. Do you know why?"

"No."

"Elizabeth Ann, I need your help."

"You have it, James. What must I do?"

"We have good reason to believe that all--and I underline the word `all'--the top people at the bank, from the head teller on up, are participating in a conspiracy to embezzle.

"In fact, Elizabeth Ann, we have reason to believe that they were the people who did those horrible things to you, as part of the conspiracy. To nail them, we need to conduct a spot check of the cash in the vault, and, for obvious reasons, we have to do it discreetly, at night."

"Like bank robbers."

"Exactly. You catch on fast."

"You don't know who else is involved. If you come during the day, they could be warned."

"Elizabeth Ann, it's hard to understand how a woman as beautiful as you are, could also be as brilliant as you are. I guess we're just stuck with it."

"Oh, James, you're so sweet."

"Let me show you something else." He left the room. When he returned, he was the man who had robbed her at the bank.

She pointed. "Percy Hornswoggle."

"The very one."

"Oh, my God! Was that part of it?"

"We had to prove we could trust you, Elizabeth Ann. We had to know you weren't one of them."

Elizabeth Ann had never felt such gratitude and relief. Luckily, she was sitting down. The fact that James and Percy Hornswoggle were the same man proved she was not the nymphomaniac she had believed herself to be. The guilt and self-recrimination fled. More than ever, she felt beholden to him. What a pity he wasn't a member of the church.

That's how easy it had been. She believed everything he said. People believe anything, however absurd, however much it contravenes their observation, experience and reason, if it is presented with sufficient authority, sincerity and panache. Despite her loquacity, which was a function of her gullibility, Elizabeth Ann had turned out to be worth every penny he was spending on her clothes and apartment. Of course, she had no idea what the plan really was. Because she believed, she had been able to convince McGuiness, who wouldn't talk.

Inside the vault, the beauty of the vista struck them dumb, even bringing friendly thoughts to Guzik. On endless shelves, there was cash to the ceiling, counted and banded, more than enough cash to put hotels on Park Place and Boardwalk. McGuiness had seen it many times through the gate and by now was blasé, so he opened the cases and dumped out the cash, the version Dr. Ghibellini had prepared. The copiers Spats had boosted had been useless for the purpose. Surely Albert Holley knew that. Why was he spreading such misinformation? You couldn't trust anyone nowadays, not even the president of the New York Reserve. Now, Spats was stuck with half a dozen copiers Jim had failed to get rid of.

It took a long time to pack the bank's cash. When they had done so, they stacked the Ghibellini version on the shelves. It was sorted and packaged, just like the bank's; indeed, the naked eye could not tell them apart. Sure, at some point someone was going to notice that Ghibellini's greenbacks were as phony as a one-dollar bill; were not printed on Crane paper, or that the chemicals were wrong, which could show up in black light, but so what? The discovery would be kept as secret as the D-Day invasion, because the bankers would fear panic and public humiliation. The bankers, the F.D.I.C. and the Reserve would become his accessories.

While they stacked, Spats and Elizabeth Ann looked out the window. It was almost 2 a.m. A passing policeman stopped to watch them work. Spats smiled and nodded through the glass. There was nothing to fear. Weren't they putting cash *into* the vault? Wasn't the guard the policeman had seen on duty the last few nights helping them? The policeman left.

"This is so romantic, James," whispered Elizabeth Ann.

Happily, the boys finished at that moment, so Spats didn't have to answer. At the door of the vault, they stopped for a long minute to consider their work. It looked exactly as it had when they arrived. It was impossible to tell that any change had been made. Again Spats produced the key.

"Mr. McGuiness," said Spats, "I want you to inspect the vault to ensure that everything is in order, and then lock it up."

McGuiness did as he was told. He was in the vault alone for a long time, so long that the boys began to tremble. Even Spats began to wonder whether something had gone wrong. At last, he emerged.

"Everything's okay."

"Lock it up."

Spats hit the button reactivating the alarm and handed him a form. "Please sign to that effect. Mr. McGuiness, it is imperative that no one learn of our visit, regardless of his title. Everything has been explained, and I rely on your discretion."

"You can do that," said McGuiness, grinning, immensely pleased to be included in this conspiracy for good. McGuiness couldn't get over how smart Slagle was. Now that F.D.I.C. had replaced the cash in the vault, it could inspect the bank's cash at leisure and the bank would never know.

Spats waited in his apartment on Sutton Place for days, doing nothing but reading newspapers and watching the evening news. The tension grew, but none of those fountainheads of information said a word. It was true: Spats had made history. He had engineered the greatest bank robbery anywhere. Not only had he stolen more cash than anyone ever had--the heist would make the Great Train Robbery a penny-ante boost--the victims didn't even know they had been robbed. Who would believe that the cash in the bank vault was phony?

After a couple of months, word came down that vault security at all the branches had been doubled. They knew. McGuiness, along with all the other vault guards, was questioned. "Slagle" had warned McGuiness that could happen. The questioning was perfunctory, because the authorities were afraid of revealing more than was known, and because McGuiness in particular was not suspected of anything. Needless to say, neither was angelic Elizabeth Ann.

All Spats had to do now was cultivate her counterpart in another major bank, and do it all again. It would be so easy. The question was, now that she was superfluous, what could he do with Elizabeth Ann? Were she anyone else, he would just dump her and disappear. Spats did not believe in long liaisons. A permanent woman caused attachments, obligations, responsibilities, and problems, problems, problems, all things that were anathema to Spats's unique, personal religion. A worshipper of liberty, even license, Spats hailed the burgeoning women's liberation movement, and contributed liberally to N.O.W. in his capacity as president of Manhattan Restorations. He had always preferred relationships based on money. Money kept a woman honest. Most women were in relationships for money, but they lied about it. On the contrary, a liberated woman contributed to a relationship for free; insisted on "paying her own way." By now, Spats had mastered women's liberation lingo, and could talk "equality" as well as Betty Friedan. Only a couple of hangovers from the discredited morality remained: he still had a horror of inappropriate language in mixed company, and insisted on holding doors open for masculine females emerging from the closet.

However, he couldn't just do as he liked with Elizabeth Ann. She knew too much. If he got on her wrong side, she could tell what she knew about the job, and someone smarter than she was--Albert Holley, for instance--would figure it out. Sure, he could just disappear, as usual, and pollinate elsewhere, but the chance was great that the all important plan would be exposed.

He also couldn't just waste her, as he had the boys in Brazil. Yes, Spats was a killer and a crook. But he wasn't a sleazebag. He had a code. A code meant that you stole to pay your poor landlady the rent. You didn't run out on her. There was "no honor among thieves," but you played fair with other crooks. Nothing had ever gone wrong on one of his jobs, but Spats always found out where the boys were when they got into trouble on their own, and bailed them out. No wonder they were so fanatically loyal. Spats's code was good for business. He killed only when the victim deserved it. Elizabeth Ann had done everything he asked. He couldn't whack her now just because she was redundant. Besides, the nocturnal Elizabeth Ann was as delightful as the matutinal version was loquacious.

He took her to dinner at one of the most expensive French restaurants in New York, an elegant setting for a kissoff. He would send her away in style, with an envelope full of cash, completely legit, printed by the U.S. Bureau of Engraving. However, he couldn't seem to get around to it. He told himself he was afraid. She was crazy about him. That was obvious in everything she did. And who could blame her? Wasn't he one of the handsomest, most brilliant and charming men God had ever put on this earth? Wasn't she always saying so? Couldn't he charm the rings off a rattlesnake? Wasn't he a dancer who made Fred Astaire look like Jerry Lewis's impression of cerebral palsy?

Suppose the shock of separation compelled her to do something crazy. Wasn't she dancing with him now like they were glued together? Her left hand was on his back, of course, but it was inside his tuxedo coat, which concealed the fact that her fingertips were exploring the top of the crack in his behind. The coat also concealed his Smith & Wesson Model 29, the "Dirty Harry" special, his favorite, enough gun to blow away a couple or three pimps in a line. Not many men disagreed with Spats in business; the last thing the few who did often heard, was his assertion that they had "made his day." Spats had one of the rare pistol permits issued in New York City--the last thing he wanted was to be caught with an illegal gun--owing to his connection with somebody important in the Police Department downtown.

He always packed it, not just because he might run into someone who had a different opinion of him than he did, but because in recent years New York had so utterly changed. Time was when a couple in tuxedo and evening gown could stroll unmolested along Fifth or Park Avenue of an evening, after the theater. No more. Civilization was collapsing. Criminals claimed the streets. It was disgusting. What were other people paying taxes for?

Her head was on his shoulder. Her hair tickled his cheek. Her scent rose to his nostrils and slowly cooked his brain. His skin tingled. The sensation was so intense, he squirmed. For the first time, Spats realized that Elizabeth Ann was an emergency. Yet, he had been trying all evening to kiss her off with no effect.

"Elizabeth Ann?"

"Yes, James."

"We need to talk about our relationship." *Relationship* was a key word. Spats had discovered it during his research in *Cosmopolitan* magazine.

Sure enough, Elizabeth Ann almost trilled like a songbird, "Oh, darling, you're so intuitive. That's just what I've been thinking." She was almost overcome. James was rich, powerful, clever, longed to father many politicians and policemen with Elizabeth Ann in holy matrimony--despite her sins--and now he was going to show her his soul. Everything was happening just as she expected. Her fear that he would think himself too old for her was gone. Elizabeth Ann's anticipation was so intense it was painful. She knew what was coming. Why else would he take her to a restaurant as good as Maxim's?

"I believe in equality. Don't you?" Spats asked.

"Equality of what?"

"Everyone says this is the greatest time in history for women," Spats said with perfect aplomb, no surprise since the line had worked many times. "You've been in bondage since creation, but today, here, now, you're free."

Elizabeth Ann's face still smiled. Behind it, a cloud, no bigger than a man's hand, appeared. She *didn't want* to be free. She *wanted* to be in bondage, to a man who, etc. Had she misunderstood?

"And so am I. The women's movement has liberated men as well as women. Frankly Elizabeth Ann, I'm tired of being used as a sex symbol and discarded. So many women these days think they have the right to take a man home. If he's stupid enough to go, he could find himself in the garbage."

The cloud disappeared. Didn't she feel the same way? He was testing her. He was tired of being hurt. How sweet! "Darling, I have the most thrilling news you have ever heard," she cooed.

Fear was in the room, hanging in the air like a handful of dust. Something horrible was coming, he knew. "What?"

"I'm pregnant."

Chapter Twenty One
Casing The Jernt

Only the immense discipline he had cultivated for so many years kept him from groaning. Despite the calculated ambiance, so perfectly modulated, so urbane and discreet--the most sublime expression of Twentieth Century western culture--Spats felt a cold wind and heard worms crawling through eye sockets in a cemetery at midnight. Why, God, why, was this happening to him? What had he done? Hadn't he been hosannaed for contributing liberally to various charities and churches along with both political parties and a couple of activist women's groups of several genders, not to mention many individuals in positions of public trust whose receipt of such largesse would have been felonious to mention? What else did God want?

He had coldly enmeshed Elizabeth Ann in his currency-switch scheme. He had initiated her for the purpose, by means of drugs and sex, into perversions she would have never dreamed of committing and didn't know were possible. For so long he had endured her Goody Two Shoes facade. That's what it was: a facade--and a reproach. He had needed it, but had shown her it was a fraud like everything and everyone else. She wasn't better than he was. The fact that she could make love as well as she did was proof.

Spats could not remember ever being so insulted. Did she really believe that Spats Davis could be suckered by such a line? Probably not, but of course she didn't know he was Spats Davis. She thought he was some poor slob with a good job, who was her ticket to a three-bedroom split level in Fort Lee, all expenses paid. So, since he was Spats Davis, why did he feel that walls were closing in?

Because she was trying to take advantage of the Code, of course. Aside from her hair, her face, her figure, her scent and pliability, her personality and competence, she was a typical female; that is to say, utterly without morals or sense of fair play, who, despite her fulsome protestations of idealism--probably because of them--would tell any lie, concoct any scheme or commit any injustice, if it got some poor bastard to the church on time. Spats had never actually met anyone as unscrupulous as Elizabeth Ann. With typical female hypocrisy, she was snuggling even closer to him now, trying to trade on his good will. With typical female hypocrisy, she had asked for nothing, which meant she wanted a blank check. As soon as he got rid of her, he would return to his sensible policy of renting women when he needed them, women who had no such things in mind.

He had never realized until that moment how truly precious freedom was. Elizabeth Ann had crossed the line. The Code no longer applied. Spats had nothing against children--if they belonged to someone else--but, despite her condition, he would feel better only when the boys told him she was gone. He would already have told them to install her in the newly poured foundation of the financial district's latest skyscraper, were it not that he needed her again for a job that would beggar Willie Sutton, which Dr. Ghibellini had said was feasible with sufficient preparation.

A couple of weeks later, they took the National Reserve tour. As they stopped at each point of interest, listening to the guide, Spats recorded each detail in his prodigious memory, paying silent deference to the expertise of Albert Holley. How typical of the Reserve to reveal what every other bank would keep secret. Its governors were experts in hiding in plain sight.

Well, wasn't he doing the same thing? Elizabeth Ann was beside him, exactly what she seemed to be, cloaking him with her virtue, scrubbed and starched, oohing and ahhing with the other tourists, radiant with the ultimate beauty of pregnancy. With her beside him, talking, talking, talking, inhibiting all thought, not one of the others could dare to guess why he was there. She was still useful, but, after this tour, in the finest spirit of equal treatment of the sexes, he would tell the boys to whack her. Besides, since she had quit her job at the bank, at his command, Spats had learned that her father, McGillicuddy, was on her trail, which made her continued presence a liability. Spats wished he could be there on her final journey, to kiss her on both cheeks and tell her it was "nothing personal, just business," but he would probably be otherwise engaged.

The Reserve was justly proud of its administration of the nation's monetary system. That was obvious in the script the young guide had been trained to recite. She pointed to the gold bars behind glass as thick as Bavarian castle walls.

"This is the world's largest gold depository: more than 14,000 tons. Sixty countries are represented here. The vault you are looking at lies almost 80 feet below street level. The door weighs 90 tons, and is a vertical cylinder with a passageway through it, set in a steel frame that weighs 140 tons. Does anyone have a question?"

"How do you ship the gold between countries?" Elizabeth Ann asked. That was one of the questions Spats had written on the paper.

"We don't. We don't need to. Transportation would be too cumbersome, dangerous and expensive, too old fashioned. When one country owes another, the gold is simply moved from the debtor's stall to the creditor's."

"How does the door lock?"

"Simple. It rotates and drops down in its frame. It's a plug valve."

Spats exulted, worried about how the boys would carry so much gold away. However, as the tour continued, his exultation dissipated, replaced by a sour funk. Wasn't it obvious why the Reserve was offering this tour? It was laughing at him. It was rubbing his face in the fact that what he contemplated could not be done, despite Dr. Ghibellini's assurances. He had never seen security measures like these in the biggest banks. It would probably be easier to get into the White House and have a bologna sandwich with the President. There were layers of clocks, locks, doors and electronics, guards and alarms. You probably had to show your fingerprints to get into the bathroom. Only the Third Army under General Patton himself, could penetrate such a vault. Only the Third Army could carry off such a haul, and then only with sufficient prayer.

His spirits fell. He became as depressed as he had been ecstatic. He glared balefully at Elizabeth Ann. The fact that the job would not come off meant that she was now redundant. She was typically oblivious, and of course was not to blame, but--like the good wife she wanted to be--she was there, and she was talking, talking, talking.

All the way to her apartment, his anger against Elizabeth Ann kindled. All the way to her apartment, she yammered while he fumed. "What an interesting tour it was. Thank you, James, thank you, thank you for taking me!" As usual, she asked for nothing, a silent reproach. There was only one way he could ever get rid of her. When he finally got home, he was furious, went to the phone and called Guzik the Goniff, who was as sympathetic as a virus and was not a good listener. There was no answer, so he settled for Louie the Enemy, who would do just as well, but had a rudimentary sense of humor as funny as a prostate exam.

"Lou, I want you to whack the girl."

"What girl, boss?"

"McGillicuddy."

"Da one wid da red hair?"

"That's the one."

"Ya want I should whack her?"

"Isn't that what I said?"

"How, boss? Any ideas?"

"No, Lou. You figure it out."

The boss was getting testy, which was Lou's cue to hang up. Of course, Louie didn't make a practice of asking the boss for advice on a hit. He was surprised. From what he had seen, the boss had a thing for McGillicuddy. Wasn't she pregnant? The difference between Guzik and Lou was that Guzik wouldn't even have wondered why Spats wanted Elizabeth Ann whacked.

Spats walked out on the terrace and enjoyed the glorious view. He showered, changed and drove across the George Washington Bridge to the road house in Jersey. It was Tuesday, almost time for the lingerie show, just what he needed to shake off the afternoon's disappointment. It was just starting when he got there, and he settled in at his favorite table for a drink. Sure enough, he began to lose himself, feasting on the wispiest garments the genius of Satan could devise, scandalously uncovering the sublimest females God ever had created. Later, he would move to a restaurant he liked on Route 17.

Then a curious thing happened. Without any warning, Spats couldn't breathe. With uncommon effort, he inhaled, but couldn't get any air. He was wheezing like a bellows, with little effect. Pulling at his collar desperately, he staggered from the road house. Maybe there was more air outside. Maybe the smoke and whisky were the problem. Yet, outside, the situation fell apart. His lungs were on fire. He had never felt such pain. Spats fell to his knees beside the building in the shadows. He knew he was going to die. Why? What could be wrong with a man as young as he was? Doom was coming for him, and there was nothing he could do but wait.

Probably there was a medical explanation for the problem, complete with titres, temperatures, deficiencies and leukocytes. Whatever, Spats thought he heard a voice. Elizabeth Ann was smiling and softly telling him goodbye. *Thank you, James. My trust in you is total. I know you are acting for the best.* Spats thought he could see her in the shadows, but her face receded as she spoke.

Whether or not he was right, he decided that his only chance was to head Louie off. Scrambling on the gravel, gasping, staggering and falling, he got to his car phone and dialed the Enemy. Something was wrong. There was too much interference. He was too far away. He limped back into the road house. All three public phones in the lobby were in use. Women jabbered into them while his life drained away. He took one by the shoulder and tore her from the phone. The silly puke stood there in amazement, screaming, pointing, trying to repair her dress, too stupid to understand that he was dying.

Now, a man was there, a large physical man. Of course, he didn't know who Spats was. He didn't know that Spats was a karate master, who could break his leg like a board. Ordinarily, he would have been no trouble, but Spats couldn't breathe and his lungs were on fire. While Spats desperately tried to get a dial tone, the man smashed him in a kidney. He fell. The man was wearing cowboy boots, and kicked Spats in the head. Spats struggled to his feet. The raucous road house music was clanging in his head.

He was outside, staggering across the gravel of the parking lot, while the man took potshots at his head. He fell. His hands and knees would be horribly abraded. He crawled. His tormentor kicked him in the torso, in the thighs and chest. The boot found Spats's face and rolled him over.

At last, he got to the trees and crawled in. His tormentor laughed and finally left him in peace. He lay there all night. He could not get up. In the morning, with the road house closed and every one gone, he was able to get to his car, and somehow drove home. Still bloody, he called Lou. There was no answer.

His jaw was broken. He was sure of that. Maybe a rib along with it. Had he lost any teeth? He was still losing blood. Yet he couldn't take the time to see a doctor. He had to talk to Lou first. He had to head Louie off. If he sat very still, he could draw enough air to stay alive. Now that he could think, he felt no animosity for the man at the road house. Spats would have done the same had someone assaulted his woman, if he had a woman. Again, the man hadn't known who he was. It didn't matter, because he could never go back there. The humiliation would be too great. In fact, never in his life had Spats been so humbled. He hadn't known it was possible.

Louie didn't answer until morning. When he did, he told the boss he had done as instructed. No, there was no doubt about it. She was gone.

"Are you sure, Lou?"

"Soitenly. Just like ya wanted. Ya want I should tell ya how?"

"No."

As he hung up, he shivered. For no reason, it was cold. Yet, now that he knew, he could breathe again. He did so, deeply, reveling as never before in the act. Everything was normal again, except that the doom remained, permeating the days.

Two weeks passed. Spats tried to shake off his regret. Regret was something he had never felt. He brooded, even neglecting to call Dr. Ghibellini. The tour that had bombed in the vault of the Reserve was bad enough, but he was alone now. Elizabeth Ann and her forgettable monologues were gone. Such peace! Wasn't that what he had wanted, especially now that she no longer was of use? Why did he now recollect her nattering so fondly? Why did remembering her resuscitate the doom? He rented a woman for $1,000 for the night, well worth every penny of the price, a woman who could have been official courtesan to Haroun al Raschid, or, with any social conscience, even someone important in Hollywood or Congress. She was boring.

For want of something better to do, Spats browsed through the newspaper. He would never humiliate Willie Sutton. He would never pull off the biggest bank job in history. To do so, he needed the Third Army, and it was unavailable. He needed a diversion, so devious, so complicated, that beside it a gambit by Machiavelli would look like a fund-raising campaign run by Mother Teresa.

A story in the entertainment section said that David Polyakov was coming to America for the premiere of the movie of his life. There was an interview with executive producer Vincent Blandino, of Superior Pictures, and another with Polyakov himself. Now, Polyakov was a multi-billionaire, honored throughout the world as a philanthropist and Nazi-hunter. Now, he had endless respect as chairman of one of the biggest pharmaceutical houses in the world. But, all during World War II, he had been the lowest of the low, a resident of Auschwitz. "Days of Valor" was the story of Polyakov's survival and transformation, the story of how a soft, pampered Jewish intellectual, a self-admitted "selfish brat," became hard enough to stay alive in hell, and how he changed himself from a spoiled, effete dilettante to an avenging witness to what had happened in the camps.

"It's a picture that will make you cry," said Vincent Blandino. "It's idealistic. It's spiritual. It's romantic. The women will love it, but there's enough war and disemboweling to satisfy a California biker. It's a story from The Bible. Mr. Polyakov is a regular Ishmael. So we kept the language to a minimum, and you can take the kids."

The story said the premiere would not take place in a theater, but in the vast tower auditorium of the New York headquarters of Polyakov Pharmaceuticals, in the financial district, by invitation only. "Mr. Polyakov suggested it, and we bought it," said Blandino, on the stage of the huge room. "We shot one of the scenes here, so it will be like seeing the picture on the set. How's that for realism?"

Spats lingered on the photograph of Polyakov. He had billions, he had power and he had it made. Of course, he was a crook. No one who had that much money could be straight. Spats didn't need to know anything about the man to know that, and, looking at his photograph, he felt the mystic tug of kinship. Certainly Polyakov was no more brilliant than Spats, no more ruthless and resourceful. The only thing that separated Spats from his billions was an accident of birth. Was it his fault he wasn't Jewish and hadn't been at Auschwitz?

About a week later, Spats happened to be in the financial district near Wall Street, to discuss an insurance scam. It showed every sign of promise, and he left the meeting in such good spirits that he decided to take a walk. It was a glorious day. "Business" had helped him shake off his recent funk. Elizabeth Ann by now was nothing but an ice pick in his heart.

He looked up and saw the massive, squat facade of the New York Reserve. There were steps, endless steps stretching away to a small door in the sky, calculated to intimidate Godzilla. There were columns calculated to frustrate Samson at his best. There were stone walls thick enough to entomb the Abominable Snowman. Somewhere up there, safe and smug, in an office he could not reach, was Albert Holley, dewlap dragging on his desk.

His good mood fled. His funk returned. Like an open mouth revealing immense teeth, the monolith was taunting him again, daring him to fight. He turned away bitterly, trying to avoid it.

There was another facade, even more imposing, elegant, not at all squat, much, much taller, like the extended finger of an aspiring hand. Spats craned like a tourist, but could not see its top. Against the clouds, it seemed to be moving, leaning toward the Reserve, as if preparing to admonish it. Why hadn't he noticed it when he recently took the tour?

Proudly carved in the marble imported from Vermont were the words: Polyakov Pharmaceuticals.

It is said that genius attacks its victims without warning. Archimedes takes a bath, no doubt expecting to doze, and issues therefrom quite beside himself and naked, shouting, "Eureka!" Newton sits under a tree, the most innocent of occupations, is beaned by an apple and discovers gravity. Conrad discovers fear in a handful of dust. Spats is struck dumb by two words carved in a facade.

So it was that the broad outlines of the plan now emerged. The details would come later. The revelation completely erased his black mood. Joy erupted. The Third Army had arrived. He suppressed a desire to kneel in thanks on the pavement, which would have made him a spectacle among the throngs, there in the capital of Mammon. Again he felt the inexorable hand of mystic kinship. This could not be an accident. There had to be foreknowledge!

He needed only one thing more. Sure enough, a few days later in the religion section of the same newspaper, a story said that churchmen were up in arms. A nutcake who said he was Jesus Christ, and had "apostles" to prove it, was curing the blind, sick and halt. Father So-and-so and Reverend This-and-that said this was blasphemy, especially when he did it on Sunday. The police said he was breaking several pages of laws, including a failure to pay certain fees and secure certain licenses to solicit. The federal government was making noises about population policy, the environment, truth-in-advertising and civil rights. The chairman of a prestigious commission warned that the "phenomenon" could reawaken anti-Semitism. A U.S. attorney pointed out that the gang sometimes conducted these sectarian performances at public institutions, thereby running afoul of the U.S. Supreme Court. And, needless to say, the doctors weren't happy. The nutcake was practicing medicine without a license, bilking the elderly and persuading desperately ill patients to postpone treatment until it was too late. Recently, one of the victims, age 92, had been found dead. According to still unconfirmed rumor, the leader had a rapidly growing account in Geneva. Lieutenant Bobby Combs, of the N.Y.P.D., told the media that the gang was hard to find and disappeared just before the cops arrived. Spats decided to subscribe to the newspaper to follow the story.

Elizabeth Ann! Her face, even her scent, sprang instantly to mind, as if there all the time, waiting just beyond the gates of awareness. He needed her, as he had before, which evoked intense delight. Elizabeth Ann could play a crucial part in the plan that now was taking shape. The fact that she talked too much would be an asset. But Spats had told Louie the Enemy to whack her. She was gone, gone by Spats's hand as sure as if he had pulled the trigger. The doom returned, oozing in from the terrace, smiling. No matter what he did, he couldn't shake it. What did it want? Why was it waiting? Elizabeth Ann was gone, he could do nothing to atone, and no one could forgive him.

Chapter Twenty Two
Prodigal Son

e have news you may think is more important than Goldstein." Yusuf paused to become portentous and leaned across Krüger's desk. "We learned in New York that you have a son."

"I have a son? A child?"

"Yes. But no longer a child. A man."

Many years ago, Krüger had willingly surrendered to the mass delirium at Hitler's speeches. He recalled with sweet nostalgia marching to the *Horst Wessel.* Who could resist it? Yet, he had always disliked the expression of personal emotion in public. In fact, after all these years, he feared it. He could betray himself with one remark, and the Jews were so vindictive without reason. Because of his life-long masquerade he had necessarily taught himself total, inner discipline, despite which, now, he had to hang on to his desk, and preview every word he said with special care. It was all he could do to keep himself from jumping to his feet. He knew that if he got to his feet, he would lose control.

"We know nothing more than that," said Ahmed. "We learned of it in the course of our investigation of this Goldstein, quite by accident."

"Where is he?"

"In the United States."

"But, who is he? What is he? How does he happen to be there?"

"We don't know that, *Herr* Polyakov. We don't know his name. You sent us there to investigate Goldstein, not your son."

Ahmed was right, but Krüger was suspicious. Suppose this man in America, whoever he was, was a fortune hunter. Many such opportunists would like to be Krüger's son. "Why has this man, my son--if he is my son--waited so long to show himself?"

"That we can answer, *Herr* Polyakov. You see, he doesn't know he is your son. The news will surprise him as much as it does you."

So, he wasn't a fortune hunter. Krüger's heart did a little pirouette. "Then you learned all this from a third party."

"Yes."

"Who?"

Yusuf smiled, revealing expensive teeth. "Would you like us to launch another investigation, *Herr* Polyakov? We know you are a generous man. We would love nothing better than to reunite you with your son, but this would be more difficult than Goldstein. And, New York is so expensive, *Herr Direktor.* The corrupt Americans have allowed the drug culture to make the city unsafe. Women on the streets either commit assaults or are assaulted. Children either beg in droves or work as pimps. It is impossible to park. Only an expensive hotel could supply the extra security we need, in view of the fact that this concerns you personally. The danger is great. We know you will appreciate the fact that we must eat carefully there. The Great Satan cooks everything with pork. We have to eat in kosher restaurants. We tell them we are Jews." Krüger shuddered invisibly. How humiliating! "And, of course, the expenses themselves, the research, not to mention a modest sum for us . . . ."

Krüger waved a pacifying hand. "You are a joy to deal with, gentlemen. You will have everything you need, as usual." He pushed a button on his desk. "Please see *Herr* Schwartz on your way out. My guess is that you will find him generous."

"A thousand thanks, *Herr* Polyakov. You are a credit to your race."

"And the proof?" asked Krüger.

Ahmed said, "The proof will be so positive, so authoritative, that, if you are unconvinced, your considerable investment--in U.S. dollars, small bills and unconsecutive serial numbers--would be returned."

"In which case, the man would never know anything about it."

"Correct."

"There are genetic tests, as good as fingerprints, admissible in court. DNA. I want them done."

"Agreed," said Yusuf. "Our source in New York, who unfortunately cannot be named at this time, says he will reveal the name of your son only to you--in person--after acceptable identification."

"*Natürlich.*"

"There is something more," said Ahmed. "The one you have sought since the close of the World War is also in New York."

Krüger licked his lips. At last! He had known all along she would be found. His hand went reflexively to the flaming scar on his cheek. "Do you have the details?" he whispered.

"They are being processed."

"Do they come from the same informant?"

"Yes."

The Arabs left. The door closed and Krüger vaulted to his feet. He could not have waited another moment to do so. He rushed to the window and looked down on Munich. He was shaking. He tried to maintain his suspicion of the Arabs, but, for several years, they had supplied him with helpful information--mostly the fruit of industrial espionage--and it had always been remarkably accurate. Needless to say, his Israeli friends and the West German police didn't know about the Arabs.

A son! This was the sign--the sign from Valhalla--that Krüger had been praying for.

Krüger finally was able to stop shaking. A modicum of sanity returned, and with it a disturbing question. Whose son was he? Was the child his, or was he an unknown son of the real David Polyakov the Arabs believed Krüger to be? Had Polyakov fathered this child before the war, before Nazi science? Krüger hadn't thought of Polyakov for years. The silly, little, Yiddish bastard! Krüger refused to consider the question. Of course the son was his! The genetic work would prove it. The discouragement, the *angst*, that had slowly been encrusting him for years, fell away like dead skin molting from a snake. His spirit soared, again as young as he was. The *Führer* would live. The *Führer* would live again.

The Arabs had said his son was in New York. Did he live there? Was he a visitor? Krüger's mouth twisted with the usual contempt. Was his son an American? What did he do there? Was he involved with Jews? Krüger trembled. If, as the Arabs had said, his son didn't know who he was, would his son reject his father? Krüger shook his head. Nonsense! There was too much proof. This was teutonic destiny.

Krüger pushed the button. Before Schwartz could answer, the question hit him with a shock. Who was the mother? Krüger didn't even have a theory. There had been so many women through the years, each one more desirable, more exciting, more beautiful and accomplished, than the last. So many. The Arabs had said his son was an adult. Was the mother still alive? Women aged so differently from men. That was why a man needed many mistresses, and Krüger was on the best of terms with every one of them. Why not? A Krüger mistress lived for a time on Mount Olympus, and, when she was replaced, she was sent away with all the treasure she could carry. For all he knew, the mother could be here, in Munich, or elsewhere in the *Vaterland.* Why had she never revealed the existence of his son? Whose wife was she? What was the relationship between his son and his mother? Did they live together? Krüger felt a flood of warmth for her, whoever she was. He wanted to offer her his gratitude in person.

He would find his son. Their reunion would be a scene from Wagner. Together, they would solve the problem of this termite Abraham Goldstein. Together, they would bring the hated Jew to his knees, and smash the Jewish-Communist Conspiracy for good. Together, they would resurrect the Führer and the Thousand-Year Reich. On their knees, the Christian riffraff would know for sure who was god! Together! The word had a mystical quality, evoking the thunder of generations of Nazis marching through the centuries, crushing nations under foot. Krüger's son would be the Spear of Destiny.

Only yesterday, Vincent Blandino had called him from New York, to say that, according to his sound men, the world premiere of "Days of Valor" could indeed take place at the company's headquarters there, as Krüger had suggested. Blandino had used every blandishment to persuade Krüger to attend. "Despite your modesty," the presence of the "real-life hero" would no doubt "max out" both the publicity and the receipts. Krüger had told Blandino that he would call in a few days with his decision.

The premiere would be in New York. Goldstein was in New York, of course, extruding Jewish filth like a cockroach in the candy. Now came the news that Krüger's son was there, and that so was the only one who could betray him, the one he had been hunting all these years. All roads led to New York. Didn't this mean he had to go? Wasn't it a message?

Schwartz was talking, but Krüger was too deep in reverie to notice. At last, Schwartz's voice came into focus. "Prepare one of the 747s," Krüger said. "I must go to New York."

Chapter Twenty Three
Messiah

From the beginning, Louie the Enemy had been troubled. He had wasted many men without a twinge, but they had been men. Men were rivals, competitors in business. Women were baubles, playthings, put here for amusement. How many men had he whacked by now? He thought it was 17, but wasn't sure. He had never whacked a woman. From the moment the boss had given him the contract, Louie had felt deepening anxiety, his mouth as dry as a Kalahari beach. As usual, the boss hadn't told him why he had to do it, and Louie had been afraid to ask. The reason might have vitiated the burning in his gut.

Indeed, not only was this woman stunning, not only was she sublimely feminine, not only did her personality make Dale Carnegie look like a bozo; besides all this, she was going to have a baby, which, typically, not only intensified her beauty, but added a superstitious aspect. What had she done to deserve a hit? Louie shuddered. Would he be cursed?

He was afraid of the boss. It was smart to be afraid of the boss. He had calmly sent many men to the wall, like the two bozos in Brazil, besides which Louie had no idea what he looked like. It was smart to be afraid of a man who could kill you with a look, but whose looks you had no idea of. So, Louie was suffering from intense, inner stress.

The boss had told him to tell her she had to go away for a while. A man would know what that meant and would protest. She did not, did not even ask for an explanation, and Louie marveled. The plan was to put her on a plane from J.F.K. to Boston, to meet her there at Logan, to drive her up into the mountains, and do what he had to do. Twenty third century paleontologists would find her body.

Louie did his best. At the wheel of the car with her beside him, he was morose. He was approaching disaster and there was no escape. His head fell low, as low as a head can fall and still see the approaching road. He was a hairy man. His beard had a beard, and resembled the classic cartoons of Senator Joe

McCarthy's "five o'clock shadow," so that his dark eyes seemed to be looking suspiciously over a hedge.

Needless to say, Elizabeth Ann noticed none of this. There was nothing and no one to suspect. There was some good in all of us. "James" had told her to go away, so she was going. When he told her to come back, she would, all for the greater glory of the bank. The only thing on her mind right now was the thing she had seen on the local evening news.

A gang of con artists of the most despicable kind was operating in town. Their targets were old and critically ill. Practicing medicine without a license, they pretended to cure, no doubt swindling numerous widows' mites in the process. Their leader even had the temerity to call himself "Jesus Christ." His followers called themselves "apostles." The authorities had launched a media campaign to warn the people about them. An investigation was under way, which no doubt would soon lead to their arrests.

Elizabeth Ann shivered. Why would somebody call himself Jesus Christ? Would people who weren't apostles say they were? She called her cousin, Bobby Combs. A policeman for many years, by now he was a lieutenant. Many times, he had told her father, Frank, the truth about stories she had seen on television, information that never came out.

Now, however, he "knew nothing." He had heard of the gang, as she had, but had "seen no paperwork." Was Bobby being evasive? Elizabeth Ann had been trained by the Treasury Department to recognize evasion, just in case a drug pusher tried to launder some cash, and she saw its signature here. Was there something about the gang Bobby was afraid to tell her? For instance, she didn't know Bobby wasn't telling her he knew the gang leader and had sat in his living room, but she smelled a dead mackerel. Using the same training, she knew that "James" was incapable of guile, and probably didn't know the meaning of the word. His conscience was a clear mountain lake, one of the many things she loved about him. He wanted her to leave town, so she was going. She had total confidence in whatever "James" said; wasn't even aware that his name should always be in quotes.

Louie let her out at J.F.K. The last he saw of her was her retreating back, as she waddled slightly into the terminal, flanked by a couple of skycaps wheeling mountains of luggage. Louie had considered seeing her to the gate, to make sure she boarded, but witnesses would have put him there, when the cops began to retrace her missing steps, and Louie was aware of his unorthodox appearance. Of course she would board the plane! Hadn't she been told to?

Elizabeth Ann did get on the plane. It did take off and flew to Newark, where it landed. Unknown to Louie, whose expertise did not extend to meteorology, Hurricane Jemima, although officially moribund, was then converting Boston to Christianity, with the result that Logan was closed. At Newark, friendly, efficient airline personnel, who loved to fly, told Elizabeth

Ann to get on a bus, so she did. It disgorged her in midtown Manhattan, where they installed her in a hotel, even gave her toiletries tagged with the airline's name (which we don't mention here because it refused to pay us a promotional fee for the purpose) and said she would be flown out in the morning, when Jemima would be savaging Atlantic Canada. Should she call "James" or her Dad? If she did, they would feel pressure to do something. She was perfectly safe here, and the airline would explain what had happened to the people "Mr. (Louis) Johnson" (Louie the Enemy) had told her would be waiting at Logan.

It was still relatively early in the evening, the weather in New York was fine and Elizabeth Ann decided to walk off the excitement. The doctor had told her to do a lot of walking, which would be good for "the old bomb bay doors." Elizabeth Ann did not understand what a couple of doors in Bombay had to do with her condition in New York--besides which she remembered from her geography that Bombay doors were somewhere in Calcutta--but obstetrics were new to her so she took the doctor's word for it.

Deep in thought, she left the hotel and walked to Central Park. Soon, she and "James" would be married. He didn't need to marry her. The baby wasn't his. By now, she understood that she had been kidnapped, drugged and assaulted, because she had been an obstacle for the embezzlers at the bank. Yet, despite the departure of her fabled virginity, "James" had volunteered. He had talked about it only last week; made her take notes about what he wanted at the wedding. She hadn't even mentioned it. He was so noble, like a knight from Camelot.

She should have left a trail of bread crumbs or a string tied to her finger. She had left the park and was in an area she didn't know. She was lost. After all, she was from Brooklyn, born and raised, which enjoyed a different culture, different language, different mores and traditions. Besides, Manhattan was so vast. To her, most of it could just as well have been central Ouagadougou. Now, there were spacious lawns stretching far away. There was a large, two-story building with many windows, an old, converted mansion, along with lesser buildings. There were many, big trees. Something prophetic was moving in the shadows.

* * *

Abe stood in the trees and waited. It was dark. It was quiet. It was too quiet. There was something in the air. The trouble was that he couldn't be sure. Lately, he had that feeling all the time. As always, Moe was beside him, listening. Did Moe feel something too?

How many months had they been doing this? Abe could not recall. He didn't want to do it, never had, but someone had to, and, as far as he knew, he was the only one who could, courtesy of God. At first, it had been easy, just a matter of walking in. Now, there was the security, the running and hiding. Why? Wasn't God making sick people well? Wouldn't that save lots of money? What did the authorities have against that?

Abe didn't understand, and didn't know anyone who did. Even police lieutenant Bobby Combs didn't, but he was able to keep Abe abreast of police plans. The pressure was certainly coming down--his picture had been on the front page again that morning; Bobby had warned him there was an A.P.B.--for which reason Abe had started to work at night. Maybe they needed to work a different city. Would the others follow him? If they left their lucrative jobs and did, where would he get the cash to operate? They were tired, exhausted, none as much as Abe. The temptation to lie low was great. In fact, shouldn't they do so until the heat had passed? But Bogart had warned that every day they rested more patients would disappear. Bogart still didn't know why that was happening.

Where were they now? Abe looked at the plaque on the little building he was near. The Workman's Circle Home for the Aged. Jews. It was all the same to Abe. Last night they had worked a Catholic establishment. Tomorrow, they would hit the Baptists. Bogart had advised him to keep the authorities off balance, in fear, always wondering where he would strike next.

Rabbi Stanley B. Garlick rose from behind the bush beside the front door, and pumped his fist, the old infantry salute indicating that Bobby Combs had picked the lock and that the coast was clear. Naturally, the rabbi had volunteered tonight. To prevent leaks, even in innocence, Abe told no one, not even his helpers, the name of a target, until they were assembled and ready to leave. That way, if a man were caught and subjected to torture, or turned out to be another Judas Iscariot, he had nothing to reveal.

Abe and Moe glided like shadows across the grass, Rabbi Garlick held the door and they went in. It was utterly dark. A door opened and closed, Abe knelt beside a bed and found a hand.

"Messiah," someone whispered.

Last night, they had talked of Jesus. Everywhere, it was the same. Abe prayed, quietly, fluently. He still didn't want to do what he was doing but by now he was good at it, sure that if something were displeasing, God would let him know.

"Oh, my God!" said the voice. "The pain is gone."

"Tell no one," Abe whispered. "Be quiet."

"I'm going home!"

Closet doors opened and closed. Abe warned again, but there was shouting. Bureau drawers were thrown upon the bed. They were in another room. Moe drew the drapes and turned the lights on. The door to the lavatory opened. A disheveled woman staggered out, tripped and headed for the floor. The rabbi dove across the bed, speared her arm with a hand, and somehow managed to keep her from falling.

Abe took her by both biceps and stared into her face. Her eyes were blank, listless, uncomprehending, victims of senile dementia--now known as Alzheimer's--and the drugs prescribed to fight it. She was expressionless, unloved, unkempt, hair akimbo. A rugged plastic band that would tell police who she was and where she belonged, in the event that she ever somehow got through the locked doors into the community, was on her wrist. Yet, Abe's gaze held her fast. She could not move. How long did he stare at her? Neither could have known. His gaze, so recently diffident, was like a sunbeam, like a laser, burning her corneas, cauterizing her flesh, revivifying her spirit.

At last, he felt the tension leave her. A light erupted in her eyes. Abe saw understanding. She smiled.

"Thank you," she said. "I'm all right." He let her go. She went to a nearby bureau, picked up a brush, and did her hair. Satisfied, she lifted the telephone and dialed.

"Bernie? Yes. Yes. Bernie. It's Adele." Adele started to shout into the phone.

Rabbi Stanley B. Garlick stood as in a trance. He saw it, saw it with his own eyes, but he still could not get used to it. Thank God, thank God, that Abe was not a gentile, whoever the voice said he was. Wouldn't the gentiles just love to get the credit!

Abe put a forefinger to his lips. "Please," he whispered to the woman.

It was useless. It was always useless. As they worked the rooms down the hall, doors opened behind them and people came out. Muttering pursued them, maturing into whispers and then actual conversation, like a wave rushing up a beach. They heard the sound of plastic hitting plastic, as inmates threw their prescription drugs into the garbage.

The wave passed them. Now, people in wheelchairs pinched and fondled as they passed, commenting with enthusiasm on the quality of their flesh, like cattle brokers at an auction. Windows were opening. People, patients no longer, were going home. Soon, the staff would be aroused, and Abe's helpers would have to hold them until the work was done. It was all so unnecessary. Yes, there was a little disruption, and several convalescent home administrators had complained that, in the wake of Abe's visits, unexpected and unwanted sexual activity had erupted among some inmates old enough to be incapable and to know better. Some patients who knew what they were doing were found in the wrong beds. Yes, it was a problem. At least there were no pregnancies. So the police sometimes found the inmates turning cartwheels on the lawns. Wasn't the salutary result worth these minor problems, especially in view of the departure of the fear?

Abe moved quickly down the hall, his feet completely healed. Almost a year earlier, Bobby Combs had found him wandering down Columbus Avenue, his shoes and money gone, his bare feet bloody. Bobby hadn't recognized him at first. When he did, he took Abe to the "Honeycomb"--that's what Bobby called his house--where, without even trying, Abe cured Bobby's wife of the twenty-year heartbreak of psoriasis. Since then, at great risk to his career, Bobby had joined the group. How else could he show sufficient gratitude for such largesse?

Abe was in another utterly dark room. Another hand found his, with a grip that betrayed its owner as a robust man in his prime. Another hand closed on his shoulder like a chain saw.

"I've got him," shouted a belligerent voice. Other equally alien voices joined him.

All the lights in the institution clicked on. The man holding Abe's wrist and shoulder in a death grip was large and bald, smiling in triumph, visions of banner headlines and hefty promotions dancing in his head. Cop was written all over him. The sound of running, flat feet indicated there were more. So full of himself was he--and so pacific was Abe--that he failed to recognize his danger. He never saw the lamp that crashed into his head, nor did he see the assortment of umbrellas, bookends, fingernails, menorahs and the like, with which he was assaulted. He was on his knees, blood flowing from his wounds, his erstwhile captive disappearing in the crowd.

"Don't hurt him!" Abe shouted.

He couldn't stay to see whether the people did as he said, because Elizabeth Ann McGillicuddy had him by one arm, Honky Ryan had him by the other, Electric Eyes Chase was behind him, and they were pulling and pushing him with all deliberate speed out the back door of the institution and away. As the gang disappeared into the neighborhood, other police arrived, among them Lieutenant Bobby Combs, notebook ready to record the amazing facts. Because of impregnable Police Department security, even Bobby hadn't known about the S.W.A.T. team.

Chapter Twenty Four
Conversion

"I don' know what happened ta her, Boss," Louie the Enemy told Spats on the phone. "Da airplane people say she never got aboard at J.F.K. da next day."

"Why weren't you at the gate to make sure, Lou?"

"She was scheduled ta disappear after Logan, Boss. Dey would have been able ta make me in New York. Dere was no good reason ta tink she wouldn' go. She wanted ta go."

Louie was right, of course. If the cops had been able to put Louie at the gate, they would have been able to tie the Mob into Elizabeth Ann's disappearance. What he had done was smart. He hadn't been trying to mess with Spats.

"You did well, Lou."

The frigid pain in Louie's gut went away. "Don' worry, Boss. I'll find her and finish it. I found a place in da White Mountains in a gully. Ya can visit her dere."

"No, Lou. Drop it. I'll handle it myself."

"Are ya sure, Boss?"

"Yes."

Spats hung up. The doom lifted. He hadn't killed her. He couldn't remember when he had felt such relief. Spats was sure he could already smell her scent. She was alive, but where was she? From the terrace of his penthouse, he could see far into Queens and New Jersey. She was down there somewhere, talking, talking, talking. What was she saying? He had to find her, not only because now he needed her to help him join the gang of kooks, but because he had to shut her up, and he could only do that if they were together. If anyone ever knew too much, it was she. Because it doesn't matter what a corpse knows, he had paid little attention to what Elizabeth Ann had heard. For the same reason, and to cement her loyalty, he had told her they would marry. She would not forget that promise. "And to think, `James,' that it wasn't my idea; that you thought of it yourself."

Now that he knew she was alive again--knew he hadn't killed her--he shook off the relief. The old irritation returned. He would use her one last time, then buy her a one-way ticket to Nepal and put her aboard himself.

Spats put his notes through the word processor, taking care not to save, so there would be no record. The kooks would be one of the diversions. Elizabeth Ann would become one of them. She spoke the lingo and was perfect for the job. She would "recruit" Spats.

For two weeks, without success, he tried to find her. It was totally unlike her to disappear for such a time, not to do as she'd been told. Spats worried and his worry became fear. Yes, she was perfect for the job he had in mind, but there were many others who could do it. Why not be done with her and pick one? Wasn't that what he wanted? He had no interest in her personally. Wasn't she more trouble than she was worth?

On the fifteenth day since he had seen her last, the phone rang. "'James?' Oh, 'James,' the most wonderful thing has happened. I went to the airport with dear Mr. Johnson, as you said. He's such a sweet man. He told me all about his family. We got as far as Newark, and they drove us back. They put us in a midtown hotel. Then I went for a walk. 'James,' I met the most wonderful people. You must meet them too."

"Not now," said Spats harshly, tuning out her voice. "Tell me where you are. I'll come."

It was bound to be some idiotic thing she'd gotten into. He didn't want to hear. He found her in an Automat on Sixth Avenue. He hadn't been in one for years. By now, he was as sweet as baklava, but he wouldn't listen. He took her hands and looked deep into her eyes.

"Elizabeth Ann, I missed you so much. Why are you so cruel?"

Elizabeth Ann marveled. Men were so mercurial. They were utter mysteries. She could never understand. How had she been cruel? Elizabeth Ann reveled in her power over him. Why did James have those bruises on his face? Why did his face look so different?

'James,' dear, sweet, mercurial and mysterious 'James,' said, "Dearest, this reunion is so sweet. It gives me the courage to say what's in my heart. While you were gone, I had time to read. I had to do something to keep from going mad. In The Bible I read how a good wife, by example, brings her husband to the Lord."

Elizabeth Ann had never heard so sweet a speech. The only thing wrong with it was that it was so brief. 'James' was baring his very soul. The intimacy was so intense, she felt like screaming. The fact that she would be the "wife" he spoke of was overwhelming. Didn't that make her a woman of The Book? She couldn't wait to tell the others.

"Oh, 'James,'" she said, through cascading tears. "You don't know how I've prayed for this. I thought I couldn't tell you; thought you wouldn't understand. Isn't that silly, dearest? This was my dream for many years, since childhood."

Spats took her by the arms. "Elizabeth Ann, there's something you can do for me."

She was happy to hear it. Doing something for her man was a Bible privilege. "What?"

"There are some people I want to know, to fellowship with." Spats had told the truth about reading in her absence.

"Who?"

Spats showed her a clipping about the little band of prophets. "I believe they are doing the Lord's work in New York. I believe that is why they are being persecuted. The world is incapable of understanding the people of The Book, because they are in the world, but not of it."

"The news media say they're hypocrites, maybe swindlers," she whispered, testing him.

"Of course they do. The natural man rebels against the Word. That's his nature. Hasn't it always been like that? I want you to find them. I want to multiply their great work."

For two weeks, Elizabeth Ann had been doing exactly that: living with the prophets, happier than she had been at first communion, but afraid that the new relationship might damage her relationship with 'James.' The coincidence of his request was clearly supernatural. Rarely in this post-apostolic age did the Lord so clearly tell people what to do. Relief flowed in and out of her, and with it her tears intensificd to deluge.

"I'm so happy, 'James.' I'll start at once."

* * *

Albert Holley was justifiably proud of his memory--he had read much and taken many courses for the purpose--so the incident understandably annoyed him. He could remember a dozen objects by number backward. He never forgot a name. But he couldn't remember what had happened that evening at the Club after he smiled and started to shake hands with Charles M. Wilson, of Manhattan Restorations. All his memory tricks failed.

The reason he couldn't remember was that Spats had stuck him in the back of the hand with a sedative that put him to sleep in the library, where they had gone at Spats's request to "talk business." Spats had put straws in his nose, and then sprayed him with something akin to latex. In a few minutes, it hardened, Spats removed the straws and peeled the latex off, leaving no trace for Holley to discover.

When Albert awoke, a doctor was examining him, and Charles was the hero of the mystery, having summoned him at once. The next morning, Holley's own doctor confirmed that nothing was wrong. For no detectable reason, Holley had "passed out." Certainly, he wasn't pregnant. Thank God the embarrassment had happened at the Club, where strict rules of confidentiality prevented media coverage. In the country's present brittle economic condition, such coverage about the president of the New York Reserve could have provoked a panic.

The incident left Holley uneasy. He had never passed out. Now he couldn't remember part of his life. Was there something wrong with his health even his doctor couldn't find? He prided himself on his control, but he had lost control. The only thing he remembered was his ambivalence for Charles, who had known what to do, but who had witnessed the embarrassment, and who had left the Club that evening with the perfect Albert Holley rubber mask.

Chapter Twenty Five
The Raid

The two unmarked cars sped into the parking lot far above the speed limit, bounced over the speed berms and stopped with a screech at the curb in the fire zone, newly painted with forbidding yellow stripes, and festooned with signs threatening parkers with deportation and worse.

The occupants extruded with conflagration in their eyes, especially those who, in violation of federal mandate, had not been wearing their seat belts, and had been repeatedly propelled against the car ceilings, further flattening their heads, leaving greasy kid stuff that could never be removed on the headliner. The thud of such contacts and the subsequent groans and exclamations could have been heard easily by witnesses, had there been any, but there weren't, and what the men said wasn't worth repeating anyway.

They were angry, but they were also happy to be free. There were six of them to each modest vehicle, burly men made burlier by the Smith & Wesson .38 specials and other brand-name hardware inside their coats, and they had come a long way ankle by knee by hip by jowl, finally realizing as they arrived that they disliked each other even more than they had thought they did.

They were important men, powerful men, lords of creation bred to inspire fear. They were also men with a mission, a dangerous combination. They were there to do business, and their arrival had obviously been well planned. Each of them proceeded immediately to an assigned position.

Unlike the others, their leader was a small, thin, man, with wispy hair and a lipless, crooked smile. Everything about him was spare, as if there hadn't been enough leftover material to make him. Yet, he was more powerful than the others. He wasn't armed, and didn't need to be. His chest swelled, a classic case of pectus cockatrivus, so that he seemed to be swaggering even when he wasn't, which was rare. He smiled the crooked smile, revealing teeth *au jus* de cigar, patted the wispy hair in place, waited until one of his men opened the heavy door and went in.

There was a reception area and a little, old lady at a desk, talking to a telephone. She hung up guiltily. Her hands flew to her throat.

"Are you Mrs. Dorsey?" asked the leader.

"Oh. No."

"Please ask Mrs. Dorsey to come here."

His voice was so unlike his looks that the little, old lady looked around to see where it was coming from. So many people made the same mistake. It was a deep voice of immense authority that could not be contradicted, a voice that should have been coming from one of the large men he led. The little, old lady turned to call Mrs. Dorsey out, but her own voice failed, despite which the unaccustomed vibrations made by so many large men in an area ordinarily frequented by children were sufficient to bring a curious Mrs. Seamus Dorsey to the desk.

"I know who you are, and I don't have the money," she said. "Why did they send so many of you? Are you afraid?"

The leader smiled, reached into his wallet and took out a card. "That's too bad." His voice was almost musical. He nodded to one of his chunky assistants, who proceeded to the door with a tool box. "You haven't kept your word, Mrs. Dorsey. You're a bad girl. You say you want protection, but you won't pay the bill. We don't want to do this, but you give us no choice."

"Who is that man?" she pointed.

"He's a locksmith, Mrs. Dorsey. We're changing the locks."

"You can't do that."

He smiled his crooked smile and fondled his wispy hair. So many "clients" had said the same thing. "We can do anything we like, Mrs. Dorsey. This building is now the property of the United States government." He handed her a card. "Sidney H. Bloberg, Revenue Officer, Collection Division, Internal Revenue Service," she read. "You need to leave now, Mrs. Dorsey. You may take your handbag."

Mouth open, she was still looking at the card. "What about the children?" she said at last.

"Not to worry, Mrs. Dorsey. They're our problem now."

Still looking at the card, Mrs. Dorsey started down the hall. "This way out, Mrs. Dorsey," said Sid, pointing at the door, not at all annoyed. So many people panicked when he came.

She started to run, and was already far down the hall near wherever she was going, before Sid realized that she was not confused and had no intention of doing as he said. This so rarely happened that Sid was taken by surprise. He heard a door slam, but hadn't even seen which one it was.

Recovering, he led his minions down the hall, trying doors. They were all unlocked but one, and the rooms were full of children. "Mrs. Dorsey," he said through it, his voice smiling. "Mrs. Dorsey, you are attempting to repossess federal property, which is a felony. Thank God I'm a generous man. Come out now, and I'll let you go."

Did she respond? Sid couldn't tell, because the hall was full of the familiar sounds of children playing. Inside, she waited on the phone. At last, someone answered.

"Police?" said Mrs. Dorsey. "We're being robbed."

Sid's veneer of gentility was showing bald spots like his pate. His generosity did not extend to fault. "Forget her," he said. "We'll starve her out. You know what to do."

Toward evening, after work, when the parents and grandparents came to claim their children at the never-profit Special Wee People day-care center for the handicapped, they found Sid seated before an open door behind a table, preventing their progeny from leaving.

"Good evening," said Sid, gesturing. "Please sit down."

"Where's Mrs. Dorsey?" asked a middle-aged man. "I'm here for my grandson."

"Of course you are. Tell me your name."

"I'm Joe Dolan. What's wrong?"

Sid thumbed noisily through a computer printout and pointed. "Dolan. Yes. Four hundred thirty seven dollars."

"What's $437.00?"

"That's how much you owe, Mr. Dolan."

"I know perfectly well what I owe, Mr. Whoever-You-Are, and I can assure you it's none of your business."

Sid chuckled. He loved his job. "As soon as you pay it, you can take your child."

In fact, Joe could see the child right now, through the open door behind Sid. A muscular dystrophy victim, he waved to his grandfather with a cane.

"Is that so?" said Joe, who was becoming nettled. "And who might you be?"

Sid handed him a card and Joe read it. His face collapsed, like a punctured parade float.

"What do you want?" he whispered.

"A check for $437.00 payable to Special Wee People."

Joe numbly produced a checkbook and began to write. Sure, he had won a Silver Star in Korea, fought a kangaroo on a bet, told so-and-so to go to hell, and streaked a Rotary luncheon wearing nothing but pantyhose and roller skates, but all that had been a long time ago. Now, Joe got a check from the federal government every month--the same government Sidney H. Bloberg represented--and he was scared. He couldn't afford to lose that check. He had heard about what happened to people who opposed I.R.S. Hadn't he read just last week about a man who had come home to find his cars and wife gone and his house padlocked? Hadn't he heard about the man who committed suicide in court?

With shaking hand, he wrote the check. As he shaped the numbers, Mrs. Dorsey appeared, having called half the numbers in the Brooklyn telephone book. Sid's mood changed. This woman definitely had an attitude problem.

"Mr. Dolan, what are you doing?" she asked, but her question was an accusation.

"Me, Mrs. Dorsey?"

"Yes, you," she shouted, ever more enraged. "I see no one here but you and this traitor."

Sid's mood changed again. She was screaming because she was helpless. Besides, Sidney H. Bloberg was not a traitor. He was a patriot. Without him, the United States government would collapse.

"I'm writing a check, Mrs. Dorsey. To you."

"Don't do it, Mr. Dolan." She pointed. "He's stolen the place. He'll just keep the money."

That's exactly what Sid was getting ready to do. "Get it any way you can" was his motto. He wasn't going to get the promotion he wanted with timidity. Recently, his manager had convened a staff meeting and told his agents to be bold.

Dolan finished writing and handed the check to Sid. Sid nodded to his men who moved the table and let Dolan's grandson out. Another parent stood before the table.

"Don't sign anything you don't want to," Mrs. Dorsey pleaded. "This isn't Belfast."

Sure, Sid could have had her removed with a nod. But, he didn't want to. He was enjoying her performance too much. She would know better next time.

Despite Mrs. Dorsey's adjuration, the woman signed, fingers shaking so much she could barely do so.

"What's wrong with you people?" Mrs. Dorsey railed. "You call yourselves Americans?"

The reason Mrs. Dorsey was so irritated was that she had been working for next to nothing for months. This was a working class neighborhood and she hadn't paid her taxes because people hadn't paid their bills. Yet, she had continued to give them service because they had nowhere else to go. If she had denied them, some would have had to quit their jobs. Now, because of intimidation she could have used but hadn't, their bills would be marked "paid," but she would get nothing.

The place was filling up with people. Certainly, they couldn't all be parents. Something was wrong, but Sid was enjoying himself too much to be suspicious.

A pregnant, young, woman with fire engine hair stood before the table. "Name?" said Sid.

"McGillicuddy," said Elizabeth Ann.

Sid shuffled through the printout. "I don't find it."

"That's because it isn't there."

Sid should have known she was a ringer, but *hubris* intervened. "No. It's all here. I did it myself."

"So you're going to keep my kiddo 'til I pay?"

"I didn't say that."

"What did you say?"

Sid thought of saying, "I said you can facilitate the delivery of your progeny by the payment of your bill," but realized that self-justification would reduce him to her level. "I'm not here to answer your questions, madam, but to collect monies due."

"In other words, you're a kidnapper, Mr. Bloberg."

"Call me what you like. We have the guns."

Elizabeth Ann smiled. "You may have the guns, Mr. Bloberg, but we have the power."

Elizabeth Ann took a chair against the wall, dainty feet together, ankles primly joined, produced a magazine called *Nursing Mother* and began to read, utterly relaxed, as if sitting in a beauty parlor waiting for a perm.

Sid was troubled. Her remark had brought him joy; it seemed to contain the prospect of violence. Sid loved violence, because it meant S.W.A.T. (Special Weapons And Tactics), participation in which had been his childhood dream until the years revealed his physical insignificance. Maybe all these people were planning to attack him!

However, the woman's actions belied his initial expectation. She was ignoring him with such fervor that her ignorance became provocative.

"Do you want your child or not?" he asked, laboring to keep exasperation from his voice.

"Mr. Bloberg, I've been on my feet all day," said Elizabeth Ann, taking off her shoes. "They hurt. Thanks to you, I'm going to relax. I didn't know the federal government provided this beneficial service, but if you're willing and able to keep my child after hours, I salute you. I may even leave him overnight."

"You can't do that," said Sid with a trace of falsetto.

Elizabeth Ann patted her rapidly proliferating tummy. "I'm an 800 pound gorilla, Mr. Bloberg. I can do anything I like."

"Good idea," said someone in the crowd.

"Keep mine, too."

"Thank you, thank you, Mr. Bloberg. You're a credit to the federal government and a credit to your race."

Silence erupted in the large room, unnatural in view of the size of the assemblage, silence that quickly became oppressive. Sid looked at the sea of faces. They were smiling at him, like cats that had swallowed an armada of canaries.

"This is federal property," said Sid. "Do you people realize you could be arrested?"

As we have seen, Mrs. Dorsey had a strong proclivity for direct confrontation, but she was flexible enough to get into the spirit of non-violence. "For what, Mr. Bloberg? For telling you how wonderful you are?"

The crowd erupted. There were titters, guffaws, even some traditional horse laughs. Sid's face clouded. He had committed himself and now he was trapped. He couldn't force the people to take their children. His men were looking at him too, S.W.A.T.-type zombies he now directed, waiting for instructions. The longer he sat there, the wider yawned the jaws of defeat.

Sid rose, beckoned to his men and went outside. "We're finished here," he said, declaring victory. "Let's go."

The men were jubilant. Sid said the operation had been a raving success, so it was. Yet, as they piled painfully into the automobiles, ankle by knee by hip by jowl, the parking lot filled with people, all in festive mood. Many surrounded the vehicles, imploring Sidney to take their kids home. As the cars screeched from the premises in haste, Sid heard them howling with delight.

Back in his office after everyone had gone, Sid sat at his desk in the dark. He hadn't felt such humiliation since the girls in his senior class voted him the sexiest male since Elmer Fudd. Why had he come up with such an idiotic scheme? Wasn't it because of his idiotic slogan?: "I'm the guy who takes your kids!" His own idiotic slogan had beguiled him. He had to stop saying it. He had to stop worrying about what those girls thought. Today, every one of them was fat, probably missing teeth and had varicose veins.

A couple of days later, Sid learned that the checks issued by Joe Dolan and the other parents to Special Wee People before the infernal red-haired woman intervened, had been returned with notations that the accounts had been closed.

Chapter Twenty Six
Dreams of Glory

"I don't want you to come," said Myra.

"I'm coming," said Sid. "I was invited."

"You're not even interested. The only reason you're coming is to annoy me."

"I've always wanted to know everything about David Polyakov. If you took any interest in me, you would know that."

"I don't take any interest in you."

"See!"

"Not only will you not tell anyone you know me," Myra said, "you will not even speak to me. When I decide to leave, I shall do so in my car. If you wish to stay all night, you may. Is that clear?"

"Why are you doing this, Myra?" asked Sid. "What's the matter?"

"You know damn well why I'm doing it!" she screamed.

"If it's change of life, I want you to know you're looking at a fountain of sympathy."

"I'm looking at an I.R.S. g*estapo* spy! You know I'm not old enough for change of life, you vicious bastard."

"I'm not an I.R.S. spy, Myra."

"You were born with change of life." The fact that they had no children was a raw wound that grew worse daily. Myra had read about her "biological clock." She could hear it ticking inside her, but it was not being wound.

"You can't have any children if you won't sleep with me."

"I *have* slept with you, God help me. It did no good. It wasn't even that much fun. You're a eunuch."

"I'm a Revenue Officer of the Internal Revenue Service. I'm a respected, highly paid official of the United States government. I'm just as much a patriot as Nathan Hale."

He *was* a patriot! Wouldn't the nation collapse if Sid didn't collect taxes? It wasn't his fault that everybody was a crook. The proof they were crooks was that they paid when he dunned them for arbitrary amounts he had invented. Would they pay if they weren't hiding something? Because they were crooks, Sid Bloberg, patriot, stood on the moral high ground, and could do anything he liked.

"Sure you're highly paid, Sid. Who else but a sewer bag would do what you do? You're a regular Judas Iscariot."

"So you're a Christian now?"

"I'm not a Christian and you're not a Jew. You're a Nazi."

"Myra, I won't tolerate these insults."

"You will."

"If it's such blood money, why do you take it?"

"Because you owe it to me, you Nazi bastard! Because I've given you the best years of my life. Because you're such a puke you can't give me kids. Because, at a party, people avoid us as if we had AIDS, and would be more friendly if we did. Because you never told me you would become what you are."

"I became what I am for ambition, for you."

"Road apples! Monkey poop! You could have stayed at the collection agency, repossessing cars. Today, you'd be assistant manager. I'd be respected. Women would talk to me at the beauty parlor. Oh, what's the use. When I think of what could have been, I go crazy."

"Then don't think of it, Myra, because you don't have far to go."

"You disgusting cockroach! To think I could have married Abe Goldstein. I could marry him today. He's crazy about me, always was. You know what he is, you Nazi bastard? He's somebody. He's a supervisor in the Department of Sanitation. I met his wife just yesterday at the Post Office. The conceited bitch."

Sid smiled the smile of triumph his quarry often saw. He had used the same technique on Myra he always used on them, and, need we add, it had worked. It consisted simply of getting them to talk, goading them, from time to time encouraging them by means of pithy comments. Sooner or later, if the victim talked long enough, he would confess. Most of the people Sid had helped put in jail, had talked their way into it.

Sid opened a folder and handed Myra a newspaper clipping about Abe and "the apostles." He said nothing; the clipping would speak for itself. There was even a photograph of Abe, years younger with more hair, which enamored Myra even more, despite which, as she read, the shame of being caught erupted on her cheeks. Even the joy of catching Shirley in a monstrous lie could not dispel it. The fact was that the man she was holding up to Sid had never been a supervisor in the Department of Sanitation. He had been a garbage man, no better than a hooligan, and now had been canned (pun intended). What kind of work was that for a Jew? Worse, he was posing as Jesus Christ, the man who invented gentiles. The remark she had made to Sid about his Jewishness collapsed.

She did not look up. Were she to do so, she knew, she would see Sid gloating, mouth open obscenely, even exposing the epiglottis, saliva on his chin, lizard tongue darting, teeth stained with cigar juice, dead eyes staring like sockets in a crypt. The fact that she had married this toad was mortifying *in extremis*. Her kiss had not made him a prince.

Myra crumpled the photograph and threw it in the garbage. "Oh, Sid, don't you think I know all this? You're so naive."

She clacked to the door while Sid scurried to retrieve the picture, and was immensely pleased to see in the hall mirror that he was wondering what she meant. If she knew it all and was not disturbed, and, furthermore, if Sid were "naive," didn't all this mean there was something to the story the *Daily News* didn't know? If so, how could Myra know it?

She slammed the door so hard, the Jello shimmied in the fridge, but after only half an hour at the cocktail party, her apprehension disappeared. She had not succeeded in keeping him away--as husband and wife they both belonged to the fraternal organization the Blandino people had invited--but, at least, Sid conducted himself as she had asked, except that he leered at her from various points in the room, as if to ask how he was doing.

They were in the financial district, in the 123rd-floor dining room--as near divine as mortal man could make it--of the New York headquarters of Polyakov Pharmaceuticals. Waiters in white waistcoats stood in flocks at every elbow, trays at the ready, prepared to satisfy almost every culinary longing. Massive tables buckled under an Olympian buffet, lacking only a vomitorium to make Tiberius at home, prepared under rabbinical supervision in the person of Rabbi Stanley B. Garlick, to the secret annoyance of those members who elsewhere discreetly partook from time to time of catfish and chicken chow mein, doing their part to maintain the Jewish reputation for tolerance. Among them were the most distinguished exemplars of New York Jewry, movers and shakers in every industry, philanthropy, racket and profession, along with some gentiles who had been attracted by humanitarian, pecuniary, scholarly, social, celluloid or other considerations, not to mention the journalists of every race, color, creed, gender, age, teleology, national origin and sexual preference, whose presence was primarily motivated by the free food and alcohol, all joyfully united in paying homage to the man who had made it possible, and in whose honor the bill-of-fare was strictly kosher.

Vincent Blandino had started out as an orphan on the streets of a dusty Italian town too poor to have tourists. He had not become the most powerful force in the movie business by leaving things to chance. The average producer would have assumed, probably with good reason, that the inspiring, romantic film biography of a man who had lost his beloved wife, but survived Auschwitz to become a world-famous philanthropist, manufacturer and Nazi-hunter--the man who owned the tallest building in New York--played by a superstar so handsome he made Robert Redford look like Quasimodo, and supported by the biggest budget in movie history, would need only routine promotion to make millions.

On the contrary, Vince Blandino did not believe in luck. The present cocktail party was one of a series he was arranging for opinion-makers before the premiere, to explain what they would see, in the same way that the network anchor man and correspondents tell you what you have just heard after someone makes an important speech. Soon, he would mount the dais for the purpose, projecting charm and power. For now, he let the truffles, the goose and crepe suzettes, along with the champagne and Mogen David, refuel and lubricate the crowd and dissipate inhibitions.

Sid Bloberg loved parties. He didn't care what the point of them was, or who was present. This was a Jewish party. With just as much panache, he could have attended a Klavern clambake hosted by the Klan. At a party, he loved to become part of one of the little groups that constantly form and dissolve. Sometimes he had to wait, because he never joined the conversation, and was so physically nondescript, but at length someone always asked him what he did for a living.

"I'm a Revenue Officer for the Internal Revenue Service."

Sid would smile obscenely when he said this, which, as the reader will recall, was one of the things that drove Myra crazy. Having said this, Sid would wait, praying that someone would ask him what it meant.

If someone did, he would reply, "It means I'm the guy who takes your kids." When he said it, Sid would smile all the way to the epiglottis.

He loved to feel the tension in the group--almost palpable--loved to hear them stutter, loved to see them seek a pretext to drift away in growing funk. It usually took about half an hour for word to get around, depending on the size of the group, after which Sid would spend the rest of the evening in quarantine. If he wanted food or drink, there was never anyone ahead of him in line. If he sat, those present would vacate and leave him all alone.

Your average man would have been mortified by this, but not Sid. Sid was not an average man. Some agents, when at parties, distorted or concealed what they did, or just lied about it. A couple even showed phony business cards. They had often felt the lash of Sid's contempt. For the same reason, Myra pretended not to know him. Sid loved the point at a party when people suddenly realized he was not an object of sympathy, but someone to fear. From across the vast room, Myra saw that he was working the crowd now.

Most people didn't realize what Sid knew. Some older agents talked about the so-called "great days," during and just after World War II, when people boasted about how much income tax they paid, and the only problems were mistakes in addition. Nonsense! The great days were now, when Sid could disrupt a party just by being there. Sid loved the fact that he had dead, fishy eyes.

People thought he was unobservant and dropped their guards. They didn't know he was just the opposite. They didn't know he knew that every one of them was cheating on his taxes. The only thing he didn't know was how. Every one of them was a felon whom Sid could send to jail, however powerful. Sid was like a rich kid in a candy store, who couldn't make up his mind. For instance, over there was a hotel impresario, who called herself a "queen." Despite the many millions she paid every year in taxes, Sid could dethrone her. Somewhere in her books a "mistake" was waiting to be found, because Sid's heroes in the Congress had made the law so complicated, it was whatever he said it was.

Outside, on the balcony, Spats studied the streets and the roof of the National Reserve through powerful binoculars. There was nothing on the roof, nowhere to hide. Whatever anyone did there could be seen from innumerable windows in the Polyakov building and others. The streets were narrow and crooked, reflecting their great age. They were deserted. The financial district was a ghost town. Spats smiled, relishing in advance the brilliance of the diversion he was planning.

"What a glorious evening," said Elizabeth Ann, beside him. "Look how far you can see into Jersey. And look the other way, 'James.' You can almost see Bensonhurst." By now, he was used to her--Dr. Ghibellini had taught him to use astral rejection to reduce her voice to a faint buzz--and he had to admit she was perfect cover for almost everything he did.

Now, there was movement in the crowd, and the others left the balcony. The lights inside dimmed, but the light outside and the enormous windows created the illusion that the assemblage was floating silently in space, high above the city.

Sid saw a woman standing near a door, thin like himself, but tall, elegant, plainly dressed in black, a woman who had been striking, even beautiful, but whom something more than age had harshened into coldness. Unlike all the others, she was not there for pleasure. She stared at them, her eyes dead, like Sid's. He was suspicious. Was she also I.R.S.?

Now, a spotlight hit the lectern. Vincent Blandino stood in the light. He was a physical man with a florid complexion, whose ensemble, jewelry and cologne could have retired the Bangladeshi national debt. He smiled, revealing the best dental implants money can buy. Waves of power emanated from him, like electricity from a generator. He was a man who made George Washington look like a victim of neurotic indecision. Without exception, the dozens of sublime women he had impregnated without benefit of matrimony were immensely grateful--despite the legality of abortion and their ability to pay, they had brought all his little bastards to term--grateful for any little souvenir. Some of them, the ones who were not on the Riviera, or back in Beverly Hills or in some other watering hole on his largesse, were in the audience.

No one introduced him--introducing Vincent Blandino would have been redundant to the max--and he began without introduction. "Imagine, if you will," he stage-whispered, "a night so bad that you know you're in hell, hell everlasting, hell eternal, infinitely painful and humiliating, and you know there is no escape. It's bad enough to be there if you deserve it, but imagine that you don't. What do you do? Do you curse God? Do you lose your sanity, like so many others?"

People already were crying and moaning. Some rubbed their arms, where the concentration camp numbers still could be read. It was a milieu Sid was used to, so he felt at home. Myra stood beside him, breathing heavily. "Oh, Sid, isn't it glorious?"

Sid looked for the woman in black. She leaned against the wall. Unlike almost all the others, her expression was cold. Near her stood a tall, young man. Sid had an aversion to tall, young men, because he was not one of them. A woman stood beside him. Sid saw a full, bare arm bent on a hip. Now she took a step, and Sid saw that she was the Taxpayer from Hell who had orchestrated his humiliation at Wee People. Since that fiasco, Sid had quaked in fear that the facts would find their way to his ravening enemies at the office.

There could be no mistaking her. Her fire engine hair was a provocation, a banner. She was even more obscenely pregnant and clearly proud of it. What was her name? Sid's left arm was tingling. He felt faint.

"As you see the Soviet troops come marching down the road to liberation, you ask yourself, 'Why did I live, while so many others died?' You hear their souls cry out for vengeance, and you know why you were spared."

Something unspeakably evil was in the room. Sid's instinct told him so, and his instinct never lied. He didn't know what it was, but instinct told him it was more than the routine tax evasion no doubt committed by everyone in attendance. Sid licked his lips. If only he could place it. The fact that the red-headed girl was present polluted the entire gathering. Was she tied to Vincent Blandino and the movie, or even to David Polyakov? Was she tied to the tall, young man?

That question, at least, answered itself when she put her arm through his with proprietary interest, whispered in his ear and left, clearly on her way to the ladies' room. Sid had never been pregnant himself, but knew that when you have to powder your nose, you have to do it. Who was the tall, young man?

Sid worked his way through the crowd and stood beside him, waiting. Spats looked down and saw a wispy, little man smoking a cigar. Sid revived. The blood and color flowed back into his face. He was on the hunt. Soon, the tall, young man would ask him who he was.

But he didn't. In fact, he looked away, and Sid saw that he was utterly oblivious, like the woman in black. Precious time was passing. Soon, the red-headed tax protester would return and confront him.

"I'm Sidney H. Bloberg," he said. "Call me Sid."

"I'm Jim Slagle," said Spats. "Call me Mr. Slagle." Was he talking down to Sid? Of course he was. He was tall and Sid was short. But was he talking down with condescension? The question often arose, and Sid never knew the answer. Sid sized him up and marked him down as an accountant. Sid had an infallible feel for people. What was Jim Slagle, accountant, who looked as Jewish as Attila the Hun, doing at this affair, in the company of an illegal Irish tax protester, yet?

The irritation dissipated. Soon, the condescending bastard would ask the fatal question: "What do you do?" Bloberg trembled with anticipation, like a groom at the door of the nuptial chamber.

Telling moments passed. Eventually, Sid realized that Slagle was not going to ask what he did for a living. Incredibly, he wasn't interested and Sid was offended.

"I'm a Revenue Officer for the Internal Revenue Service," he blurted, immediately sorry he had done so. Doing so without being asked was like pleading for attention, and Sid Bloberg was a proud man. Thank God Myra had not been there to hear it.

Sid hadn't known it could get worse, but it did. For the first time, the tall, young man actually looked at him. His eyes were alive, unlike Sid's and Sid saw derisive laughter in them.

"Hey, that's great," he said. "You're the guy who takes the kids."

Spats was truly amused. Many people he knew said the income tax was oppressive, but of course he had never paid any, so he had no complaints. Sid realized he had been wrong about Slagle. The proof he had been wrong was the fact that Slagle knew his slogan. Slagle was intimidated just like all the others, wasn't he? Everyone was. The trouble was that everyone was taller than Sid. Everybody seemed to be talking down, even when he wasn't.

"Did you see the lady who was here a minute ago? About the size of the Queen Elizabeth, the one that floats?"

"Yes," said Sid. "I saw her."

"We're Bonnie and Clyde," said Spats. "We're in the rackets too."

Sid recoiled as if slapped. He was *not* in the rackets. He was a public servant, fighting chaos in the trenches. Mind churning, he struggled to prepare a sharp retort, but he rarely needed a sharp retort and therefore wasn't used to preparing them. Before he could recover, the ocean liner returned, and Spats bumped her into pier like a tug against the wall. She pointed.

"Sidney H. Bloberg, Revenue Officer, Collection Division, Internal Revenue Service. You're the man who takes the kids. Darling 'James,' this is the man I told you about."

Her remark ordinarily would be a compliment, but now Sid took offense. Besides, she was talking almost loudly enough to interrupt Vincent Blandino, not an easy thing to do.

"A man as important as you are probably doesn't remember me, Mr. Bloberg. I'm Elizabeth Ann McGillicuddy, but you don't have to remember that, because I won't be for long. I see that you've met my fiancé, 'James.' Isn't this an absolutely lovely party? The setting is just inspiring to the max. In fact, ..."

Sid waited until she reluctantly drew breath, then broke in. "McGillicuddy. Is that a Jewish name?" It was the closest he could come to sarcasm.

"Lord have mercy, no," she said. "It's as Irish as alcoholism. But I sympathize. We've been butchered too."

"So, what brings you here, Mr. Bloberg?" asked Spats. "Is this a raid?"

Sid tried to sound bland. The time for sarcasm was past. Now came dissimulation. He knew what he had to do. He was always at peace when he had a plan. The evil that emanated from this couple was intense, but they were not alone to blame. The room was festooned with evil. It stood in the air. There were tax crimes here, yes, but also other things almost as bad, such as murder. Tomorrow morning, Sid would be running down the data on Slagle and McGillicuddy, alias Bonnie and Clyde. If there were a can of worms here, Sidney H. Bloberg, Revenue Officer, would open it.

"My card," said Sid, handing Spats one of them.

"Mine," said Spats, responding in kind. Spats was well aware of the puerile game Sid was playing, but couldn't believe that a man so physically inoffensive could be dangerous. Sid put the card in his wallet and patted it lovingly.

The voice of Vincent Blandino rolled on, but the room faded out, and the dream took over. Sid was sitting behind a desk as big as a Navy carrier. There were many photographs with laudatory autographs on the wall, even one from the President. There was a name plate: "Sidney H. Bloberg, District Director." He was talking on the phone, saying, "Yes, Mr. Secretary."

When Sid's mind returned to the 123rd floor of Polyakov Tower, Blandino was still speaking, but Bonnie and Clyde, and the woman in black, were gone.

Myra was there. "I saw you with those people, Sidney. How did you get them to talk to you?"

Chapter Twenty Seven
Under Cover

"How many years have you been with us, Sid?"

"Nine," said Sid. His voice sounded unlike itself. He was not sitting behind the desk of the District Director. He was sitting in front of another desk, hat in lap like a supplicant, and the man questioning him with badly veiled irony was a manager brought in from Washington, who was a couple of years his junior. Sid didn't even know the man's name.

"And may I say, sir, that you have done a fine job." He reached across the desk and shook Sid's hand. "Is there anything you want to tell me, Sid?"

"Only that I like your tie."

"Thank you, Sid. I picked it out myself. I know you said that to impress me, and you have."

Of course Sid had said it to impress him! Sid had learned how to do that in the Success Management course. That's how he knew they were sending him a message. Sid did the same thing himself, all day, to an endless stream of "clients." He was a master at sending messages he could disavow if accused. Now, "they" were doing it to him. He had only one rival for the only job that would have meant a promotion, so of course his rival was firing a shot across his bow. Nothing could have surprised him less. Without seeming to, the idea was to put him on edge, where he could make mistakes.

Did they know about the fiasco at Wee People? They had to. Too many people had been involved to keep it secret. Sid couldn't kill them all. Obviously the fiasco was the reason for this meeting. Why didn't this bastard from Washington mention it? He didn't mention it precisely to keep Sidney on edge, the same thing Sid would have done.

"You conduct yourself like a man worth impressing," said Sid, making clear the fact that he was speaking of himself.

"I'll leave you my card," said the visiting dignitary, who left.

The Name of the King
182

Sid returned to his cubicle. It was obvious to him that he had to strike a blow, and do so quickly. Without one, the promotion he had sought for so long was in doubt. But what could he do? The data on McGillicuddy sat on his desk now. He had looked through it with eagerness that quickly turned to disgust. She had worked in a bank. She had always paid her taxes. In fact, the government owed her $69.43, because of a mistake she had made in addition. Her father was a supervisor for the Department of Sanitation. Her record was as clean as an operating room. He had found nothing at all on James K. Slagle, no returns, but also no telltale 1099s that would require them. Maybe Slagle should be turned over to C.I.D.

He looked through the glass across the vast room. Sid knew that in the far corner, too far to see, his rival, Alexandra Freitag, was smirking, like the man who had come from Washington. Alexandra wasn't a patriot, like Sid. She was a foreigner, an alien. How had it happened that she was able to challenge Sid? What mysterious force was protecting her? What kind of man would encourage a woman who had bad teeth accompanied by mausoleum breath magnified by bubble gum, a complexion that had launched a thousand quips, purple nails gnawed to the knuckle, fingers impregnated with nicotine to the wrist; and all the allure of a cholera victim in the final throes of dehydration. Why did she hate Sidney so much? Why didn't she go back to Russia, where she came from? She was probably a Communist, who had joined the Service to destroy.

Sid felt sorry for himself. He had been born too late. Long ago, before his time, during the bad, old days of anti-Semitism, the Jews had been a "minority," but there had been no "entitlements," no programs, no crocodile tears about the "deprivation" of his childhood. Now, the benefits flowed from Washington like extruding bologna, but the Jews were no longer a minority listed on government forms. It wasn't his fault he wasn't Black, Female, Hispanic, Oriental, American Indian or Other. It wasn't his fault he wasn't handicapped. He had asked for an official ruling, as to whether the Jews could be Others and was denied. Sid had to rely for advancement on his own treachery, dissimulation, avarice and cunning. He hadn't gotten where he was on favors. Wasn't he a computer *maven*? Wasn't the Service using some of the software he had developed? Wasn't he solving the problem of its antiquated technology? He was saving the Service literally tens of millions of dollars. It wasn't his fault that the prehistoric mainframe kept failing.

He looked at the newspaper. Very few people read the newspaper the way he did. Sid had no interest in foreign policy or fashion, sports, medicine, crime or sex. He didn't care about other countries or war and was utterly bored by the most important section in any newspaper: the comics. He read the newspaper to see who had appeared at which social events, who had bought or sold what, who could afford what, why, and, most important, who deserved investigation by

Sidney H. Bloberg, Revenue Officer, Collection Division, Internal Revenue Service.

There was a photograph. Sid saw a face he recognized, and some indistinct shapes in the glare of a flash bulb. The story said that the picture had been taken by a camera like the ones used to memorialize bank robbers, installed at a hospital to collect evidence about the "Jesus jerks" now terrorizing the elderly.

Sid gasped. The girl in the picture was Elizabeth Ann McGillicuddy, whose file sat on his desk now. The photograph caption said she was part of the gang. Was James K. Slagle also a member? What happened to the tens of thousands of dollars the story said the people were paying for their services? Was that money being declared on someone's return, and, most important, were the taxes being paid? The exultation that Elizabeth Ann's data had dissipated returned, and with it the evil Sid had felt in her presence. Again Sid was astounded by the power of his own intuition. If you assume people are crooks, however beautiful and charming they are, you are rarely wrong.

Imagine the doors that would open for the individual who caught the "Jesus Jerks." Sid saw the doors now, soundlessly yawning to reveal the massive desk, long enough to launch a U.S. Navy carrier attack, on which he saw the heavenly name plate: "Sidney H. Bloberg, District Director." In fact, he didn't need to imagine. The story said as much. Sid smiled. He knew what to do. He unleashed his intuition and could almost see Freitag's face, spit and nicotine encrusted on her lips, making Myra look like Bathsheba when David caught her bathing.

Ten days later, Abe stood at the main entrance of a large mental hospital in the Bronx, pretending to conduct a conversation with Honky Ryan. It was a few minutes after noon. Many people were going in and out. Moe had made the point that, by now, the authorities were expecting them to strike at night. Bogart had conducted reconnaissance and paved the way with fake credentials. The hospital would be unable to find out where they came from. They were waiting for James to give the signal that the video cameras had been disarmed.

At the beginning of their mission, Abe had been surprised when men like James appeared. Not any more. Abe no longer even asked who they were. The video cameras had become a problem, so James had arrived. Abe knew that Elizabeth Ann had brought him aboard, but that was all he knew, and he didn't ask. Abe didn't even know his last name. He certainly didn't even wonder why James knew exactly how to neutralize the cameras. Someone had been needed, so James had been sent. Abe had given up trying to understand. Things just happened. The only thing he couldn't accept was the fury with which the powers-that-were fought his mission. What were he and his little band doing wrong? The voice could explain it, but it hadn't talked to Abe for months.

Now, here was James coming out the door, kneeling to tie a shoelace, the signal that the cameras had been disarmed. The "Jesus Jerks" filtered in, pretending to be visitors, proceeding to assigned positions, staked out in advance. Bobby Combs, their spy downtown, had insisted they increase security, because of what he had heard there. The powers-that-were were furious. They called the group "jerks" but pressure from the top had driven them to frenzy. This would be a new experience, and a test. Abe had never done a mental case. Would his powers work?

He was walking down a hall with Spats and Moe, Bogart also at his side. Gibberish and strange cries came from the rooms, and Abe stopped where he heard the most disturbance. Bogart unlocked the door. A man was there, face in a corner, blood spattering from his nose, thrashing about in a straitjacket, groveling on the floor, fighting with a chair, uttering sounds that meant nothing, obviously unable to say what demons possessed him. He was a new patient. Bogart knew nothing about him.

Abe gently put a hand on his head. It was a cool hand, a soothing hand, and, instantly, the man became placid and cried. His shoulders heaved. He sighed. Abe was impressed. By now, he accepted the fact of his powers, but he never knew for sure what would happen. A tangible presence seemed to fill the room.

The window was open, and from outside they heard a crash, then the inevitable shouting. The terrible New York traffic was claiming new victims. Horns blew. There was another crash. They heard the mortal cries of one or more animals *in extremis*. Whatever was happening out there was surely the opposite of the peaceful spirit in the room.

From the beginning, Spats had known this was a scam. The fact that Elizabeth Ann had fallen for it was proof. But, what kind of scam was it? So far, he hadn't seen any money. Abe didn't ask for any. People just took care of him, people like Spats. He never gave an order--indeed, his temperament was mild, sweet, almost childlike--yet he had immense authority, so much that he didn't need to give orders. What was Abe's racket? Spats knew every scam there was, and had run most of them, but this one he couldn't figure out. Against his will, he was impressed. Wasn't he seeing all this with his own eyes? What better testimony could there be? It was difficult to do, but Spats shrewdly doubted his own eyes, knowing that, if he waited long enough, the fix would show up.

"What must I do to be saved, your lordship?" the man whispered.

"There's nothing you can do," Abe whispered. "If you ask, it's already done." Abe wondered. What was the meaning of what he had said? "Would you like me to take this thing off?" he asked, fingering the straitjacket.

"Yes."

The man bowed his head and cried, his tears washing away the madness. Abe looked at Bogart, who nodded, utterly nonplused. How could he report what he had seen to the *Journal of the American Medical Association*? In fact, there wasn't even one colleague with whom he could discuss it. He also couldn't discuss the fact that in the last week alone, three more of his patients had disappeared. The hospital administrator he had asked about them had been evasive, even afraid. They had simply "left." They were "vacationing in Europe." Their relatives had "picked them up." A colleague who specialized in geriatrics had mentioned something similar at a seminar. Why weren't the media investigating that? Why weren't the authorities denouncing it? Bogart decided to visit the Hall of Records.

Completely restored, the former victim turned. It was Sid, smiling in anticipation of the removal of the straitjacket. He had gone under cover. An investigator who really wants to know something must go under cover at some point. It had been easy to follow Elizabeth Ann for days. She had outsmarted herself. As she had said, she was an 800-pound gorilla, with a forest fire for hair. It had been easy to discover where the gang would strike next, and almost as easy to win the cooperation of the hospital. After Sid called Chief of Police Fatima al-Shekel, just in case, the bureaucrat in charge had acceded, had even been obsequious, no doubt in part because of some monkey business on his Schedule C. Besides, he had been favorably impressed by Sid's stoicism and spirit of sacrifice. It had been hard to sit in a straitjacket for hours, without even being able to scratch his nose. The wall had been inadequate for the purpose; not until he found the edge of metal protruding from the bench had he found peace, uttering crazy cries of joy at his deliverance. The solution, while blissful, unfortunately ruptured several zits, with the result that, when the others arrived, his resemblance to Rudolf the red-nosed reindeer was profound. The experience had almost driven him insane.

Needless to say, Sid had said nothing about his mission to his colleagues at the office. The jealous bastards there would have sabotaged it; a memo would have arrived, reminding him that such an undertaking was the province of the Intelligence Division. So, he had simply taken a couple of weeks well-earned leave, telling Myra he had to leave town for the Service.

He knew of course that unidentifiable pressure from the top had driven all segments of the metropolitan New York law enforcement community to a frenzy, but they had failed to stop the jerks. Their S.W.A.T. teams had been useless, along with their intelligence and main frames, precisely because the people running them were large, muscular and stupid. They had failed, but Sidney Herman Bloberg, Revenue Officer, Collection Division, Internal Revenue Service, soon to be District Director, had found, and was now penetrating, the gang.

He wouldn't move too quickly. Impatience could be fatal. First, he had to find out who belonged to the gang. Then, he had to find out where they got their money and buried their bodies, and, most important, whether they filed returns and paid, paid, paid. In the end, he would return in triumph and present the gang tied with a bow. What would Myra say then about Abe?

He and Spats smiled at each other. As Sid had expected, "James" was a member of the gang. "James" knew he worked for I.R.S. So what? The diabolical cleverness of Sid's plan not only didn't require him to deny his employment, but to use it. Sid had done his homework.

Abe finished removing the straitjacket, and tossed it on the bed. Sid rubbed his hands and wrists into sensation. The sound from the nearby intersection outside intensified. Moe left to find out what was happening.

"I'm alive, thanks to you," said Sid. "For the first time. Until you touched me, I was dead."

"It isn't because of me," said Abe.

"If you hadn't touched me, I'd still be dead."

"All I am is a tool."

"Abe, do you know who I am?"

"I know you're rotten with sin, like everyone else."

"Do you know which rotten sinner I am?"

"No."

"I'm Sid Bloberg."

Abe had not seen Sid for many years. Of course, he had changed. Abe knew he was an exalted government official. Shirley had made that so clear. What was Sid doing here? In the old days, before the voice, Abe would have hurried home to tell Shirley about the straitjacket. Now, he didn't care. He hadn't seen Shirley for so long. He missed her. By now, the bad times had faded from memory. Where was she? What had happened to his children?

"What happened, Sid?"

"Abe . . . ." Sid hung his head again. "I'm a tax collector, a publican." Thank God Sid had become a Bible scholar for the mission. Before he hit The Book, he had thought a publican was an English bartender.

"I know. The people demanded government. They weren't satisfied with God, so they're being punished."

"Abe, I'm not a tax collector any more. They kicked me out. Because I wasn't crooked."

"No one's perfect, Sid. Don't worry."

"They threw me in here. I thought I'd go crazy."

"You're all right now."

"But, you don't know how bad I've been. Mr. Slagle, don't you remember me? I'm the guy who takes your kids."

"Yes. I remember you."

"Please, Mr. Slagle. Forgive me!"

"I do."

The minute Spats saw him, he knew this was a sting, so that was all he said. He was furious. Sid's presence meant that a bust was coming down. When? If it came too soon, Spats's effort would be wasted. The job would not come off. No one on earth knew what Spats looked like except his mother and Elizabeth Ann, and Sid knew Elizabeth Ann, so there was danger. Thank God the doctor had told Elizabeth Ann to stay in bed. Sid was trying to ingratiate himself, collecting information, asking endless questions. Spats would answer all of them, trying to delay the bust. The Polyakov premiere was coming soon; after it, he and Elizabeth Ann would disappear.

They were walking down the stairs, filtering out as they had come, Sid looking as sane as psychiatrist George Bogart beside him. Other former patients were standing on the lawn. Some were at the telephones, telling loved ones to pick them up. A large crowd was on the corner. Moe appeared, breathing hard.

"The cops are here, but not for us." He pointed. "That's the mother of all collisions."

They piled into their cars and turned on the radio. ". . . the mother of all collisions," said an authoritative voice, "compounded by the appearance in traffic of a load of pigs, thought to have escaped from a truck inbound from Secaucus. Terrified and confused, they ran to their deaths in the traffic oinking like swine, with the result that harried drivers smashed into each other trying to avoid them. Our correspondent on the scene reports that the northbound roadway is presently covered with medium pork chops."

Spats was impressed. The diversion was something he could have thought of himself. Abe had said nothing about it.

Chapter Twenty Eight
Sisterhood

ould somebody tell me, would somebody please tell me, how a terrorist gang can operate in broad daylight, for this long, in New York City, and get away with it? Would somebody please tell me that?"

The Chief leaned across the long, oval table on her knuckles and glowered at her commanders. They couldn't look at her. They knew she was right. The thing had started as a joke, escalated to an irritation, erupted as a problem, and now had metastasized to an emergency, but all they had were some newspaper photographs.

"What in hell are we? Does any one know that?"

The Chief was angry. She was harried. The doctor had told her to stay off her feet. Light flashed like thunderbolts from her medals and the jewel in her tooth. Personally, she didn't give a damn if some nutcakes invaded an old-age home and spent some time with the inmates. Weren't such institutions constantly pleading for people to do that? So what if the inmates wound up dancing on the lawn? This was New York City, for God's sake, not Peoria. The Chief would go head-to-head, nut for nut, with Los Angeles, any day of the week.

But she was only the Chief, and the pressure was coming down from so high up even she didn't know where it started. Now they had invaded a nut house and liberated one of their own. A dangerous lunatic in a straitjacket had escaped. The pressure was even worse. Why? She couldn't understand why this was so important that it had temporarily shut down Operation Spats Davis--the biggest bank robber since Willie Sutton--even though nobody even knew what he looked like. Now the farce was threatening her considerable reputation in social work, minority rights, fund-raising and crisis-management, just when she was getting ready to run for mayor, which was to be the crown jewel of her distinguished career. For just one instance, it was she who had pioneered the unisex rest rooms at headquarters. It was no surprise that she had a national reputation as an innovative reformer.

"Steinmetz, you're supposed to be in charge of this, God help you. What do we know? Not what you think. What do we *know*?"

"We know two things, Chief," said the Manhattan commander. "We know that the man who started it and runs it is Abraham Goldstein."

"Abraham Goldstein, fellow Semite, whose tribe stands falsely accused, even by some here, despite denials, of trying to send the prophet Jesus to perdition."

"Chief . . . ."

"No offense intended, Steinmetz. Needless to say, I'm not speaking for attribution, just in case, despite our best efforts, there are some media here." The Chief had done her homework. Not only did she know when not to speak for attribution, a skill for lack of which many distinguished careers had been lost; she even knew that the word "media" is plural. Even many of the media bastards didn't know that. "Let me see Brother Goldstein's rap sheet."

"There isn't any," said Steinmetz, remaining impassive, which wasn't easy. Steinmetz couldn't wait to vote against her; she was a traitor to her race, besides which he had developed a prostate condition owing to the Chief's rest room reforms. It was a disgrace and a discomfort for the Manhattan commander of police to have to journey out to Ali's Original Indian Bloody Mess, where the comfort stations were rigidly segregated and hygienically maintained as they had been in New Delhi--despite the vigilance of the Health Department of the City of New York--whenever he needed relief, while the Chief could retire when necessary to a private Jane, complete with hot tub and imported French bidet, that belonged in the Waldorf-Astoria. The press knew all about the scandal--they ate at the Bloody Mess themselves--but wouldn't expose it because they were perverts. Steinmetz also didn't happen to believe that a chief of police should be pregnant. A chief of police should command, should demand, should swear like a sailor and chain-smoke cancer cigarettes. Well, wasn't the chief doing all that? In fact, she was even more hysterical than usual today. Why?

"No rap sheet? You're telling me, Steinmetz, that a man who is terrorizing the city of New York--and who has completely paralyzed the Police Department, thanks to you--doesn't have a record?"

"About 7 years ago, he got a parking ticket, which was later thrown out. For 9 years, he's been a garbageman with the Department of Sanitation."

"All right!" the Chief pointed a manicured finger in triumph. "It's coming into focus. Those garbage bastards are a bunch of racketeers. And you can't fire them. The city never should have agreed not to cut the number of trucks. Steinmetz, what the hell is wrong with you? Didn't you know that? Didn't you know they agreed to kick back 25% of the savings from those two-man trucks? That costs us $16.5 million a year. Didn't you find all that on Mr. Abraham Goldstein's rap sheet, Steinmetz?"

She was campaigning for mayor even here. Economy in government was one of her issues. The Chief smelled victory. She would still be pregnant on election day, which was not an accident, and New Yorkers would seize the chance to choose her and score another first. Sure, Los Angeles mayor Bradley was Black and was Beautiful, but was he pregnant? Was he a single mother? She rested her multiplying midriff on the conference table to prove the point.

Cover all the bases. That was her fundamental principle of governmental science. Promise whatever anyone wants, unless he has no votes, in which case stand firm. By the time the facts caught up with the promise, she was long since gone. Thus, she had appointed Steinmetz Manhattan commander to please the Jews. Needless to say, he was still complaining. She had integrated the rest rooms to please the faggots and her fellow feminists. She had converted to Islam to please the Muslims. She didn't know Islam from slam-dunk, but the fact that a white woman would do so had endeared her to elements of the large New York black community. Indeed, wouldn't her child be half black? Five times a day, she abruptly departed from wherever she was for "prayer"--even though she didn't know praying from a mantis--which not only impressed the congregation, but concealed her potentially embarrassing present need to spend considerable time meditating in her unintegrated private rest room.

Yet, she was also smart enough to smell fear. The incumbent mayor had named her Chief, thinking he would thereby score a coup. "If you can't dazzle them with brilliance, baffle them with buffalo chips," was the theory of statecraft his parents had spent many thousands sending him to the John F. Kennedy School of Government at Harvard University to learn, and, until now, they had always been thousands well spent. Too late, he realized he had created a Boris Karloff monster, who had escaped from the lab and turned upon her maker.

Chief Fatima al-Shekel, *née* Naomi June Rosenberg, had learned everything she knew from her mentor, so she knew he was now preparing a counterblow. She had done everything she could to prepare for it, but she was nervous. Albert Holley sat in the room, behind her where she could not see him. He was an enemy, of course. That was why he sat behind her. Hadn't the mayor asked her to let him participate?

But why? What did the Goldstein gang have to do with the National Reserve? Albert Holley clearly was part of the mayor's plan, despite which Chief Fatima had let him see and hear some of her campaign strategy, along with her complete control of these male commanders. It certainly could do no harm to show him her mastery of the issues. Perhaps by sheer force of charm she could convert him to a double agent-in-place. Wouldn't that be a stunning joke on the mayor.

But he was sitting behind her, in a corner, not saying a word, and his very unobtrusion was obtrusive, in the same way that the unknown is often more frightening than the known. The hair was rising on the back of her neck. Should she take her mirror from her purse, pretend to check her face, and study him? No, Holley would see her do it and would chuckle at her puerility, while the commanders would chuckle because she was "a woman, after all." Damn right, she was a woman, and she was in charge!

"Forgive me, Mr. Holley," she said, turning to face him, typically confrontational, easing her belly off the table. "I realize that in the heat of battle, public zeal and the frenzy of professionalism we have been ignoring you. We are not used to visitors here in the War Room, especially none so distinguished. Would you care to comment or have anything explained?"

Albert Holley's smile never left his face, even when he slept. His dewlap gently brushed the knot on his tie by Givenchy. Naomi June cum Fatima could barely suppress an expression of disgust.

He said softly, "May I say, madam, and gentlemen, that, while I came here fully prepared to be impressed, I was not at all prepared for the breathtaking competence you show."

There was an appreciative murmur from the assembled commanders. With just one, short sentence, Holley already had them in his hand. He was president of the New York Reserve for good reason.

"May I take a moment to explain my presence, Madam Chief?" He did not bluster, like the others. Speaking softly, he made them listen.

Fatima bowed. His dewlap dangled as he talked. If he embraced her, would it touch her skin? If it did, she knew she would scream and throw up. Surely he must see her shudders.

"I'm here at the invitation of your gracious Chief as a representative of the business community of our great city." His voice came from his mouth--almost simpering--but his mouth was still smiling. How was that possible? Fatima decided he was a wimp.

"You have impressed me. Now, please, permit me to impress you. We are well aware of the effort you have expended in your hunt for the anarchists. The fact that they are still at large is troubling. Already, we see signs of instability in the economy. Some of our medical facilities--world-renowned for good reason--have been disrupted. A couple of days ago, a delegation of some of the most distinguished medical practitioners in this country expressed their fears on the subject in a seminar at my club. Only this morning, the executive director of a large group of retired people called me to announce his concern. The pharmaceutical industry, in particular, which yields billions of dollars in revenue--some of which finds its way to your department, may I add--has been endangered, which has international ramifications. Among our foreign members, for instance, is the distinguished David Polyakov, chairman of the company that bears his name, which is a powerful economic force in this city and the nation. Our fear is that the victims of this gang could delay, or even forego, the tested therapies and approved medications they need."

Steinmetz raised a hand. No! Fatima fixed him with a rapier glance and willed him to shut up. Albert Holley turned to him and nodded.

Steinmetz said, "When we finally find these people, and we shall, under the inspired leadership of our Chief, what will they be charged with?"

Albert Holley was impressed. What *would* they be charged with? The subtlest, legal minds in the city were now working on the problem, and the best they had come up with was trespassing, sedition and practicing medicine without a license.

"I don't know what you mean," said Holley.

Fatima took command. "Commander Steinmetz no doubt alludes to one of the stoutest planks in my present campaign for mayor: economy in government. What he means, Albert, is that if we are to expend the resources we shall need to catch this gang, we must have enough good and righteous charges to choke a giraffe. Without them, the mayor won't be able to justify the expense."

Albert Holley's smile broadened. He hadn't met Fatima before today, and hadn't expected her to be so obtuse and coarse. Why on earth had the mayor appointed her?

"I guess I just don't know what they've done," said Steinmetz.

Fatima al-Shekel shuddered with power. She was squeezing the mayor's testicles in a vise, and the more she did so, the better she'd look. Albert Holley's dewlap danced, and she didn't blame it. She no longer cared what Steinmetz said.

"I appreciate your candor, Madam Chief," Holley said. "I must say your reputation for plain talk is deserved. I have just this morning visited with the District Attorney, who assures me you will have what you need. In fact, if I may say so, all great problems are great opportunities. That belief is the fountainhead of the modest success I have enjoyed. A political meeting would of course be inappropriate here, but the biggest problem the Goldstein gang has created is in Washington, D.C. Surely you understand."

"No." What else could she say? She didn't understand. "But if you tell us what you're talking about, I'll listen. I have too much to worry about here to wonder about Washington."

"Of course you do. You probably don't have time to keep abreast of the fact that the war on cancer is now approaching denouement. I was in Washington last week and dined with the President and First Lady." Holley looked from one to the other. "May I speak in confidence?"

"Of course," said Fatima, not mentioning her suspicion that a spy was in the room. How else did Goldstein know everything she did?

"The President will soon present Congress his proposal for national health insurance."

Steinmetz rapped on the table. "Hear, hear."

"But the Goldstein gang could make the need for such a program redundant."

"Why?" asked Fatima.

"Why would we need the benefits such an economical program could bring, including eternal gratitude to government, if a fool and his clowns can walk into a hospital and convince desperately ill people they are well? The President could be embarrassed. The Congress could be embarrassed."

Fatima snorted. "You couldn't embarrass Congress if you caught it naked as a jaybird in bed with a pelican."

"Imagine the rewards waiting for the police chief and commanders who succeed in bringing this conspiracy to a halt--who put the man in the straitjacket back where he belongs."

A murmur rustled down the table like a breeze through Johnson grass. At last they understood.

Steinmetz shook his head. "Mr. Holley, we've been trying. The trouble is these jerks are not career criminals."

"Why is that a problem?"

"It's a problem because they don't associate with other crooks. And they've been able to outguess us. It's almost supernatural."

"Earlier you said you know two things. You've told us one. What is the other?"

"We have a photograph. The lady in the photograph is Elizabeth Ann McGillicuddy. As you see, Elizabeth Ann McGillicuddy is pregnant, and by now is probably as pregnant as it is possible to be." Steinmetz looked pointedly at the Chief, who typically was resting her tum-tum comfortably on the table, and, for obvious reasons, involuntarily felt a sisterly kinship for Elizabeth Ann.

Fatima said, "The photograph you are looking at shows the subject participating in one of the Goldstein operations."

"Her record typically is clean," said Steinmetz. "She worked in a bank. She is close, very close, to a businessman who is so clean he doesn't even have fingerprints. Her father is a supervisor at the Department of Sanitation."

"Would it be true, commander, that a man without fingerprints doesn't want to be found?"

"Could be."

"Why doesn't he want to be found? Who is he?"

"We don't know."

Fatima said, "Your trouble, Steinmetz, is that you don't know how to listen. Thank God I finally found time to take a look. Abraham Goldstein is a garbage truck driver. Frank McGillicuddy is a garbage supervisor. Doesn't that tell you anything?"

"This case stinks?" asked Steinmetz.

"As I've already told you, it tells us that the conspiracy is centered in the Department of Sanitation. Don't you see that? The bastards are bored. They sit around half the day with their fingers in their ears and collect $40,000. Damn it,

Steinmetz, didn't you know that Allah makes mischief for idle hands? No wonder the garbage isn't collected. Did you know the rest of the country calls us Garbage City? I was at a police convention in Minneapolis recently. That's what they said."

"So, what do you want us to do, Chief?" Steinmetz asked.

"What do I want you to do, Steinmetz? How the hell did you ever get to be commander?"

"You picked me, Chief, because you're such a brilliant leader of men."

"You're right. What I want you to do, Steinmetz, in case you didn't know, is go to the garage where those sanitation bastards keep their trucks and pick up Mr. Goldstein. I want you to bring Mr. Goldstein here."

"I tried that long ago, Chief. It didn't work."

"Do you mind telling me why it didn't work, Commander Steinmetz?"

"No. I don't mind at all."

"Steinmetz . . . ."

"It didn't work because Abraham Goldstein is now on psychiatric leave."

"Well, of course he's on psychiatric leave. Where would you expect a man who thinks he's Jesus Christ to be?"

"Chief, I would expect such a man to be in deep *kimchi*. Even Jesus Christ, who thought he was Jesus Christ and was right, wound up in deep *kimchi*."

"Did you go to his home?"

"His wife kicked him out, because he says he's Jesus Christ. She doesn't know where is."

"Does he have any friends?"

"Moe Stern. Another garbage truck driver. Disappeared."

Holley said softly, almost whispering, "You said earlier, Commander Steinmetz, that the gang can outguess you. Suppose there's a leak."

Fatima jumped to her feet and put her tummy on the table. "Impossible, Albert. Are you calling one of my commanders a spy?" The men looked from one to the other, uneasy.

"Commander Steinmetz said himself they are not career criminals. Could someone in the Department have misplaced loyalties, be confused?"

The possibility of spies had never occurred to Steinmetz. Could one of the commanders, or someone he was close to, be one of the jerks? Goldstein looked so normal. He could be anyone. Steinmetz made a note to ask Bobby Combs to look into it. He and Bobby were thick as thieves.

The commanders left the conference room, newly inspired. Fatima, too, tried to leave, but Holley put a hand on her arm.

"I know you will do what is necessary, Madam Chief. Please accept my respects in advance." He bowed and kissed her hand. Fatima was sure she could feel his dewlap dragging on her fingers. She stiffened, revolted by waves of disgust, praying to Allah that she would not throw up. As soon as he left, she went to her private, sexist rest room and did so.

Later, she sat at her desk depressed. The time had come to call in the S.W.A.T. teams, with all the civil liberties problems they would bring. They were like mad dogs with fleas. They had nothing against the Constitution, if it didn't get in their way. And guess which enlightened police chief would have to clean up their mess.

The telephone rang. She took off her ear ring and put it on the desk. "Hello, Chief? May I call you Fatima? This is Alexandra Freitag, I.R.S." Fatima thought of hanging up. What did those bastards want? Even within the law enforcement community, they were pariahs. She actually picked up her earring. Yet, this was a woman, and Sisterhood was stronger than whim. Freitag talked while Fatima listened. While she did so, Fatima had the odd impression, despite the deepening shadows, that it was growing lighter. The birds began to sing. She heard music.

Chapter Twenty Nine
Tax Man

Sid put his favorite song on the turntable and began to dance, by himself. Myra wouldn't join him. It was "Tax Man," by the Beatles. He loved to hear how his English counterpart taxed British streets, seats, heat and feet. Such was the intensity of Sid's patriotism, that he believed the government should confiscate everything--the tax should be 100%--except for what the people needed to stay alive to make more that the government could tax. Sure, the Beatles were being sarcastic. The more sarcastic they were, the more he loved it. They were sarcastic because they had made all that money singing about dope, and probably were bloody well flummoxing the limey I.R.S. Sid turned on the television and swaggered to a chair. He deserved to swagger. Soon the world would know.

He wore the surplus jungle suit from Nam he had bought while wearing impenetrable sunglasses in an Army-Navy store, along with official camouflage face paint, spit-shined combat boots and the .45 auto stuck in his Sam Browne belt, slide cocked, magazine full, a round in the chamber, waiting only for his thumb to depress the safety so that it could terminate a target of opportunity with extreme prejudice--ready for anything, anywhere, any time, anyhow. This was the real Sid Bloberg, patriot, only a platonic reflection of which his victims and colleagues ever saw, because God had not made him big enough to be a member of S.W.A.T. Only these four walls and only Myra saw what he really was.

The evening news was on the screen, along with a picture of Abe Goldstein. A voice explained how much Abe was wanted.

Myra cried softly, dabbing a tissue to her eyes. "Poor Abe. Poor, poor Abe."

Sidney H. Bloberg, patriot, turned off the Beatles and smiled in triumph, tapping on his side arm. "What about poor Abe?"

Myra didn't know and couldn't answer. Abe was a witness to her disappearing youth, which was too silly to mention. If she did so, Sid, the Nazi, would laugh.

Fatima al-Shekel, Chief of Police, was talking on the screen.

"Traitor!" Sid yelled.

She, too, smiled in triumph, even more inflated, thanks to physiology, than Sid. A microphone in a masculine hand, appeared at her lips. "Chief, can you tell us where the investigation into the Goldstein gang stands?"

"As you know, I cannot comment on an investigation in progress. Something I say could jeopardize my men. Very shortly, perhaps this evening, I shall have a historic announcement on the subject. I think the people will be pleased. Suffice it to say at the moment that the city again stands in debt to our dedicated police officers on the streets."

Sid laughed. "So you're going to have an announcement, you bitch?"

"Why is she a traitor?" asked Myra.

"Why? Because when she and I went to P.S. 166, she was Naomi June Rosenberg."

Sid strode with purpose around the room. Tomorrow morning, at his own press conference, he would expose them and tell Naomi the traitor and her police where they were. He knew them all: George Bogart, M.D., the psychiatrist; Rabbi Stanley B. Garlick, another traitor to his race; James K. Slagle, which was probably not his real name because he certainly wasn't the F.D.I.C. official he claimed to be; and police lieutenant Bobby Combs, the spy. Sid planned to make the announcement in his office, and lusted to see Naomi June's expression when she heard about Bobby. With one press conference, Sid would squash her like the bloated insect she was, would do the same for the alien slime bag Freitag, would put I.R.S. in banner headlines as the premier law enforcement agency in the country, and, most important, would give himself a death grip on the promotion that would lead to the holy nameplate.

Sid had been surprised to find that there was no tax aspect to the case. The gang was making no money on its raids. It was supported by big donations from big-earners like Bogart and "Slagle." Of course, Sid had checked their tax returns; they weren't taking deductions. Sid had to admit he didn't know what they were doing that was illegal, but his job wasn't morals, it was law enforcement. He was "just doing his job." He had played their game, dissembled, pretended to be one of them so well they believed it, and now he was dissembling for Myra, trying with difficulty to withhold the news until she saw him tomorrow on the 50 inch screen. Then he would find out who "Slagle" really was, and why he didn't file.

There was a peremptory knock at the door, made by a man with a heavy fist, who was coming in whether you liked it or not, and for whom the knock was an annoying formality. Sid had knocked on many doors like that himself.

"Mr. Bloberg!" said an authoritative voice, the same voice Sid used when he visited a "client."

Who the hell was that? Who dared knock like that at the door of Sidney H. Bloberg, Revenue Officer, Collection Division, Internal Revenue Service? Sid got mad, stomped to the door and threw it open, so hard that the knob slightly enlarged the hole in the wall he had made during previous conversations with Myra. Four meat eaters stood on the mat she had bought in Hawaii, all in the terminal phases of monstrous pituitary excess, U.S. Choice arteries pumping inexorably toward massive coronary thrombosis, galvanized by years of headline *hubris* absolving them of any insult to the Bill of Rights on behalf of THE CHILDREN and the WAR AGAINST DRUGS. They were stooping slightly, as if preparing to enter a doll house.

"Who the hell are you?" asked Sid. He knew who they were; S.W.A.T. was written all over them. He had led many a raid just like this with men from whom they had been cloned. Why were they here? What did they want? Behind them, Sid saw others in full combat gear crouching on the lawn.

The behemoths at the door did not answer Sid's question. Although his jungle suit and face paint did offer some cover, they were not sufficient to conceal him completely, and the behemoths struggled to understand what they were looking at.

"He's got a gun!" somebody shouted. Sid never found out who it was. They came through the door like "crap through a goose," as George Patton would have put it. Furniture splintered. The television set fell from its stand and went dead. Myra screamed. Sid was on his back on the carpet. The Sam Browne was gone and the .45 with it, destined for a property room tagged as evidence, along with the jungle suit.

He was in his underwear, but the invaders were replacing the jungle suit with a new garment. What was it?

"Myra!" he shouted. "Get to the telephone. Call!"

She ran as directed to the telephone, finger poised at the buttons. "Whom shall I call?"

Whom *should* she call? The police? Ridiculous! Weren't they the biggest abusers of human rights in the country? Weren't they abusing Sid right now?

"Call the office!" he screamed.

"Shut up, Sid," said a voice.

"How do you put this thing on?" asked another.

Whatever they were doing, they were finished. Lifting Sid like a putter inside a golf bag, they left.

"Myra!" Sid shouted. "Myra!"

Sid's voice faded into louder voices, slamming doors and screeching tires. In a moment, all was again like the developer's brochure that had brought Sid and Myra to this peaceful, suburban refuge years before, far from the crime, pollution, racial amalgamation and taxes, taxes, taxes of the city, so far that no one who hadn't been there would have believed the outrage had taken place.

Myra was touched. The last thing Sid had said was her name. Didn't this prove that, despite everything, despite his utter lack of charm and consideration, his dictatorial and insulting manner, his bad breath and hostility to foreplay, his baldness and belching at table, he still loved her? Myra sank to the couch in reverie, tinted with the satisfaction that the strutting bastard had finally gotten what he deserved and now knew how it felt to be a doormat. The question of who had taken him away did not arise.

By morning, after a frightful evening without television that felt like "Night of the Living Dead," during which in panic she had read the erotic parts of a best-seller by Laura Ingalls Wilder, Myra had mastered herself sufficiently to call the bunco artist called Repair Man, who replaced the violated set in time for her to see Chief of Police Fatima al-Shekel, who filled the screen, pointing to Sidney H. Bloberg, Revenue Officer, Collection Division, Internal Revenue Service, who wore a straitjacket.

Doing a bad job of keeping herself under control, Fatima said, "I'm pleased today to report the first break in the Goldstein case. The problem is more serious than we thought. These people have even infiltrated the federal government, as you see. Most of them don't look like criminals. They could be anybody. There is no reason to panic, but, with some exceptions, as in this case, they look like you and me. This is Sidney H. Bloberg, I.R.S. Revenue Officer, an important member of the gang, a victim of the delusion they share."

Sid Bloberg did not look like himself. Despite his pectus cockatrivus the swagger was gone. His remaining hairs were askew, exposing the bald facts. His eyes, ordinarily so alert despite the dead look, saw nothing. There was fear on his face, disgust and betrayal. The director cut to a close-up of Freitag's tobacco-stained teeth, spittle flying from the paint-encrusted lips, joy blowin' in the wind of her dinosaur breath.

"We never suspected a thing," said Freitag.

Nothing was more powerful than Sisterhood. Fatima loved I.R.S. Until now, she had never fully understood how much. She remembered thinking of hanging up on Freitag, and shuddered. Fatima made the silent promise to stop concealing income on her tax return.

"Ask Bogart," Sid screamed. "He's one of them!"

The camera cut to George Bogart, M.D. "No, I'm not surprised. Many patients think the doctor is the villain. It's a normal symptom of the disease."

That night, the national news showed Sid's arrest. Every detail had been recorded by Sid's next-door neighbor, who smiled and smiled, but was an illegal tax protester, and knew that he would nail Sid if he secretly recorded him long enough with the mini-cam he had bought for the purpose. The S.W.A.T. officers who had conducted the raid were surprised and delighted to see themselves brutalizing Sid. Maybe the coverage would help dissipate the mystery of why they "didn't get no respect."

* * *

George Bogart, M.D., was sad, to the bone and spirit. The moment of truth had come and he had failed. He had lied about Sid. Sid had told the truth, but the psychiatrist, in weakness, had lied to save himself. In the old days, Bogart would have seen his own psychiatrist, but that religion had failed, as had everything before it. Now, Bogart himself had failed--Sid had trusted him and been betrayed--and he was weary. The others had tried to reassure him, blamed his lapse on the flesh and reminded him of Peter, but he would not be reassured. He recognized in himself the symptoms of clinical depression, compounded by his recent discovery at the Hall of Records. Every one of the patients who had disappeared was dead, the ones who had "gone home," and the ones who had "left for European vacations." He had seen the death certificates, all of them. The "relatives" who had come to take them away had lied. Did the victims have anything in common? *Were* they victims? Bogart was not a detective, and didn't know, except that all the documents apparently had been prepared by the same man. Did his discoveries mean anything? Should he report them, and, if so, to whom? Bogart had been betrayed, first by psychiatry and now by himself. Maybe he should just give himself up and tell the authorities he was a member of the group, as Sid had said.

"What would that accomplish?" Abe had asked.

"It would free Sid."

"No," said Bobby Combs. "It would just discredit you. Sid would stay where he is."

As a psychiatrist, Bogart had been a valuable recruit, providing respectability when it was needed, and funds to pay the bills. All that would be lost, were he to do as he proposed.

"Have you asked yourself why you want to do this?" asked Abe.

"To atone."

"I've read that when Teddy Roosevelt went to a wedding, he wanted to be the bride; when he went to a funeral, he wanted to be the corpse."

Bogart nodded. Of course! He had been humoring himself. He hadn't seen it. Yet, Abe, without a psychiatric residency, even without a degree, had explained it. Tears came to Bogart's eyes.

"Suppose Sid talks?" asked Bobby, of no one in particular.

"About what?" asked Honky Ryan.

"About us. They'd know everything." Bobby became morose. Like the criminals he had arrested for many years, he had never thought he could be caught. In the darkness, he saw disgrace and the end of his career. For the first time, he realized what it meant to be committed to a cause. Was it worth even the total cure of his wife's psoriasis?

"No one would believe him," said Tom Chase. "No one believed what he said about George."

"The *people* wouldn't believe him," said Abe. "The government would. The government says he's crazy, but doesn't believe it."

"We're finished," Bobby whispered. "They can make anybody talk."

"Not Sid," said Abe.

"We need to free Sid ourselves," said rabbi Garlick. The rabbi had visited Sid, and been mortified by what he had seen. Sid was one of his people, like Moe Stern, and always bought the most expensive seats. The rabbi had been amazed when Sid became a member of the group. He didn't know what to feel about it, but Sid's present status certainly reflected on the rabbi.

"Yes, we do," said Abe, "but we don't know how."

Spats smiled. "Let me figure something out."

A couple of weeks later, precisely at noon, Sid sat on the cot in his private quarters in the state hospital for the criminal insane, staring blindly at his hands. The authorities were taking no chances. In the time since his arrest, he had passed through several textbook phases. He had banged his head on whatever was available; screamed his innocence to the walls and his interrogators until they heard his voice depart. He had never experienced such frustration, even as a child. A month ago, he had exercised considerable, growing power. Now, he had less authority than a five-year-old. He had lost everything: wife, career, reputation, livelihood. But, he was innocent! He had been framed by the alien feminoid Alexandra Freitag!

No one listened to him. No one believed, just as he had never believed when he was trying to build a case of conspiracy and his own "clients" had tearfully told him they were innocent. He had never known or even wondered how they felt. Until now. Now, the only things anyone wanted to know from Sid were the names of the other members of the "gang."

Yet, there is a limit to how long the mind can sustain an emotion. However prodigious, there was a limit even to Newton's mental force. After a while, the wellspring of Sid's indignation ran dry. He began to realize that Freitag was just a symptom of his own overweening ambition. Hadn't he concocted the scheme that had led to his demise? Hadn't he outsmarted himself? Wasn't he a wise guy, who had ignored so many pleas like his own? Didn't he refuse to "fifty-three" a target until he was dead? Hadn't he tried to shut down that center for the handicapped? Thank God Elizabeth Ann had intervened. Didn't he deserve what was happening? Wasn't he as guilty as they said he was? Hadn't he been doomed from the beginning? Sid had been humbled as low as a man can be, and he couldn't save himself.

He stopped banging his head against the wall. He stopped screaming and began to cry. His interrogators saw the tears and knew they were a trick, which kindled their investigative zeal to fury.

"Talk, you little bastard! Give us the names!"

Someone help me, Sid pleaded, knowing as he did so, that no one would. Why would someone help him? Sure, George Bogart had condemned him. He was worthless. He deserved to be condemned. Myra had called him a Nazi. That's what he was.

But he hadn't talked. He hadn't talked because in the shadows at the ceiling he saw Abe's face. He had treated Abe contemptuously and run him down to Myra, but Abe had welcomed him, excused him, protected him. Were Sid to talk, he would earn Abe's lasting contempt, and would deserve it. Bogart and the others would call him traitor too. Myra would find out. He would lose her. Maybe he already had.

So, he said nothing. Silence was his final refuge, the last piece of flesh on the bone.

"Okay, you little bastard," said his tormentors. "We'll just let you stew."

They had secured him in the straitjacket to a chair anchored to the floor, his back to the rectangular glass peephole reinforced with chicken wire, and left him strictly alone.

"It's for your own good, you lousy traitor. If you split your head on the wall, you won't be able to give us those names. Don't go crazy, now. Take all the time you need."

He was a traitor if he didn't talk, and would be a traitor if he did. Was he crazy already? He didn't know. By now, the reality he had always been so sure of was a Chinese puzzle. He certainly was damned. Savoring the peace of being left alone at first, he knew only that his tormentors were the enemy and that he had to endure. After a while, the solitude he had welcomed became a torture. However bad it had been the first time, he had arranged it. It had been part of his plan. Now, he was utterly powerless in fact, outsmarted, without hope.

He was dozing, when the door opened. "Who is it?" he called.

Bogart was there, with a couple of others, and they walked around the chair to face him. "Sid, we're here to help."

Sid smiled. Tears were on his cheeks. "George, I didn't talk."

"I know you didn't, Sid. Abe said so." Bogart touched his shoulder and saw that he was calm. There was peace in his eyes, peace without narcotics, electric shock, psychoanalysis and Zen. Bogart couldn't understand the mystery. "Sid, I'm sorry I said what I did."

"You had to say it, George. You had to protect Abe."

Bogart began to undo the straitjacket. Sid shook his head. "Don't do that, George. You'll get into trouble."

"Abe has other plans."

The tears cleared, and Sid saw Myra. She, too, was crying, into a handkerchief. Now that Sid had been humbled, her frustrated maternity found voice. She fell on his neck, complicating Bogart's efforts to liberate him. "What have they done to you, dearest? Come to Mama."

"Sid, this is 'Harry Houdini,'" said Bogart. "He'll take your place."

"Harry Houdini" gloated and prayed that Bogart would hurry. He couldn't wait to get into the straitjacket. This was the chance he had been waiting for to silence the skeptics for good, including Bogart himself. Bogart had never been able to cure "Harry." Now, he was glad. "Harry" was meant to perform this noble service. Later, would he know what he had done?

Despite Myra's interference, Bogart got the job done. "Remember," he told "Harry," "you can't leave until sundown."

"Harry" smiled. "Trust me."

Since he wasn't Harry Houdini at all, but Terry Ash, Bogart knew he would be there a long time, but played along. At the door, he turned to inspect. From the rear, in the straitjacket, Terry closely resembled Sid, especially after the job Jim Slagle had done. Jim was sure a man of many talents.

"Good luck, 'Harry,'" Bogart called.

"Luck has nothing to do with it, doc. You'll see."

Bogart locked the door. They left, Sid between them, still at peace, reveling in the freedom to move. No one saw them. No one saw them get into a car, or saw the car slowly depart. No one saw the car drive up a ramp into a truck. When the switch finally was discovered, at the end of the day, no one would be able to explain it. "Harry" would tell them it was all his idea. By now, after a couple of weeks of deep hypnosis, he believed it himself.

By the next morning, Sid and Myra were safely installed in a farmhouse in gorgeous, rural Pennsylvania, with new names and new lives. Myra wouldn't know it for a while, but she was pregnant. Sid was already at work on something new.

Bogart was in his office when he heard the news: "Police authorities today confirmed that Sidney H. Bloberg, renegade I.R.S. agent, has escaped again. The room at the state hospital for the criminal insane, where Bloberg had been held in a straitjacket since his capture, was still locked, but the straitjacket was empty, and Bloberg was gone.

"How he did it, and whether anyone else was involved, isn't known at this time, but Chief of Police Fatima al-Shekel says the Department has several strong leads. Bloberg is a member of the gang known alternately as 'Jesus jerks' and the 'Goldstein gang,' the leader of which is suspended garbage truck driver Abe Goldstein, who says he's Jesus Christ."

So, Terry really was Harry Houdini. Bogart was more in awe than ever. Where had Terry gone?

Chapter Thirty
Unmasked

Horst Krüger debarked from his private 747. As his foot hit the tarmac at J.F.K. International Airport, he was sure he heard an echo. Why not? he chuckled. Wasn't he a conqueror, coming to take charge? The echo was the voice of history, beckoning to him.

His skin tingled. Tiny needles of disgust danced on his pores. He wore white gloves. Anything he touched here in the world's largest Jewish city, had probably been contaminated by Jews, and was crawling with Semitic microbes. Because of mongrelization, anyone could be a Jew. Of course, he took pains to maintain his cover. Without waiting to be asked, he told people his gloves were necessary because of his "allergies." He didn't tell them what he was allergic to.

The limousine entourage was waiting, complete with police escort, and he sank into the cushions. With the doors closed, the tinted windows raised and the air conditioning, he was largely insulated and could observe at leisure. Soon, they crossed the Tri-Boro bridge and were cruising down F.D.R. Drive, skillfully evading the peasants who had no police escort and so had to obey the speed limit. No doubt most of them were Jews. Krüger was one of the few people in Europe who knew that Roosevelt "had been a Jew." Reagan and Bush, who both wanted to be President, "were Jews." Most Americans were Jewish Bolsheviks; the two words went together. Such a pity! Colonial Americans had considered making German their national language. Why had their descendants committed racial suicide by instituting policies that had destroyed their genetic pool?

Yet, the "research" that "proved" all this had come from here in the United States. There were real, Aryan men in America despite the Jews. Who were they and where? Was O.D.E.S.S.A. active? Krüger longed for the camaraderie of association with the Organization Der Ehemaligen SS-Angehorigen, which that bastard English novelist--what was his name?--had exposed, but of course it would be too risky.

They were off the freeway, creeping through the financial district, at the very foot of Polyakov Tower, about to enter the private parking area beneath it.

Krüger saw a furious crowd, shaking fists and shouting. They were throwing things, whatever came to hand, out of control, barely restrained by police. Krüger saw a flash of color. Was it what he thought?

"Stop!" he told the driver through the microphone. Krüger's order was almost redundant. Because of the uproar, the cavalcade had to stop anyway, across the street from the Reserve.

Krüger got out, leaving his entourage in wonder. He never mixed with *hoi polloi*, yet here he was, wading through a crowd of them, actually making contact. They didn't know that he was as mystified as they were. All he had seen was a patch of color on a garment. Krüger worked his way through the multitude, gently pushing them aside, knowing full well that most of them probably were Jews, praying that the Führer would protect him. What were they so exercised about? The last time he had seen such fanaticism was at Warsaw, where the wretched refuse had killed so many Party members.

Then he saw them, extruding the pseudo-innocence of collective pride, smiling in the face of hate, standing at military attention, not many, just a squad, more than enough to prove their superiority; standing as their spiritual forefathers must have stood just after noon in the Munich courtyard of the former War Ministry and before the Feldherrnhalle on November 9, 1923, suffering Jewish catcalls in the *putsch* that put the Führer in Landsberg am Lech prison. Krüger feasted on their boots, tall, so shiny they reflected like the expensive mirrors in his castle. They wore the majestic uniform of the SS, with red on the armbands and the swastika in black. Some of them were *totenkopf.* He saw the Iron Cross. Incredibly, they were young--even the leader was no more than forty--with no possible, personal recollection of the movement. Didn't this prove the Führer was alive? Krüger was sure he saw Hitler's face on a Tower wall. Was this what the religionists called an epiphany?

Indeed, physically they looked not at all Aryan. They weren't blond. Most of them weren't tall, and had the wrong noses. Some were distastefully overweight, definitely not crack troops. They were swarthy. Could they be Mediterranean, even--Führer help us!--Semitic? Yet, they were in uniform, and they were there, enduring insults. What else could motivate this most unlikely squad of Nazis but the spirit? Krüger's own spirit soared.

The leader gave a command--in English, unfortunately--but he gave it. A flag appeared, a large flag defiantly putting the swastika where it belonged, *über alles*. Krüger licked his lips. His mouth was dry. He trembled. His desire to stand with them--in uniform--stand and bellow orders *auf deutsch*, was a lust more intense than any he had ever felt for sex. He shook with the effort of trying to restrain himself.

The leader gave another command. The squad began to sing, the *Horst Wessel*, of course, this time in German. They had memorized it. Krüger opened his mouth to join them, already feeling his lungs fill with the avenging wind that would become the sacred tune, reveling in the a capella music of his voice. He literally had to close his mouth with his hands to stop himself, and knew that he would die. *When will it end, mein führer*?

The leader gave an order. Krüger heard the familiar sound of marching feet. His brain ordered his tingling soles to join them. The fact that he restrained himself was another triumph of the will. Soon the little group was gone, and the crowd along with it.

Such a demonstration would be unthinkable in Germany, thought Krüger. Needless to say, the Jews controlled it, and had neutered the greatest nation known to history, so that it was now perverted rabble. Adenauer had been a Jew. Erhard was a Jew. So were Brandt and all the others. But here, here in the world's largest Jewish city, the spirit lived. Krüger knew this was an omen.

"Anything wrong, Mister?" Krüger realized his hands still covered his face. He withdrew them. A policeman was there, of some minor rank, judging from his shoulders. Kruger saw a nameplate: Combs.

"Nothing, officer. I . . . just . . . you see, I was a concentration camp inmate during World War II. Who were they?"

"Just a bunch of kooks."

"What do they want here?"

"Somebody made a movie about a guy named David Polyakov. The premiere's coming up and the sewer bags don't like it."

"Why do you let them do it, officer? Isn't a Nazi demonstration in New York like yelling fire in a theater?"

"It's something called the Bill of Rights. Ever heard of it?"

"I've heard of it, but it shouldn't apply in an emergency."

"That's the best time for it." Foreigners! They just didn't understand.

"Are they any threat, Mr. Combs? They didn't look like Nazis in the movies."

He was right. Movie Nazis were slender, tall and blond, aristocratic. So were most of the kooks at the meetings Bobby had policed. On the contrary, these just now had been smallish and scruffy to the max. Bobby had been near them. One had even stunk. Bobby was not an expert on Nazi racial theology; in fact, because he had slept through the subject at St. Agnes under the tolerant eye of Sister Mary John, his expertise in genetics was confined to the fact that the Irish are superior, but he knew enough to know that something was amiss. He would easily have recognized Louie the Enemy--Bobby had arrested Louie twice--had not Spats himself arranged Louie's makeup and ensemble, sufficiently authentic to impress Vincent Blandino.

"They're probably down to the bottom of the barrel," Bobby said.

"Bottom of the barrel. I don't understand."

Krüger didn't understand, but brightened. The National Socialist influence no doubt had something to do with the presence of his son. The Nazi renaissance would start here, in New York. How appropriate! The Bill of Rights was the weakness they would use. The fact that the Americans revered such a perversion was proof they were corrupt. Thank God, who is a German, for it. The more things unfolded, the more Krüger saw they were ordained. His heart sang and he turned away, smiling at the young men all around him. His son could be any of them, tall, blond, robust, Aryan. The Arabs had said his son didn't know, and Krüger had told them not to tell him. Kruger wanted to see the expression on his face when he found out.

The first thing he did in his palatial suite at the pinnacle of Polyakov Tower was call the Arabs.

* * *

"All right, he's here. Now what do you want us to do?" Chandler was irritated all right. Why?

They looked at each other, puzzled. "What do you do with a Nazi war criminal? We want you to lock him up."

Chandler smiled. "You want me to lock him up. For what?"

"We just told you," Ahmed said in disbelief. "He's a Nazi war criminal. Didn't you know that?"

"Sure, I know it. I've known it for years."

Yusuf got mad. "You've known it for years? Then what the hell is wrong with O.S.I.? Why did we go to all this trouble?"

"You've been under cover. We do that every day."

"Maybe we should start at the beginning, Mr. Chandler. My name is Sheldon Finkelstein. This is Shlomo Mayerberg. As you know, we're with Mossad. For some years, commissioned by the P.M. himself, we've been posing as Ahmed and Yusuf--we speak fluent Arabic--in a highly successful campaign to unearth Nazi war criminals."

"We know that."

"It seems you know everything, Mr. Chandler," said Finkelstein. "How?"

"You have your spies in O.S.I. and the Agency. We have ours in yours. Professional courtesy."

"Then let me repeat what you already know. Krüger is by far the most important of these gangsters who has not been brought to justice. Not since Eichmann have we chased an animal like this. Krüger killed the real David Polyakov, of course, along with many others exterminated in conditions so horrifying that other Nazis thought him sadistic. Only Himmler himself outdid him in savagery. Indeed, it is fair to say that Krüger outdoes even Himmler, because he is not just hiding, like Eichmann or Mengele. He is using his stolen identity to influence policy. Of course Kurt Waldheim is doing the same thing. How a Nazi officer got to run the United Nations is beyond me. In that position, he has done much to benefit his fellow National Socialists; despite which Krüger has done more on behalf of his own goals."

"If what you propose is so easy, Mr. Finkelstein, why didn't you move on him in Munich?"

"He has made many friends there," said Mayerberg. "He isn't just another Nazi using an assumed name. We couldn't get away with it."

Chandler nodded. "And you thought we could."

"Exactly," said Finkelstein.

"In fact, why don't you move on him in Israel? He's always there."

"It would be embarrassing. Several very influential Israelis would be exposed as dupes."

Chandler nodded. "Gentlemen, I assume you know as much about O.S.I. as I do about Mossad. We are an agency of the Department of Justice, charged with finding Nazi war criminals within our jurisdiction. Do you know what our biggest problem is?"

"The Nazi underground?" asked Mayerberg.

"Not enough money," said his partner.

"Our biggest problem is the Bill of Rights. The Bill of Rights will remain our biggest problem, because it spawned Miranda. Our struggle to nail Demjanjuk with K.G.B. evidence, has been a living hell."

"For which you will always be remembered in our country," Mayerberg said.

"Someday, someone smarter than you and I will figure out how to get rid of the Bill of Rights. Tell me, gentlemen, have you heard of it?"

Finkelstein smiled. "I could embarrass you, Mr. Chandler, but I won't, because I share your frustration. I was professor of law at Columbia before I emigrated to Israel, and I revere the Bill of Rights."

"I'm what you would call a Pharisee," said Mayerberg.

"Then you certainly remember, professor, that, because of the Episcopalian fanatic Patrick Henry and his ilk, we must operate within certain rules, such as the Federal Rules of Criminal Procedure, *inter alia.* Did they teach the rules of evidence at Columbia, professor?"

"Yes, I did."

"Then, maybe you could tell me, as an admirer of the Bill of Rights, how we could nail Krüger's *cojones* to the wall, without getting arrested ourselves."

"Let me save some time, Mr. Chandler. We have proof."

"What proof do you have?" Chandler said cautiously.

"A witness."

Chandler chuckled sarcastically and rose. "Someone who will testify that the present Mr. Polyakov is the man he saw wearing an SS uniform in a concentration camp. Someone who will testify that Polyakov's earlobes resemble Krüger's. Someone nobody ever heard of, who will go word against word with the world's most famous, living philanthropist. Damn it, Mr. Finkelstein, we need documents, photographs, facts."

"No, we don't."

"We don't?"

"No."

"When and where did your witness last see Krüger?"

"In 5706. In Switzerland."

"Fifty seven zero six. What year is that?"

"To you, 1945."

"Do you happen to know what year this is, professor?"

"Fifty seven forty one."

"Nineteen eighty. Your eyewitness hasn't seen Krüger for 35 years. You're a professor of law. What would Melvin Belli or F. Lee Bailey do with that? You wouldn't recognize your own mother if you hadn't seen her in 35 years, even if you were breast-fed."

"My witness is Mrs. David Polyakov."

Chandler sat down. "So you found her."

"Yes, we found her. As you know, Krüger has been paying us to find her."

"How much does he know?"

"Nothing, of course. He wants her dead."

"Where is she?"

"Here."

"In New York?"

"Yes. She's been here all along. Do you think she might recognize David Polyakov?"

"What has she been doing? Why hasn't she come forward?"

"She thought nothing could be done. Is she right, Mr. Chandler?"

"How long were she and Polyakov married?"

"A few years."

"Did they have any children?"

"No."

Finkelstein had long since decided not to tell Chandler she had a son. If he did, the Department of Justice would take the son away from the professor, whose disgust for the U.S. government's record in catching Nazi war criminals was unbounded, and was the main reason he had emigrated to Israel some years before. The Bill of Rights had never hindered prosecution of the foulest serial killers before. Why now? Some said that O.D.E.S.S.A. had infiltrated Washington even to the point of substantial influence. Finkelstein had no proof of that, but could not explain the sorry record. Chandler seemed eager enough, but could be squelched by his superiors. It was better to keep a weapon in reserve, especially the weapon that had brought Krüger to America. Besides, her son was a nogoodnik who had completely discredited himself, which an expensive law firm could use to impeach her testimony; and Krüger would have the most expensive law firm in New York. It was better to keep the son secret until after Krüger was exposed.

"Let's see. They were married a short time, they had no children, and she hasn't seen the new Polyakov for 35 years. Is that your case, professor? Is that what I'm supposed to take into court?"

Neither Finkelstein nor Mayerberg answered. They knew Chandler was right. Krüger had been Polyakov longer than he had been Krüger. Finkelstein had been hoping to sell Chandler a case he would not have bought himself.

"You said Krüger killed Polyakov," said Chandler.

"Of course."

"Where?"

"In Switzerland, we think."

"You think! Where in Switzerland?"

"In the mountains."

"Well, that narrows it down. All we need to find are some mountains in Switzerland. Could I safely assume there was snow? No, gentlemen, it won't work. I want to nail this bastard as much as you do, but, let me remind you, we'd get only one chance. If the judge throws us out, do you think we could ever get back in?"

Finkelstein still wore a brave face, but was weary. They had sought Mrs. Polyakov for years. Mayerberg was a *sabra*; his family was intact, but Krüger had killed most of the Finkelsteins. Finkelstein had convinced himself that, when they found her, they could finally go home. He was tired. He didn't want to pose as an Arab any more. His meetings with Krüger always gave him an attack of colitis. This quest had made him old. He had come here thinking they could nail Krüger and quit, but in a few minutes Chandler had blown his little delusion apart. And Chandler was a "friend." What would an enemy do?

"What more do we need, Mr. Chandler?"

"Believe it or not, it's easy."

Now it was the Jews' turn to laugh. "Easy?" said Mayerberg with contempt.

"People like Trifa and Artukovic were tough, because we had to prove who they were. All you have to do is prove who Krüger isn't. If we can prove he isn't Polyakov, we've got him."

"How do we do that?"

"All you have to do is find David Polyakov."

Chapter Thirty One
The Beast

It was bright enough for a parasol outside, but she sat in the dark, protected by heavy drapes. She never left the apartment, hadn't for many years, with one exception. Her son brought her groceries and paid the utilities and rent. Long ago, he had argued with her. Now, he had given up. She watched television and read the newspapers, looking for one story; it never appeared. She waited for the telephone to ring. When it did, it was her son, or, most of the time, a telemarketer selling a free vacation package for only $695, plus tax.

Echoes of her departed, classic beauty lingered like an aura. Indeed, as far as she knew she was still as beautiful as ever. She was remembering--more than remembering--living the day on the mountain. Every day, she lived that day again, suspended, waiting, leaning forward in her chair, in a type of hibernation, and, when it ended, she lived it all again.

The men in the easy chairs were the only men who had ever entered her apartment, except her son and the Italian. She knew what they were doing and approved of it--even had known some victims in the older one's family before the war--but they had tried for two years before she had let them in. They alone knew who she really was; knew that the name she used, picked from the New York telephone book because there were so many Goldsteins, was a *nom de guerre*. If they had found her, couldn't Krüger?

"It's useless," she had said.

But professor Finkelstein had been so persistent, so sincere, so dedicated, and he spoke Yiddish. Now, he was back from his meeting with Chandler, and she knew he had failed, as she had told him he would.

"It was everything we hoped it was and more," Finkelstein lied. "All we have to do is find your husband."

Frieda Polyakov looked at him in wonder. "Find my husband, who has been murdered for 35 years?"

"If we can find your husband, we can prove that Krüger isn't who he says he is."

"How could I find him?"

"You must go there. You must search the area. Just being there could bring your memory back to life. You could discover something. A document, a photograph, a record. In Switzerland a body just doesn't disappear. Somewhere, somebody has a record."

"How do you know I was in Switzerland? I don't. If I was in Germany, what's another body in the snow?"

After they left, she sat trembling. She didn't want her memory to come back. If she did as Finkelstein asked, the day on the mountain--the only day she lived--would be worse than ever; but if she didn't, and the evidence was there, Krüger would arrive in hell without stripes, and the blame would be hers. The thing she lived for would be gone and she could not lament it.

Terror shook her by the throat. For the first time, she realized she was afraid to find the proof. She knew if she found it she would be trapped in the day on the mountain, no longer able to get out.

She needed only a few minutes to pack. How long do you need if you have nothing? She reached for the telephone to call her son. No, he wouldn't be there. He never was. Guilt joined her fear, clawing at her conscience. Because he was what he was, she had never been able to love him. The fact that what he was, was not her fault was irrelevant. She was a Jewish mother and felt guilt. His present activities were no surprise, despite the fact that he had no idea who he was. Exchanging boasts about their sons with other Jewish matrons at Hadassah meetings and Mah-Jongg games was not for her. "My son, the con man," she bitterly heard herself saying. All the times she had talked with Finkelstein and the younger man, she had dreaded the possibility that they would ask about her son. Thank God they had not. The shame of discovery would have been too great.

* * *

"Don't hand me that crap!"

Fatima al-Shekel leaned across the table on her knuckles toward McGillicuddy, who paled. No one had talked to him like that since Father Gillespie, many years ago, who had found the young McGillicuddy sadly deficient in catechism. Certainly, no one had dared say anything remotely resembling it since McGillicuddy had become Francis X. McGillicuddy, managing presence in the Department of Sanitation, City of New York.

Yet, here was this crazy woman the mayor had appointed police commissioner saying it, and McGillicuddy had to take it.

"I don't know what you're talking about," he repeated.

"You don't know what I'm talking about," she mimicked, becoming Bad Cop. Her provocative tummy punctuated her remarks. What did she have on the mayor? Fatima al-Shekel put a picture before McGillicuddy. "Exhibit Number 1. Abe Goldstein, who says he's Jesus Christ, but is a terrorist. Abe comes to us not from Galilee, but from the Department of Sanitation, where his boss is Francis X. McGillicuddy.

"Exhibit Number 2. Elizabeth Ann Wilson, *née* McGillicuddy, a member of the Goldstein gang, whose father is Francis X. McGillicuddy, and whose husband is Charles Wilson, a builder, who is also a member of the gang, and who has been pretending to be a vice president of the F.D.I.C. Exhibit Number 3. Moe Stern, Goldstein's St. Peter, whose boss at the Department of Sanitation is Francis X. McGillicuddy.

"Whom do you think you're screwing with here, McGillicuddy? I know damn well the Jesus Jerks operate out of the Department of Sanitation. You jerks just don't have enough work to keep you busy over there, since you screwed the city with that criminal contract."

Fatima stuck a bejewelled finger in his face. "When I become mayor, you greedy . . . ."

"Now, look here, Madam Commissioner . . . ."

"When I become mayor, you greedy bastards will go to work. Please give that message to the next meeting of the jerks. So, you see, McGillicuddy, the only thing I don't know is whether you're a member of this gang of terrorists yourself. Are you, McGillicuddy?"

"Certainly not!"

Fatima relaxed, and became Good Cop. Her voice trilled, telling McGillicuddy the problem had been solved. By means of clever police interrogation techniques, she had elicited the subject's admission that the gang was where she said it was, and that he was not a member. She sat down.

"Where is Moe Stern?"

"I don't know. Disappeared. Hasn't been to work for a couple of years."

"Where's Abe Goldstein?"

"Ditto Abe. Underground."

"Did Abe ever tell you he was Jesus Christ?"

"No, but Moe did."

"What did you do?"

"Not a thing. Under departmental rules, a man's religion is his own business--as long as it doesn't interfere with his duties--even if he's Jesus Christ."

McGillicuddy began to sweat. He hadn't broken any rules, but even in jail Abe could accuse him of discrimination, and there would have to be a hearing. In a hearing, an innocent man could be condemned.

"I don't give a damn about your rules! What happened?"

Fatima shouldn't have had to be asking these questions. Their answers no doubt were in Goldstein's file--but Goldstein's file had disappeared, proving Albert Holley's theory about a spy at police headquarters.

"The Assistant Commissioner told me to send Abe to a psychiatrist, so I did."

Praise be to Allah! It was a place to start. "What is the psychiatrist's name?"

"I don't know. Human Services handles that. Isn't it in his file?"

"Yes, Allah damn it! Of course it's in his file."

"Then why are you asking?" McGillicuddy smiled, not knowing she couldn't tell him the file had disappeared. The tide was turning. The soldier of the cross would subdue the bloated harlot of mystery Babylon.

"Where is Elizabeth Ann, McGillicuddy?"

"I don't know."

He didn't know anything about Elizabeth Ann. He thought he'd known her all these years, until she'd become a victim of this cult. Now, she was gone--ruined, beyond redemption--and he hadn't seen her for months. Saints preserve us, it was more than a year! Never would he stand beside her in St. Patrick's at her wedding.

"Frank, I'm going to level with you," Fatima said softly. "This gang is tearing the city apart. It could hurt my campaign. The mayor is yelling for my *tucchos*. I need a volunteer to take the heat."

"I certainly hope you find one, Madam Commissioner."

"I *have* found one, Frank. Don't you understand? Thanks for volunteering. The campaign will not forget. When I take office, one of my first official acts will be to make sure you keep your job. Go to church. Confess the part you played in the conspiracy. The church will forgive you. I will forgive you--if you give the Police Department all the praise."

Francis X. McGillicuddy, Supervisor, Department of Sanitation, City of New York, found himself walking up Mott Street in Chinatown, and crossing Canal, where Mott would become Little Italy. He had no recollection of how he had arrived there. The last thing he remembered was Fatima getting to her feet. Had the shock of what she said caused him to black out?

Like one of the Four Horsemen, terror rode his returning consciousness. The woman was crazy. It was sensible to believe she would do anything she said. As police commissioner, she probably could arrange to have him fired, despite Civil Service.

But how could he confess he was a leader of the gang? It wasn't true, and wouldn't he be fired anyway? He kept walking, afraid to do anything else.

For a long time after he left, Fatima sat at her desk. She had set things in motion. She would shake something loose. She reached for the telephone, and quickly established that the psychiatrist Abe had seen was Dr. George Bogart.

Bogart was the psychiatrist accused of membership in the gang by I.R.S. clown Sid Bloberg. Was this a coincidence? The hair on the back of Fatima's neck rose.

* * *

The problem wasn't just trying to remember something she hadn't seen in 35 years; the problem was the fact that almost everything had changed. There was more of everything, more building, more technology, more people and their cars. Only two important things hadn't changed: the teutonic penchant for lederhosen and hiking, especially in the mountains, which protected her from the curiosity of any hidden Nazis; and the train.

Despite all the changes, the train to Munich was still there, and it was the place to start. If she took the train, perhaps she could find the road and the tree where Krüger had put David out. If she found that place, perhaps she could find the inn. If she found the inn, perhaps she could find the lodge. If she found the lodge . . . .

She shuddered. She was alive again. She had been dead for so long, entombed in her New York apartment. Now, she felt the things that made life so unpleasant: fear, pain, hope, guilt. She was here to find something, but didn't want to find it.

She had flown from Kennedy to Frankfurt, picked the train up, and took it to Munich. She rented a car and headed south, up into the mountains. She parked, got out and hiked, not even knowing she was on the right road. Other hikers hailed her and she returned their greetings. She looked like a woman in her sixties, hiking for her health, whose beauty had faded, but whose elegance and assets had not.

She found nothing. The trees looked alike. The snow did not change. There had been no landmarks. When she and David had passed here so long ago in Krüger's limousine, they had had eyes only for each other. Now, she couldn't ask anyone whether this was the place they had left her husband 35 years ago. The inn where Krüger had left her wasn't there; if it was, she didn't recognize it. Maybe it had been remodeled. She went to several newspapers and read their back issues. Weeks later, she still had found nothing.

Wherever she stopped, she asked the same questions. "How old is this inn?"

"It was built in 1893."

"Almost ninety years. I was here toward the end of the war, but I don't remember it. Has it been remodeled since?"

"Yes. Twice that I know of. I was here when they did it in 1971."

"So beautiful. Is there anything to do in the neighborhood?"

The innkeeper smiled. "No. People who come here don't want anything to do."

"Yet, you have a newspaper. Surely there is local news."

"The newspaper is a sham, *Frau* Goldstein. Nothing ever happens here."

"Were you in the war?"

"Yes, I was in the war. Far away. As you see, it cost me an arm. But the war didn't happen here. We read about it."

"In the newspaper, which is a sham and prints no local news."

"Precisely."

Was it the right inn? It was in the right place, in an alpine town near the main road, but she remembered nothing. Could her room have been the one? Yes, but she didn't know. She sat in the dining room, alone, at a little table. She had been alone for so long, all the time she was dead, and had liked it, but now she was alive, and it hurt.

A woman stopped at her table, a woman about her own age. "May I join you?" she asked tentatively, expecting to be dismissed. "I'm alone too."

"Please," said Frieda.

"Thank you. Should we speak German, or do you prefer French?"

"As you wish."

"Pardon me for overhearing--I was getting my mail--but I couldn't help chuckling at your conversation with the *concierge*. I am Marguerite Duchamp, from Lyons. I come here every year."

"Call me Frieda. I live in New York. Why did you find my conversation so amusing?"

"There is a gentleman's agreement not to mention what happened."

"Nothing ever happens here, and isn't printed. Didn't you know?"

"Yes. I know. But I'm not a gentleman."

"What was it?"

"The body. Such a scandal. It would be so bad for business. We didn't know whether we'd be murdered in our beds. How much do you know about the avalanche, *Madame*?"

"In New York we have the Crash, we have the crime wave, but we do not have the avalanche."

"The avalanche is a beast. We walk softly, we whisper, hoping to appease it, trying not to wake it--but we fail. In the face of all logic and experience, we forget. The deadly beauty of the snow ensnares us. Someone speaks. Someone shouts. The *fohn* blows. The rains come. An eye opens. The beast awakens, roaring. Have you ever heard it roar? No? I lived through a tornado once, in Kansas. Americans call Kansas the alley of tornadoes. I was passing through. It was frightful, horrendous. But it was a force of nature. This, this is the roar of something living, primeval, from the ooze, something furious because we puny mortals have dared set foot in its domain.

"It rushes down the slope, destroying everything before it, uprooting majestic, ancient trees like toothpicks, entombing whatever unluckily or stupidly stands in its path. Nothing can withstand it. Nothing can escape. Soon it sleeps again. All is calm. The intruder gives no more offense. He is gone, buried. He will not be seen again. He sleeps within the bosom of the beast."

"And the body?"

"Yes, the body. Forgive me. I forgot. Sometimes the beast sleeps only for a moment, a night that could last 40 years. Then, provoked again, maddened, it moves on. Do you know what happens then?"

"Its secrets are revealed."

"Exactly. The things it buried are uncovered, perfectly preserved, as if returning from a sojourn outside time. Last week, there was thunder, no rain, just a single thunderclap. The beast awoke, moved on, foolishly searching for the fool who dared offend it. And there was the corpse, wedged into a tree stump."

The *schnitzel* Frieda had ordered was as superb as Marguerite had promised. Frieda chewed as long as she could--as long as she chewed, she couldn't talk--then, reluctantly, swallowed.

"Who was it?" she asked.

"That's the mystery, you see," said Marguerite. "No one knows. No one is missing. No one claimed it."

"Can't it be identified?"

"No. It was horribly mutilated, no doubt by the beast. It had no face. An arm was missing. The doctor said it had been buried for many years. Anyone who could identify it could well be dead. He has only a bizarre theory. Because the corpse was circumcised and missing an arm, and because of something I don't recall about the clothing, he believes it could be someone left over from the war, if you know what I mean."

"Yes. I think I do. But here in Switzerland?"

"Those were insane times. Switzerland was a target of intrigue. We lived here then, to avoid the war. We'll probably never know who the victim was or how he got here. Of course, the doctor is Jewish, which could be coloring his judgment."

"Yes. It often does."

"I see you understand. I'm happy. We lost so much, so much business. I blame the Jews. Were it not for them, there would have been no war."

"Could I see the body?"

"Ugh! Why would you do that?"

"I haven't told you. I'm a writer."

"How interesting. I've always wanted to be a writer. One of these days, I'm going to sit down and write. What do you write about?"

"The war."

"How interesting. Still, you can't see the body. It's been cremated. The mayor promptly returned the dust to whatever god it worshipped. It would have been bad for business, you see, which I understand. Except for the corpse, nothing has happened here since the war. The *concierge* told you the truth."

"But, surely there are records."

"Gone. Remember, I lived here. I have relatives at city hall."

"I wonder where it happened. I'd like to see it."

"What a pity. I'd take you there, but I leave tomorrow for Lyons. This is the final evening of my week. It happened the night of my arrival. I've never seen such a racket. It was like the *Bourse* in Paris. Anyway, it's too far to go, and the only way to get there is to trek. But, I tell you what, if you promise to engage a guide, I'll draw you a map. Here, *garcon*, please clear this away."

Frieda was dressed and waiting the next morning for dawn. The lunch the cook had packed her the previous evening was ready. The *concierge* had risen to see her go. Ordinarily, he would have warned someone embarking on such an expedition to take a guide--as Frieda had promised Marguerite she would--citing such dangers as the one that had recently provoked the uproar. By now, however, Frieda's putative literary career had discreetly permeated the little town, so the *concierge* knew she was probably crazy, and said nothing, despite the fact that his nephew was available.

As soon as there was enough light, Frieda set out, map in hand. It was cold, but the unaccustomed exertion made it pleasant. The sun rose, and she undid her coat. It was quiet. The only thing she heard was her boots, crunching in the snow. Towering all around her, watching, was the beast, the beast and the beckoning horror of the day.

She walked for several hours. At last, much farther than she remembered, there was the stone arch the map promised, and the broad, treeless field. She sat against a tree in the shade and ate. She couldn't remember enjoying a meal more. There was a little carafe of wine. It was relaxing.

She was on her feet again, load a little lighter and refreshed, trekking in the snow. A long time passed without event, much more time than the trip had taken so many years ago. Had the Beast changed the topography? Nothing ever happens here, she told herself. It was now the shank of the afternoon, and she realized that, if she didn't return to the inn immediately, and perhaps even if she did, it would be dark before she arrived. If she didn't return, would they send someone after her?

At last, in the twilight, she saw the remains of the lodge in the trees, and looked a long time, afraid to approach. Most of it was still buried in the snow, but what remained of the roof was usable as a lean-to. Trembling, sticky, tired, she crawled in. It was dark now, and there were no stars. She heard a distant animal lament. The wind rose. She heard it sigh. Blowing snow obscured her view. She was so sleepy. She couldn't stay awake.

When she awoke, it was bright day, and she was uncomfortable. She was lying on something she had been too tired to notice the night before. She crawled out into the sun, and pulled it with her. It was a long-handled ax, the blade rutted, rusty and stained. There were tens of thousands like it, but she had seen this ax before.

She stood, staring at the ax, and the day of horror returned, as she had known it would. The horrid ax had summoned it. She was shaking, utterly out of control. Thank God she was alone. She dropped the ax and took her head in her hands, trying to quell it, but her hands were shaking uselessly too.

As she had feared, she no longer had to remember. She was living the day of horror, trapped. She could not get out. She staggered, wringing her hands, moaning. *Addonai, please. Help me! Help me!*

She saw something half-buried in the snow. Last night, in the twilight, she hadn't noticed it. Or, had the blowing snow revealed it only now, another of the secrets the monster had decided to disgorge?

What was it? Something else she'd seen before? Mesmerized, she approached, fell to her knees and began to dig, fingers freezing, clearing snow, until she realized what it was.

She recoiled, jumped to her feet and began to scream, trying to provoke the beast, praying that the beast would bury it again, and her along with it. As she had feared, she was totally, irretrievably insane.

Chapter Thirty Two
Baptism

Francis X. McGillicuddy, late high protuberance of the Department of Sanitation of the City of New York, prayed on his knees before the representation of St. Francis for guidance. It didn't come, and he despaired of his vow to stay there until it did. Despite the cushions, his knees were sore.

He was trembling, struggling feebly in a closing fist. He had never been so desolate. The suddenness of the disaster had left him no time to prepare. If only he had understood politics. If only he hadn't panicked. He should have known he was being bushwhacked. He should have sought advice; but in the brackish pond where he had been head mackerel, he hadn't needed advice.

As Fatima had demanded, he had written the letter, confessed he was Abe's leader, credited Fatima's police work for exposing him, thanked her for explaining how wrong he was, and asked the people of the city for forgiveness. As Fatima had predicted, the revelation was a coup, fading all the heat, including all the major talk shows, even making a contrite McGillicuddy a star.

Fatima hadn't told McGillicuddy what she would say at the press conference; hadn't warned him he would be fired. But he had been. Yes, under the rules there would be a mandatory hearing. Yes, she had promised he would return to her administration in glory, but his permanent record would always bear the stain. Fatima hadn't explained that he probably would be disgraced in the church. What did she care? Wasn't she an Ayrab? McGillicuddy bowed low in the alcove, before the statue of St. Francis, trying to hide, half-expecting to be thrown into the street, despite the fact that he had taken a circuitous route to this distant church in the Bronx, where no one knew him. He was searching for a sign. Surely St. Francis, his namesake, would give him a sign!

He looked up and his mouth fell open. Was he seeing what he saw? He rubbed his eyes, trying to remove the tears. St. Francis was crying too. McGillicuddy saw tears on the statue's cheeks. Its eyes were wet. In fact, it was smiling. He looked around furtively. Did anyone else see it? But it was very late at night; he was alone. Because of the impending collapse of Western civilization, foretold by thinkers from Oswald Spengler to the ayatollah Khomeini and Walter Cronkite, even the staunchest believers, who used to worship at all hours, now feared assault, battery, robbery and rape, along with panhandling, prostitution and Driving While Intoxicated, on their way to church. So, no one else was there to tell McGillicuddy he was crazy.

The tears were still flowing, and the smile along with it, as plain as the nose on McGillicuddy's face. Didn't they prove that St. Francis of Assisi approved of him, and looked with favor on what he had done? Didn't they prove St. Francis was sorry about his plight, sorry about what the rotten, scheming bastards had done to him, including the Ayrab she-wolf who had killed our Lord and Savior and was a traitor to her race? What else could they mean? The fist that had been strangling him opened and was gone. He could breathe again, and realized he had never understood what a joy it was. He cried even more. The simple things cost nothing, and yet were so much more important.

As the statue looked down at him, a plan came to mind, his plan, not the heathen whore bitch Fatima's. Soon, someone else would see the tears. Pilgrims and the media would arrive. Whoever had first seen the manifestations--whoever had first reported them--would get the credit. Whoever discovered them would be there as cicerone. His sins would be forgotten. He would be redeemed; probably even restored to the Department of Sanitation.

McGillicuddy turned the plan over and over in his mind and could not see a flaw. Hadn't he conceived it in the presence of St. Francis? Wouldn't the saint tell him if something were wrong? McGillicuddy heard angels caroling in an arrangement for organ by Bach.

A spotlight on a wall brilliantly illuminated every feature of the statue. McGillicuddy found a ladder in a shed on church grounds, climbed up and unscrewed the bulb with much fingerblowing, to the point of darkness. The face of St. Francis receded in the shadows. He found an old, ragged but serviceable, vestry cloth, hung it between two wall lamps in front of the statue, and laid the ladder down before it. No one could even guess the statue was there.

Pleased with his work, McGillicuddy hurried from the sanctuary and went home. As he drove off, Father Romagna arrived to make his evening rounds, always on the lookout for vandalism. What was the country coming to, when houses of worship had to live again in fear, as he had lived in Fascist Italy? Only last week, a few blocks away, someone had painted swastikas all over a synagogue. Father Romagna--the son of a World War II anti-Nazi hero in Genoa--had thundered against the "reviving Nazi threat" from the pulpit; then led church members to the synagogue to help clean up, followed by gefilte fish and pastrami on rye. Some members of his flock had suggested that the church doors be locked when not in use, to inhibit potential vandalism. Never! Recently, some Nazis in full uniform had brazenly paraded in the financial district, and the *padre* had had to pray without ceasing for strength to avoid the scene, where, he was sure, he would have lost control. Who was behind all this? He would love nothing better than to catch them *in flagrante delicto*.

With these gloomy thoughts, Father Romagna entered the sanctuary, and saw immediately that something was wrong. The lighting was different. The spotlight on St. Francis of Assisi was off. He found and worked the switch near the confessionals to no effect. The statue was not only in the dark; it was concealed behind a ragged cloth. A ladder on its side prevented approach.

At last, Father Romagna understood. He smiled and nodded. Only that morning, after several fruitless attempts, he had finally discovered the origin of the mysterious leak in the 96-year old structure that could have caused irreparable water damage to the statue. Father Romagna had been a plumber in civilian life, and the leak offended his expertise. Of course he had reported it at once.

Now, here they were already to repair it. Father Romagna was utterly amazed. These things ordinarily took weeks, and, when he complained, he was usually told that the Roman Catholic Church had endured since Peter, and probably would survive a few weeks with a drip.

In the morning, he would call with unaccustomed praise. Thank the good Lord the problem would be solved before some nutcake noticed the unwanted moisture and started talking about "a miracle."

* * *

McGillicuddy hadn't known it was possible for a human being to feel so bad. He had felt bad after the Fatima incident, yes, but the fallout from that fiasco had only cost him his job, his prestige, his pension and power, things of this world. He could blame all that on the whore of Babylon. Now, he had come close to losing his immortal soul, and he had done that to himself. He had acted blindly as usual, without bothering to check. Yes, Father Romagna had lost his temper; but everything he had said to McGillicuddy was true. McGillicuddy had embarrassed himself. Worse, he had embarrassed the Church. The Church hadn't thrown him out, of course, but his reputation as a "prominent Catholic layman" had been replaced by furtive smirks. Because of that reputation, children in the church around the corner, asked in catechism who founded the Roman Catholic Church, had often replied, "Frank McGillicuddy." They would do so no more, and it was his own fault. In fact, hadn't the trouble started with what he'd done to Abe? Wasn't the same thing now happening to him?

There was nothing he could do. He had stupidly burned his bridges to the Church and was bound for eternal perdition. Father Romagna hadn't said that, but McGillicuddy knew. Until the end of time, God would force him to listen to acid rock music at top volume in hell. His criticism of Elizabeth Ann now charred his cheeks with shame. Nothing could be done. No one could help him. Who could help a worm so low?

The telephone rang. So deep was his funk that it rang a long time before he heard it. No one called him any more. Who would call an utter fool? He grabbed his coat and left. The phone was still ringing. Whoever was calling would never know he had been there. As he descended in the elevator, he realized what he had to do.

The trouble was that he didn't know of a river in the metropolitan area that wasn't polluted. He didn't mind dying. He wanted to die--dying was the only way to stop the horror--but he didn't want to die in a sea of garbage, used condoms, mutagenic bacteria and human refuse that the Department of Sanitation was too corrupt to pick up. He wanted cool, clear waters to close over him, water certified as safe to drown in by the Department of Public Works. He wanted to sink to the bottom, where Elizabeth Ann would never find his body.

He drove north, along the Saw Mill River Parkway. It was a pleasant day, cool and sunny. Such a waste. His car was running hot. The radiator needed flushing. So what! He turned off the parkway. He was on a dirt road.

Then there was a lake hidden in the trees, cool, calm, clean, inviting, and no doubt very deep. No one was about. McGillicuddy knew this was the place.

He left the car and waded in. The question arose of what the dear, departed President Kennedy would think. He suppressed it. President Kennedy had never suffered like this. Soon the waters would close over him, ending this farce. Thank God he couldn't swim. Already, it was up to his knees. At thigh level, he was already between the two worlds. His pain disappeared, and the world of corruptible flesh along with it. His eyes stared, but did not see. He kept walking, making good progress. The thought occurred to him that perhaps he should have left a note, but it was too late. Goodbye, cruel world! He walked a long time. The water rose to his waist.

At last, he was climbing from the water in confusion, dripping, shivering, staring across the lake at his car, and he realized that it wasn't deep enough to do the job. He had called Abe incompetent, but he had been talking about himself. What do you call a man so incompetent, he can't even commit suicide?

So, what should he do now? Walk back across the lake, and get even wetter than he was? Are you crazy? What would that accomplish? He struck off along the shore, but the picture postcard foliage that made the lake so deliciously private made his portage a chore. Branches whipped his face. Sticky things were there, along with muddy traps. Something noisy lived in the tall weeds along the shore, invisible but carnivorous. His ankles were aflame. The Chamber of Commerce of whatever town had jurisdiction was concealing all this. The trip hadn't seemed so far, but two sweaty hours passed before he saw the car.

The day was just as sunny and pleasant, but now he was cold. He shivered. As he sat again in the car, he heard himself squish. The seat would be ruined.

Since he was at fault, the insurance would not pay. His $75 shoes had been almost new when he left his apartment. Now, they looked like mud canoes. If he'd had any sense, he would have taken them off. *Yes, you idiot, and had your feet cut to shreds.* He resolved with renewed vigor to finish the job. Should he go home and change clothes? No, he wouldn't return to Brooklyn a failure.

When he awoke, it was dawn. The rim of the sun was just topping the trees. He was stiff, cold, sneezy, uncomfortable. Now was the time, before he came down with pneumonia and had to go to Emergency, which would probably hurt his insurance. Many people drowned in their bathtubs. A distant relative had done it, too drunk to breathe. Statistics proved that bathtubs were far more dangerous than loaded guns. The only way to neutralize the danger would be to register them and train responsible adults in their use, replace them with mandatory shower stalls, prohibit bathtub sales to individuals under 18 and require a three-day waiting period, or simply forbid people to bathe alone. Needless to say, the acquisition of tubs through the U.S. mails would be forbidden.

He descended again to lakeside. He would walk out into the water again, and at waist level lie down. He crossed himself and did so, face up. It was hard to do, but at last the healing waters closed over him. Sure enough, he heard soothing voices. He felt a hand on his back.

Then, someone was lifting him. He was a big man, not easy to lift. Again he stood on his feet. To his surprise, he felt immensely refreshed. The water subsided. His eyes cleared. He could see.

"Hello, Frank."

It was Abe, the same Abe McGillicuddy had always known, Abe at peace and with a new authority.

"You came," said Elizabeth Ann tearfully, nearby.

McGillicuddy hadn't seen her for months. All that time, he had been practicing the lecture he'd planned, stern but loving passages on duty, sacrifice, morality and God. Of course, that was before Fatima and the "miracle" of the tears.

"Abe, I'm sorry."

"For what?"

"I betrayed you."

"You had to do what you did, Frank."

McGillicuddy had never known the Jews were so forgiving. The realization touched his guilt and inspired unembarrassed tears. Abe's serenity was awesome. His presence was no accident. "What are you doing here, Abe?"

"Celebrating. Tom Chase suggested it. Honky thinks it will catch on." Abe walked off. McGillicuddy saw him immersing many others.

"Daddy. Daddy. Daddy." Elizabeth Ann kept repeating his name.

"Lizzie." That was all he could say. His voice broke. Tears came again.

"I knew you'd come."

"How?"

"I called. You'd already left. James wants you to work for him."

"James?"

"My husband."

It was true. Spats had calculated, wrongly, that marriage would shut her up. He had told her she would be married in church, so they had flown to Vegas and been married in a chapel on the strip. The ceremony had not diminished her forensic excess.

"I didn't know."

"In deference to you and the baby, I went ahead and did it." McGillicuddy saw that she was holding an infant. "Would you like to hold your granddaughter?"

"Yes."

"James is an undercover agent for the Federal Deposit Insurance Corporation. A bank can't go broke without his imprimatur. I don't know what you'll be doing. It's secret. James assures me it will be much more important than collecting garbage. James was so pleased to learn you were available. Daddy, what happened to your face? It's full of scratches."

McGillicuddy was happy to hear that he was going to work for a man who had an imprimatur.

Chapter Thirty Three
Fool's Gold

Now that the night was here at last, the anticipation was driving Spats berserk. He fought to stay calm. The complicated plan was going well, too well. Nothing had gone wrong. This meant that something would break down, but, since it hadn't happened yet, he couldn't fix it. What would it be?

He had made his rounds for the last time a few minutes ago. The trucks were in place. Louie and the others were in position. The equipment worked. The greatest bank heist in history soon would begin, a job so exquisite that the victims perhaps would never know they had been robbed--and even if they did, would not admit it. The spurious "gold bars" were waiting in the trucks. When it was over, the bank would find them in its vaults, where they were supposed to be, while Spats left for his new life in Rio de Janeiro, just in case, where there was no extradition for a man who had fathered a Brazilian child, even a man who had been accused of murder. His new identity was ready, carefully constructed over many months. "James K. Slagle," "Spats" and Charles Wilson would be history. So would Elizabeth Ann, who was not Brazilian and spoke no Portuguese. McGillicuddy would have to find still another job.

Spats looked at his watch. His mouth went dry, so dry he couldn't swallow. It was time to put the plan in motion. He lifted the telephone and placed the call.

"Naomi June?"

"This is Chief of Police Fatima al-Shekel. Who the hell is this?"

"This is somebody who's going to tell you where the Goldstein gang is right now, if you want to know." It was an Irish voice, so Fatima knew it was phony. The Irish accent was the easiest to duplicate.

"Who gave you this number?"

"Do you want to know?"

"What I want to know is who the hell you are."

"Goodbye."

"All right! Where are they?"

There was no time to trace the call. Fatima had never expected she might have to tap her own phone.

"Happy Acres Scientific Nature Spa, Allerton Avenue in the Bronx."

"Are they all there?"

"Every one of them, except Sid Bloberg. Remember him?"

"What the hell do you want?"

"Just the satisfaction of knowing I've done my duty as a citizen."

"Camel dung!"

Spats hung up. Bastard! She'd try to find him later. Was he telling the truth? Sure he was. Instinct said so, and her instinct never failed. He was a fink, a gang member, who had turned against the others. Fatima told her criminology students all the time that betrayal was a characteristic of the psychopathic mind. She lifted the telephone again. If only the election were tomorrow, instead of a few weeks. When the news hit the street, she could be elected mayor by acclamation.

"Steinmetz! Alert the media! We're going to the Bronx!"

With considerable pomp, Fatima descended to her car. The trip to darkest Bronx would be a long one, from police headquarters on Center Street in Lower Manhattan to the F.D.R. Drive, north to the Tri-Boro Bridge, and then up Bruckner Boulevard to Happy Acres. She would be gone for most of the evening.

As she left, Spats arrived, consummately attired, a few blocks away, at Polyakov Tower, and presented his elegantly engraved invitation. The great hall was teeming with inspired conversation. Everyone who claimed to be somebody was there, and Spats moved among them, carefully pronouncing his name, making many favorable impressions.

"Charles Wilson," he told Albert Holley, extending a hand. "We met at the Club."

"Of course. Manhattan Restorations."

Holley remembered him with mild unease. Months ago, Charles had called the paramedics and perhaps saved his life, so Charles could testify that Holley had a weakness and wasn't a god. But he was a god. Hadn't he created himself? That was why, despite his gratitude, Holley hadn't called Charles with proper thanks.

"I'm impressed."

"Memory is indispensable to success in business, Mr. Wilson."

"Please. Call me Charles. If I may call you Albert."

Spats was pleased. People would believe a man with a reputation for good memory, when he said Spats had been present, especially if he was chairman of the New York National Reserve. Holley didn't know it, but he was about to make history. He, too, was impressed. Charles hadn't mentioned the incident at the Club, which showed good judgment.

The house lights dimmed, brightened and dimmed again. People started finding their seats.

"Would you care to sit with us, Charles?"

"Thank you, no. I'm waiting for someone. She's late."

"My wife's always late. When she arrives, I call her the late Mrs. Holley. I don't know why she objects."

Spats was lying, of course. He wasn't waiting for anyone. He sat a couple of rows behind Holley and waved. Soon, it was dark. Credits were scrolling majestically up the screen. Spats had taken care to learn that the hymn to Polyakov starting to unfold would require 191 minutes plus an intermission to do so. He silently gave thanks to Polyakov that his life had been so eventful and long, and, of course, to Vincent Blandino, who, in deference to world Jewry, and to the millions Polyakov had paid to help finance this work of art, had chosen to tell every minute of it. By the time Spats left, everyone exposed to Blandino's hosanna was too preoccupied to notice.

Spats found a telephone, dialed another number and hung up. By the time he reached the street, he heard the singing. It was lovely, masculine, irresistible, victorious. It made him so happy, he felt like joining in. In a few minutes, the detachment came around the corner, in perfect formation, uniforms beautifully pressed and creased, singing a Nazi marching song, worth every dollar he had paid. With singing and uniforms like that, he couldn't understand why everyone was so hostile to the Nazis.

Happily, everyone was. A large group of Jewish *hoi polloi* was there, already enraged by the news that a detachment of Nazis was actually marching on the Tower to protest its use by a publicly held corporation to honor "Jewish trash." The Nazi demand for an injunction to prevent it was still awaiting action in federal district court in Foley Square. A proper brawl was shaping up. Before he realized that the "Jesus Jerks" could be used to lure Fatima out of town--which was essential--Spats had circuitously hinted to Abe that perhaps the little band should lead the loyal opposition in the street, but Abe, thank God, had modestly declined, saying that his mission was to bring peace, not a sword, and Spats realized he was right. So, adopting the Jewish accent he had learned like a native on the Lower East Side, Spats had called the Jewish Protective League, and other civic groups like it, urging them to fight.

Spats stood among them. "Are those bastards allowed to do that?" He pointed, aghast.

"The American Civil Liberties Union says they are," said one of the Jews. "But we're allowed to kick their *tucchos*."

"Well, whatever, that means, I hope you do."

The Nazis were performing well. Damn right, they were! They had been trained for weeks and were being paid like *gauleiters*. Bastards! He had had to pay the Nazis, but the Jews were there for free. Before he had even hired the

Nazis, his own men, Louie, Jim and the others, had marched the same route, in uniform, to test its practicality. There had been quite a scare when they saw Bobby Combs. Thank God he hadn't recognized them.

Far above, padding like a panther on the roof, Krüger heard the singing too. His soul brothers were coming to protest, as well they should. He exulted, but this time without frustration. This was a historic evening. There was a presence in the air. Krüger knew his son was near. The Arabs had said they soon would meet, after the premiere. Together they would return to Germany, where Vörst reported he was making dramatic progress with the Führer. The new tissue had turned out to be perfectly suitable, as Krüger had promised it would be. The Führer would chortle when he learned that Krüger was making sure it was all Jewish, as in the old days. With characteristic audacity, he had revived the plan in the world's largest Jewish city, where no one would notice if some old Jews disappeared. The logistical problems he had feared were minimal. Up to the last moment, Vörst had still insisted on young girls.

Krüger stood erect. Soon, he would descend to the grand ballroom and accept the adulation of the Jews and their Christian lickspittles. The moment of vindication was approaching at which he could reveal himself.

In the Bronx, the chief of police pointed at Steinmetz. "Where the hell are the media?" she fumed.

"Bobby Combs called them all. They said they're covering the preview."

"What preview? What the hell are you talking about, Steinmetz?"

"The movie, chief. The celluloid biography of David Polyakov. His lives, his loves, his triumphs and tragedies, his service to the wretched refuse yearning to breathe free, a story calculated to bring tears even to the eyes of Martin Bormann, starring . . . . "

"All right, Steinmetz. I remember."

It was such a joy to humiliate Fatima, the apostate, with the story of a fellow Jew. Steinmetz couldn't wait to see the movie. Soon, in the ballot booth, he would vote against her. The lust to do so was more intense than sex, although it must be said that, as the husband of Rosalie, Steinmetz hadn't had any sex worth mentioning for years.

"That's where they are."

There wasn't any point to this without the media. She had already expended the media dividend she had made from McGillicuddy. She needed something new. The gang was completely a media invention. They had been screaming for Abe's head. Now, because of brilliant police work, she had it, and the media pukes typically didn't care--simply because Polyakov gave them better food and drink--despite which she had to humor them. The New York press made a herd of jackals gorging on rotten intestines look like lunch at Happy Acres. Thank Allah, Spats Davis was apparently on vacation while all this was going on. All she needed was another embarrassing bank robbery.

"Where is he?" she asked.

Steinmetz pointed. "In there."

In the next room, Abe smiled as she closed the door and sat down. She said nothing for a long time, trying to make him ill at ease, a technique she taught to her students of advanced interrogation. Yet, Abe just kept smiling, apparently perfectly relaxed, as if she were an old friend, and they were sitting in his living room.

"Are you Abe Goldstein?" There was genuine doubt in her voice. This man looked so inoffensive. She had expected more of a man who had disrupted the City of New York.

"Are you asking who I am in time?"

"As opposed to what?"

"Eternity."

"Let's start with time."

"Sure. That's who I am."

"Who are you in eternity?"

"The people say I'm Jesus Christ."

"Why did you decide you're Jesus Christ?"

"I didn't. I don't want to be Jesus Christ."

"Then, how do you know that's who you are?"

"God told me. He said I was Jesus before the foundation of the world."

"Abe, let me give you some advice. Cooperate. Stop playing games. If you stop playing games, I'll see what I can do."

"I like games. Can we play one? Do you know Toad-in-the-Hole?"

"Are you the man who's been causing all the trouble?"

"No. Has there been any trouble?"

"Have you and your people been going to the hospitals and rest homes, like this one?"

"Sure."

"Why? What are you doing here?"

"We're visiting."

Fatima smiled. She pointed. "You're giving them medical treatment."

"Wouldn't that be illegal?"

"Ah ha! So you do know that much."

"Sure. Of course, that's not what we do. I don't know anything about medicine."

"Then what do you do?"

"We lay on our hands?"

"Exactly. You lay on your hands, and they recover. You're treating them. Then you take credit for the cure. You aren't kidding anybody, Abe."

"I didn't think I was. Thank you for confirming it."

"How many people have you cured, Abe?"

"I haven't cured anybody. My Father in heaven does that."

"Abe, for Christ's sake . . . . "

"Thank you."

". . . you're a Jew."

"Yes. Most people don't know that."

"Haven't you embarrassed your family enough?"

"You mean Shirley?"

"Yes. Shirley." Fatima beamed. She had made contact. All she had to do now was make sure Abe kept talking.

"The only reason Shirley's embarrassed is that she didn't know I'm a Jew. As soon as she understands, she'll come back."

"How could your wife not know you're a Jew?"

"What about you, Naomi June?"

"My name's Fatima."

"That's what I mean."

"Abe, look. There are just the two of us here. What you tell me won't go outside this room. How much are you making? I'm just curious. I'd like to know."

Fatima enunciated with special care, and wished she could tell Abe to do the same. Although the room by now was completely wired, she wanted to avoid any chance that the stenographer couldn't understand what was said.

"You're talking about money?"

"Yes, Abe. Money. Convenient, green pieces of paper. National Reserve Notes. The crap that Albert Holley puts out."

"We don't make anything at all."

"How much have the people paid you? What's the total?"

"Oh, they don't pay us anything. You don't pay anything for grace."

"If they don't pay you anything, how have you been living?"

"People take care of us. We let them, as long as they expect nothing in return."

Abe smiled, divinely at ease. From the beginning, they had told him he'd be caught. He had expected to be caught. Now he had been, and the next chapter was beginning.

"You're entitled to a telephone call, Abe. Who's your lawyer?"

"Woe unto them. I don't have one. Do I need a lawyer?"

"You're facing 500 years in jail if you don't cooperate. I'd say you do."

"Five hundred years. A blink of the eyes. Is the food any good?"

Fatima shuddered. This was the testimony the jurors would hear in court. Thank the good Allah she wasn't the prosecutor.

She left the room and told Steinmetz to take Abe and the others downtown. As she did so, Spats looked at himself in a side view mirror of one of the trucks parked behind the National Reserve Bank, across the narrow street from

Polyakov Tower. He looked more like Albert Holley than the latter did himself. The latex face mask fit perfectly, down to the dewlap. Holley still didn't know--and would never know--why he had fainted at the Club months ago. The hair was just right. For months, Spats had been studying Holley's mannerisms and voice, his gait and attire. Albert would be flattered if he ever found out. Now that the caper was in progress, all Spats's nervousness had gone. He looked at his watch.

The portable telephone beside him rang. "Hello."

"Is this the Automat?"

"No."

"Sorry. Wrong number."

Spats hung up. Louie's call, originating in the unknown city beneath the city, 80 feet below the street, on time to the minute, meant that the National Reserve's telephone system was now in the fine Italian hands of Dr. Ghibellini. Spats lifted the phone and dialed the security captain's night number.

"Yeah?" So impenetrable was the security, that the captain didn't even identify himself or the company he worked for.

"Fred? Is that you? This is Albert Holley. I'm calling you from home."

Spats could almost see Fred buttoning his coat and smoothing his tie. If there was one voice Fred knew as well as his wife's after all these years, it was Albert Holley's. Fred knew of Holley's fascination with memory, and always tried to impress him with his own.

I'll call you right back, Mr. Holley."

"Don't bother buttoning your coat."

Fred found Holley's home number on the list, and called him, pursuant to the security protocol developed by the foremost authorities in town. The phone beside Spats in the truck rang. Sure enough, "Holley" answered. After all these years, Fred knew Holley's voice as well as his own.

"Albert Holley."

"This is Fred, Mr. Holley. At your service.'

"Fred, I'm coming in shortly with a piece of equipment."

"You may have some trouble getting here, Mr. Holley."

"Is something wrong?"

"Not a thing. Outside is a different story."

"What's happening there?"

"A movie premiere across the street. A traffic jam. You could get caught in the middle of it."

"I better get started. Thanks, Fred."

After he hung up, Spats waited a while, to give "Holley" time to arrive. He was sitting in the lead truck. He got out and looked at them, half-a-dozen eighteen-wheelers in a line, all neatly packed to the roofs with utterly gorgeous bars of the metal Dr. Ghibellini had developed that could not be told from gold.

When the heist was over, Holley would have no way of knowing what had happened; if he did discover it, he would keep it a secret.

"Are you ready, Dr. Ghibellini?" Spats asked.

Ghibellini nodded. "*Si. Prego.*"

He was as inspired as Spats. He, too, wore a latex face mask, regretting only that he had had to shave off his Van Dyke for the purpose. He had never been so happy. Only now, in his sixties, had he discovered his proclivity for crime. Often these days, he lamented the lost decades over a bottle of good wine. As a young man in Palermo, he had rejected the efforts of many to recruit him. His father had tried, but Enzo hadn't listened, even ignoring his mother. Thank God he had come to his senses in time. He had learned the biblical injunction to obey one's parents the hard way. In just a few months, thanks to "Giuseppe," he had also learned how the modern world worked. His masterpiece would now unfold. He would use part of his share of the heist to pursue his Equal Employment Opportunity Commission complaint against the university for sexual harassment and ethnic discrimination, which already had sent several members of the administration screeching down the hawsers.

Spats led the way up the ramp. Behind him and Dr. Ghibellini, a couple of men in uniform wheeled the machine on the table. He stopped at the small, heavy steel door, so the cameras could see who he was. Of course this place had never been taken. it wasn't just a bank; it was a fortress, a tomb. It didn't even have any windows.

The door opened. Fred was waiting for them. Spats shook his hand and pointed. "Help them, Fred. Would you? That's a good fellow."

They were wearing uniforms just like Fred's, but he didn't know them, so he was interested. "Where are you guys from?"

"They brought us in from St. Louis."

"How come?"

"We don't know. It must be big."

"What's it all about, Mr. Holley?'

Spats gestured. "Fred, this is Dr. Tobias Greenson, from National Reserve headquarters in Washington. Dr. Greenson's visit here is completely confidential, but it is official business. If it were a military matter, it would have a 'Q' clearance. I rely on your discretion. Understood?"

"Sure."

"Please ask the others to report to the third floor conference room and stay there."

Fred activated the public address system and did so. Fourteen other guards under his direction were on duty. They assembled where Fred told them to go, wondering what was up, happy for this chance to exchange the latest theories about virginity, frigidity, nymphomania and sports. Soon after the Hawk filled the conference room with gas, they fell asleep, some in midsentence. They would awake the next morning with painful headaches, a side effect Dr. Ghibellini, unfailingly humane, had not been able to delete.

"What do we do now, Mr. Holley?" asked Fred, unaware of all this.

"We go down."

"You want to see the gold?"

"Correct."

The door to the vault weighed 90 tons, and was a vertical cylinder set in a steel frame that weighed 50 tons more. It locked by rotating and descending in the frame, like an ordinary plug valve. Fred went through the mandatory protocol. The door rose and rotated. A passageway opened through it.

He was not at all surprised by this visit. Now that it was happening, he expected it. About a year before, unknown to Spats, Holley had paid a similar visit, accompanied by a comparable official. Fred had been, not suspicious, but watchful. Was something wrong? If something was wrong, would Fred be blamed?

That was the last thought he had. When Spats, Ghibellini and the Moose left the passageway through the door, Fred was sitting in a corner on the floor, eyes closed, comfortably waiting until morning.

Spats's voice caught in his throat. The gold stood before him in stalls, 14,000 tons stacked taller than he was, stretching away endlessly in room after room, each bar catalogued and numbered, each stall labeled to show which country or other entity owned it. When that ownership changed, it was simply moved from stall to stall. Taken together, it was a large portion of all the gold ever mined, the repository of several millennia of labor. It shimmered. Spats was sure it exuded a psychic force. He had seen it before, of course, on the tour he had taken with Elizabeth Ann, but then he had been standing on the covered bridge two floors above, separated from it by glass that could have laughed at a plasma torch. Now, he stood beside it almost near enough to touch, and the emotion in his breast was holy. This was the temple of the only god he worshipped. Spats hefted one of the 1,000 ounce bars, enjoying its weight, stifling the desire to sing.

Enzo had smiled when Spats told him the target. His eyes had closed, so his photographic memory could boot up. His head had moved rapidly from side to side as he read what was there.

"'Atomic number 79,'" he read. "'Atomic weight 197. Melting point 1,063 degrees Centigrade. World production from 1493 to 1955: 1,730,000,000 ounces. Total bulk: a 50-foot cube. Largest nugget ever found: "Welcome Stranger." Weight: 2,500 ounces. Found in Victoria, Australia, in 1869. Electrolytic refining.' Hmm 'Alloys. Nitric acid. Amalgam. Mercury. ". . . any excess of mercury over 60% makes the amalgam pasty."' Hmm. Look at this. *Molto interessante*. 'When auric oxide or a gold solution is treated with concentrated ammonia, a black powder is formed called fulminating gold.

(2AuN. NH3.3H20). When dry it is a powerful explosive, since it detonates either by friction or on heating to about 145 degrees Centigrade; it should always be handled with great caution.' *Encyclopedia Britannica*."

The Moose put the machine where Dr. Ghibellini wanted it. "It's all yours," said Spats. Ghibellini went to work.

Enzo had explained it to him carefully. Although it was never mentioned to the people on the tour, the gold was protected by a doomsday security system known to only a few people like Holley. Even Fred and his men were not aware of it. The gold could be picked up and admired where it was without danger. Spats had just done that. However, any attempt to remove the bars without disarming the system, would trigger a hurricane of concentrated ammonia, via hundreds of artfully hidden spouts, thereby converting the metal into fulminating gold, which, subjected to intense heat, would explode. The god Spats worshipped would be transubstantiated but not hurt, blasphemed by sticky pieces of human flesh, bone and brain tissue which specialists would have to remove. Better that, than a successful bank robbery, was the theory.

The theory had never been tested because the guards and some executives, along with several trusted employees, were the only people close enough to do so, and they hadn't tried. They had been told that any attempt to take the gold off the floor would be considered theft and be severely punished.

Only Albert Holley and his deputy in New York, the chairman of the National Reserve in Washington and several others there knew how to disarm the system. It was not based on any guerrilla war-type trip wire--nothing so primitive--but on a complicated combination of gold's atomic weight, atomic number, specific gravity (pure gold: 19.3), magnetic properties and valence. That was as much as Spats understood, and he still wasn't sure he remembered it, but, he didn't have to. That was Dr. Ghibellini's department. The only thing worth knowing was that the system created an electronic field based upon those properties of gold, which if violated went boom, and that Ghibellini's machine could find the frequencies the system was attuned to, shut them off and then change them. It would take about twenty minutes to clear each room. Spats looked at his watch and made a telephone call.

Far above, at street level, the Jews and Nazis were refighting World War II, with results that would be profitable for emergency medical centers around the city. In the Grand Ballroom at the top of Polyakov Tower, Albert Holley sat in total darkness between his wife and Vincent Blandino, marveling at David Polyakov's rhapsodic story. Albert had tried again to persuade his friend Charles to sit beside his wife--suggesting that the lady he was waiting for join them--but, with characteristic modesty, Charles had declined, no doubt electing to watch in a distant row of immovable seats, shoulder to hip with *hoi polloi.*

In the Bronx, Chief of Police Fatima al-Shekel was announcing the arrest of the Goldstein gang--almost all of them--to an impromptu press conference sparsely attended by the second-string reporters and videotape teams the city editors and evening news shows downtown could spare.

And, in the sky over Polyakov Tower, Abe's face appeared, smiling benignly at the celebrants, combatants, observers and police, just as it had so often on the evening news. Many among them were not familiar with recent, revolutionary developments in the science of aerial holographic technology, and took the apparition for a "sign." Compared to the trucks, the waiting choppers and the phony bars of "gold," the "sign" had been easy and inexpensive to arrange. People Abe had touched arrived with their families and friends for a better look, some of them angry. Word of his arrest had just hit the street.

The history books call this "the greatest traffic jam in world history," far surpassing ancient Rome, Gimbel's bargain basement or the ladies' room at the Super Bowl. From Houston Street south to the tip of Manhattan, the city was in gridlock. Nothing moved in or out, except the people who arrived from Brooklyn and New Jersey in rowboats and motor launches. The Staten Island ferry was shut down. As far north as Eighth Street, the main drag in Greenwich Village, police were waving cars away, pursuant to radio directions from Fatima al-Shekel in the Bronx, who was fuming. These are the facts, revealed here for the first time, from the files of the Greater New York Convention Bureau and certain whistle blowers who, because of their sensitive positions in Room #206 at N.Y.P.D., cannot be named.

Still farther above, Krüger went inside and turned on the theater television, to see the media coverage of the premiere the Jewish New York press was providing. Instead, he saw Abe Goldstein's smiling face. The fact that this Yiddish louse had been on television almost every day since Krüger's arrival, was proof of how utterly corrupt and diseased the Americans were. Goldstein's face was so clearly the face of the classic kike. It was intolerable. Krüger quickly turned the television off to escape it.

Spats looked at his watch. There had been no rush; the movie gave them three hours plus an intermission, but thirty minutes had already passed and Dr. Ghibellini still had not cleared the room. Spats began to pace. At this rate, they would run out of time. They would not be ready when the choppers arrived to take the trucks out.

Another half an hour passed. Ghibellini worked with total intensity at the machine. Spats's simmer became a boil. At last, Ghibellini turned to him, shoulders raised, palms extended, mouth open, nose wrinkled with dismay.

"It won't disarm."

"What the hell do you mean?"

"It won't behave as it did in the lab. The frequencies . . . ."

"So, what are you telling me?"

"I need to go back and figure this out."

Spats became calm. That was one of his virtues as a leader. The worse things got, the calmer he became. "Maybe you don't know what's involved here, Gibo. Maybe you don't know what I've invested in this. Are you telling me we need to scratch the mission?"

"The next time we come . . . ."

"There won't be a next time, Gibo. They'll know we were here. They'll redo the security. Whatever you find will be worthless. You said this would be no problem."

The loss would be enormous. Spats had invested most of his considerable fortune. Someone had to die. Spats could not imagine a better candidate than Gibo. The guards would find pieces of his corpse when they awoke.

"Let's just take the gold," said Gibo, starting to come apart.

"And be blown up?"

"If the system won't disarm, maybe something else is wrong."

If Spats killed Gibo here, he would never solve the mystery. His only hope of finding what had happened lay in letting Gibo find it. Gibo had never failed before.

"Keep trying," said Spats. "If you haven't found it when the choppers come, we'll leave."

He couldn't find it. Despite the emission of many interesting signals, considerable fluctuation of the gauges, and several flashing lights, Dr. Ghibellini was no closer to a solution when the Jolly Green Giants thumped in perfectly on time. Spats woodenly took his seat in the lead truck. It took but a moment to connect the grappler; then the chopper lifted off, as smooth as a medevac in Nam.

Many people in the neighborhood saw the choppers and the trucks, but the turmoil made it impossible to concentrate, and they were gone so quickly that the witnesses weren't sure what they had seen. Every aspect of the plan had worked perfectly, with the minor detail that the switch had not been made. Ghibellini's beguiling but worthless metal was still parked in the trucks.

In the Tower, the premiere ended. The lights came on, revealing tears in many eyes. Little was said as the audience left. What could be said about an experience beyond words? People shook Blandino's hand, speechless.

Spats sat around for several days, knowing time would have to pass before he could recover from the shock. Needless to say, not a word appeared in the newspapers. At last, he called Ghibellini.

"Do you have the answer, Gibo?"

"Yes. The answer is quite simple, the only answer possible. If only I had thought of it down there."

"Damn it, Gibo, what have you got?"

Shouldn't Gibo be jubilant? He had the answer, but he wasn't. He was still confused, which did nothing to dissipate Spats's irritation.

The Name of the King
238

"The numbers tell the story," said Ghibellini. "The specific gravity, atomic weight and chemistry. The only possible reason the system did not respond, could not respond--the only possible reason the numbers did not match--is that it was keyed to a different frequency."

"Meaning what?"

"You've been deceived, my friend. The metal in the National Reserve's basement isn't gold."

Chapter Thirty Four
Identity Crisis

Krüger looked around the room, smiling, waving, surrounded by attorneys, pretending that the entire proceeding was a farce, as if it were a social occasion, his rage growing with the pretense.

He was still trying to recover from the shock. A few days ago, he had been what the Americans call "the toast" of New York. The mayor had given him the "key to the city." According to *Variety*, the movie of his life, "Days of Valor," was "boffo b.o.," far outdoing "Acne Frenzy." A three-hour, three-part "Conversation with David Polyakov," was presently airing on the highest-rated television interview program in the country. Only yesterday, his company had won an award from the mayor for public service, and a contract from the U.S. Army. The Goldstein gang had been stopped.

Yet, here he was now, the target of a hearing conducted by the Immigration and Naturalization Service, to determine whether he should be deported for allegedly lying about the question of whether he had ever belonged to a group that advocated the extermination of a minority. His lead attorney, a specialist in immigration law, had told him it meant nothing. It wasn't even a criminal matter. The fool didn't understand that, if successful, it could start a flood.

Of course, it wouldn't be successful. Krüger didn't need his attorney to tell him the government was stalling. They had no case at all, which made him nervous. Surely they were smart enough to know that. But wasn't Chandler, of I.N.S., smiling at him? Did he know something Krüger didn't?

Yes, he did, and he was waiting for it. Finkelstein had convinced him it was true. If he could just hit Krüger with a flesh wound, the next time and venue would be easier. At least, that was the theory. If Chandler couldn't prove it, he was history.

An assistant bent and whispered in his ear. They were ready. Chandler rose. "Commissioner . . . ."

The commissioner stopped him with a hand. "Mr. Chandler, let me say a word before you start. This is an extraordinary proceeding. I don't remember one like it in all my years of service to the Service. This is not a court of law. Although an agency of the Department of Justice is conducting it, this proceeding should be considered quasi-judicial. The only reason I agreed to it, Mr. Chandler, is that you demanded it. To justify it, I'm going to demand an even higher standard of proof than a court of law would require, and, in deference to Mr. Polyakov, we shall conduct this hearing in executive session. Mr. Chandler, is that agreeable?"

"Perfectly, commissioner."

Krüger's lead attorney nodded at the court reporter. "Commissioner, as long as we're making a record, could it show that Mr. Polyakov, who is something of a newshound, which he admits, has not requested that the media be excluded?"

"Let the record show that, madam reporter," said the commissioner. "Be that as it may, they will be excluded anyway. If Mr. Polyakov has no fear for his reputation, I do."

"I do have a procedural question," said Chandler. "Since we have no rules that govern a higher standard of proof, may I safely assume that the Federal Rules of Criminal Procedure will apply?"

"Mr. Chandler, we already have a tower of assumption here that would rival Babel, but, if Mr. Polyakov's people have no objection, I'm sure we could proceed on that basis."

The attorneys surrounding Krüger bowed, smiled, preened, made deprecating gestures and had no objection. Why bother objecting to something that is so palpably a fraud, something that will turn its perpetrators into pitiful object lessons?

"Commissioner, our purpose here today is modest," said Chandler. "We make no pretense of proving the identity of the subject of this hearing. That would be irrelevant to the present purposes of the Service, and we shall do it later, in another forum. Today, however, we shall initiate that process, by establishing that the subject of this hearing is not who he says he is; that he lied on his application for admission to this country."

"What did he lie about?"

Chandler pointed. "Commissioner, this man is not David Polyakov."

John Weaver Yates III, Kruger's lead attorney, senior partner at Yates, Harris, Bluestone, Foreman and Rice, was on his feet. Like all his lesser colleagues there, he didn't know his client wasn't David Polyakov, so the belligerent rectitude of ignorance, combined with the bloated contentiousness endemic to his ilk, produced a manner that made Mussolini look like Shirley Temple, and was worth every penny of his itemized bill.

"Commissioner, at this point may I add something constructive?"

"I wish somebody would." The commissioner was uncomfortable. He had been told that Polyakov would be a witness in a hearing of extraordinary importance to the Service. He had not been told that Polyakov was the subject of the hearing. He had not been told that Chandler would say Polyakov had lied. The commissioner looked at Chandler balefully. He had been snookered. He couldn't wait for this thing to end, so he could retaliate.

"I realize we are governed here by the Federal Rules of Criminal Procedure," counsel chuckled, "but in the interests of time and tide, lunch and tennis or golf, as the case may be"--the other attorneys tittered--"may I suggest, commissioner, that we simply ask Mr. Polyakov who he is."

"A productive suggestion," said the commissioner. "And since we have already made a mockery of procedure, I don't see any harm in it. Mr. Polyakov, would you mind sitting here? There's no need to swear him. Are you comfortable, sir?"

"Yes. Thank you."

Chandler saw that he had already burned a bridge. The enmity flowing from the commissioner was palpable. The commissioner had given him victory in the rules, and then taken it away. Well, hadn't Chandler deceived him? He could not go back.

"Proceed."

"Would you identify yourself, sir?" asked Yates.

"I'm David Polyakov."

"How old are you, Mr. Polyakov?"

"I'm 68."

"Have you always been David Polyakov?"

"Yes."

"Have you ever been anyone else?"

"No."

"Where were you born?"

"In Poland, in 1912."

"Mr. Polyakov, what position do you presently occupy?"

"Among other things, I'm chairman of Polyakov Pharmaceuticals."

"Have you ever won any awards for public service?"

"Oh, yes, a couple."

"A couple, Mr. Polyakov? Isn't it true that the government of Israel has given you the highest honor it can give a civilian? Isn't it true that a hospital and many other things in that country are named for you? Do you deny that, Mr. Polyakov?"

"No, I don't deny it. You've got me." Both of them were chuckling.

"Mr. Polyakov, have you any idea why someone would seriously believe you are not who you are?"

"I can't imagine. A business rival, perhaps. A victim of the war who is suffering a delusion. A blackmailer who hasn't yet asked for money. It is difficult to deal with anonymous charges. I believe in your country you call it McCarthyism."

"That's exactly what we call it. One more question, Mr. Polyakov, which I'm sure will lay this thing to rest. Can you prove who you are? Do you have anything on paper?"

"Yes, I have much paper, many documents. My birth records. The Nazi files. The Allied paperwork after the war. It's all available if needed. But I don't think it will be. I have something else. May I show it to you?"

Krüger took off his Givenchy coat and folded it neatly on the chair. He took the diamond link specially designed for him, worth about $9,000, from his left cuff and put it on his coat. He rolled up his sleeve, and pointed at his arm.

"There, your honor. My concentration camp number from Auschwitz."

At the sight of the horror, the hearing room grew still. No one spoke for a long time. Even the attorneys in attendance stopped preening. The commissioner looked away. Never had anything so evil been seen in the room. Krüger held out his arm. "The Nazis kept such good records. Would you like to check the number, Mr. Chandler?"

The commissioner cleared his throat. "Mr. Polyakov," he said at last, "let me apologize on behalf of the United States government, the Attorney General and the Immigration and Naturalization Service. The fact that you have been subjected to this embarrassing waste of time is an outrage. I hope you understand that when someone makes a charge, the government must respond. Be assured at least that the person responsible for this outrage will pay. Are there any more questions, Mr. Chandler?"

"I have no questions, commissioner. But I do have a witness. May I ask her to come in?"

"Get it over with, Mr. Chandler. Mr. Polyakov, please step down, if you like. Take a moment to restore your attire."

Chandler signaled to the back of the room. The door opened. A woman came in, a tall woman in her sixties, who had been beautiful, still was impressive and moved with a dancer's grace. She carried a long, rectangular package. Chandler waved her to the seat recently vacated by Krüger.

"Would you tell the Commissioner your name?" Chandler said.

"I am Mrs. David Polyakov."

Was it she? Krüger could not believe it. Yes, she was regal, but Krüger saw no trace in her of the Frieda he remembered. The Frieda he remembered was young, as he still was, blonde, virginal. This woman was old, much older than he. There was no trace of color in her hair. Of course, he had been hunting her for 35 years. For some of those years, at least, he had been paying the Arabs to find her. They had failed, but now she had simply walked in. How could that be? Krüger became aware that his attorneys were twisting in their seats in consternation.

"Can you prove that, Mrs. Polyakov?"

There didn't appear to be any emotion in her actions, as if all emotion had long since drained away. She opened her large bag and took out a folder. "Everything is there."

"Mrs. Polyakov, were you an inmate at the Nazi concentration camp called Auschwitz?"

"Yes."

"Mrs. Polyakov, I apologize for my next question. I hope you understand why I must ask it. Do you have the Nazi number on your arm?"

"Yes."

"Would you show it to the commissioner?"

"All right."

For 35 years, she had worn long sleeves to conceal it. All that time, others had told her to have it removed, because "you need to forget." The skin could not again be made pristine, but the number would be gone. She had refused. She *didn't want* to forget, *couldn't* forget. Now, she pulled up a sleeve and laid her arm on the commissioner's desk. He barely looked at the offensive brand. He couldn't.

Chandler handed her a document from the file. "Mrs. Polyakov, I hand you a document, and I ask you to identify it."

She held it by diagonal corners between thumbs and forefingers, making as little contact as possible. "This is my Nazi record from the camp."

"Does the record contain your name, date of birth and family history?"

"Yes."

"Does it contain the same number you just showed the Commissioner on your arm?"

"Yes."

Chandler took the document from her, and put it on the Commissioner's desk. He asked, "Was David Polyakov your husband?"

"Yes."

Yates was whispering nervously to Krüger, taking the farce seriously at last. Who was she? Krüger could not answer. He had no physical attraction to this woman whatsoever; but, of course, she had not enjoyed the benefits of Nazi racial science for the last 35 years. So far, she hadn't even glanced at Krüger.

"How long were you married, Mrs. Polyakov?"

"Seven years."

"Why seven years?"

Krüger's lead counsel was on his feet. He had come here in the belief that this would be some sort of joke, for which someone who didn't get the message would be punished. Conducting an adversarial proceeding with this pip-squeak Chandler, who made less in a year than Yates paid snotnoses in training bras just out of law school, was embarrassing. He had brought along four such attorneys, with and without bras, expecting them to conduct the hearing under his supercilious direction. When David Polyakov was paying the bill, one could bring enough attorneys to inspire Jesus Christ to violence. By means of various emoluments and blandishments Yates had established a discreet liaison with one of them, for whom a training bra could not do justice, primarily because she was so egregiously up front. Until this point in the hearing, he had been in reverie about what he would do to her later.

Now, without warning, the proceeding had metastasized, and, for some incredible reason, Polyakov couldn't help him. If there was one word that summarized Yates's success, it was "preparation." Know your case by heart. Never ask a question if you don't know the answer. Don't introduce a subject, unless you know all about it. All well and good, but the present booby trap threw all that wisdom in the garbage. He had no idea what was happening. All he had was an intuition, based on the fact that Polyakov had never mentioned a wife.

Yates said, "Commissioner, it appears that, whoever the lady is, brother Chandler's plan is to navigate her into areas that the late Senator McCarthy used to infest. May I ask that she be sworn?" Yates didn't know what the point of that would be, but he had to do something; had to take the risk that "brother" Chandler would know he was stalling.

"May I remind the commissioner that Mr. Yates's client wasn't sworn?" Chandler shot back. "Mrs. Polyakov does not object to being sworn, and, in fact, is eager to be sworn, but I ask the commissioner to take judicial notice of the fact--pardon me, commissioner, I ask the record to reflect--that the man who says he's Polyakov was not."

"Commissioner, I object to Mr. Chandler's characterization of Mr. Polyakov."

"Your honor, the identity of the man who says he's Polyakov is the subject of this hearing."

"All right," said the commissioner. "Swear her in and let's move on."

"Mrs. Polyakov, why were you married to your husband, David Polyakov, for only seven years?"

"He was murdered."

"At Auschwitz?"

"No. After."

"When?"

"April, 1945."

"The war was still on, but would end soon, in May. The Nazis closed Auschwitz in January, to escape the advancing Russians."

"Yes."

"Mrs. Polyakov, who killed your husband, David, and why?"

The question severed her fragile contact with 1980, where she was painlessly dead. Like a voyager lost in deep space, she drifted back to 1945, where she was horribly alive. She had warned Chandler this could happen. She had told him she couldn't tell it all. She never had. She couldn't tell the whole thing to anyone, not even God. Chandler had assured her she didn't have to.

"Horst Krüger." She whispered the name.

"Who was Horst Krüger?"

"He . . . killed . . . my husband."

"What did Krüger do for a living at the time?"

"He . . . was . . . a senior SS killer at the camp."

"Is this the same Horst Krüger who has been sought ever since for his crimes against humanity?"

"Yes."

"Tell us about the murder, Mrs. Polyakov."

"We made an arrangement . . . ."

"You and Krüger."

"Yes."

"What was that arrangement?"

"We would give him our money in Zurich in exchange for our lives."

"Did you give Krüger your money, Mrs. Polyakov?"

"Yes."

"Did Horst Krüger give you your lives?" She was here to tell her story, but Chandler was having to drag it from her with forceps.

Frieda bowed her head. "No."

"No?"

"He killed us . . . ."

"Killed you?"

". . . and has impersonated David ever since."

"The presence of the real David Polyakov would have made that impossible."

"*Natürlich.*" Her perfect, colloquial English was leaving.

"Did you see Horst Krüger kill David Polyakov?"

"*Ich* . . . I saw David's body. Krüger was there. He boasted about it. I saw the ax he had used."

"He killed your husband with an ax?"

"*Ja.*"

"Mrs. Polyakov, do you see Horst Krüger, the man who killed your husband with an ax, in this room?"

"Objection!" Yates shouted.

"*Ja.* I see him."

"Let her finish," said the commissioner. His interest was reviving.

Frieda pointed. "There."

Chandler said, "Let the record show that Mrs. Polyakov is pointing at the man who calls himself 'David Polyakov.'"

For the first time since her arrival, she looked straight at Krüger, and he saw her eyes, the same eyes he had seen on the railway platform in Munich long ago, the Aryan eyes of the glorious, young woman he remembered, cold, pristine, like ice-blue mountain lakes. Her eyes had not changed, except that now they contained an emotion beyond hatred, an emotion beyond emotion. It was she, the only one left who possibly could hurt him; the one he had sought for 35 years since D*er Tag*. Krüger looked away, trying to suppress his lust for vengeance, trying to maintain his smile. Were the Arabs just incompetent, or traitors? His hand went to his face; his fingers traveled along the jagged scar, like an alpine road across his cheek.

Yates smiled. Experience took over. Knowledge took over. Yates had read a lot about the camps. Despite the palpable emotion in the room, Chandler hadn't proved anything. He hadn't proved that Polyakov was Krüger. He hadn't even proved that Polyakov was somebody else. All he had was a crazy woman with a number on her arm.

"Commissioner, may I ask the lady a couple of questions?"

"We want no cross examination here, Mr. Yates. This is not a trial."

"Of course not, commissioner. Just a couple of questions for the record. Madam, you've said you were married to David Polyakov for seven years."

"Yes."

"How many years did you both spend in concentration camps?"

"Four."

"More than half your marriage?"

"Yes."

"During all that time, did you ever see your husband?"

"No. The Nazis."

"Of course. The Nazis. Later, after the Nazis, how much time did you spend together?"

"A couple of days."

"And you haven't seen him for 35 years."

"*Nein.*"

"Let me see whether I understand this, *meine frau.* You and your husband spent a couple of years together; four years later, another couple of days. And you haven't seen him for 35 years. *Nicht wahr*?"

"*Ja. Ja.* But I'd know him anywhere."

"You'd know whom anywhere, Mrs. Polyakov? Whom are we talking about now?"

"Krüger."

"Commissioner," said Yates, "I have no wish to make light of what the lady has told us, no desire to embarrass her. The number on her arm proves that, like Mr. Polyakov, she has suffered much. Her sincerity is touching. Obviously, she believes what she is saying. I raise the question of whether it is true. I raise the question of what that suffering has done to her, precisely because Mr. Polyakov is an innocent man. I raise the question of whether what we are talking about could be some sort of estrangement.

"There is no need to recite again Mr. Polyakov's record of achievement. It has been mentioned here. It is available for guidance and inspiration in every library worthy of the name. Let me simply remind the commissioner how faulty the memory is. Eyewitnesses often can't agree about what they saw a week ago. After 35 years, most people could not recognize their mothers. After 35 years, Dante would not recognize Beatrice. After 35 years, Tristan wouldn't recognize Isolde. And, after 35 years, it's just possible that a woman who has suffered much, a woman who has been wronged, a woman who feels abandoned, doesn't recognize a man she was married to for less time than some people are engaged.

"Commissioner, I know this isn't a trial. All I ask is that we be reasonable. Isn't it reasonable to ask whether the lady is mistaken? Yes, the lady has numbers on her arm--but so does Mr. Polyakov! So does Mr. Polyakov, commissioner! His arm tells the story. His arm tells the story! If my question is reasonable, and I think it is, are you willing to run the risk of destroying an innocent man, a man who has built an international reputation hunting down the very people who caused the lady such grief?"

The room became quiet. Chandler smiled and tried not to smile too much. Yates had taken the bait and run with it. Chandler would have done the same thing. This was the time.

"Do you have anything else, Mr. Yates?"

"No, commissioner."

The emergency was past. Yates and his people were smiling and preening again. Krüger marveled at his attorney's brilliance. What a splendid Nazi he would make!

The commissioner said, "This hearing has been most uncomfortable. It springs from a tragedy that perseveres even 35 years later. Both of these good people are victims. One of them is mistaken, no doubt sincerely mistaken, but we don't know which one and probably never will."

"Commissioner?" It was Chandler. "I believe the lady has something else." He nodded. Yates, Harris, Bluestone, Foreman & Rice was alert again.

All this time, there had been a package on her knees, neatly wrapped, like something she had bought in a duty-free shop at the airport in Munich. It was rectangular and a couple of feet long. She unwrapped it gingerly, without tearing the paper, the way a woman unwraps gift paper she plans to use again. Inside was a clear plastic container, which she put on the commissioner's desk.

He looked at it, and his emotion changed, from the tired sympathy he had recently expressed, to horror. Despite himself, he shrank against his chair.

The commissioner was looking at Polyakov's arm.

* * *

She had screamed for a long time, pulling at her hair. When a modicum of sanity returned, she had stared at David's arm and cried. Because of the cold, Krüger had been able to do nothing but barely cover the body. The avalanche had buried it. Krüger had not been able to sever the arm. The beast had done so, and buried it far from the body. The climbers who had found the body hadn't found the arm. The beast had hidden it, waiting for her, knowing she would come.

It was perfectly preserved, thanks to 35 years of deep freeze. The charred skin had not deteriorated. The number had not faded. It was just as clear as it had been that day at war's end, waiting all this time for its rendezvous with Krüger.

She had to take it to New York, but how? Any authority who found it on the way--police, airport security or customs--would take it away. There was also the problem of refrigeration.

It was all she had left of David. Shuddering, eyes closed, she touched it. "*Ich bin hier, liebchen,*" she whispered.

She packed it in snow, stowed it in her backpack, and was able to get it safely to her room at the inn. She paid the bill, loaded the rented car and drove to Zurich, where she found the proper container, learned about dry ice, and began a new career of lies. She was a "physician" who needed to "transport a specimen." A "patient" was "running out of time" in New York. Her story was so outrageous, it worked. Driving like an old lady, she set out for Munich. There, airport security looking for Middle Eastern terrorists made her open all her bags. The arm was there in plain sight, underneath some lingerie, but they ignored it. Had she wished, she could have smuggled aboard enough *plastique* to destroy the Eighth Air Force.

Finally aboard the non-stop flight, she couldn't relax until they were airborne. Over the French coast, the captain explained that "a mechanical" would force the flight down at Heathrow. The passengers were bussed to the city, where they spent the night at a hotel. The next morning, back at Heathrow, on line to check in, Frieda was escorted to a small, quiet room. A middle-aged man waited there, looking out the window, smoking a pipe. On the desk was the arm, still in the container.

"Mrs. Goldstein?"

"Yes."

There was no need to play games, or even to wait for his questions. She sat at the desk, rolled up her sleeve and pointed at her arm.

He nodded. "Where did you matriculate?"

"Auschwitz. The arm is my husband's. It's needed in New York at a war criminal's trial."

"Who is the criminal?"

"Krüger."

"Horst Krüger?"

"Yes."

"So they finally found him after all these years."

He handed her the container. "I took the liberty of adding some dry ice. I hope you don't mind, Mrs. Goldstein."

"No." She smiled. "I don't understand."

Now it was his turn to undo his sleeve and show her his number, and, for the first time, she noticed his name on the desk plate: Hyman Cohen. "Sobibor," he said. "My mother and sisters didn't make it. The Nazis are everywhere, but so are we. I just wanted to make sure who you are."

* * *

No doubt the commissioner was imagining it. The numbers on the arm seemed to be throbbing with light. Still seated with his attorneys at the table, Krüger nervously fingered his scar. It flowed south, blood red, throbbing like the arm. The room was still unnaturally quiet.

At last, the commissioner said, "Why don't you tell us what this is, Mrs. Polyakov?"

"Go ahead," said Chandler. "Tell him."

"This is David Polyakov's arm," she said. "Krüger tried to destroy it when he killed my husband that day; tried to hack it off with the ax. He couldn't, but the avalanche finished the job. The evidence has been buried, waiting, for 35 years."

"How did you happen to find it, Mrs. Polyakov?" asked the commissioner.

"The avalanche moved on. They told me this happens all the time."

Chandler said, "Commissioner, the arm doesn't prove that this man is Horst Krüger, but it certainly does prove he isn't David Polyakov. Please compare the numbers."

"Your honor, this is preposterous!" Yates shouted, forgetting himself. "There's no proof it's even human. For all we know, it's a prosthesis, an invention."

"That can easily be determined by the pathologists," said Chandler. "May I suggest that we subject the arm to rigorous tests."

The commissioner brightened. Chandler's suggestion was good. By adopting it, the commissioner could wash his hands of the problem. It would go to the courts.

"I protest, commissioner," said Yates. "We came here today out of respect for your office. We weren't told we'd be tricked into playing the butt of a silly farce."

Chandler said, “Commissioner, could the record reflect the fact that neither Mrs. Polyakov nor I regards this proceeding as a farce.”

"Your comment is so noted, Mr. Chandler,” said the commissioner. “Have you told us everything, Mrs. Polyakov?"

She nodded. "Yes," she lied.

Chapter Thirty Five
Breathing Together

Albert Holley looked at the six men around the table. Together, they controlled most of the economy of the United States. What they didn't control wasn't important, and they didn't control it simply because it wasn't worth bothering with, and because it did the very important job of preserving the illusion of Free Enterprise.

"Gentlemen," he whispered. He whispered because they were meeting in a conference room where everything was said in whispers, but the intended heard. It was a dark place, with heavy furniture and drapes, polished and portentous, where speaking in a normal voice would be *gauche*, even *outré*. The conference room belonged to an informal, little group, whose membership made it the most powerful, private organization in the United States. Although many media lions belong to it, all members must sign a pledge of confidentiality to encourage free discussion, so nothing that happens there has been revealed--until now.

"Thank you for coming. No doubt you are wondering whether the occasion of your august presence is as important as I said it was. The truth is, gentlemen, that I couldn't tell you on the telephone how truly crucial it is, even over the scrambler. We face the most dangerous threat since that priapic, smart aleck Jack Kennedy proposed that we leave South East Asia, and start printing United States Notes. Of course, fate removed him."

Bryson Fagley, the industrialist, whose seminar on Free Enterprise had made him fairly well known in “conservative circles,” nodded. "And a damn, good thing it did. The Reserve could have been destroyed."

"Yet, you say this thing is worse," said Wilfred Bronson, a "private investor," whose name never appeared in the media.

"Gentlemen, ten days ago the National Reserve's integrity was compromised."

"Good lord, Albert," said James Parnell Maxon, "are you trying to tell us some metal has disappeared?" Maxon was the theoretician of the little band of prophets. A man of consummate mildness, he was known to the outside world as a "college professor," which in fact he was.

"I wish it were that simple, James."

"Albert, what in hell are you talkin' about?" asked Shorty Longstreet, who was six feet four inches tall. Longstreet was the senior senator from a southern state, was flamboyant without trying, and had won a well-deserved reputation as a "staunch anti-Communist."

"Unauthorized people got into the vault."

"You mean they broke in?" asked Longstreet.

"No. They walked in."

"How the hell could that happen, Albert? Don't you have security?"

"Security admitted them, because their leader was my double. He wore a mask so lifelike, even down to the dewlap, that even Fred Kravitz, who knows me well, couldn't tell the difference. He compromised our telephone system and spoke with my voice as well as I do. The tape of the telephone call Fred made to me at home, which is the mandated security protocol, proves it. Let me play it for you now."

There was a tape recorder on the table and Holley got it going. The others heard the conversation between Spats and Fred. "Is there anyone present who wouldn't have believed that's my voice?"

"Are you sure it isn't?" Fagley asked.

"Does Edgar Bergen have an alibi?" asked Shorty.

"I'm confused," said Bronson. "What did they do when they got in?"

"We don't know. They used sophisticated drugs to knock out Fred and his men. I do have a theory."

"Let's see," mused Maxon. "They broke in, or, rather, gained admittance, obviously after months of preparation, presumably to steal the metal. They left without it, which you regret. Albert, I think you do need to tell us your theory."

"They did come to get the metal. They did prepare for months. Whoever they are, they are men of genius. They orchestrated the most complicated diversion since the Inchon Landing, with the help of Jews, would-be Nazis, an aerial holograph, the Goldstein gang and the Polyakov movie premiere, which I attended. Everything worked perfectly--until they discovered that the metal in the vaults isn't gold."

The friends coughed and shifted in their seats. Suddenly, the air was cold, as if a ghost were there. If Albert Holley had ever lacked their attention, he certainly had it now.

"So they know," whispered Fagley.

"How did they discover it?" asked Maxon.

"You told us it was undetectable," said Bronson. "We decided to move forward on that basis."

"We don't know," lied Holley. He had decided not to tell them about the machine. Holley never told all he knew. Fred was the only one of them who had seen it, and Holley had told him to forget it. "Right now, that's not important. They found it wasn't gold and left. Which means, gentlemen, that there is now at least one man who knows there is no gold in the vaults, who knows we replaced it with lesser metal and who knows the gold is somewhere else. Do you all realize what this could mean if it gets into the media?"

"It won't get into the media," said Dick Ballantine, the man from Big Oil. "We own the media. The only media we don't own are the talk shows and the newsletters, and we don't want them."

"Why not?"

"They're a valuable safety valve, Albert. They prove we have freedom of the press."

"Are you willing to risk your liberty and property on that, Dick?"

Maxon said, "If it gets out to any extent, the markets will destabilize, before we want them to. The runaway panic we've been planning could start before we're ready. We could lose control. Although there's nothing behind our currency, the people think it's the gold. If they think the gold is gone, the National Reserve could collapse. All the effort we've invested in destabilizing the Middle East could be squandered, along with the vast, virgin Russian market, pleading for cheap goods. We couldn't very well impose fiscal discipline on the rest of the world if we lose it ourselves. We could also lose access to the educated but economical labor of the Far East. International coordination could be crippled."

"The guy who did this thing is probably looking for the gold right now," said Longstreet.

"Could our shipments from Colombia through Panamá be affected?" asked Ballantine. "They are presently our biggest source of revenue."

"Dick, they could be stopped."

Maxon said, "If that happened, we couldn't sustain the war on drugs. The banking regulations we've worked so hard for could be lost."

"Gentlemen, may I say something?"

"Of course, brother Krüger," said Holley.

"We can talk about this all evening, but we need to restore our security, and the fact is we can do that only with a final solution. We must find the man who did this and destroy him."

An approving murmur crept around the room. Leave it to good, old Horst to seize the problem by the throat.

"I think we know that, Horst," said Maxon. "How would we do it?"

"The man who did this has considerable, scientific expertise. I wish he worked for me. He also knows a lot about banks. Maybe we are talking about more than one man. Does anyone come to mind, gentlemen?"

Despite the gravity of the emergency, Krüger was at peace. He always enjoyed these meetings with his confreres. They thought they were using him. *Let them think that*! By the time they found out what was happening, it would be too late. By now, the cultural degeneration that was an essential element of the takeover was irreversible. The campaign to seize control of the doctors was advancing. Americans were such fools! You could sell an American sodomy, if you called it "following too closely."

"There are lists we could consult," said Maxon. "Spats Davis is the best known bank robber in town."

"Could he have done this?" asked Krüger.

"He is very thorough, but we don't know what he looks like and we don't have any prints. 'Spats Davis' is probably a *nom de guerre*. He could be anyone, and probably is."

Now that Krüger had put the solution into words, Holley became aware that something was bothering him, something in his memory he could not recall. It would come with time.

"The longer this man lives, the greater the danger," said Krüger.

"I'll put everyone I have on the problem," said Holley. "On another subject, Horst, I'm sure I speak for all of us when I say how happy I am that the recent misunderstanding was resolved. People get such strange ideas."

"'War criminal,' indeed!" said Fagley. "Preposterous!"

Everyone chuckled. "Your assistance was invaluable, gentlemen," said Krüger. "Especially yours, Senator."

Longstreet said, "I'm told poor Mr. Chandler is adapting nicely to his new job in Nome."

In the end, the bizarre dispute had come down to the question of whom to believe: a dilapidated arm with no one to speak for it but a crazy, old woman no one ever heard of; or a complete man with enough reputation for a few Nobel Prizes, and many friends in high places, for whom election as Chancellor of his country would have been a step down.

"What happened to Mrs. Polyakov and the arm?" Bronson asked.

"Mrs. Polyakov has disappeared again," Krüger said. "When we find her, I am sure we can reach an understanding. I kept the arm as a memento."

It was true. He had brought David's arm to Vörst at the castle, where it hung in a place of honor beside the portrait of the Führer, permanently preserved in a vacuum container.

* * *

McGillicuddy waited in the reception room as directed. He was as high in the hierarchy as he had ever gone--the office of the president of the New York National Reserve--but his faith was fading fast. He had sat in so many reception rooms and seen so many people. All the questions and conversations had been useless. He was no closer to James K. Slagle, Senior Vice President of the Federal Deposit Insurance Corporation, than he'd been at first; except to discover that there was no such man.

Elizabeth Ann had disputed that, of course. "James" was "under cover." The F.D.I.C. people had been told to say he didn't exist. She had read some books on intelligence. That was how it worked. Against all reason, she had chosen to believe that his disappearance was connected to his work. Had something happened to him?

Needless to say, McGillicuddy was not taken in. He had been suspicious of "James K. Slagle" from the start. A man who wouldn't get married in church was probably a Communist. Abe had assured him "James" was okay, but he was different from all the others in the group. McGillicuddy had done what "James" had liberally paid him to do, but still couldn't understand what it had to do with F.D.I.C. It, too, was probably connected to his "under cover" work. Everything was. Well, Francis X. McGillicuddy was there to say that he wouldn't let this man keep victimizing his daughter.

"Tell me your story," smiled Albert Holley, when McGillicuddy at last was seated in his office. It was a vast room. There were groups of sofas, judiciously placed, so that several conversations could be conducted at once. The one McGillicuddy sat on was so soft, so yielding and enveloping, that, when the time came, it would require quite a struggle to get up, despite the fact that his feet firmly rested ankle deep in the carpet.

Holley had heard his story of course, from the lady McGillicuddy had told it to on the phone, but he wanted to hear it in person. This would be an unusual visit. People did not see the president of the New York Reserve unless they didn't need to drop his name. But McGillicuddy's story sounded worth hearing.

"My son-in-law is missing," said McGillicuddy.

"I'm sorry to hear that. Your daughter must be distraught."

"No. She believes what she likes."

"But why come to me? I'm a banker. Shouldn't you tell the police?"

"I've done that."

"Then why come to me?"

"Should I tell you?"

"Yes. Why not start at the beginning."

"Sure. I was born in Brooklyn, in Sheepshead Bay, but my people come from Ireland. Did you know that?"

"I guessed it."

Francis worked his way up through his childhood and first communion, his courtship and marriage, his career in environmental science, finally arriving at his daughter's disappearance and mysterious marriage, his unwilling confrontation with Fatima, his stint as a disciple and the loss of his job, where he had been quite important, if he said so himself.

"I called F.D.I.C. You'd think they'd have heard of a senior vice president, but they said the name was not familiar. My daughter says of course they'd say that. He's working undercover. She's not worried, you see."

"Very sensible. What is he working to expose?"

"He never said. Lizzie says he exposes irregularities in the banks."

"What kind of irregularities?"

McGillicuddy whispered, "Sometimes cash disappears from the vaults. Sometimes it happens all the time."

"Embezzlement?"

"Yes."

"I didn't know that. Your son-in-law found out?"

"So he says."

"Maybe the embezzlers found out who he is. Maybe something happened to him."

"That's what I was thinking. Or, did he just disappear?"

"Whom does he say he works undercover for? F.D.I.C.?"

"All I know is he helps Abe Goldstein. Like the night of the movie."

"The hymn to Polyakov?"

"The very one. Knowing my talent for supervision, he asked me to look after the hollow graft system, a technology I could explain if you like. We put an image of Abe in the sky, which was blasphemous idol worship, if you ask me. Of course, I played along to see where he was going."

"What do you know about Abe? Is he a con man?"

"Abe wouldn't know a con if it stole the shoes off his feet."

"Yet, he says he's Jesus Christ."

"He doesn't say he's Jesus Christ. A voice says it. Abe doesn't want to be Jesus Christ, for which I'm grateful, if you want to know the truth. He was drafted."

"And the miracles?"

"They happen. Many have been cured. I didn't believe it either 'til I saw. He's good on senility. He's a sweetheart on tumors. I know he's an expert on the heartbreak of psoriasis."

"So, how do you explain it?"

"I don't, Albert. Could I call you that?"

"If you believe all this, why did you recant?"

"Fatima told me I had to. She said if I refused I'd lose my job."

"I think I could be helpful there, Francis. I know a few people in high places. Perhaps I could make a few calls. If I were you, I'd stop worrying. Tell me, what is your son-in-law's name?"

"Slagle. James K. Slagle."

"Thank you, Francis. You have been such a help."

When McGillicuddy had gone, Holley sat a long time at his desk, staring out the tall windows at the East River traffic. James K. Slagle. Obviously a pseudonym. Whom did he represent? Some rogue element within F.D.I.C.? Impossible! No such group would have enough clout. Another agency of government? The Bureau? The Agency? Only one conclusion made any sense. Somewhere at the top, there was a traitor. Could it be one of the six? The thought was so intolerable, Holley had to hold his head. Who was he?

Charles M. Wilson. Manhattan Restorations. Where had they first met? At the Club. Hadn't he been alone with Charles? Of course! Holley's loss of consciousness had been part of the plan. That was what Holley had been trying to remember. Charles had knocked him out for some reason. Why? Had Charles's purpose at the premiere been to make sure Holley didn't leave during the operation at the bank, or simply to establish an alibi? Of course none of the metal was gone. The penetration had not been an attempted robbery at all. Somewhere at the Reserve there was a leak. Wilson, or whoever he was, had been there to investigate. Was Charles "James K. Slagle?"

Holley lifted the telephone. "Manhattan Restorations."

Chapter Thirty Six
Lifeguard

"Do you know why I brought you here, Abe?" Fatima said at last. "Just the two of us?"

"No," said Abe. "But since you brought me here, I guess you'll tell me."

"Abe, we've decided to let you go."

"All of us?"

"Yes."

"Does that mean we won't go to jail?"

"Correct."

"Fatima, I just want to tell you what a fine person you are, and that I probably would vote for you if I voted, which I don't, because I'm sure the mayor is as fine a person as you are. So, I stay out of politics. By their fruit ye shall know them, which probably means you'll go to hell, but of course your destination is foreknown, so you can't do anything about it anyway."

"Abe, if you have any complaints . . . ."

"Not one. I've made some good friends on your staff. They've treated us so well. I do have one question."

"What's that, Abe?"

"If you're letting us go, why did you spend so much time, effort, and money, which you don't have, to arrest us?"

Fatima shuddered. "Politics."

The mayor, the City Council president and the district attorney had triple-teamed her. "What shall we charge these people with, Fatima?" the latter had asked.

"There are probably a dozen good and righteous charges. Use them all."

"Such as."

"Money."

"How much money have you found?"

The truth was that Fatima had found none. People gave them money, but there was no fraud.

"Who would testify against them, Fatima? The people you found dancing on the lawn? In fact, who would serve on the jury? Did you remember that, despite our best efforts, we would still need a jury?"

"What about trespassing?" she had asked in a small voice.

"We couldn't get criminal. Are you prepared to tell the people you went to all this trouble and spent all this money because Mr. Goldstein walked on the grass?"

"There's always practicing medicine without a license."

"Good idea! Do you have a witness?"

"Certainly! Hundreds."

"By any chance, chief, would you be referring to the people Mr. Goldstein saved from senility, stroke, syphilis, dandruff, and the thousand other evils the flesh is heir to?"

"There are two conditions," Fatima told Abe now.

"I don't like conditions. They cause discord. I like things one way or the other."

"First, you have to stop what you're doing."

"Stop helping people?"

"Whatever you call it. No more laying on of hands. No more cures. No more taking money from the mouths of struggling Park Avenue specialists with mistresses to support. No more spitting in the face of organized religion. No more dancing on the lawn."

"You said there was a second condition."

"The second one is more important. We want you to get out of town."

"Leave New York?"

"Correct."

"Where would we go?"

"We don't know. We don't care. It's a free country. As long as it's not here. If you're Jesus Christ, you should get used to being run out of town."

"A good point. I'll tell the others."

"There are many people who don't like you. Did you know that?"

"Most people don't like me, Fatima."

"If you leave, the chances are good they'll cool off. If you don't, well, the police can't be everywhere."

* * *

Frieda sat in the dark, as usual. It was soothing. She had sat in the dark for many years, waiting, suspended in a limbo between life and death. Now, the waiting was over. There was nothing left, no reason to continue this farce. In its own way, this was worse than the camp. There, at least, there had been hope. Here, there was nothing. She should have let Krüger kill her, so the avalanche could cover her with David.

She had told Finkelstein and Chandler it wouldn't work, even if she had the arm. Krüger also had an arm, he had billions and he had powerful associates. Who was she beside him? Hadn't they made a movie of his stolen life? Wasn't it making millions? She recalled with disgust attending Blandino's media blowout at the Tower, hoping to discover something she could use. Krüger was "Polyakov," but she hadn't even used David's name for many years.

Yet, she had done everything they asked, hoping against reason that a confrontation would finally bring Krüger down. Instead, Krüger had laughed in her face. All she had accomplished was to prove she was alive, to show him what she looked like and tell him her address--so he could send his thugs to kill her as he had killed all the others who could have identified him. She hadn't even bothered to go home from the hearing. Now she was living, if one could call it that, in a furnished room in Brooklyn.

Only the chance of a minor victory was in her power. She could deny Krüger the satisfaction of killing her, by doing it herself. What she was living wasn't life, anyway. She had no friends. The only family she had was her son, and she couldn't bear to look at him. Her life had been ruined, and she had ruined his. She had never been able to give him the things a child had the right to expect. No wonder he had turned out as he had.

She called him. He wasn't there, of course, so she left a message on his answering machine. She left a note he would find when he visited her next, inserted all her cash except what she needed to get where she was going. A taxicab was passing the apartment building and she took it to the subway.

An hour later, she was walking across the Brooklyn Bridge in the rain. Good. The rain added to her feeling. The city lights became vague. Even the traffic noise receded. Out here, suspended between populations, it was easy to believe she had already set sail.

She kept walking. She certainly wasn't going to pick a place and sit there for a while, giving crowds and local media and Fire Department rescue teams the time to gather. She would walk to the center, halfway to Manhattan. When she made her move, she would go right over.

Now she was there. She climbed up on the fence, still physically lithe and youthful, stood at peace for a moment, enjoying the small pleasure of the rain on her face. Then she stepped forward and fell.

Suddenly, the wind was screaming around her. She turned over and over. Would she be killed by the impact? To her surprise, she was not afraid at all. Then there was a thump and she was in the water, swept along by the current. She hadn't realized how strong it was. Don't swim, she told herself. Long ago, she had been a strong swimmer; had won prizes in school. Had it not been for

Hitler and the war, she would have made the German Olympic team. She hadn't been swimming for years, but one never forgets. She tried to go limp and make herself sink.

* * *

"Charles, I need your help. Again."

It was another scam, of course. By now, Spats knew that the metal in the vaults wasn't gold, which could only mean that Albert Holley had replaced it. He was a crook. Spats was reassured. He didn't trust men who weren't crooks. What kind of crook was he? Wasn't the gold supposed to back the money? Spats knew he was closer to the mystery that had plagued him all his life than ever. By the time Holley called him at Manhattan Restorations, Spats had a plan.

"Do you need to restore something, Albert?"

"Charles, I need an alibi."

"An alibi for what?"

"I need to be in two places at once."

"Albert, I have enough trouble just being in one place at once. What's it all about?"

"We have reason to believe that someone is stealing gold from our vaults."

So Holley suspected him. So what! Suspicion wasn't proof. Holley was clever. But he wasn't positive. If he were positive, he wouldn't be playing this game. If he were wrong, he would reveal too much. Spats decided to play along.

"How could someone do that?"

"We don't know. The only thing we know is that metal is missing."

"I've taken your tour. Whoever could get past security like that is a genius."

"He's such a genius, he's done it more than once."

"Twice?"

"Even more."

"Wouldn't that mean it's an inside job?"

"That's exactly what we think."

"Anyone inside who could steal metal more than once, would have to be very high on the hog. Am I right?"

"Yes."

Holley smiled. Charles was lunging for the bait. By now, of course, Holley had looked into Charles, and found that the only thing genuine about him was his name. There was no birth certificate, which meant he had been born at home, or in another country. There was no Social Security number, no military record. He owned no property, not even a car. He filed no individual tax returns. Holley's investigators had found no prints.

"Is it you, Albert? Are you a bank robber? Is that why you need an alibi?"

"Some people here think so."

"Why, that's ridiculous, Albert. It is, isn't it?"

"*You* know it's ridiculous, Charles. *I* know it's ridiculous. But some who want my job think it's perfectly sensible. They say I did it during the premiere."

"The Polyakov premiere?"

"Yes."

"But you were there. I saw you. I saw you when it started, and when the lights came on you were still there."

So Charles wasn't there. Holley's deception was already bearing fruit. He hadn't been there when the lights came back on. He had been closeted with Krüger discussing the need for national health insurance. Why would Charles lie about something so commonplace--unless he himself had left the premiere to rob the Reserve?

"They say I left the premiere when the lights went down, stole the gold and was back in my seat when it was over."

What a puerile, transparent gambit. Spats's respect for the Reserve president diminished somewhat.

"I could tell them . . . ."

"It would do no good."

"Then, what alibi could I provide?"

"Charles, could you impersonate me?"

"Maybe. In thirty years. How long can you wait?"

"Over the telephone. When whoever is doing this calls, he will think I'm at home. But I won't be home. I'll be right here."

"Albert, I'd like to help, but I'm no good at voices. I don't think I could do yours."

"You don't have to, Charles. You'll have laryngitis. You'll cough and whisper. The conversation will be short. Whoever calls will only want to establish I'm there."

"Shouldn't somebody in the Reserve do it?"

"Remember, Charles, it's an inside job. I don't know whom to ask."

"When do we start, Albert?"

"Tonight."

"How long can you keep the lid on?"

"What do you mean?"

"Well, how much gold is gone?"

"We don't know yet. Considerable."

"Doesn't the departure of considerable gold leave a large, empty space? Won't someone notice?"

Holley smiled and pulled at his dewlap. "Charles, I'm sure you understand that this tragedy could trigger a disaster. I ask you to treat what I tell you now with the utmost discretion."

"Of course." What disaster? Spats wanted Holley to explain, but since the latter assumed he already understood, he couldn't ask.

"To forestall that disaster, we have filled that large, empty space."

"I don't follow."

"We've filled it with base metal, masquerading as gold."

Spats whistled. His deception had already borne fruit. Holley had confirmed what Spats had only suspected. "So there's no gold in the vaults of the National Reserve!"

"I didn't say that, sir," Holley said shortly.

"Of course you didn't. I beg your pardon. I misspoke. Whom do you suspect?"

"At the present time, no one is under suspicion."

"The way I figure it, whoever did this--and keeps doing it--is plugged into your security. He knows all your codes and passwords, has all your keys. The guards know him. If they didn't, he wouldn't be able to haul off the gold. Maybe he's one of them. My guess is we're talking about only a couple or three people. Shouldn't you tell the police who they are?"

"It isn't as simple as you think it is, Charles. There is politics."

Holley exulted. Telling "Charles," or whoever he was, the truth, had deflected his attention from what he had found, or, rather, not found, in the vaults. It had explained the presence of the base metal, and it had cleared Holley. "Charles" would not even be aware of it, but slowly he would be drawn into the web. This would be better than terminating him, as Krüger had suggested. Krüger's suggestions always veered in that direction.

"I do have a question, Albert. Why me?"

"Intuition, Charles. Intuition tells me you can do the job."

* * *

"Shirley? Shirley!" Abe knocked on the door. It opened slowly. She was standing there, a smile on her face until she saw who it was.

"So you found us," she said coldly.

"May I come in?"

"If you like."

How long had it been? Neither could remember. So much had happened. They were different people. Abe, of course, was Jesus Christ. Shirley, too, had changed. She was not the same woman she had been long ago, when she locked Abe out of the house. The women's magazines hadn't explained how hard it was to raise children without a man in the house, however decrepit or crazy he was.

She had been chastened, and she was mortified. Abe saw shame on her face. Despite all this, she was angry. Weren't her motives the best? Why, then, was she suffering so much? Was this her reward?

"You can't stay," she said. "I have to leave."

"No problem. I'll come along."

"You can't do that, Abe. I'm going to work."

"Gee, that's great, Shirl. What do you do?"

"I'm an executive, if you must know."

"What do you execute?"

"Lingerie."

"French underwear?"

"That's not what I said." Leave it to Abe to cheapen everything. What else could one expect from a garbage man?

"Whatever you said, I'm happy about it."

Typically, he couldn't see how she was suffering. How obtuse he was, how insensitive! "I want to thank you, Abe."

"You're welcome, Shirl. For what?"

"Because of you, I found out who I am."

"Shirl, that's great. I didn't even know you didn't know."

"Sure, you didn't. That's the problem."

"Who are you, Shirl?"

"See? You still don't know. I am woman."

"Gee, that's great, Shirl. I am man."

"I'm powerful. I'm efficacious. I'm competent."

"Sure you are."

His agreement was immensely irritating, because the more she said the more hopeless she felt. "I don't expect you to understand."

"Shirl, It's my turn to thank you. I was worried. I didn't know you'd be so happy."

"Well, I am!"

"Shirl, let's get together."

"You're talking reconciliation?"

"Yes."

"I got a divorce."

"No problem. Let's get married."

"Get out of here!" she screamed.

"I came because I have to leave town. The mayor says I'm a menace to society."

"He's right. I wish I could vote for him twice."

"Wouldn't that be illegal, Shirl?"

"If you don't leave, I'll cry."

"You're crying right now."

"I'm going to call the police, Mr. no name."

"The chief is one of my friends, Shirl. She won't be happy to hear you want to vote for the mayor twice. Why don't you just pack some clothes and come along."

Shirley pushed him out the door and slammed it. In a few minutes, he was walking up the street, as he had long ago, when she had refused to let him in and burned his clothes.

A long, black car pulled up beside him. The doors opened. Some large men got out and pulled him in. He was seated between them, their hammy arms and shoulders almost touching, and the car was already going fast.

"It's very nice of you gentlemen to give me a lift," Abe said.

"It's the least we could do for Jesus Christ," one said. Raucous laughter erupted in the car.

"Who are you?" Abe asked.

"Didn't you know? I'm John the Baptist." There was more coarse laughter.

"I'm pleased to know you."

"He's pleased to know us," said "John the Baptist." The car erupted. Everything anyone said was funny.

"It's a nice night for a ride," said Abe. "I'm enjoying this."

"We knew you would."

"New Yorkers are such wonderful people," said Abe. "So friendly. So helpful. Always there to give a man a lift. I'm sorry I have to leave."

"We are too."

"Is this the Brooklyn Bridge?"

"That's what it is. This is the place."

The car stopped. They all got out. "What are we going to do here?" asked Abe.

"I'll give you a hint. I'm John the Baptist. Can you swim?"

"No. But I can wade."

It was raining. By now, it was late, so there was little traffic. Here at the middle of the bridge, the city seemed distant. Its lights were vague. "John the Baptist" and the other man hurried Abe to the fence.

"Any last words?" asked "John."

"Only that I enjoyed our visit. I hope we meet again."

Without any fanfare, they threw him over. It was cold on the way down. Suddenly, there was wind, and, sure enough, it whistled. Turning over and over, seeing light and darkness, Abe became disoriented during the long trip.

He hit like a flapjack and sank, then surfaced with difficulty, coughing and sputtering. His heavy clothes made it impossible to swim, which he couldn't do anyway. He sank again. None of his life flashed before his eyes. The only thing in his mind was the memory of what a nice man "John" was.

Some distance away, Frieda was finding it difficult to drown. She couldn't seem to make herself do it. She was so at home in the water. She couldn't make herself swallow. She was floating effortlessly, like the Olympic champion she could have been. She was beginning to realize she had made a mistake, when she saw and heard the man hit the water. He surfaced after a while, coughing, sputtering and flailing with no effect. Soon he would be gone.

She swam to him easily, turned him on his back and put an arm under his chin. "Don't struggle," she said. "Be calm. It's all right."

He did as instructed, and she swam for the lights, as if she had been swimming every day for years. Even more to her surprise, she had purpose again. She had to bring this would-be suicide ashore.

The drizzle became a downpour. There was thunder. Lightning lit the clouds like cotton candy lamps. She couldn't see or hear anything else. She swam and rested, swam and rested. However, the lights were farther than they looked. In the rain, they were deceptive. She was fighting the current, which was very strong. The man she towed was heavy; his clothes were waterlogged. She tired. After a while, she could make no more progress, expending all her energy to stay afloat. The current was sweeping them out to sea. It was dark. No one could see them. Perhaps she could have reached the lights alone, but that would have been contradictory and pointless.

Chapter Thirty Seven
Reunion

"When?" Krüger asked.

Ahmed-Finkelstein had just told him the news, and his heart sang as it had every morning at Auschwitz. His son was coming. His son was coming *here*, to the Tower--tall, triumphant, Aryan, blond! Krüger exulted, and the anger he had felt for Finkelstein fled. Taking quite a chance, "Ahmed" had reminded him of all the successful missions, pointed out that they were "only human," and pleaded that they would have found Frieda if Chandler had not. As Finkelstein had gambled, the news about Krüger's son drove everything else from his mind.

Just before the "Arab" arrived, Krüger had seen Abe Goldstein on television again. He was out of jail. He had been told to leave town. The media were Jewish, and reveled in giving valuable coverage to one of their own. So, for the umpteenth time, Krüger had suffered Abe's Yiddish face. By now, involuntarily, he almost knew Abe's biography by heart. He used the same principle of repetition himself in his advertising. Now, he was a victim of it. It was intolerable. His son lived here. Why? How did he stand it?

"Next Monday morning at ten, *Herr* Polyakov."

"Here. In my office."

"Yes. Is there anything you want us to tell him?"

Krüger waved. "Tell him that someday all of this will be his."

"The American dream," said Ahmed-Finkelstein.

"*Jawohl.*" Krüger laughed. What a good joke. The "Arabs" didn't suspect how good it was.

Now that "Ahmed" had given him the news, Krüger couldn't wait for him to leave. He wanted to put on his magnificent, black SS uniform, complete with all his medals and insignia of rank, which he had kept perfectly preserved at the castle all these years, and always brought with him to the Tower. Over the years, it had become a talisman of sorts, akin to Hitler's Spear of Destiny. Because of his continuing youth, he still could wear it as comfortably as he had long ago at

Auschwitz. Today, it inspired him to do his best thinking. He longed for the day he could wear it for his son. He wanted his son to know who he really was. Someday, soon perhaps, his son would wear the same uniform. They had so much to talk about, so much to plan. Krüger found the anticipation exquisitely painful. He wanted to take the uniform out right now, fondle it and try it on.

"Why must we wait so long?"

"He has been away. On business."

"Excellent. Have you seen him?"

"Not only have I seen him, *Herr* Polyakov; he asked me to tell you that he is looking forward to the reunion next Monday, and wishes you strength through joy."

Krüger laughed. It was a satisfying laugh, warming, the kind the Jewish psychiatrists say is good for mental health. The more he heard, the surer he was that this was his son. By means of these ignorant Arabs, his son had communicated a key Nazi slogan, which proved that father and son were *simpático*. Soon, they would be reunited. They would be together at last. Their reunion would be a scene from Wagner. Together they would complete the destruction of America and the Jews.

"And the papers?"

"Here. Everything you need to satisfy yourself. May I say, *Herr* Polyakov, that he is a son you will be proud of." Finkelstein handed him a thick manila envelope.

Krüger handed him an envelope in turn. "You have done well."

"The news about the woman is not as good. She has disappeared again. We have reason to suspect she committed suicide. She left all her things in her apartment. She even left a note."

"For her sake, I hope you are right. She would be better off. For decades, since the war, she has tormented herself--and bothered me--with a delusion. No doubt because of her suffering in one of the camps, she actually believed that I, David Polyakov, am a Nazi named Krüger."

"Absurd," said Ahmed-Finkelstein.

Everything was up to Finkelstein now. Despite Polyakov's arm, they had failed, as a bitter Chandler had expected. Chandler was gone, ruined, another casualty of the war. Finkelstein wasn't sure what the meeting would produce, but was hoping it would inspire Krüger to incriminating excess. Of course, he hadn't told Abe that. Finkelstein had decided to do whatever it took to nail Krüger, legal or not.

The day came. It was ten o'clock. Krüger sat at his desk in the huge swivel chair, staring out the tall windows behind his desk at the city far below. It was a glorious day. The sun spackled everything with color. The harbor teemed with commerce. Money flowed like a tide into the Tower. He had never felt so robust. On his desk the console beeped.

Reunion
269

"Your ten o'clock is here, Mr. Polyakov."

"Send him in."

The tension was intolerable. This would be the greatest day in his life since he had met Hitler. He had studied the paperwork. There could be no doubt. The man who would walk through the door was his son. There was a discreet knock. The door opened and closed.

"Father?"

No one had ever asked him that. Its novelty was exquisite, almost painful. There was a question in the voice, as there should be. His son was asking for acceptance. Krüger joyously swiveled his chair around and rose.

"Yes, my son."

It was Abe.

There could be no mistake. It was the face Krüger had seen time after revolting time on television--he knew it by heart--but this was worse. On television, all they had shown was Abe's face. Now, here he was in person, and Krüger saw the whole man. He was short. Stubby legs supported a large torso. He was balding. What was left was not blond. His broad smile revealed bad teeth, and he was not Aryan, but Jewish, Jewish, Jewish.

Was this some monstrous joke, or just the biggest mistake of all time? Krüger was standing in his own office, higher than any other in New York, surrounded by all the accoutrements of power, yet he felt trapped. He shrank away as Abe advanced across the room.

Abe's eyes were raining tears. He could not see. Krüger felt the force of his love, like a deep river flowing toward him. Since earliest childhood, Abe had asked about his father. Everyone had a father, even if he wasn't there--except Abe. If a father wasn't there, it meant he was dead, or divorced, or had deserted, even disappeared. Just having the right word to apply was reassuring. Yet, Abe hadn't had it. He had asked his mother time and again about his father, and she had not replied. She had no relatives, and said little of herself. Eventually, he had stopped asking, but the hurt remained. Without a father, he had no history, no temporal connection; he was outside time, a nomad, a wanderer, without country, without loyalty, with no place to lay his head.

Then, a week ago, without warning, Ahmed had arrived, from Germany he said, with news of Abe's father. Indeed, he had proof, in the large manila envelope Abe was carrying right now. His father was David Polyakov. Abe had heard of David Polyakov and had seen his photograph, but little more. The fact that, as his son, Abe would be the sole, instant heir to billions, give or take a billion, had not yet occurred to him. When it did, it would be supremely unimportant.

The only thing that mattered was that now he had a father. Abe wanted to know everything about him. He looked forward like a child to all the wonders he had missed, to years of getting acquainted and camaraderie, basking in his father's glow. Why had his mother so cruelly denied him this, almost as if she were ashamed? Were it not for Ahmed, Abe never would have known.

"Father," Abe said again.

"What are you doing here?" Krüger said harshly. "How did you get in?"

"I'm Abe, father. Your son. Here. I'm supposed to give you this."

Abe held out the envelope containing the documents. He had been incredulous, suspicious and afraid to be hurt again, so he and Ahmed had gone over them together. The documents had convinced him. Ahmed had told him to give them to his father.

As Abe extended the envelope, Krüger realized what this was. Abe was a con man, wasn't he? That's why the little kike was on television every day. He was probably milking the Christians for millions, and Krüger had no argument with that. Theirs was a weakling, *yid* religion, a religion of defeat. They *deserved* to be victimized. The fact that this Goldstein was impersonating the king of the kikes, Jesus, for the purpose, was amusing. When the *Reich* was restored in all its grandeur, Christianity would be exterminated, along with the *Yids*.

Wasn't it obvious what Abe the con man and whoever was behind him were doing? They were working a pedestrian variation of the old "missing heir" scam. Often, years after unsolved disappearances, brutal kidnappings and assassinations, "missing heirs" appear. Weren't there half a dozen or more "Anastasias," claiming to be the long lost daughter of the murdered Nicholas II, lusting to get their hands on the Russian imperial family's billions, still drawing interest in British banks? Weren't there a couple of "Lindbergh babies," now grown to adulthood? Long after the French Revolution, weren't missing Dauphins constantly coming out of the *gateau*? Marie Antoinette and other victims of those swindles were often no longer there to defend themselves, but Krüger was here, and, by Hitler, was perfectly able to do so. He would rather throw his billions down the toilet, than give them to Goldstein and his ilk.

Krüger swatted the envelope away. It flew across the room and opened. Documents erupted, like frightened birds from a coop, and roosted on the furniture.

"Father," said Abe, surprised.

"I am not your father!" Krüger screamed. "You are not my son! Get out of here, you little *Yiddish* bastard, and tell your bosses the scheme didn't work."

"Father. Please."

"Get out, you crook!"

Krüger slapped him forehand and backhand across the mouth. Abe's nose spurted blood. Krüger shoved him hard. He fell. Krüger kicked him in the groin, and kept kicking him as Abe crawled to the door. It was such a long way, and this was worse than almost drowning. This time, no one would save him. Could he make it?

At last, Abe crawled out into the anteroom and Krüger slammed the door. Abe lay there a long time, choking, coughing and gasping for air, ribs and kidneys on fire, Krüger's accusations echoing in his ears. No one came to help.

Abe's father had denied him. Why? Because his father was David Polyakov, a Jew, a victim of Auschwitz, but Abe was Jesus Christ. Could there be any other reason? The voice had done this, the voice Abe had last heard long ago. Because of the voice, Abe would be denied his father. Was it for this his mother had saved him from drowning? It could not be! It was too cruel!

It was not too late. Abe's only chance was to tell his father he was not Jesus Christ. *Father, I am not Jesus Christ.* That was all he had to say. But he couldn't. Who was Abe to argue with God? Despite the pain, he got up and tried the heavy door again. It was locked. He banged on it and shouted.

"Father! Let me in! Please don't do this. You are making a mistake."

Abe kept banging on the door, shouting that his father was making a mistake, until he was dragged away by a couple of large men in uniform. The next thing he remembered, he was walking, or, rather, shambling, up Central Park West. How had he gotten all the way up there from Wall Street? He wandered into the park, sat on a bench near the zoo and stared glassily at the passersby. His middle was on fire. It hurt with every breath. He was alone, homeless. His wife had kicked him out. Now, so had his father. No one wanted him, and there was no one to help. He lay down and passed out. When he awoke, it was a lovely fall day, a lion was roaring, his middle still hurt and his shoes were gone again.

For a long time after Abe stopped shouting and banging on the door, Krüger had sat alone at his desk, head in hands. The dream was over. He had no son. He would never have a son. For months, he had been waiting for the Arabs to deliver. This was the result, this abject humiliation. Fear gripped his throat. Did anyone know? Could what had just happened there get out? No, he had taken pains to be discreet. Some people in his executive offices could be wondering how a bum like Abe had won access often denied the lords of creation, but no one knew why he had come.

Someone had to pay for this. Ahmed came to mind. Who else? Hadn't he taunted Krüger with the vile canard that Abe was a son he could be proud of? Was Ahmed working for someone else? Who? On the other hand, Ahmed thought Krüger was Polyakov, a Jew. Wouldn't a Jew want his son to be a Jew? Ahmed was not a Christian, but a Muslim, and no doubt didn't appreciate the differences between the biblical religions. Couldn't his remark about Abe have been perfectly ingenuous?

The papers! The proof that Abe was who he said he was. The proof he had demanded. It still roosted on a sofa, a coffee table, a lampshade and a rug. Krüger didn't want to look at it. He wanted to pick it up and put it through the shredder. He would have done so, easily, had there been a witness, but, alone, he could not resist.

He gathered up the papers and read them again. They were exact copies of the documents Ahmed had given him. There was the blood comparison to which he had contributed a sample, the DNA analysis, the hair, all the latest techniques and technology used in Hollywood paternity cases, almost as good as fingerprints. It would have been absurd to try to trick the chairman of the world's largest pharmaceutical house, but, to be sure, he had had his lawyers check their authenticity. Krüger had long anticipated reveling over them. Now, he felt disgust. What Abe had said was true. As Ahmed had promised, Krüger was his father.

Then who was the mother? The electrifying question returned. How could any woman whom Krüger would honor with his favors foal such a son as this? Chromosomes did not lie, but experience did. Could Goldstein prove Lamarck's theory of inherited acquired characteristics? Suppose he and his mother had been separated. Suppose he had been kidnapped and raised by someone else. This was New York. Could the Goldstein disaster--almost a mutation--be the result? Indeed, who was Goldstein? Krüger could not recall any woman of that name. Could that help explain how Abe, who--according to the paperwork--was Aryan to the bone, had turned out to be a sniveling, little kike?

He put the papers in the safe and called the Arabs. There was no response. The next day, still in shock, Krüger flew to Munich. A week passed. He did business by reflex. His mind was still suspended, so shaky he did not visit Vörst. Then Ahmed arrived from New York.

"Goldstein says you kicked him out. I told him he was crazy."

"I did kick him out."

"Why?"

"I didn't believe him."

"You did not believe the papers?"

"Not enough."

"You said they were conclusive."

"I was wrong."

"Would you believe his mother?"

"Have you found her?"

"Yes."

Krüger came alive again. One way or the other, this thing would be resolved. "Who is she?"

"We don't know what she called herself when you knew her."

"We must meet."

A couple of weeks later, Ahmed called him from New York. "Next Monday morning, she will be at the Statue of Liberty."

"Why there?"

"She wants to take some pictures. She doesn't know that you may meet. You will be able to observe her discreetly in the crowd, and decide whether she is worth talking to. Maybe her face will excite your memory. After 35 years, she no doubt has changed. We need you to identify her and decide whether to proceed."

"I'll be there."

Chapter Thirty Eight
Vengeance

Crowds of people were on the ferry, despite the nasty weather. Was she one of them? Krüger pulled his hat brim low. A slot remained between it and the ample, upturned collar of his Aquascutum raincoat, buttoned at the front to keep out glances and the fog. Supremely alert, he stalked her through the vessel. She was not aboard. Neither was Ahmed, who would finger her. No doubt that meant they were already on the island. Why were so many idiots going there, on a nasty Monday that was a school day? The fog was so thick, there was nothing to see. Krüger was glad for them. He could easily be anonymous.

Would she want money? Probably. What else could she want? Would he give it to her? He had always been generous to former lovers, but this one was the mother of Goldstein the *Yid.* On the other hand, she hadn't approached him. She had never approached him in the 34 years since Goldstein's birth. Maybe she didn't want anything, and it would be best for Krüger simply to observe her but not approach. That was all he would do, if Goldstein in turn would forget the crazy idea that Krüger was his father. Despite the evidence now stored in his safe at the Tower, Krüger had decided that Abe was not his son.

The ferry was nearing Bedloe's Island. The Statue approached, towering out of the fog. Kruger smiled. It was an appropriate place to meet the mother of *Yiddish* trash, the ultimate symbol of the mongrelization that was the hallmark of the degenerate American culture. "Wretched refuse," my *tucchos*! Appropriately, the Statue was a gift from the faggot nation, France. And wasn't that wop automobile tycoon raising money to restore it? Needless to say, Krüger had never set foot on Bedloe's Island.

A guide was there, giving some of them a tour: "From the base of her foundation to the tip of her torch, she is a tad over 305 feet tall. Her right arm is 42 feet long. Forty people can stand within her crown. She weighs 225 tons. The ladder to the torch has been closed to the public since 1916."

Vengeance
275

Krüger carefully explored the perimeter, averting his gaze from the Emma Lazarus poem on the base. At last, he saw "Ahmed," discreetly pretending to read a Park Service brochure. Finkelstein was nervous. They were going to get Krüger today, but he didn't know how, except that they were going to do something illegal, the prospect of which frightened professor of law Finkelstein. It was up to the woman now. It had always been up to the woman. Finkelstein hadn't dared to ask whether she could do it. What was her plan? Finkelstein had asked her to explain. She had refused. Why on earth had she picked the Statue of Liberty? Finkelstein had tried to talk her out of it.

"She's upstairs," he whispered.

"Where?"

"At the lamp."

"At the top?"

"Yes. On the catwalk."

"The guide says it's been closed since 1916."

"It is."

Krüger smiled. "`I lift my lamp beside the golden door.'"

"I'm sorry?" said "Ahmed."

"A line from a poem. Unlimited immigration. So American. How do I get there?"

"Take the elevator. Then the stairs. Then the ladder. It's a long climb, nothing for a man in your superb condition. There's a saw horse and a sign at the bottom of the ladder. Ignore them."

"I don't like it. Suppose we are alone."

"No problem. The fog is thick today. You won't be able to see your own arm. She won't see your face. Here. Take this flashlight."

Krüger did as he was told. The stairs were steep, but no problem. As "Ahmed" had said, he was in such good shape. He was getting younger every day. Now, he was at the foot of the ladder that led to the lamp. The sign was there, as "Ahmed" had said: "Closed." He ignored it. There was a little gate. It was unlocked. He was alone now. It was quiet. He was in the Lady's arm, then her hand. It was hot and humid. Talk about "yearning to breathe free!" He heard his footsteps on the rungs--nothing more.

At last, he pushed the trap door open, climbed up and stepped out. He closed the door, looked up and saw the lamp, glowing in the fog. That was all he saw. "I lift my lamp beside the golden door." He could not excise the hateful poem from his mind. The fog was as thick as any he had ever seen, like a *schnitzel*, something he could cut a slice of. He waved his hands and saw billows of it move. He couldn't see the famous skyline, couldn't see the harbor or the ground, couldn't see the Brooklyn docks or Jersey flatlands. Of course, he was standing on a small, round, open catwalk below the lamp, that ordinarily offered extraordinary views of those things, but since he had never been there and couldn't see, he had no way of knowing that. For all he knew, he was standing on a meteor fragment in deep space. How could she take pictures in so much fog? Because of the fog, it was as cold on the catwalk as it had been hot and humid in the arm.

"Hello?" he said.

A horn sounded in reply, infinitely mournful, lost in the mystery of the fog. Despite its sadness, it was happy, proof that someone was alive. He waited a long time, hand on the rail of the fence for reassurance, but there was nothing else. He pushed the switch and lit the flashlight. It responded, but the beam was useless.

The rail went in a circle, and he edged around. Maybe she just hadn't heard him. "Hello?"

Krüger was just about convinced she wasn't there. Perhaps she wasn't. Maybe she had gone down before he came up, while he was talking to "Ahmed." Maybe "Ahmed" was mistaken, and she had stayed below, never come up. Goldstein was 34, so, whoever she was, she had to be a woman about sixty. She wasn't young, like Krüger. Maybe the climb to the lamp had been too taxing. Unlike Krüger, she wasn't expecting to meet anyone. Krüger edged back along the rail to the trapdoor. The foghorn called again. He shivered. The fact that he was close to so many people, yet alone, was unnerving. This had been a mistake.

It happened with a speed that defied comprehension. A shadow rose up. He heard a couple of determined footsteps--not feminine at all. A figure hurtled toward him through the fog. Above the figure, not visibly connected to anything, was a pencil of light, bright, slender, like a laser. A roar came from a throat. With any warning, he could have prepared. He could have set, both feet planted, knees slightly bent, and responded. He could have evaded. He could have used the flashlight. Not only was he young, he worked out every day in Munich or the Tower, was in tone and condition that a man of 35 would have envied, and had been a martial arts master since his SS training in Berlin.

But whoever was attacking with such fury, was like a phantom in the fog. Krüger was disoriented, utterly taken by surprise, still unsure of what was happening. Was he under attack? What was the shining object? Was what was happening even related to him?

He dropped the flashlight, backed up with alacrity and climbed over the rail. There he would be safe, until he found out what was happening. Perhaps because of condensation, the greenish catwalk metal he was grasping was wet and slippery. He lost his grip and fell. His hat flew off. His side hit something hard; he didn't know it was one of the statue's fingers. He would have an aching kidney in the morning. He flailed out. His feet kicked hopelessly in space, failing to find another finger, but his strong hands found a purchase. He would be all right. He had only to hold on, climb up and back over the rail, and then confront the spectre that had done this.

He looked up and saw nothing. The fog was still so thick. He could barely see the catwalk a few feet above. Was the phantom waiting? What did he want?

"Who's up there?" he called.

There was no answer. Instead, he heard the phantom climbing down. Relief replaced Krüger's fear of the unknown. The phantom was climbing down to help. Whoever it was had not been attacking him at all. There had been a misunderstanding, a mistake. Even now, Krüger heard the phantom tying something to the fence, obviously a rope or chain he would use to reach the victim.

"Here!" Krüger shouted. "Here!"

Still there was no answer, but the phantom was moving down a finger, holding to the rope. Help would be there in a moment. Despite the fog and the chill, Krüger would have liked to doff his coat--now it was uncomfortable and heavy--but he could not spare a hand.

"Hurry!" he shouted, manfully suppressing panic.

The spectre, now quite corporeal, was climbing down the rope. Krüger saw its back. Close enough at last, it turned, close enough so that, even in this historic fog, he could see who the phantom was.

Krüger was looking up at Frieda. There was no chance of mistake. Her eyes were all he had to see, despite her age still as clear as ice cubes in a glass. The same Aryan eyes he first had seen at the railway station in Munich. The eyes that had tormented him. The same eyes he had seen at the hearing his attorneys had aborted. It was she.

"I'm here, my love," she said in German, true Aryan *hoch deutsch*, not the horrid Yiddish perversion. She was smiling down at him. Her voice was a caress.

"Frieda . . . ." he whispered.

She cut him off. "*Sprich du auf deutsch*!"

"Certainly, *meine liebe*. As you wish. Is it really you, Frieda?"

"Yes, my love. It is I. I came to you, as you said I would, after 35 years. You knew better than I."

"I'm so relieved, dearest. I'm glad you're here. Such a charming coincidence."

"Oh, it's no coincidence, *mein Hauptsturmfuhrer*. But, it is charming. I'm glad I'm here too. They said you wanted to see me. Do you?"

"I've been so worried, so afraid, Frieda. They said you had drowned."

She nodded. "Yes. They were supposed to say that. They lied."

"Lied? What do you mean, Frieda? I don't understand."

Krüger didn't understand, but he was wearing a heavy coat, he was hot, he was hanging from Miss Liberty's index finger, and he had no time to figure it out. She was smiling at him. He could literally feel her emotion, as he had recently felt Abe's.

"You're still so lovely, Frieda. As lovely as the day I first saw you at the station."

Frieda chuckled. "You're teasing."

"No."

Frieda had lied. She said she had. So could he. He didn't think she was still lovely, at all, but the fact that he was saying so took effect. He remembered.

* * *

They were tramping across the snow. The sun was low. It was bright, too bright to see. By now, she had no idea what time it was. The hope of seeing David dispelled her exhaustion, despite her misgivings, which were useless. Were she to voice them, Krüger would protest with gusto. *If you don't want your husband, you don't need to come*, he would have said. In the face of logic and experience--but with David's life at stake--she had to take the chance Krüger was telling the truth, and so far he was doing as he promised.

He had never felt so fit. He broke into song. He had a good voice, which Frieda resented, and she listened with disgust to a medley of his favorite Nazi marching songs.

"What a glorious day, *liebchen*!" he announced after a spirited rendition of the *Horst Wessel*.

He was impressed. She was right behind him. She was much stronger than her husband. She was a woman of spirit. How had a woman of such spirit ever married such a weakling? Despite the glory of the day, Krüger felt nervous, maudlin to excess, afraid she would insist on throwing everything away.

"I am confident, *liebchen*, that when you talk with David--when he tells you himself--you will see that his proposal is the best thing for us all. You need time, time to realize that. Thank God I am so patient. You will see."

She did not reply, of course. He knew she wouldn't. What answer could she give a madman? They crossed the pristine, open field, then the stand of leafless trees. At last there were the evergreens, and, within them, the lodge. The sun was fading. Soon, it would be dark. She broke into a run. She passed Krüger.

"Go ahead, my love," he shouted. "He's waiting."

She broke through the trees into the clearing. Someone lay in the snow before the lodge. It was David. She knelt at his side, vision further impaired by bitter tears. He had come all the way from Auschwitz to die here in the snow. She would never feel his living body next to hers. Their putative reunion had been fruitless, unworthy of the name.

Krüger strolled up. "You see, *liebchen*? He did not wait for us. He knew you'd try to argue with him."

Her husband's face was turned the other way. As the light disappeared, her vision cleared and she saw he had been maimed. His head lay in a pool of blood.

His face was gone. One of his arms was horribly charred. More blood and gore suffused an elbow. She could be sure the corpse was David's only by consulting the untouched numbers on his arm. He would have been better off in Auschwitz.

She looked at Krüger, unaware until this moment that it was possible to hate someone like this. She was shaking. A pain in her chest made it impossible to breathe. She groaned. *Please, Unnameable One, don't let me pass out.*

"I have kept my word, *liebchen,*" Krüger said. "You are together. No doubt you want to be alone. *Nicht wahr*?"

Without another word, he turned, walked up the steps to the lodge, went inside and closed the door. Lights came on. Soon, there was music. A woman was singing "Lili Marlene," and Krüger joined in. Smoke was coming from the chimney. She smelled cooking food.

Still on her knees, she screamed. She kept screaming. She had only enough sanity left to know she was insane. Even all through Auschwitz, she had not known evil such as this. She jumped to her feet, rushed up the stairs and in the door.

He looked up. He had just been putting plates out on the table--two plates. The presumptuous Nazi bastard had known she would come in.

"Ah, there you are, Frieda. Please. Sit down." He gestured, smiled, like an urbane host in a townhouse off *Unter den Linden.* "If you're half as hungry as I am, you could eat all four of these."

He set a pot on the hot pad between the plates and took the cover off. Steam erupted, along with what to Frieda was the foul stink of pork.

"Pig's knuckles and sauerkraut," he said. "One of my favorites."

Across the room, an American Victrola was slowing down. He wound it up. The woman on the record sang "Lili Marlene" again. Krüger returned humming it, and ladled the pork onto their plates. Frieda sat, dizzy, afraid she would fall down. Beside the fireplace, leaning against the stone, she saw an ax. It was a longhandled ax, old and rusty, a relic left by the woodsman who had long since disappeared, perhaps swallowed by an avalanche. The blade glowed like a finger of light. Frieda saw a stain on the stone beneath it.

She prayed. She hadn't prayed all the time she was in Auschwitz--life had been idyllic there; prayer had not been needed--but she did so now. *Addonai, Nameless One, I am helpless. What is right? I know I've died and am in Hell, but you have power even here. Show me what to do.*

Krüger handed her some *schnapps*. "*Prosit.*" She took it and they drank. "Splendid!" he roared. The alcohol revived her and helped dispel the dizziness.

"Eat something, *liebchen*. You need your strength."

She did need her strength for what she had to do. She was acting automatically, by rote, in shock, but she knew that he was right. She ate, not even bothering to grimace. Kruger feasted on the sight. Frieda eating pork was as good as he'd expected. He filled her glass. She drank.

"Now I shall stink like you."

"*Jawohl*!" he roared. "There's nothing like good pig's knuckles to make a girl romantic! In a moment, I shall start reciting Heine. '*Ich weiss nicht was soll es bedeuten, das ich so traurig bin* . . . .' So beautiful! Did you know he was a Yid?"

"I want you to bury him," she whispered.

Her desire that Krüger bury David was what she had burst into the lodge to scream. The thought of David lying unprotected in the snow was intolerable.

"Impossible, my love. I tried. We're too high up. The ground's too hard."

She rose. "I'll do it myself."

"All right. There's a shovel. It's dark now. In the morning you can try."

It *was* dark. He was right again. She shuddered. His rightness was consuming her. Krüger took her by the wrist. She tried to pull away without success, and he drew her to his lap. He caressed her hair.

"Your beauty is returning with the spring," he said. "You are defying time."

She got up, broke loose and headed for the door. He caught her. "Do you know how much I love you, dearest? There is nothing I wouldn't do for you, nothing I haven't done."

He pressed his mouth to hers. She bit. Krüger tasted blood and licked his lips. "I love your spirit, Frieda," he breathed. "Spirit is the most important aspect of a woman. You are a gorgeous mare galloping across a green field."

She tried to make the door again. Krüger grabbed a handful of her hair, made her bend and run around him, and swung her forcefully into a wall. Her breath departed. She slid onto the floor.

Krüger was on top of her, breathing in her ear, reveling in the scent he had given her to wear for David. "*Liebchen*, for old time's sake, I'm going to show you what love is really like. I owe you that. I don't think you know. How could you know, married to that spineless, little kike?"

She still wore her parka, and he lovingly undid the buttons, which revived her. She had to get out of the cabin. She had to get away. She struggled free on hands and knees, trying to get up. He caught an ankle, and was on top of her again, kissing her neck, his tongue exploring one of her ears.

"This is part of it, my dear."

She fought, kicking, twisting, slapping and scratching. Krüger loved it. If a woman yielded right away, he left her. The fact that Frieda struggled would give savor to his conquest. She was running out of energy. What more could she do?

He took her parka off. Then her sweater. Beneath it, she wore a blouse he had given her at Auschwitz, stolen from a corpse. He pulled the collar roughly. Buttons spattered him like teeth. The blouse fell open, he tore it off and threw it in a corner.

"Do you realize, my love, that, even after all these years, I've never seen you in your bra? You're lovely."

She crossed her arms in fruitless modesty. "Please. Let me go. You have everything you want."

"Not everything, *liebchen*. There is something more."

"You're mad. You're even crazier than I thought you were."

"Yes, dearest. Mad about you." He was placid, even smug, paying her no mind, as if what he was talking about was predestined like the sunrise.

She was screaming again. "You disgusting toad! You piece of *drek*! You murderer! You've taken everything we have. We did everything you asked. You broke your word. You *Nazi* pukes always break your word. You speak of honor, but you have none. All you are is horrid slime."

"I gave you my word I would teach you to love, dearest, and I shall."

She charged him, with a fury he had never seen before. Even he was frightened. She drove him back, off his chair. She bit his hand. Her teeth clicked, reaching for his throat. Her arms flailed, seeking flesh and bone. At last, she found some hair. He could not pry her loose and she tore it from his scalp. He shouted, more surprised than hurt. She was crazy; yet she dared to call him mad.

Krüger kicked her in the stomach, then smashed her in the jaw. She hurtled across the room into a mirror. It broke in many pieces. The frame fell off the wall. Legs useless, she tottered into the fireplace tools and collapsed.

She was sitting at the table again, when consciousness returned. The Victrola was playing another song she didn't know. Krüger was filling her glass again with schnapps. Something was wrong with her face. Her jaw was throbbing and askew.

Krüger held a shard of the mirror up before her. "Look, dearest. See what you have done. You're such a naughty girl. Did you bring a brush and makeup?"

Her jaw was broken. Her face was swelling up. A purple knot was on her cheek. Her back was on fire, a memento from the fireplace. She was naked but for panties. What had happened? She could not recall taking off her clothes.

Krüger lovingly caressed her breasts. She could not move. She could not stop him. All she could do was watch. He played until the nipples hardened and stood erect like polished knobs. The sensation was intolerable. She knew if he continued she would faint or go insane. With great difficulty, she raised her hands and gently covered his. The relief was so intense she cried, but the intimacy of the fact that she was now pressing his hands on her naked breasts inspired him.

"Frieda," he whispered. "They are superb. No artist, no Gaugin, no Titian, could do them justice. You are even more beautiful than I dreamed you are. I'm so glad we waited. I'm so happy that you care."

He put the glass in her hand. "Drink." She did as she was told. The alcohol was good. It helped the pain, but, because her jaw was broken, some of it ran down her cheek.

"Come, darling." Krüger wound the Victrola up again. "Let's dance."

He pulled her erect, held out her arm and made a lively show of dancing; but her body was out of control. Her limbs did not work. She sagged against him, but for which she would have fallen. Krüger felt her shudder.

"How thoughtless of me, sweetheart," he said. "You're catching cold. I must warm you up."

He carried her to the alcove and put her in the bed. It was nothing special, but there were clean sheets, goose pillows, along with several heavy quilts and it was heavenly beneath them. If only she could lie there quietly and die. As she thought this, she realized how ridiculous it was. In today's world, minding one's own business was a mortal sin.

Krüger threw more wood onto the fire. The room was pleasantly warm. What else was he doing? She couldn't even turn her head to see. He threw the covers back and gently pulled her pants off. Then she felt him sliding in beside her, and he was naked too.

Suddenly, his face was between her legs and his tongue was doing something she had never heard of. He straddled her, put his arms between her legs and bent them. Something huge was jammed into her mouth. There was a horrid smell. She couldn't move. She couldn't see. She couldn't breathe and she was choking. Yet, despite her revulsion, she was flowing like a river.

After a long time, he got off, turned around and kissed her, his face dripping slime, which stank. He forced his tongue into her mouth. He was everywhere, kissing, stroking, squeezing, licking, and everywhere he was she had to yield.

Why was all this happening? In Germany, before the war, she had been raised to be discreet. As a young wife, she had been private, taking no offense and giving none. She had never been involved in politics, had joined no anti-*Nazi* groups. Yes, her husband had money. Why was that her fault? Hadn't David and her father worked well into the night? What had she done besides being there? What had she done to Krüger? How had she offended God?

He put her legs over his shoulders, so that her heels were bouncing on his back. Then, he was inside her. She had so little to remember, so little to compare. She had been married a short time, a time of political disruption, of business travel and short separations. Then she had been thrown into the National Socialist maelstrom. She was as close to virginity as consummation can be. Now, as Krüger entered, her brief experience returned, but she was not prepared for this. Krüger entered farther than she had known was possible. On and on he came, expanding all the way, until he reached the place that never had been touched. Despite her wish to die, she was afraid, certain she'd be maimed. Surely it was impossible for a person to survive this.

If this had never happened, of course there would have been nothing to compare. She was not comparing now. She couldn't, because, in self-defense, her brain had stopped, leaving her nervous system to function on its own. Yet, her flesh remembered. David had been so different, so fastidious, almost tepid.

"You are utterly sublime, *liebchen*," he whispered. "Had I known how truly sublime you are, I could not have waited all this time."

She screamed. Krüger rammed her head into the board, and thereby entered even farther. She screamed again, struggled and tried to get away, the horror of being violated compounded by the fact that the monster wasn't circumcised. Her struggles inspired Krüger to do more. Again and again, he rammed her head into the board, at last holding her there like a butterfly impaled.

She moaned, bit her lip and tossed her head. A warmth she had never felt erupted deep inside her.

"Now you know what real love is, *liebchen*. Do you see?" He shook her. "Do you see?"

"Yes."

"Admit you never have been f--ked like this before."

It was true. "I never have."

"Say it!"

"I never have been f--ked like this before."

The warmth cascaded like a consuming fire down her limbs. She felt the intensest pleasure she had known. It was a fleeting sensation. Had she not suppressed it, the pleasure could irrevocably have dragged away her soul. It was a feeling of the flesh, not the mind and spirit, but the fact that she had felt it evoked horror and then shame. Krüger was total evil, yet so much he said was true, and the pleasure she was feeling was his work. *Please. Help me. Help me!*

"I'm so glad you chose to stay, *liebchen*. It is a wise decision. You will see. This is the first day of our new life together. Mr. and Mrs. David Polyakov. You must call me David."

"*Jawohl, mein commandant*."

"*Sehr gut, meine frau*. You are hopelessly in love."

"I am hopelessly in love."

All through the night, he entered her, turning her to suit his pleasure, using her in sheer delight. The loathsome, indescribable feeling returned. She could no more have deflected it, than she could have flown up to the moon. The warmth gave way to lassitude, compounded by her injuries and shame. At last, toward morning, her strength, such as it could be, returned, her mind began to function and Krüger fell asleep. By now, of course, it would accomplish nothing,. but she desperately wanted to wash. Washing would create the illusion that she could cleanse herself of Krüger; but there was no water. She got out of bed unsteadily, with caution. She hurt everywhere. Now was the time to rid herself of him.

Then she saw the ax beside the fireplace. How appropriate! The ax was waiting for her. David's blood, now dry and dark, gave witness on the blade. She crept across the room and got it, then returned. Krüger was snoring, conscience clear, enjoying the well-deserved rest of an honest workman, unaware that Frieda had survived and was herself again.

She raised her arms as high as they would go. Maybe he sensed something via the air currents in the room. It is impossible to say. He stopped snoring and sat up, not yet awake, eyes working but not yet plugged into the brain. What he saw was a beam of light, pencil-thin, as the lamp caught the blade. The beam approached, expanded, rose and disappeared. He realized what it was, too late.

She struck with the fury of a millennium of vengeance. As he rose and stuck a hand out to deflect it, the blade smashed into his unprotected cheek. A trough of fire erupted on his face. Frieda still held the ax, and Krüger saw his blood on it. Blood was everywhere, spouting from a hundred geysers. He tried to speak. Did he succeed? His ears roared like a train. He saw two Friedas, then four, then nothing at all.

Krüger slid to the floor on his back, mouth open. Frieda threw the ax. It skittered across the floor to the fireplace. More than anything else in the world, she wanted to get out of there, far from Krüger's corpse, yet she forced herself to realize she would freeze naked in the snow. She dressed, fast enough to silence the most demanding husband impatient to depart, and went to the door.

As she opened it, Krüger noisily stood up. She screamed. One side of his face was raw meat. His clothes were soaked with blood. Sheets of gore festooned his corrupted flesh. He swayed, blinking, trying without success to clear his eye, but he shambled toward her. She threw the door open and jumped down the stairs. He followed, reaching for her, tottering, blood spattering the snow.

"Come back, Frieda," he called. "It is time to die."

She shrieked. She had forgotten David's body. She stood beside it now. Krüger was approaching. Whenever she was with her husband, she was torn away. She couldn't even remain with him now that he was dead, couldn't even bury him.

"Goodbye, darling," she whispered.

Then she was running, running for her life, crashing through the snow, running with the shame and horror, tempered by the knowledge that she had left her mark forever.

* * *

"I'm happy you think I'm still lovely, *liebchen*," she said. "I was afraid that all these years of American decadence had made me old."

"Nonsense," Krüger said. She *was* old, old and repulsive. How on earth had she ever captivated him so? She was also insane. All he had to do was keep her talking. An opportunity would arise, and he would take it. "You are every bit as charming as you were. Even more attractive."

"I know. You're so sincere. You always were. No one ever f--ked me as you did."

"Frieda, about the hearing. I didn't want to do it. It wasn't my idea. My attorneys . . . . I . . . ."

"Nonsense. You had to do it. I was trying to destroy you. What else could you do? No hard feelings, I always say."

Krüger was encouraged. It was going his way. She was being sensible. However, she was making preparations of some kind.

"What's that, Frieda?"

"This? It's the ax you used on David's arm. The ax I marked you with. The day you killed my husband. The day you f--ked me on the mountain. Remember? I left it as it was, except the blade. I had an expert sharpen it, didn't trust myself. It's a real art, I found out."

"What are you going to do?"

"What I should have done thirty five years ago."

He still didn't understand, but didn't have to. The rope was tied around her waist. She held it with one hand. With the other, she held the ax, which was also on a leash. She swung and missed. Krüger heard it slash the air. She swung again, and hit the metal near his arm.

"Someone will come!" he shouted. "You'll be caught."

"No one will come," she said. "The arm is closed. There was a sign. Remember?"

"I have a man downstairs. He will come."

"Finkelstein? He's mine."

"You're crazy, Frieda. He's an Arab. His name's Ahmed."

"No. He's from Mossad."

Krüger gasped. He understood. "Ahmed" was a double agent, a traitor in the pay of Israeli intelligence. What had she called him? Finkelstein! No wonder everything had gone wrong. Finkelstein and his partner had told him about Abe to lure him to the United States. They were agents of that bastard Wiesenthal's. No wonder they had never been able to find her. They were Jews, and one could never trust a Jew.

Frieda swung again. The ax flew from her hand, but she used the leash to retrieve it. Krüger understood that no one would help him. He had to save himself. She swung again, he lunged for the long handle and the blade nicked a finger. There was blood on his hand.

"What's that, *liebchen*?" Frieda asked. "Blood?"

Again she swung. He removed a hand just in time to avoid contact, and hung for a moment by the other. The blade clanged hungrily against the metal. The same thing happened again. If only he could climb up. If only he could pull her down; but he was rolling craps against the house. Sooner or later, he would lose, and she was not in any hurry.

"Frieda, let's talk."

"Good idea. I love to talk. I haven't talked in years."

"Let me take care of you and Abe. Remember him? Our son. He is our son, isn't he?"

"Yes. He is our son. But he is Jewish."

"So what, Frieda. That's all past. Now we must live for him. I'll give you everything I have."

She swung and missed. "It's already, mine commandant," she said. I'm Mrs. David Polyakov. Remember?"

At last, however incompetent she was, the ax bit through the Aquascutum coat, through the Harris tweed jacket made for him on Saville Row, through the initialed shirt, into an arm. He screamed. The blade was every bit as sharp as she had said it was. He felt a searing pain.

"Which arm is it, commandant?" she asked.

"This one," he whispered. "The left."

"The left. Good. That's the one I want."

"Frieda, please. Can't you forgive?"

"Yes. I can forgive."

“Can you forgive me?”

“Certainly. I forgive you.”

She swung again and found the target. She swung again. The blade was chewing up his arm.

"You God-damned *Yiddish* bitch!" he screamed.

She laughed. "You forgot *untermensch* and mongrel, *liebchen.*"

The arm was numb. He could not hold on much longer. He was dizzy. He couldn't move anymore, so he was easier to hit, and he was out of schemes. She knelt and swung again, a stalwart blow that caught him in the elbow. They heard a crunch. The arm surrendered Kruger's weight, still resting on the statue's finger. Frieda seized it by the hand and withdrew it from the shredded garments. The number--David's number--was there.

She laughed. "The Americans have a saying. ‘I’ve got your number.’ Now, I have your number, *liebchen.* David's number. You owed me that. *Auf wiedersehen.* That's all I want."

"What about me, Frieda?"

"Well, what about you?"

"Frieda, please," he rasped. “For the love of God. Help me up. You have the arm. You have the number. That's what you want."

"Pray to your god. Ask him to help."

She climbed up and over the fence, carrying the arm, surprisingly youthful. She was standing on the catwalk, looking down. She really meant to leave him. He had lost all the blood he could. He was at the gates of shock. His remaining hand was trembling in protest. His brain was shutting down. At last he understood that his famous resourcefulness had ended. He had pulled his last rabbit from a hat.

"It's over," he whispered. "I die with the joy of knowing that I ruined your life and that you are still alive to suffer."

Krüger let go and instantly disappeared in the fog.

Chapter Thirty Nine
Collapse

The financial debacle lasted many months. Even today, some years later, there are lingering effects: banks seized by F.D.I.C.; savings & loans collapsing; personal bankruptcy and unemployment; mansions and Mercedes auctioned by the dozens, for quarters on the dollar; officials on their way to and from country clubs maintained by the federal government for the purpose, to name a few. The reader is familiar with them, and may well be enjoying this modest narrative as an inmate.

So much of what we read in our history books is false. The authorized version of the deliberately concocted misunderstanding at the Bastille that launched the French Revolution, is of course an utter fraud. So was the tripe told us about the horror of the Lusitania, which was loaded to the gunwales with munitions. The official version of the Japanese attack on Pearl Harbor is of course a lie, along with the Gulf of Tonkin Resolution. Glasnost and perestroika are as phony as a one dollar bill. Indeed, the reader has seen that history would have told us David Polyakov lived a long and fruitful life; we would have believed it had not his widow intervened. Both Prime Minister Benjamin Disraeli and President Woodrow Wilson wrote that true history happens behind the scenes, and is often quite different from what we are told.

Most of the truth never will be known. Some of it emerges. Defectors surface on the crest of discrepancies and often leave them worse, viz., the assassination of President Kennedy and others. The version the schoolchildren eventually learn is the one that has the most, or the most powerful, adherents.

For all these reasons, we tread with trepidation on the present can of worms. Not being professional historians, we wisely take their advice, and offer here only what appears to be generally accepted, with the usual proviso that, while we are grateful for their help, without which this analysis could not have been computed, our wife is of course solely responsible for any bloopers the historians may discover.

The affair apparently began in a bank in Pakistan, where it would have been confined had the institution not been plugged into the early phases of the international fiscal system that President Bush would later call the New World Order. A suspicious loan led to another, which led to another, utterly egregious arrangement, in which branches around the world collaborated to pressurize several Third World governments by means of threats to disinvest, the result of which was chaos in the markets on the downside.

The discount window was open when it happened, which triggered the law of large numbers and a damaging spike in interest rates. Leading economists with access to the White House predicted action by the Council of Economic Advisers, and it was soon forthcoming, despite which corporate raiders made a killing in *deutschmark* arbitrage. Needless to say, Big Oil was involved.

Subsequent investigation disclosed the malevolent influence of the international narcotics racket, which used the bank to buy shaky governments like *wampum*. Happily, Karachi acted when it did. For years thereafter, cyclical analysis behaved erratically, which hampered capital accumulation to the point of critical mass, where it started downhill. All in all, the situation looked grim for foreign bonds.

It was generally agreed that the hero of the affair was the new chairman of the National Reserve. Founded to insure stability in the nation's currency and markets, the National Reserve System, under his inspired leadership, performed exactly as designed. At precisely the right point, the chairman raised the discount rate and dramatically reduced the float, which guaranteed that federal funds would quickly follow suit. The *coup de grace* was his now famous pronouncement on the margins, in which he promised that the Reserve would henceforth require a more realistic spread. Investor confidence returned quickly, and those who foolishly did not believe him found themselves short the puts and calls, or, worse, with Not Sufficient Funds.

At the historic press conference, National Reserve Chairman Charles M. Wilson explained as follows: "Ladies and gentlemen, I have a brief statement. Then I will take your questions. I think you need to know that my nomination by the President as Chairman of the Reserve at this critical time, is no coincidence. Rather, it is a mandate. We have recently seen how close to disaster the world economy came, precisely because of the lack of international coordination that the Reserve has long been warning about. Without that coordination, individuals who lack any sense of community, motivated solely by personal gain, find easy access to illicit profit, as in the sordid affair just concluded.

"I take it as my mandate to bring closure to this egregious situation. We are stewards here, custodians of the people's homes and livelihoods. The Reserve must scrupulously maintain the most elevated levels of ethics and protection. I have no wish to be a policeman, but if policing is required to bring discipline to our economy, I shall grit my teeth and do it. The first crop of convicts caught in the Karachi scandal is already on its way to prison. There will be many more. Let word go forth from here this day to every closet robber baron, that uncontrolled free enterprise capitalism--trampling the people's rights untrammeled--no longer will be tolerated. Let me add that Police Commissioner Steinmetz has promised his complete cooperation.

"Toward this end, we are presently collaborating closely with the central banks of the G-7 nations. We are striving to bring the struggling nations of eastern Europe into the fold. By the turn of the century, we expect to see a true world community in place, the most important element in which is massive reeducation. Of course, the process will require many conferences and treaties. Please help yourselves to the material on the tables in the rear, which will give you the details. Let me assure you that the National Reserve System has a carefully constructed plan. Thank you. I'll be happy to take your questions."

Spats smiled an invitation, perfectly at ease with the New York press. The sea of reporters looked up at him with kinship. Only a few of them understood what he had said; only a few knew there was nothing to understand. The conferences and treaties he had mentioned would be boring. They wanted red meat. Who was in bed with whom? Who was Charles M. Wilson in bed with? He certainly looked good enough to be in bed with someone, unlike Albert Holley, the dewlapped antique president of the New York Reserve, who stood smiling and flapping beside him. Rumor had it that Holley had recommended Wilson to the President for the job.

Even the columnists who specialized in business didn't understand, none of which caused any concern, because all of them knew the National Reserve always got favorable spin, which was mildly frustrating, because even if they did find out whom he was in bed with they couldn't print or broadcast it. Wasn't everybody who was anyone on each other's boards and a member of the group?

"Mr. Wilson, may I ask a personal question?"

It was the lady from *Free Woman*, the monthly magazine, to which male colleagues often added "But Expensive." It is superfluous to say that they did so *sotto voce*; failure to understand that feminism was presently *de rigeur* had already landed many a man in the dust bin of chauvinism. Her recent piece on the art and science of masturbation, for women of (business) affairs on the road, had won a prestigious, journalistic award, along with the approbation of women's groups that declared men largely superfluous and medical organizations fighting to contain AIDS. She would be no problem.

"Be my guest."

"We know so little about you. In the haste of your nomination and confirmation, there has been no opportunity to ask."

"No problem. Mr. Holley here thought of me because of my long experience in business and banking. You will find my résumé along with the other material on the tables in the rear. On behalf of the President, he asked whether I'd be able to put those business interests in hibernation and be willing to serve. The only woman I sleep with is my wife, Elizabeth Ann, whom I'm insane about, and who is sitting over there."

Spats pointed at Elizabeth Ann, who was tumultuously pregnant again, and therefore more radiant than ever. Her father had been wrong, because he was so protective. Charles had been undercover as she said, which explained his disappearance. It had been wrong to suspect him. His reappearance in triumph as the new chairman of the Reserve was proof and vindication. The idea that Charles would dump her was silly. Didn't he tell her all the time how insane for her he was? Didn't he give her everything? Didn't he do all this because Holley had told Spats how important it was to have a gorgeous, loving wife? To protect her Daddy from inevitable, bad feeling, Elizabeth Ann hadn't mentioned McGillicuddy's suspicions to Charles. She tittered now at Charles's sweet remarks, but the lady from *Free Woman*--who did not need H.L. Mencken to tell her when something wasn't Politically Correct--did not. Albert Holley's face was bland.

"Her Dad is Commissioner of Sanitation Francis X. McGillicuddy, who has promised to clean up the garbage with me and Mr. Holley, president of the New York Reserve. So, you can see I picked the right wife."

Automatic pencils whirled across the steno pads, recording every word. Were anyone else to give such an evasive, self-serving reply the New York media would skewer him like a crawfish. His corpse would be thrown under the Queensboro bridge, where hobos would fight for his cuff links and clothes. His head would adorn a spike in Times Square, until the pigeons ate his eyeballs and picked it clean of flesh.

"We're told that Police Commissioner Steinmetz's predecessor isn't happy; that she was forced to resign after the mayor was safely re-elected. How does her departure relate to the collapse?"

It was the man from the nation's newspaper of record. Holley had taken pains to warn Spats about him. He was one of the few who understood everything, and he certainly was "part of the program," but, because he had made a good living, while still in college, as a circus geek, killing chickens with his teeth, he sometimes lost control when he smelled blood. Doctors at the paper managed this proclivity with drugs. Of course, he hadn't been "told" anything. He was fishing.

"Not at all," said Spats. "She asked to move on. After the birth of her child, she needed something less hectic. She left in triumph after driving Spats Davis even farther into hiding, and forcing the Goldstein gang to quit. Ms. al-Shekel is quite happy as U.S. ambassador to Iraq, where I'm told she's learning religion from President Saddam."

"You mentioned the international narcotics racket. Could you explain how it contributed to the recent disaster, and what you intend to do about it?"

"Did I? Sure. I think it's fair to say the Karachi caper could never have gotten off the ground without it. Funds in branches around the world were used to buy raw opium from the Golden Crescent, and cocaine from Medellin. Later, heroin made from that opium turned up on the streets of Paris. The cocaine came here. Where do you get your coke? Maybe some of you are using it. Funds coming the other way were laundered, used to buy substantial positions in the market. The racket already controls many household names. I wish I could say more. The thing is now in court.

"What do we plan to do? We know these people are selfish to the max. Our children are at stake. Whatever we can do to protect them makes sense. The Reserve proposed the limit one can withdraw from an account without reporting to the federal government. We helped design the form. The Reserve developed the concept of structuring, in which evading or attempting to evade, or appearing to evade, or trying to obey, federal reporting would be a crime."

"What about the Bill of Rights?" someone asked.

"It seems to me that privacy is secondary, when our children are the targets."

Holley unobtrusively put his hand on Spats's arm. He had gone too far. There wasn't any point in casting pearls before swine.

"We're told they compromised your records," said a network correspondent.

"They tried," said Spats. "We've already taken steps to put everything on floppy. We're invulnerable. It doesn't matter what they do."

"Is the disappearance of David Polyakov related to all this?" asked the man from the newspaper of record.

"Ladies and gentlemen, there is no doubt whatsoever in our minds that Mr. Polyakov has been kidnapped. You all know he has been our point man in the war against narcotics. The racketeers hope to win that war by silencing him, by intimidating us. Everyone needs to know--and I hope you will communicate our firm commitment--that they will fail. A dragnet, the likes of which hasn't been seen since Jack Webb, is now combing the city. Mr. Polyakov will be found. We won't be intimidated, and we shall win this war. We're going to cut their peckers off."

Holley and the others were quite pleased with his performance. He was young. He was handsome. He was immensely charming. He had read the statement they had prepared with exactly the right missionary fervor. Hadn't he spent a couple of days memorizing it? The press conference put to bed the last of Holley's doubts, despite Spats's extravagant choice of phrase in some cases.

Usages like "Be my guest," the Karachi "caper," selfish "to the max," and "cut their peckers off," really didn't project the image the little band of prophets had worked so hard to cultivate for the National Reserve. In the same general category was public mention of sleeping with his wife and accusing the working press of using coke. Of course the scummy bastards used coke! Coke wasn't the worst thing they did. The trick was to communicate to them one's knowledge of that fact without mentioning it. Holley had never heard of Jack Webb, but intuition told him he should likewise not be mentioned. Of course Spats needed seasoning. That would come with time.

He had done a perfect job with Krüger. The little group of friends clearly had no wish to find him, and there certainly was no dragnet for the purpose, but it had been prudent to say there was. Thank the good Lord he had disappeared, whatever the reason. His activities during the late World War had always made Holley uneasy. Albert had nothing against them personally--*chacun a son gout*! he always said--but the danger was great, despite decades of expensive, favorable propaganda, that he could be exposed. Holley was hoping Krüger would stay disappeared.

How many of us enjoy the luxury of achieving our ambition? Spats was one of the favored few who had. He had everything in life he wanted. He was precisely where he wanted to be and was doing exactly what he wanted. The aggravating mystery had been solved.

Holley told him, “Charles, we have made the sun stand still. We have committed the miracle of reversing cause and effect. You are now a moving part of the only business on earth that rewards failure, and the greater the failure the greater the reward."

Why was it then that Spats felt hollow? Doom was closing in again, the same doom that had almost destroyed him when he had thought Elizabeth Ann was dead, dead by his own hand as sure as if he had murdered her himself. Maybe the reason was the suspicion that he had been talking utter nonsense. So what! So what if he had! Who cared what the truth was anyway? There was no such thing.

"You don't like what I'm doing, do you?" he asked Elizabeth Ann. In the old days, before this horrible thing had happened to him, he never would have asked for her opinion.

"Charles, I don't know what you're doing, but, whatever it is, I'm sure it’s for the best, and I’m behind you."

She too had changed with marriage and pregnancies. The intolerable nattering was gone. She was serene. She had even accepted Spats's latest change of name with equanimity.

"Don't play games, Lizzie. You know damn well what I'm doing."

"All right. I'll stop playing games. Yes, I know what you're doing."

"Well, damn it, what do you think?"

"What do *you* think, Charles?"

"If you're going to be critical, the hell with it."

"All right, Charles. The hell with it."

"You have everything you want. Why in hell are you complaining?"

"I don't know, Charles. I'm probably out of control."
“Well, stop it!”
“All right, Charles. I’ll stop.”
"What else could I do?"
"God only knows."

Chapter Forty
Victory

All the way down inside the statue, with the arm inside her coat, she expected to be seized, but nothing happened. The fog was so thick, and went down to the ground. Krüger hadn't shouted. No one had seen or heard the corpse. By the time it was discovered, Frieda and Professor Finkelstein had long since left the island. Indeed, they had left New York.

The part of the body the National Park people found on Bedloe's Island, could not be identified. One of the arms was of course missing at the elbow. The corpse was further mutilated by the fall. The clothing was hand made and expensive, even the shoes, but there were no labels, not even any wallet, just $3,817 in big bills, which was sequestered at a Manhattan hospital, pending next of kin, and wound up in the coffers of the bankrupt City of New York. Krüger had often left the office in this manner, when conducting a sensitive mission like his abortive meeting with Goldstein's mother.

The fingerprints of one hand were available, of course, but Krüger was not an American, and the Federal Bureau of Investigation could not find a match. The only thing the forensic pathologists were sure of, was that the corpse had belonged to an aged man who looked even older than he was: about 95. Had a man so old gone to the Statue of Liberty alone? Needless to say, this meant that something had gone wrong with Vörst's rejuvenant. Even Krüger's cousin Bernhard, in Germany, now dead, would not have been able to recognize him. The mystery was mentioned on the local news that night, and remains unsolved on the books of both the federal government and the City of New York. There was no reason to connect it to the even more aged, utterly senile gentleman found wandering without supervision in one of the red light districts of London, muttering in German. The Polyakov story of course was banner headlines. There was nothing to connect the aged corpse found on Bedloe's Island with Polyakov, who of course was a much younger man. Recently, a television psychic reported that Polyakov had been seen in a café on one of the Greek islands, in conference with Aristotle Onassis and President Kennedy. The disappearance made the movie about the famous philanthropist an even bigger hit. It made even more money, which Frieda spent with special zeal.

Frieda burned Krüger's arm in an oven. It was entirely consumed without difficulty, after the addition of sufficient charcoal briquettes. After 36 years, she physically felt the curse lift. Through the Wiesenthal group, she learned that David's arm had been found in refrigeration in the Polyakov castle in Bavaria. On condition that not a word reach the media, West German intelligence released it. She said kaddish, sat shiva, and arranged proper interment. West German intelligence did not reveal to her or to anyone the discovery of a subterranean *Nazi* shrine at the castle, complete with an eternal flame that had failed because of non-payment of the gas bill, and a field marshal's uniform on a throne filled with putrefying tissue that stank to high heaven. The problem was solved by the local health department.

A couple of months later, Finkelstein came to her office in Polyakov Tower, to tell what he knew. Frieda was now chairman of the board. She had been a logical choice, in view of her husband's "disappearance." The board had approved without comment to ensure continuity and protect the shareholders. George Bogart, M.D., the prominent psychiatrist, was president and chief executive officer. Bobby Combs, recently retired from the Police Department with honors, was chief of security. Important jobs had also been found for Thomas Chase and Horatius Ryan.

"The decision was made at the highest levels in Jerusalem not to tell either of you at the time," Finkelstein explained. "You are not professional actors. Had you known the truth, the splendid job you did would have been that much harder. It was crucial that you both give a convincing performance."

"I still don't understand," said Frieda.

"We doctored Abe's records."

"His medical records?"

"Yes."

"Why?"

"Krüger was not his father. We had to prove he was."

"That's ridiculous. Of course he was."

Finkelstein opened an attaché case and handed her a file. "These are Abe's medical records. Look at the numbers. These are Krüger's. As you see, they don't match. According to the genetic fingerprints, it's impossible. In fact, according to the experts, this is better than fingerprints.

"Mossad went to work. They're very good. These are the records we gave Abe and Krüger, spurious, but absolutely genuine, doctored by sympathetic physicians here in New York. But, of course, we didn't need them. Because of his problem, Krüger would have believed anything we gave him, no matter how amateurish it looked."

"What problem?"

"He was sterile. Apparently, one of the sterility experiments with radiation at Auschwitz went wrong. He wouldn't believe the doctors. Through the years, he tried to impregnate many women. He blamed them when they failed to conceive. We knew he'd believe us."

Frieda sat in silence a long time. "All these years alone, I thought, I thought . . . ."

"I know. What you thought was logical. But it was wrong. I truly regret the suffering it caused--but we got Krüger."

She smiled. "Thank God for that. But, you see, dear Professor Finkelstein, despite your numbers, no one else could be the father. There was no one else. Do you understand? *There was no one else*! So much for your Mossad."

Finkelstein shrugged. "I'm sorry."

As he spoke, Frieda finally realized the implications of what he was saying. "If you're right--if Horst Krüger was not Abe's father--who is?"

* * *

Sid pointed at the screen. Abe saw a tiny, smiling face, a squiggle, a jumble of symbols he didn't recognize. "I used the computer in the office once," he said. "It ate everything. McGillicuddy was furious. He said I was illiterate. I guess I still am. Since then, I use a ball point pen, or a nib and an inkwell."

"It's really very simple," said Sid. "All you need to know is that it improves on the Pakistani Brain."

"Sid, you spent Polyakov money improving the Pakistani brain? Why not the Jewish brain, where there is room for improvement? What have the Pakistanis ever done for you?"

"Abe, the Pakistani Brain is a virus."

"You improved a virus? Sid, as you know I'm stuck with being Jesus Christ for now, but when the real McCoy shows up he's going to be very disappointed to hear it, not to mention my mother."

"Abe, do you know the difference between a worm and a virus?"

"A worm makes holes in the ground and crawls through your eye sockets. A virus is an invisible disease."

"Correct. They also mess up computers. They destroy data. The difference is that viruses can replicate themselves. The trouble is that you can only introduce them on the phone. Sure, you can get them in on floppies, if someone takes them in. They can reinfect a system after months at the bottom of somebody's desk drawer. But you have to get them in. Abe, do you know what you're looking at?"

"The truth is, I don't."

"You just happen to be looking at the end of life as we know it."

"Sid, would that be so bad?"

"It can erase everything on a computer disk, even from outside. It doesn't have to get in."

"You mean, no records?"

"None. The only problems I haven't been able to solve are the noise and rotation. Anyone who understands could spot us. What should I do?"

"Where is all this taking us, Sid?"

"We already have prostheses. In a hundred years, today's prostheses will be as primitive as Captain Hook is now to us. When a guy is half man-made, or more--and you can't tell the difference--will he be man or machine?"

"And his soul, Sid? Will that be man-made too?"

Sid chuckled cautiously. "Souls are not my line."

Sid was as close to heaven as one can get and still be here on earth. He and Myra lived there on the farm, he spent all day on his computers, the authorities were no longer looking for him, and Myra was pregnant again, which had fatally shaken his faith in atheism. Sid's personality had changed. He was at peace.

Abe left the barn they had converted to a laboratory, crossed the grassy compound and walked into the woods. The day was sublime. Sun and shadow danced among the needles on the piney forest floor. A breeze caressed his face. A sweet aroma hung like perfume in the air. Birds he could not see serenaded in the trees, and his feet crunching underbrush made a pleasant sound.

Yet, he was morose. They had no money worries. Checks he hadn't asked for kept arriving from Polyakov Pharmaceuticals, enough to buy Sid all the equipment he dreamed of, enough to support Abe and Moe, more than enough. They couldn't spend it all. The checks were signed by his mother, Frieda Finkelstein. That was all he knew.

But, he had lost his purpose, at least temporarily. What should he do? They had left New York as Fatima had ordered. They were high up in the wilds of a mountain state, remote enough to daunt a hillbilly. They were safe. Everyone had forgotten about them. Should they leave the compound and work another city? Abe had lost the ability just to live from day to day. Without purpose, he was a windsock, drooping without wind, a rainbow without color, a mother hen without an egg.

My son.

Thank God the voice had waited until he was walking through the pine trees. He fell like a rock, but the needles prevented broken bones. He lay spread-eagled, face down, waiting. He hadn't heard the voice for several years. He had almost forgotten the fear he felt now. Perhaps, had he been given some warning, he wouldn't be shuddering as he was. He dug his hands into the pine needles, trying not to move.

Yes, Father.

You have done well. I am well pleased.

Abe heard music in the voice. It was rich with good humor. He believed what it said. Since the incident at the Tower, Abe had been afraid that, when he next heard the voice, it would be angry because he had called Krüger father. Now, the fear began to dissipate.

Thank you, Father.

My son, I have another job for you.

Another job, Father?

That is what I said.

The voice was so calm, so deep, so sympathetic, yet so commanding, so amused--which proved it was impossible to contradict--that Abe was afraid to ask what was wanted. How had Moses dared to interrupt?

Command, Father.

Thank you, my son. I was hoping you would say that. I was sure you would. You are no longer Jesus Christ.

Abe cried. Tears of joy were on his face. He rolled over on his back, exulting.

Oh, thank you, Father. Thank you. Thank you. I was never very good at it. You needed someone taller, Father, someone better looking with more hair, someone smarter, who could preach--a leader--someone whose tongue doesn't get in the way. There was too much responsibility. I just wasn't good enough.

I know you weren't. That's why I picked you.

Why, Father?

So everyone would know I did it.

They know, Father. I told them.

I know you did, my son. Now, it is finished. You are no longer Jesus Christ. You are Patrick Henry.

* * *

They were in a truck and they were coming down from the mountains in rural country, going north on an interstate. Electric Eyes Chase, who had the best eyesight, was at the wheel. Honky Ryan was in the other seat. Abe and Shirley rode behind them, sitting side by side, even holding hands as they had done when courting. She was smiling at him, thanking God for giving her the courage to give in. The dream was the reason, the dream that told her it was the will of God that she be Patrick Henry's mate. The dream had told her to read Patrick Henry's famous letter to his daughter Anne. The dream had told her to come here to this mountain state. Why *this* state? She knew no one here. She had never even been here. Her amazement when Abe opened the door, responding to her timid knock, had left her speechless. He had just stood there smiling, waiting, letting her recover.

"Don't you want to kick me out, Abe?"

"Why would I kick you out, Shirl?" He was not at all surprised. Had he expected her to come?

"Because that's what I did to you."

"How mad at me would you be if I suggested something new?"

"Abe, I was wrong. You can be anyone you like. If you like, you can be Jesus Christ. After all, he was one of us."

"Could I be Patrick Henry?" Then, he had explained.

It was a large panel truck, heavily curtained and full of expensive electronic equipment. On top of the truck, there was something that resembled a radar screen at rest. They drove in silence. Now that they were nearing their destination, after so many hours on the road, tension was building.

They were entering a city. They left the interstate. They crossed a bridge. Electric Eyes knew just where he was going. Just for practice, he had already made the trip several times. Despite the tension, he drove slowly. He didn't want to have to explain anything to the police.

They stopped at the top of a hill. There was a good view of the target. Electric Eyes looked at it for a long time, smiling. Then he started down. Still some distance from the triple rows of ten foot-high fences and, behind them, the armed guards, he parked, carefully scanning the government architecture typically intended to intimidate. Sid smiled, feasting on the sight, and looked at Abe. Sid nodded.

"Ladies, are you ready?" Abe asked.

"Yes," said Shirley. Abe's voice was like a trumpet. The voice she remembered had been nondescript. He seemed to stand taller. She didn't understand it, but reveled in the change.

"Ready," said Elizabeth Ann, fondling her tummy, smiling at Myra, who was just as pregnant. Sid had tried but failed to persuade her not to come.

"Gentlemen, are you?"

"Ready," said Dr. Ghibellini.

"Let's do it," said Spats, still chuckling about the wire service story he had read in the morning newspaper about his "disappearance." The only incident that rivaled it in modern memory was the disappearance of industrialist David Polyakov. A sidebar explained what the National Reserve chairman does. A companion piece explained that "foul play" was suspected, despite the discovery of "substantial irregularities." Spats had never been so happy. Elizabeth Ann had said nothing. He still didn't understand what was happening to him. Next week, he and the others would put the exquisitely constructed plan to expose the Reserve into motion, and he would be even happier.

His gang, abandoned, would go on to other things. After a difficult period of adjustment, symptomatized by denial, then despair, rectified by psychiatry, Guzik the *Goniff*, using another name, would become executive director of a tax-exempt foundation leading the fight for gun control. Jim Stink would become a top salesman for an exclusive line of men's toiletries. Louie the Enemy would make millions selling junk bonds for one of the nation's most prestigious brokerage houses. After the crash, he would run a "bring your own sheets" motel, with rates by the hour. The Hawk and the Moose still live peacefully in Attica as wards of the State of New York, all expenses paid. None of them would ever see Spats again.

There was only one problem: the voice. How long had it been calling to him? Weeks? Or was it months? It was inside his head, but it certainly wasn't his own. Whose was it? What did it want? It was a commanding voice, a voice of total authority far greater than his own, serene, without a mustard seed of doubt, which, combined with the fact that he couldn't shake it, made him tremble, something he didn't often do.

Saul! That was all it said. *Saul*! Who the hell was Saul? Spats could think of only one man with that name, a little punk who made book on Avenue A in New York. Was he the one the voice was calling? Was it all a mistake, a wrong number? Why then did the voice persist, endlessly patient, even disrupting conversations he was trying to conduct?

Spats was frightened, as he had never been before. Of course had told no one, not even Elizabeth Ann. But he didn't know how long he could resist. He was tempted to answer. If he did, would it stop?

"Sid, are we close enough?" asked Abe. "Will it work this far away?"

Sid smiled, went to the consoles, sat down and pushed a button. The consoles came alive and booted up. The screen on the roof of the van started turning, accompanied by a pulsing, electronic signal. Sid nodded. Dr. Ghibellini pushed a button. A calliope began playing, obscuring the sound.

"Aim it right at the sign, Sid," Abe commanded. "Then strafe the building."

"Roger that."

Abe and Moe put on their uniforms, including the coin changers. So did Spats. "Moe, did you remember to fill these things with change?" Abe asked.

"Roger that."

Abe opened the side door. Leaving the women aboard to help Sid and Enzo at the consoles, Abe and Moe and Spats got out. The truck was already surrounded with children, even some parents, attracted by the loud circus music, the large, multi-paneled, glass dome turning on top of the truck, concealing the screen, and the big, red letters on its sides. Spats opened the freezer and the three of them started selling ice cream, making change.

Now came the test. Sid hit a key and turned a dial. The signal intensified; it would have to stay that way for hours. The patrons at the truck kept on buying ice cream, oblivious, dancing to the music around the truck. Abe wanted to cheer, but discipline intervened. Behind the ten-foot fences, in the path of the beam, people hurried on their mission, grim but completely unharmed, unaware of what was happening.

They sold ice cream all afternoon. It was hot. At last, the pace of commerce slackened, and they were able to feast their eyes on the majestic sign:

United States Government
Department of the Treasury
Internal Revenue Service
NATIONAL COMPUTER CENTER

The End

About the Author

Aloysius P. Sharon was born and raised in Brooklyn, the product of a union between an orthodox Jew and a former Roman Catholic priest--but emigrated to Israel in time to participate in the Six Day War. He stayed to launch a distinguished career in the military (he took part in many commando raids) and, later, became equally well known as a journalist. Anti-Israel and anti-Catholic circles have accused him of being an agent for Mossad and the Vatican. He is certainly a legend to Israeli intelligence, and has hunted Nazi war criminals for years. The late Ian Fleming encouraged him to write, and he is the author of a definitive work on military intelligence. He is the father of six children and lives in Israel and Scotland. He and his family could be in danger, were we to show you his photograph. *The Name of the King* is Mr. Sharon's first novel.